ALSO BY LAURA BRIGGS

One Day Like This

one winter's day

LAURA BRIGGS

Bookouture

Published by Bookouture in 2018

An imprint of StoryFire Ltd.
Carmelite House
50 Victoria Embankment
London EC4Y 0DZ

www.bookouture.com

ISBN: 978-1-78681-675-7
eBook ISBN: 978-1-78681-674-0

For Jacquelyn,
who loved the wintertime
and especially loved the snow.

Chapter One

Ama sifted flour into her bowl, sending a cloud of it airborne, scented sweetly with cinnamon and cloves. Her first autumn treat of the year, from her online side business Sweetheart Treats to its latest customer—a batch of miniature spice loaves, to be decorated with an apple glaze, each one boxed as a gift for attendees of a fundraiser.

Unlike the loud atmosphere of her family's restaurant the Tandoori Tiger, the kitchen at Wedding Belles, the Southern event planning firm where Ama now worked alongside her friends Tessa and Natalie, was quiet, except for the sound from Ama's laptop, which was playing a DVD of *Bride and Prejudice*. It had just reached the wacky musical number devoted to Mr. Collins's marital quest as Ama slipped her wet ingredients into the flour's well.

This was the only Bollywood film that Ama truly loved—she enjoyed a few others, but she wasn't as big a fan of them as her mother and auntie, who were positively diehard viewers. They adored the musical sequences and even liked the more outrageous stunts of the late-night Indian action flicks. Sometimes Ama would watch these with them, paging through a cookbook as she enjoyed the sound of her family's laughter at the onscreen antics. But she wasn't big on action films herself, and when it came to love stories, Ama had one very specific rule: the more impossible the romance the better.

That was probably why the stack of DVDs that entertained her as she stirred her latest batch of cookies for a birthday party included *Serendipity*, *While You Were Sleeping*, and a few Hallmark Christmas movies she had sneaked from her sister Rasha's collection. Movies with mismatched protagonists and star-crossed lovers were a must for someone with Ama's romantic ideals, and the Bollywood favorite she was watching right now was a perfect fit.

Designer cookies with a pumpkin-vanilla glaze… and was it mini chrysanthemums she was painting on them, or foxtail feathering? She searched through her sketches to refresh her memory, sliding aside her latest wedding-cake designs. There was her favorite of them all, the Birds of Paradise cake that she still hadn't found the perfect customer to appreciate.

What about herself? Fat chance of that. Ama laughed at the idea of finding anybody to fall in love with her—unless her auntie forced on her some matrimonially desperate boy she met at the laundromat, for example. But as for love at first sight sweeping her away and making her dream of a lifelong future with someone come true… she would probably find a customer for this cake long before then.

Love at first sight. A first kiss under the stars. A glance from across the room that forms an instant connection and changes everything in the world. Ama would take any of these scenarios, or any alternative that was completely magical and spontaneous. In short, anything but a sensible match with someone carefully screened by her overly protective family. If he was on an Indian matchmaker's dating site, if he thought you could find your lifelong mate through traditional channels of matrimonial ads, he wasn't the boy for her.

Mr. Darcy and Lizzy's story was onscreen again. Ama turned up the volume and propped her chin on both hands for this part, smiling as she watched. This was the only way that two unlikely matches could or should ever come together, and that's what she loved about it.

Chapter Two

Natalie's black pencil brushed over her latest design sketch with quick, feathery strokes, deepening the shadows of the chocolate brown halter gown, which Natalie envisioned embroidered with a gold and green vine decorating the left half of the neck strap and bodice. Perfect for an autumn charity ball or an office Christmas formal, she thought. Now, if she could just convince someone else of that, too.

Her own outfit was an advertisement for her skills both as a designer and as a seamstress: a sheer, silky peasant-style blouse with fitted wrists and open elbows and shoulder slits that let a glimpse of skin be seen. Flowers were hand-embroidered along its wide scoop collar, held closed by a couple of pearl buttons—a dressy twist with her casual suede skirt and vintage straw platform sandals with brown ankle laces. She'd tried to sell the blouse once in her former boss Kandace's shop, but it had ended up being buried behind a line of black vinyl capes her boss had designed—deliberately hidden there, Natalie knew, behind the shop's least successful item at the time.

At least she was getting some use out of it now—and a few compliments to boot. She reflected on this as she sipped her cappuccino in the little coffee bar close to the university where she studied part-time for her degrees in fashion design and business. This was the urban district of Bellegrove, the Southern city that managed to capture small-town heart in the historic homes and quaint little boutiques that outnumbered the modern business complexes at the heart of its business quarter. Even a modern street like this one bore hints of the city's old-fashioned charm, from the magnolias and dogwoods on the cafe's wall mural to the soul-food joint on the corner, and the flyers for this weekend's 'Merry Christmas, Baby' blues concert in the park.

Lots of other students were at the coffee bar today—most of them younger than Natalie, who had spent her college years working in her family's Italian bakery—and she loved the vibrant atmosphere as much as they did. Including the *extremely* cute teacher's aide who had just walked in.

"Earth to Natalie. Tell me those brain cells are totally focused on the pad in front of you," said Cal, her former coworker, who had just rejoined her with his skinny latte and a low-fat soy seaweed cookie. They'd worked together at Kandace's Kreations—a horrible fashion boutique—until last summer, and had remained great friends.

"Ew. You're eating that?" she said, wrinkling her nose.

"I'm trying to be good. I've been bingeing on chocolate for two weeks straight, since Kandace is working us like her personal slaves to finish autumn inventory. I have never sewn soooo many hideous orange-patched flannel shirts in all my life." He opened a packet of sugar substitute and sprinkled it over his coffee and the dry-looking seaweed cookie, making a face as he took a bite.

"Is she that behind in production? What about the fashion show?" Natalie asked. The December fashion revue was only a few weeks away, and most of the city's major designers wanted their creations to parade down its runway for the sheer prestige, not to mention the publicity in the local fashion journal.

"There's no way we'll have her winter fashions completed in time, so Kandace won't have a thing to do except sneer at the competition," said Cal. "But I thought maybe a *certain* someone might finally be contributing something?" he hinted.

Natalie closed her sketchbook. "Uh-uh," she said. "I've sewn one dress for my personal collection, and that's it. If I go, it's strictly to network." Her last two dresses had been wedding gowns—not her most brilliant creations, but the important part was the exposure. *Her* name was on the labels worn by those brides, and it was all thanks to her friend Tessa's idea for Bellegrove's most unconventional and unique wedding planning firm. Known as Wedding Belles, it was more or less a 'one-stop shop' for would-be brides, providing everything for their big day from the cake to the gown, and anything in between. It was run by three girls, three genuine artists dedicated to providing the perfect day's most crucial pieces, as Tessa would put it. Ama handled the cakes and all things catering, Natalie designed and consulted on bridal couture, and Tessa… well, she was in charge of everything else.

"You are going, though?" persisted Cal about the fashion show. "Say yes, Nat, please. It'll be totally unbearable if it's just me and Tony and Celia hanging out together, commiserating about the horrors of Kandace's Kreations."

Until this year, Natalie had always played the part of faithful assistant to the boutique in question, accepting Kandace's tongue-lashing with the best grace she could muster as she struggled to solve the designer's last-minute fashion emergencies. But not anymore, and for that, Natalie was immensely thankful. No standing by and smiling—or rather, biting her tongue and trying not to roll her eyes—as Kandace savaged the more talented competition in the show or clung fawningly to the few critics who took her work seriously.

"I'll be there, probably," she reassured Cal. "Providing I'm not working or anything. Here—I even printed some business cards to hand out. You know, so I could look professional?"

She pulled a few from her billfold and held one out to Cal. She'd printed them herself a couple of days ago. *Natalie Grenaldi. Simple, Chic, Timeless Designs.* A little black pencil silhouette of a girl in a fashion gown to one side, copied from one of Natalie's own sketches.

"Yay! You used *my* words for this card," said Cal. "I'm flattered, truly. Can I keep one?"

"Keep a dozen," said Natalie. "Just not where Kandace can see them lying around, all right?"

"Are you still afraid of the Wicked Witch of the West?" said Cal. "You're her ex-employee, Natalie. You don't owe her any loyalty, so you don't need to tiptoe past her when it comes to your career."

"Maybe," said Natalie vaguely. Kandace wouldn't be understanding, to put it mildly. For all her ex-boss's mean remarks about her designs, Kandace was more than a little bit jealous of anybody's talent. Anybody, even a nobody whose dresses had only publicly graced herself, her family and friends, and a few bridal parties thus far.

"So, big plans for the weekend?" Cal sipped his latte, knowing for Natalie that plans meant only two things—either she was participating in one of the Grenaldis' endless Italian traditions of family gatherings or baking for a living, or yet another of Natalie's casual, fun, and flirtatious encounters had asked her out.

"Nothing too big," said Natalie. "Jake and I aren't seeing each other these days. I decided he's more interested in sunbathing beauties on the beach than me."

"Oooh, too bad. It's his loss. He totally doesn't deserve you."

"Thanks," she said. "I'll be a little more careful before I say yes to the next surfer. Try to avoid anybody who plans to stab my heart or my pride." Not that Jake had been anything special, but they had dated longer than most of Natalie's relationships lasted. She had found him fun and loved spending time with him... until he revealed the feeling was not mutual, that is. Natalie's openness when it came to romance did not extend to being someone's last-minute date of desperation after another girl said no.

"Someone better will come along," said Cal sympathetically. "A girl as gorgeous as you can't stay single. It's a crime." He took another bite of his soy cookie, then abandoned it. "I can't. I just can't," he muttered with a sigh.

"Tell my mother that I'm a viable commodity," said Natalie. "She thinks I'm almost over the hill, and I still haven't found a steady boyfriend who would make a great father for her eight imaginary grandchildren."

"Eight grandchildren?"

"She's Italian," said Natalie. "What can I say?" She took another sip of her coffee and flipped open her sketchbook, finding herself mulling over Cal's hints about the December fashion revue. What would it be like to see her designs in a runway show? It would be exciting... and way braver than anything Natalie had ever done, since her first official dress sale had been this summer.

Natalie Grenaldi, fashion designer. Her own label, her own fashion house. A much bigger dream than even this first step as Natalie Grenaldi, fashion consultant and designer for the Wedding Belles.

"Plans for Thanksgiving?" asked Cal. "If you want, you can join the rest of the gang—Marcel's making a tofu turkey and his famous cranberry stuffing, then we're decking the halls at Sadie's apartment with some *totally* kitschy holiday ornaments she bought last week at a basement sale."

"And have my mother kill me for skipping her dinner? Not on your life."

Chapter Three

At the Wedding Belles' headquarters in the historic downtown of Bellegrove, proof of success, albeit modest success, adorned its walls. Tessa had photographs from all four of their wedding clients framed as big black-and-white images in the foyer. Paolo and Molly looked joyful beneath the shower of petals from the ornate fire escape balconies above, while another smiling couple, Tim and Reese, were posed beside one of Ama's cakes, decorated with delicate gilded candy butterflies.

An impromptu snap from their last wedding featured the newlyweds beneath a beautiful canopy of autumn leaves drifting on the wind, which Tessa had just finished hanging in the foyer. She climbed down from her ladder and inspected it with a smile of approval.

"Perfect," she said. "Ama, move the one of Kelly and Clark a little to the left, will you? It's a tiny bit crooked."

Ama nudged it slightly to one side. "Better?' she asked. "You know, I only have a couple more minutes to help before those cupcakes are ready." She pointed to her wristwatch timer.

"I know. I'll be done before then, I promise," said Tessa, biting her lip. "Maybe I should have an extra one printed and framed of Kelly and Clark's cake."

"Maybe we should just find another client," said Natalie wryly. She had just entered the foyer, her class satchel filled with business and fashion textbooks slung over her shoulder.

"We will," said Tessa. "New businesses always have a tiny slump right after their initial success. It's a proven fact. Look it up in your textbook if you don't believe me."

Natalie rolled her eyes. "I think we're getting mown down by Weddings 'R' Ours a couple of streets down," she said gently. "They've got the edge right now, Tess. They plan birthday parties and retirement dinners on the side. And our word-of-mouth theory hasn't exactly paid off with hoards of clients."

Their last official wedding had been John and Ella in the first week of October: a local apple orchard with straw bales for seats, and a weathered two-story barn rental space on the grounds for the reception, with smoked brisket, homemade rolls, and a local vineyard's wine selection on hand. Ama had created a spice cake with caramelized apples between layers, naked sides, and simple candy-glass leaves for the top ornament. The bride had worn a plain but elegant white dress with a pink sash, her smile radiant in the large sepia-tinted photograph that hung among the display on Wedding Belles' wall: an image of the bride walking down the autumn leaf-strewn aisle.

Since then, a handful of customers had ordered baked goods from Ama's side of the business, including the latest batch of cupcakes for a wedding shower, and Tessa's services had been tapped for planning a surprise last-minute engagement party for a nearby restaurant owner. But an event for all three of them? A full-size event that would help them stay competitive? Not for six weeks now. Long enough that they couldn't help but feel a little nervous that four clients simply hadn't been enough to put them on the map.

"I know," said Tessa. "Relax. I have a plan."

"A plan?" said Ama. "For getting more clients? Are we putting a trapdoor in the walkway outside?" she joked.

"No, we're getting a billboard," said Tessa. "Look. There's one available on the main bypass to the heart of the business district." She opened today's paper to the ads section and showed them the notice: *Billboard for rent, prime location, reasonable payment plan.* A telephone number was printed at the bottom.

"Tess, those billboards cost a fortune," said Natalie. "You do remember that we're still paying off this decrepit old building, right? Which would you rather have—a nice billboard or heat in your new digs this winter?"

She was referring to Tessa's two private rooms upstairs, where the wedding planner had taken up residence in order to concentrate all her earnings into the Wedding Belles' headquarters and business. Even if it meant giving up her privacy and the guarantee of a washroom with running water at all times, luxuries that this building did not offer its only full-time resident.

"We won't have to worry about either one if we don't have more clients, right?" retorted Tessa. "I called the rental company that owns the space and it's not that bad, Natalie. Here's the cost proposal, and here's the design I had in mind. I sort of doodled it last night while watching reruns of *Rich Bride, Poor Bride.*" She handed both women a sheet with the little sketch on it, and the quote from the billboard's owners.

Natalie made a slight face. "I guess it could be worse," she said. "It's more than our advertising budget for this year, though."

"I thought we were taking out some ads in the bridal magazines instead," said Ama.

"Well… we will," said Tessa. "We'll do both. It'll pay off in the end, you'll see. All we need is one high-profile client to help secure our reputation in the event planning community."

"But I thought the ad in *Local Bridal Trends* was really pricey," began Natalie, who was now searching through her satchel for an older quote from her business partner.

"Let's not worry about that right now, okay?" said Tessa. "I've got it under control—you just need to worry about the alterations you're making on the wedding gown for that bride who hired you last-minute for her self-planned ceremony. And the decorating project, since we clearly need to spruce up our image a little for the holidays."

Ama's usual smile had dimmed a little. "Tess, I agree with Natalie," she said. "We're taking a big risk if we spend too much money. I mean, we are still paying our unofficial fourth partner, too."

As if to illustrate her point came the sound of a Skilsaw buzzing to life in one of the building's closed-off rooms. The building contractor and all-round handyman Blake Ellingham had done more than fix their building's faulty wiring and floorboards. And though he might roll his eyes at this reference to his honorary partnership in their firm, it was more than a little true. From the beginning, Blake had been helpful, after all—even stepping into the role (albeit begrudgingly) when their fourth partner had quit, to save the Wedding Belles' first ever paid event from turning into an utter disaster.

Although he had stuck to carpentry duties since that first wedding, it didn't stop Tessa and the others from thinking of him as part of their creative team. And—though she would never, ever admit it aloud—it didn't stop Tessa from thinking of him as something more than merely a hired craftsman who could leave them at any time.

"He's not working for peanuts," contributed Natalie. "He keeps threatening to bring in some sort of antique shelf facings to spruce up that room, whatever those are."

Blake's skills as a restoration contractor were at odds with both the budget and the eclectic tastes of the Wedding Belles, who were fine with the 'un-period' metal spiral staircase and the sunny 1940s yellow and green in the newly installed kitchen, none of which belonged to the building's original interior.

"Plus, we *kind* of promised him a cut of our profits," said Ama. "Not that he'll ever make good on that promise. Or that we'll never again need a guy in a suit to spruce up our image, right?"

"I know all of this," said Tessa. "Why do you guys doubt that I'm on top of the situation? It just so happens that I do have a plan to pay for all this which won't touch our profits."

"How?" asked Natalie.

"I'm paying for it myself," said Tessa. "I have a job on the side, and the money I'm making will cover the billboard for a month. So there. You don't have to worry, see? It won't be a burden on our fragile expenses *or* our partnership's budget."

Her partners exchanged glances. "What job?" asked Ama.

Tessa's expression became coy—or cagey—but it was impossible to tell which one. Was that a slight blush on her cheeks, or just the sunlight reflecting off her gingery-red hair?

"That's for me to know," she answered loftily. "Let's just say that I'm helping out a friend on a sort of... consulting basis... and leave it at that." She smiled. "See? Nothing to worry about."

"If you say so," said Natalie, who still sounded a little disbelieving. "So what kind of sprucing should we begin with? A bigger autumn wedding display in the window? Christmas trees in the parlor?" She held up one end of a leaf garland sporting orange silk aspen leaves, and the dusky, speckled pinkish-red and yellow of Bradford pears. Tessa's fall wedding vision held lots of seasonal pastel shades, from Pink Lady apples to Princess de Monaco roses mixed with soft orange, coral, and red-shaded peonies, and delicate corn husk flowers in the same shade trimming the fake two-layer wedding cake on display.

"I think we should do a white wedding for Christmas," said Ama. "With lots of silver and maybe some graceful elements like birch trees for accents, or a big floral centerpiece with mistletoe and paperwhites. Or we could do a big red-and-green display with the classic shades."

"You're really getting carried away with this idea, for someone who doesn't celebrate Christmas," said Natalie with a grin.

"I like Christmas," said Ama. "Gingerbread cookies and trees decorated in the stores, and all the candles and bells and snowflakes, and the really big nativity outside the cathedral. It's my parents who stick to strictly traditional Indian holidays in the home. Me? I'm happy to celebrate both kinds." She planted her hands on her hips as she studied the display window. "Maybe I could make a huge iced gingerbread mansion with little lights in it, and lots of sugar glitter."

"In my house, the Christmas tree isn't even up for discussion until after the last bit of my mom's Thanksgiving feast has been eaten," said Natalie. "Until then, the only decorations in my house are brown paper turkeys cut out of grocery sacks by my cousins' kids. And those awful clay turkey place-card holders that me and Roberto made when we were in grade school."

"I longed for paper turkeys as a kid," said Ama enviously. "And real turkey with sage dressing. My mom always fixed *bhakra* curry, my dad's favorite. Thanksgiving's not the same when your turkey's dressing is seasoned with turmeric and comes with rice, either." An electronic beep trilled persistently in the room. "My cupcakes," declared Ama, racing to the kitchen as the timer beeped. "Oh no—these are the ones for the birthday party on Saturday, and I've burned one batch already!"

"Are you sure you have this covered?" Natalie glanced at Tessa. "Everything?" She lifted one eyebrow, watching to see if Tessa squirmed under scrutiny.

"Of course," Tessa answered, without any visible twinges of doubt. "You just worry about the next window display. Bring a couple of the latest wedding dresses downstairs for the new window, right?"

She moved aside the sketches on their reception desk, ones for fall weddings that had never materialized. The newest of Ama's cake designs was festooned with glittery marzipan leaves in red and spicy orange. It was accompanied by some sketches Tessa had made of a country church decorated with the display garlands and flowers, with glittering pumpkins in shades of blue, pale orange, and rich burnt red matched with the delicate Pink Lady apples and pastel-shaded Indian corn bundles.

Natalie was adjusting the bridesmaids' gowns on show—a few lucky finds from Natalie's home closet of fashions past that she had tweaked to be more fashionable now—and turned one of the silk floral bouquets to a nicer angle.

"I think I have a gown that will be perfect for the Christmas one, if I finish the hem tonight," said Natalie. "I guess we should find some fake snow or something."

"I brought tons of old decorations from my mom's store room," said Tessa. "She decorated like a fiend for the holidays when she still had that big house to show off. Snowflakes, garlands, the whole collection. There's even a tree from one of those end-of-the-year retail sales."

"I'll go sort through piles, I guess," said Natalie. "Let's change the display over Thanksgiving weekend, okay? I know you might be busy, but I don't want Ma force-feeding me leftovers while chiding me for not having made fruit buns or spice cookies or something for the big dinner. If Ama doesn't have big holiday plans, that is."

"Second-generation Indian-American in a traditional family, remember?" Ama called from the direction of the kitchen, where the clatter of pans suggested her cupcakes were ready to emerge from the oven for the cooling period.

"Stuff's in the sitting room," said Tessa, as she gathered up the hammer and picture hooks she had been using for the foyer's new art. Natalie pushed open the door to the closed-off room at the same time as the handyman opened it.

"Why is there a Christmas tree in my workspace?" Blake asked. A pair of safety glasses was propped on his head, holding back his unruly cinnamon-brown mane of hair. Sawdust and bits of rotted wood decorated the shoulders and sleeves of his worn blue flannel shirt. At the sight of him, Tessa turned quickly on her heel and began stowing away the picture-hanging supplies as if they were unsightly clutter.

"No reason," answered Tessa over her shoulder. "It'll be gone in another week. Just throw a plastic tarp over it if it's in the way."

"So long as you don't mind wood rot and fiberglass in your Christmas decor," said Blake. "I have to take the whole windowsill and surround out today, because two guys from the crew I'm working with volunteered to haul off the grisly remains."

"Is that the crew from the old bank building with the storm damage?" asked Natalie.

"My paying gig, you mean. How nice of you to remember," said Blake. "Yes, it is. And they've offered to bring the new one. *If* you sign the purchase receipt, so I can go pick it up from the yard. You're signing it, right?" He glanced from Natalie to Tessa, as if to emphasize his hint. "We have a deal."

"Right. Our deal," said Tessa. "I'll sign away, I promise."

"Good. It'll be here by Wednesday," he said. "I'll have your wall back together by Thanksgiving, scout's honor." He started to leave, then paused. "Is that my hammer?" he asked. Tessa hid it behind her back.

"No," she said. "I don't think so." Blake looked unconvinced before he retreated into the sitting room again.

Natalie raised one eyebrow. "Can we afford whatever that window thing costs?" she asked.

Tessa sighed. "It's that, or pay him money out of guilt," she said. "Which do you think pinches our bank account less?"

"So long as he doesn't make me paint over my wall mural, I'm happy," answered Natalie.

✳

Four dozen vanilla cupcakes, frosted with swirling icing, gold-glittered, each decorated with a single gold candy fleur-de-lis on top, were nestled in bakery boxes for delivery to the wedding-shower client by Ama herself early Saturday morning. That was after she stopped by the baking supply shop to pick out some new round gold sprinkles and some edible glitter, both for dusting some red-and-orange winterberry clusters she was making with colored white chocolate beads and dark chocolate stems.

Meanwhile, Ama's latest customer's order—cupcakes from Sweetheart Treats—was cooling at the family restaurant's kitchen today, rather than at the Wedding Belles HQ. These were big red velvet ones waiting for spiced cream cheese icing and the aforementioned winterberries; three dozen in total to be served at a women's luncheon at the Dogwood Tearoom the day after tomorrow. Ama was hoping to find something new to add an extra kick to the frosting, as somehow cinnamon didn't seem quite special enough for this batch.

Lately, she had been spending her Saturdays off from Wedding Belles in the new ethnic market at the south end of town, where her family's favorite Indian vendors had moved to set up shop near some Thai stands, some Taiwanese and Chinese spice stalls, and a host of other new flavors that Ama hadn't yet experienced in the world of cuisine. Her brother loved to branch out when it came to flavors—not that the Tandoori Tiger's menu often reflected this—and Ama herself was always on the lookout for something unique for her baked goods. Plus, she loved the excitement of the new location, full of new scents, diverse faces, and the electricity of cultures blending and melding in one location.

Today's dessert selection at the Tandoori Tiger was one of her father's favorites: an Americanized version of banana *halva*, which was served with an additional sweet sauce of melted butter or *ghee* and a little dusting of cinnamon across the top. She garnished it with a side of bananas in a brown sugar glaze, which seemed a little excessive in her opinion, but her father loved excesses. "Americans like it sweet," he always insisted—and that was one thing they had in common with her Punjabi immigrant family, even if the flavors they were used to were different.

"Order up," she said, as she placed one of the finished desserts in the kitchen window, ringing the bell. She arranged more slices on the next plate, her father hovering at her shoulder.

"Add some of this," he said, pushing forward a container with some sweet and spicy pecans in it, with an orange hue from the spices and sauce that her brother Jaidev had used in roasting them. "It's a good color. The customers will like them. And put on some little candy squash—pumpkins—from the container there." He pointed toward the glass canister across from Ama, where the dessert garnishes were kept, including some sticky candy corn pumpkins her brother had bought at an end-of-Halloween sale.

"No, Papa—that's too much," she protested. "It's sugar overload."

"No—it's for autumn," said her father. "We should make pumpkin desserts next week. And put some of those little candy leaves on them you put on your cupcakes, too." He lifted his big rice pot from beneath the counter, not hearing Ama sigh as she added a sprinkle of nuts and a little candy pumpkin to the top of her next order. Her father had changed the dessert of the day on the chalkboard to read 'festive fall halva' with a badly drawn turkey next to it. That part made her smile a little.

"I can't believe you haven't said anything yet," said Rasha, who was arranging mint leaves around the edges of some turmeric-infused quinoa on a vegetarian plate.

"About what?" Ama asked.

"About your match. The online one."

Ama's smile vanished, and the world ground to a halt despite the double order for banana *halva*, one with marshmallow cream on top. "*What?*" she said, dropping her spoon on the table.

"Dad didn't tell you?" said Rasha, who looked surprised. Jaidev let out a groan.

"No, he did *not*," said Ama indignantly. "Was anybody going to tell me about it?" she demanded, staring at the rest of her family in turn.

Her father had placed an ad in the matchmaking section of an Indian journal for her at the end of summer, and created a profile on an online matchmaking site, all of which Ama had chosen to ignore up to now. No one would respond, she told herself, but now *this*—an actual reply to whatever badly written description of herself her father had crafted to solicit an acceptable, likeminded Indian boy.

"A nice boy responded to you on the computer this week," said Ranjit casually. "What's to explain? He sent a question, I sent an answer."

"Papa, you know how I feel about this," said Ama, suppressing a groan.

"Ama, two more desserts," her brother reminded her. "Hungry customers await."

Her auntie tapped the spoon against the pot of clarified butter. "Don't look so sour," she said. "It's good news. It means you're being noticed now. We'll find some nice boy for you, at last."

Her auntie had introduced her to virtually every 'nice young boy' she had met since Ama was sixteen. Most of them had been related to friends of her auntie, or friends of friends, although there had been the occasional random boy her auntie met at the grocery, the laundromat, or even the dentist's office, whose coerced phone numbers and half-hearted coffee invitations Ama had been dodging for years.

"But I don't want to meet him," said Ama. She dolloped marsh-mallow cream a bit too forcefully over the brown sugar sauce, where it slid away. "I'm sorry, Papa, but I told you I wasn't interested in matchmaking sites when you insisted on doing this."

"Ama, just give it a chance," coaxed her sister. "Who knows? It could be a fun experience."

The kitchen door opened. "A customer wants to know if we have fresh fruit to top the yogurt," said Ama's sister-in-law, Deena.

"Did you explain to them it's not dessert?" asked Jaidev, as he minced green onions beneath his knife's blade.

"No. They want fruit and they're the customers. I'm not going to give them a lecture on Indian cuisine," she added with a laugh. "So do we have fruit or what?"

"Blueberries in the fridge," snapped Ama. "I'll get them. And I really mean it when I say I don't want to be matched with someone. Doesn't matter who he is, or how much money he makes, or how many Indian restaurants his family owns. I'm serious, Papa." She gave her father a look, one that matched the stubborn determination set deep in his own gaze. It took a lot for Ama's good humor to evaporate, so not even her father said anything at this moment, although Ama could sense a few glances being exchanged by her family members, even with her back to them.

Of course, the lunch crowd might be part of the reason why no one argued with her, she told herself, as she slammed the fridge door, and pretended to be busy peeling open the blueberries' container.

She was not meeting this boy. She meant it—really and truly. Her father *knew* how she felt about ideas like matchmaking; he *knew* how she felt about love and romance being breathtaking and spontaneous for her. As far as she was concerned, that little slip of information about someone being interested in her profile could stay a secret, because she intended to ignore it from this moment forward.

She pounded milk dough balls for tomorrow's *gulab jamun* with more force than necessary that afternoon, until she felt better. Then she baked two pumpkin spice cakes and let them cool, dicing them into cubes. If her father wanted pumpkin for dessert, maybe an Indian-inspired trifle would be a good choice, with lots of cream, sugar syrup, sweet milk sauce, and spicy apples.

"Smells good," said Rasha, who had come downstairs for a container of pineapple from the fridge. "Can I try some?"

"Be my guest," said Ama, who was spooning the layer of apple into the trifle dish. "This is just a trial run."

"Mmm. I like it. Very seasonal," said Rasha. "Can we put spicy nuts on top?"

"I was thinking maybe crushed brown sugar candy," said Ama. "That's what Papa would like." She added a drizzle of the *halva's* banana sauce for now.

"You shouldn't be angry at him, you know," said Rasha. "He's just trying to help. He really thinks it's for the best."

"I know, but he's totally ignoring my feelings," said Ama. "Match-making isn't for me. He just keeps insisting, and I don't want to hurt his feelings over it. But I don't want to be talked into a relationship I'm not interested in, either. I want him to accept this fact about me and move on. Is that too much to ask?"

"You're single. That's not happiness in Indian culture," said Rasha, shrugging. "That's not happiness in our family, either. You can't blame him for trying to fix it."

"With a bunch of strangers emailing me?" said Ama. "Does anybody else we know think that would fix things?"

"Auntie Bendi," said Rasha, and giggled. "And every other Indian family in the city who still thinks old-fashioned traditions about marriage are the best. Come on, Ama. It's not so bad. Maybe Papa's actually going to find your perfect match."

Ama rolled her eyes. "Are you being serious?"

"Let's find out," said Rasha. "You *know* you're curious."

"No way! I don't want to look." Ama covered her eyes as her sister pulled her toward the stairs. She had pretended the awful profile didn't exist—she had stuffed the journals with the copy of her father's ad as deep into the restaurant's dumpster as she could.

"One little peek," coaxed Rasha. Ama's sneakers stumbled on the step one below the top as her sister pulled her into the office room, which held the business computer and all the restaurant's receipts and old menus.

The matchmaking site was at least more modern than her father's choice of an Indian journal, and didn't feature as many sari-clad potential brides as Ama imagined, although every other guy looked exactly like the I.T. badges of all her parents' friends' successful sons. There were listings for horoscope matches, for matches by social caste or religious beliefs, and even matches for personal interests, such as careers, or favorite pets. Rasha logged in using her father's password, which he kept in an old recipe box.

"Oh my gosh. Look at this awful dress, Ama. At least Dad picked a better photo for you than this girl picked for herself," said Rasha, making a face over the fashion selection worn by a girl on the website's homepage testimonials.

"Ew. Is that fabric sewage green?"

"Oooh, that boy is totally cute. Think he's the one who emailed you?"

"Don't." Even giggling, Ama cringed at this reference to her prospective suitor.

The profile for herself was every bit as terrible as Ama imagined. She groaned and buried her face as the photo appeared on the screen—a new one that her father had obviously scrounged from one of her siblings' phones, of Ama in her sister's pumpkin-colored *salwar kameez*. Her face was too round and her short hair flipped out too much on its ends, and the tree branch in the background looked like a big clawed hand reaching to grab her head.

"Let's see… here's your profile info," said Rasha, fingers clicking across the keyboard.

"Which probably says I'm homely, a good curry cook, and have a degree in fabric weaving," said Ama, peeking through her fingers.

"Oh, here it is—your matches," said Rasha triumphantly. "This one with the message envelope must be the guy who emailed Dad.

Look—look, Ama," she said, poking her sister in the shoulder. "He's not so bad. 'I saw your profile, and you sound like a nice and interesting person. Would you like to exchange emails and learn a little about each other?'" she read aloud as she opened the account's inbox.

Ama peeked upwards. "Oh no," she groaned. "He's real."

"Of course. Papa wouldn't sign you up somewhere with internet trolls and catfishing schemes," said Rasha. "Let's look at his profile. He has a college degree. He likes Indian food... comedies..."

"He's way out of my league," said Ama. "He's educated, he's successful. He's not going to ask me out, he's probably just testing the email function before he emails some... some Sanskrit poetry major from Harvard or something."

"Some of these guys are pretty cute, Ama," argued Rasha. "Maybe you should give this thing a chance?"

"Can you imagine our aunt looking over my shoulder as I email them?" asked Ama. "Telling me to double-check my spelling, but not to sound *too* smart because men like nice girls—"

"—who don't talk about things that have nothing to do with cooking a good pot of rice or picking a nice girl for their sons," finished Rasha, as they both giggled over one of Bendi's typical pushy and old-fashioned suggestions.

"Awful," said Ama. "All of it. It's all awful. I refuse." Reaching over, she closed the web browser as the advertising picture of smiling young Indian matches who looked like catalog models filled the screen. "If Papa doesn't delete this thing, then I will."

"But what if Papa's onto something here?" said Rasha. "Some of these guys look good to me."

"And they all have one thing in common," said Ama. "They're exactly the kind of guy our family would push me to pick. I don't want to pick somebody for suitability or compatibility or whatever." In a conventional Indian cultural marriage, you chose to make other people in your life happy as well as yourself. Making a choice to please her parents or somebody else's wasn't Ama's picture of happily ever after, and seeing her profile made her *definitely* sure of this fact.

"You can't delete it. Papa would kill you," protested Rasha.

"Let him," said Ama. "It's better than going through with any of this." She clicked to close the persistent ad for a cultural matchmaking site that had sprung to life again.

Chapter Four

The smell of freshly sawn lumber filled the air as Tessa struggled upstairs with a box of potential cake toppers to add to the shelf in her office. No whirr of an electric saw, however—but that was because the handyman was in her office, replacing a rotten piece of trim above the doorframe, as Tessa discovered when she smacked the door into his ladder.

"Ouch. Watch it below," he said, steadying its frame.

"What are you doing in here?" said Tessa. "I thought you weren't working in my office today." The agreed-upon project for this week was the dismal condition of the hall outside it, where Blake had expressed extreme concern for the last vestiges of the termite damage.

"I wanted to fix this little bit here so you can paint," he answered. Tessa walked around to the adjoining office to enter through the side door of her own.

"I'm done painting, so you don't have to worry about it," she said, placing the box on her desk.

"You're done?" he repeated.

"Yes. Romantic Blue on two walls, cream on the opposite one," said Tessa. "That's what I picked out." She sat down behind her desk, tossing her shoulder bag beneath it.

It still felt a little awkward, being alone around Blake. She couldn't explain why. It couldn't be from the kiss, she thought.

That kiss. The one they had shared after the Wedding Belles' first event became a success. Alone together in a beautiful garden, champagne glasses in hand, Tessa had leaned over to kiss Blake on the cheek—and somehow miscalculated, ending up in a liplock that stole her breath away and set her heart aflutter with more than just a few wishful notions.

Just a simple mishap born from a friendly gesture. They had both enjoyed it, accident that it was, right? No need to talk about it, or make a big deal about it, especially since Blake had never brought it up. Then again, he hadn't been around to discuss it, since after Molly and Paolo's wedding, he'd left almost overnight for a carpentry gig in Virginia. And *that* had been what spelled disaster for all those little butterfly notions of love in Tessa's brain, post-wedding kiss.

A favor for a friend, he'd said. The chance to work on a genuine antebellum mansion. He would only be gone a week or so, and he promised to stay in touch while he was there, though he didn't say if it would be for personal or professional reasons at the time. And Tessa didn't ask, though she was dying to know if he'd felt those same sparks between them in that garden that day.

"We'll talk," he'd said. "I'll call you." With a look that, at the time, made Tessa shiver to the core of her soul… although it was probably just the lingering effects of the kiss that did it. That's what she had decided, in these weeks without exchanging anything more than a few emails between them, friendly enough, but with a slight awkwardness behind them due to what hadn't been said after that kiss. Or was she imagining things again?

Those sparks had plenty of time to cool in the month and a half Blake was in Virginia. The job's time frame stretched beyond the deadline, with each rotten beam or faulty wiring job from some World

War II-era electrician. When his phone call came, it went to Tessa's voicemail; her return call, an eager press of the button—reproached by her sensible side—was rewarded by a conversation in which they talked about anything but romance.

The last email from Blake before he returned? A business one about the plans for restoring the rest of their headquarters. Not a word between them about electric sparks, growing attraction, or having dinner together on a restaurant's candlelit patio. With six weeks of no face time, those seconds in the garden slipping into the past, it was almost easy to believe they were exactly where they were before that little slipup on her part.

Which was for the best, Tessa thought. Time apart had cleared her head, strengthening her resolve to remain a 'reformed romantic,' as she had styled herself since college's romantic failures. No spontaneous kisses or so-called magical connections were going to leave her heartbroken like other times in the past. Better to stay friends and colleagues with Blake than take another trip down disappointment lane. No need to complicate things or blow one tiny little incident out of proportion. Even if Blake seemed so very, very worth the risk at times, when she caught herself thinking about him while she was supposed to be writing business emails.

If Blake thought she was going to bring it up at some point, he was mistaken. She could work around it for weeks more, maybe months, until it was entirely erased from memory, rather than reveal that a part of her was glad it happened—and wished he was, too.

"The original color was green," Blake said, a moment later. Tessa broke away from her thoughts, which had carried her far from the issue of romantic blue's historical inaccuracy. A few taps of the carpenter's hammer fastened the new trim into place. "I found it under the paint layers when you peeled off the old wallpaper. I thought maybe you'd like me to see if I could match it."

"Why? I just painted," said Tessa. "Don't you like lavender?" In her opinion, it was a perfect color, whereas the original green might be some noxious shade that would drive clients from the room.

"It's just the green's original," he said, slotting the hammer in his tool belt. Once again, Tessa knew the contractor was despairing that their decor choices were wandering off the building's historical path. "About the air vent, by the way," he continued, tapping the ornate metal transom grate above his head. "Its hinges are a little rough, and I know you said to take it down, but are you sure?"

"Sure? As sure as I can be that I don't want it falling on somebody's head," said Tessa with a short laugh. "Down it goes. There's a new one behind the door. The lightweight white metal grate in the box."

"I know." He didn't curl his lip with distaste, but Tessa detected it in his voice. She decided to ignore it, as usual. "It's too small. But maybe I can make it work."

He climbed down from the ladder and folded it. "I won't be here as often starting next Tuesday, so I'll make sure the wall in your hallway is covered before then," he said.

"Where will you be?" Tessa looked up from her computer screen with surprise. Not that she should find this statement surprising, since the Wedding Belles weren't his only clients, were they? He'd proved that the moment he asked for time off to take the gig in Virginia. It made perfect sense that he wouldn't be here whenever a better-paying opportunity presented itself.

In truth, to think that he wouldn't be in their building most days—a presence that she was always subconsciously aware of, like a steady, comforting detail that belonged to this place—left her disappointed and dismayed. Even that tiny little accident with the kiss hadn't changed it. She'd grown used to him being close by again, the sound of his hammer's taps, the whirr of the power saw and drill in the next room, so it felt strange to think of silence…

Cut it out, Tessa, she scolded herself. Next thing, she'd be finding excuses for him to stay. For example, to paint this room some hideous Victorian shade of green.

"I'm starting the new job over on Springer Street," he said. "It's a major renovation uptown—I'll be pulling together a crew, tracking down hard-to-find fixtures that are missing from a couple of rooms. I might not be around for a while, so I don't want to leave you with a mess that your clients won't appreciate."

"I see." Tessa's voice seemed tiny and quiet compared to before, strangely enough. "Thanks. I appreciate that. I mean, we appreciate that. Of course."

"Sure. I'll prep it for paint. You have a color picked out already, probably. Neon pink, something called 'Valentine Special.'"

She ignored that little bit of sarcasm too. "So, this new job is an old building, I gather?" she said. "Something with a little more authenticity in its decor?"

"To a 'T,'" he answered, whistling as he gathered up the stray splinters of wood from her floor. "You really should come and see it sometime, though. But give it a few weeks, because it'll take us that long to make a real dent in the place. I have to rip out part of the ceiling in the dining room and the modern partition between the old study and the library. It has to be back in place before MacNeil comes in to work on the decor before the holidays."

"MacNeil?"

"The decorator. Mac's one of the best I've worked with, so this client doesn't mess around. But don't worry. I'll still try to come by here a couple of times a week when I'm off, so I can finish up the work on the office next to yours, and that problem area we talked about downstairs."

"The tiny room that's supposed to have that really ugly wallpaper around the fireplace?"

"That's the one. And it's a Victorian print, by the way."

That was the room Tessa envisioned painted in a shade called 'Valentine Red.' The future show room for mock cake designs and potential toppers, formerly a storage site for old store mannequins. Blake, however, obviously preferred the original wallpaper, a once-bright 'flowers and birds in cages' motif that was waterstained to the point of creating bulbous bird heads on some of its feathered friends, and which had faded the pattern's decorative diamond lattice to a color shade resembling watery grape juice. He had shown her paint swatches before for era-appropriate colors, including more shades of green that Tessa found dubious. Perhaps Blake felt the house's original owners had exceptional taste, or that authentic details trumped personal style somehow, but Tessa had other ideas.

He leaned over Tessa's shoulder—who hadn't even realized he was behind her at that moment, since she had been pretending to look for her stapler in the drawer while she processed Blake's announcement. Aftershave and fresh-cut lumber scented the air surrounding her personal space, a strong pair of arms almost encircling her as he clicked her laptop's mouse on the browser and typed a few words in its search box. Tessa had grown very still, and very aware of the bicep brushing against her sleeve, the scruffy jaw and overly long waves of brown hair mere inches from her cheek as he leaned closer to type.

If she closed her eyes, she knew what she would be imagining right now. Fortunately, Blake located the website he was searching for before it could happen.

On her screen was a picture taken of a large three-story mansion from a bygone era of architecture. Bay picture window, large porch wrapping around its front, pillars and rails festooned with bunting for the Fourth of July. White paint, dark roof, and a brick chimney to one side, the whole house surrounded by an immaculately landscaped lawn.

"That's the house," he said as he withdrew. Tessa could see the little historic plaque beside the front door. Actually, she could see everything about the picture more clearly, now that Blake was on the other side of the room again, collecting his ladder.

"Wow," she said. "It's really—something."

"If 'something' means 'grand' and 'historic' in the broader sense of the words," surmised Blake. "It's all those things and more. I don't always get this lucky when it comes to my projects, so I'm looking forward to really making it shine."

"I'll bet," said Tessa. "Congratulations."

"Thanks," he said. "Come by and see it sometime. I'll be there most days, and the doors are open." He was whistling again as he left her office, collecting some tools first from a pile by her door.

It was gorgeous. And, inside, it was probably exactly the kind of place Blake thought this one should be, down to the proper walnut banisters and Tiffany-inspired dormer windows. No late-addition metal spiral staircase to be seen in a place like this one—or modern paint colors like 'Romantic Blue.'

She closed the browser window. If that was what Blake preferred professionally—steady payments, professional artistry, no offbeat creative quirks like this place offered—then good for him that this client had hired him. And it wasn't like the Wedding Belles needed him full-time, did they?

The answer was no, of course. For the life of her, Tessa couldn't figure out why some part of her persistently felt that the answer was yes instead, since that made utterly no sense at all.

Chapter Five

A cloud of curious smells surrounded Ama as she entered the restaurant's outer hall, which contained the stairs to her family's private apartment, the fragrance of her marketplace visit mingling with that of the jasmine rice that had been cooking in the kitchen that morning. No smell from her father's fire, however, which meant he wasn't grilling the chicken for tonight's special yet, weirdly enough.

"Jaidev, I brought you some new spices," Ama called. She shrugged off her blue cardigan as she set down her shopping bag. "This new Hispanic stall outside the whole foods store had some amazing chipotle, and they were handing out samples of this black pepper rub at the—"

"There you are!" hissed her sister Rasha, hurrying downstairs to meet her. Right behind her was Ama's mother Pashma and Ama's auntie—instantly, Ama smelled trouble instead of spices. Was it an emergency? Was someone hurt? Or was it—but it couldn't be—

"Here I am?" she answered suspiciously.

"*He's here,*" hissed her auntie. "In the private room with your father—"

"Who?"

"The guy from the website!" said Rasha, who would be squealing with excitement if not for her lowered voice.

Horror filled Ama. "What?" she said, her voice louder than she intended. "No. No, this is a joke. He can't be—" Her brain drained itself of sensible replies. "How?"

"Papa invited him," answered Rasha simply. "When he emailed back."

"What? Why?" Ama moaned.

"Hurry up and change," said Pashma, interrupting. "You can't meet him looking like that."

That someone who had replied to her father's online ad for her was *actually* here? Had actually arranged to meet her? It didn't seem possible somehow.

"Tell me this isn't happening," said Ama. "How could he do this? I told Papa I wasn't interested in meeting any of those people, no matter how great they sound." Her voice was growing too loud, because her mother and Rasha were pulling her upstairs, and away from the dining room. Where, presumably, the guy in question must be talking with her father.

"Come on, we have to get you fixed up," said Rasha. "His family's been waiting for fifteen minutes."

"*Family?*" *Oh no.* It was even worse than she thought. He had brought his parents along for the first meeting, like an old-fashioned couple meeting to evaluate the match. It was bad enough to be part of an online dating website that matched her with suitable strangers, but even worse to meet her would-be in-laws on the first date. Wasn't the internet's modern way of connecting people supposed to eliminate those sort of conventional setups? Who in their family had made the horrible mistake of teaching her father how to use a computer in the first place?

Are you fixing up my hair and clothes? Or fixing me up with a lifelong commitment? Ama's heels dug into the stairs. "I don't think I can meet a stranger without warning like this," she told them. "Let's just apologize and find an excuse for them to leave, okay?"

"Do this for your father, to make him happy," said Pashma. "He's so happy that a nice boy answered. Give him this chance, Ama."

"He didn't even give me any warning, though," said Ama in protest.

"He's a nice boy," her auntie Bendi assured her, as she pushed open the door to Ama's bedroom. "True, his family is from the south… and a *little* dark…"

"I don't care about that," Ama assured her, thinking how the same kind of prejudices seemed to crop up in every culture across the world. "I don't care what he looks like or where he's from… I just don't want to meet a stranger to discuss whether or not we should date."

"You should appreciate this opportunity to find someone," her aunt scolded her. "It's not as if a rich Punjabi boy is going to come beg you to marry him, is it? So we fish in a bigger pond."

"His family is from Tamil Nadu, and he has a good job and a college degree," supplied her mother.

"He's in I.T. for one of the major financial firms downtown," said Rasha excitedly. "It's a *great* salary with benefits. Sanjay says it's the biggest international trader in the city. This is perfect, Ama."

Ama waved away the blessing from Rasha's accountant husband. "Then how come he hasn't found a nice girl already?" she asked, as her family shoved her onto the bed, with Pashma already opening her closet's door. "Why do they want to meet me?" Were the groom's parents so very set on finding a match for him that they would let their son meet a potential wife from a totally different background?

"He was sick a few years when he was younger. Nothing contagious by now," assured her mother. "But it put him behind the rest of the young men his age."

"Mono," said Rasha. "Bendi, do something with her hair—the pins are in the box. Ama, the clothes have to go."

"What's wrong with the way I look?" protested Ama. She gestured toward her outfit, which was a perfectly cute embroidered peasant blouse and a blue paisley skirt paired with some wooden-soled Dutch clogs she had found at a secondhand clothing shop.

Her mother stepped back, she and Rasha holding a sari between them as if unveiling a painting. A bright green one with an orange sari shirt and underskirt, and orange and gold embroidery detailing it to create a garment exactly like the sort her sister would have picked out from an online garment retailer. Which was where it had come from, Ama knew full well.

Ama shook her head. "It's not me. I don't want to wear something just for the sake of impressing someone else." She held up her hands, defensively warding it off. "Please, just pick something else. Something more casual."

"It's just the one time," insisted her mother.

"A cousin of his mother's goes to the hairdresser my friend Sheeta visits, and she says that his family is very traditional," Bendi explained. "They will expect us to be traditional at home too. We don't want to offend them, do we?"

"You would look *soo* cute in this!" said Rasha enthusiastically. "Just try it on, Ama. For me. You've never worn it, and it's a perfectly good dress."

"Hold still," said Bendi, slapping Ama's hand away when she tried to stop her hair from being pinned back. "Pashma, where are the sari pins?"

"Mine are in the little makeup case on the table," answered Rasha. "Grab the tube of lipstick too. This is going to be so much fun!"

"Fun?" echoed Ama.

"Hurry! We can't keep them waiting!" said Bendi anxiously.

Ten minutes later, they were downstairs in the restaurant's private tearoom, in Ama's own private dating nightmare.

It was a scene from *Bend It Like Beckham*, Ama thought grimly—or maybe a chapter from *A Suitable Boy*, which her mother had been listening to in audiobook form this past week. Probably in mental preparation for this afternoon, when her family would sit down in the private dining room across from the Devar family with their eligible son.

World's most awkward tea. She had heard stories before from friends of hers who had modern arranged marriages—how the first meeting between families of the prospective couple would feel stiff and be only polite small talk until somebody managed to break the ice of formality. They all laughed about it later—and Ama laughed with them—but always with the secret resolution it would never be *her* in that scenario. And *they* probably hadn't been forced into a traditional dress just to appeal to strangers, either.

"He's cute," Rasha had whispered a moment ago, peering into the tearoom through the doorway curtain's crack, as Pashma tweaked a few of Ama's hairpins in place. "This is so exciting. It's just like that scene from *The Namesake*, Ama—think, this could be your perfect match!"

"Yeah. Right." Sarcasm, although Ama was almost never sarcastic. She could hear her father's voice, getting too loud in his usual fashion when he was nervous. This was going to be horrible.

Feeling uncomfortable in the formal sari and with a hairpin sticking her in the scalp, Ama resisted the urge to squirm a little, sandwiched between her mother and auntie on the little love seat. Across from her sat the dignified-looking parents of her prospective suitor: a man with a medium skin tone in a nice suit and tie, and a woman in a redesigned modern *salwar kameez* that could almost pass for business casual.

Clearly, 'traditional' for the Devars was sensible, sedate, and modern with a touch of India, and nothing like the impression her aunt had painted from a friend's words. Ama knew they, too, probably hadn't pictured her or her family like this—in their flashiest choice of saris and too much lipstick, her father in his embroidered cotton linen and Jaidev the same. Jaidev, who smelled strongly of *masala dosa* and whatever spice he had used to rub down the meat this morning, which blended with the fragrance of her mother's tea. They seemed to have morphed into a giant Punjabi cliché from a Bollywood movie for this occasion.

What had her father *put* in that online ad about her prospects? Did he say her family was secretly Punjabi royalty? That they owned a chain of Indian restaurants across the U.S.?

Her suitor sat next to his parents, and appeared to be deep in thought as he listened to their relatives bantering about American food and traffic. Or maybe he was conducting a serious study of the loud Oriental carpet beneath his feet, one her mother had insisted on buying for the restaurant at a cheap bazaar sale.

"Tamir was very bright and gifted as a boy," his father Narain was now saying. "At the top of his class when we moved to America. Everyone believed he would go to MIT when the time came—but then, the illness delayed his education. He's now behind in his career goals, but he is working very hard to catch up with the other young men of his age. I'm sure he'll achieve a promotion very soon."

Narain was in designer retail, Ama had learned, managing two or three different stores for one of the big chains. His wife Deevana was only a semi-traditional Indian housewife, who taught classes in classical artwork at a cultural studies center. Tamir was their bright and only son, the engineer who'd graduated from a respectable northeastern university a few years ago.

His complexion *was* a little dark by Indian caste standards, which could explain why his successful parents were having trouble finding him a wife, since Ama knew that some families might be prejudiced against darker skin tones. Plus, the fact that he had fallen behind academically would be a problem for others from his social sphere, who would expect a young man of his age to have climbed higher on the corporate ladder.

Not with her family, though, who had no degrees, only a knack for running restaurants successfully. Her matrimony-hungry auntie would be willing to embrace him as family right now, even if he were fourth in line for promotion at the nearest dry cleaner's.

"Do you work in the restaurant?" Deevana asked Ama.

"Yes, but—" Ama began, before Pashma gave her a quick poke in the side.

"Ama is a wonderful cook," said Pashma, who obviously still believed in the 'traditional' description as given by Bendi's friend. "She makes good curd rice."

"You should taste her *kadamba sambar*, and her *dosa* with chutney," volunteered Rasha.

She had never cooked *kadamba sambar* in her life, and her *dosa* was weak at best—Ama knew these were dishes selected to appeal to the prospective culinary tastes of their Tamil Nadu guests.

"And her chicken curry," contributed Jaidev, who winked subtly at Ama. She stopped herself from glaring at him.

"We are vegetarian," announced Deevana. An awkward pause from Ama's family after this.

"She can make good curry with vegetable too," supplied her father Ranjit, coming to the rescue. "Put it on a banana leaf, and Ama can make it seem like a feast for the tongue."

He looked thrilled, beaming at his daughter whenever he thought their guests were busy with their tea. He had been dying for years to have tea with a nice young boy interested in her, she knew. Finally, he had an official prospective suitor materialize on the scene, meeting her in a traditional Indian family setting, right down to the Darjeeling tea poured in the saucers and the 'no shoes indoors' policy.

If it wouldn't have broken his heart, Ama would have been tempted to run from the room—and not just because the parents across from her did not look overly excited at the prospect of the Bhaguts as their in-laws.

She could bet they really wished their son had picked somebody else from his matches.

"Are you a graduate from a college or university, Ama?" inquired Deevana politely. "Your father's email did not mention your education." An email crafted with lots of backspaces and single-digit tapping by Ranjit, undoubtedly, with Pashma hovering over his shoulder to contribute and correct.

"No," answered Ama honestly, and couldn't help but see the subtle exchange of glances between this boy's parents—doubtful ones. "I decided against college a few years ago. I preferred baking."

"I am sure you are a very bright young woman, nonetheless," contributed Narain, still polite. But Ama knew that it was probably a stigma for him, her lack of a degree, just like it was for a lot of affluent multi-generational Americans too.

There must be an auntie *really* pushing Tamir to find a wife.

"I thought about culinary school for a while. But I own my own business now," she added, before Pashma or Ranjit could stop her. "I'm the baker and cake designer for an event planning service."

"That sounds very interesting," said Narain, who didn't look particularly interested at all.

The young man, Tamir, glanced directly at Ama for the second time, and twitched his lips into a smile—polite, bland, and with a touch of shyness that suggested all that recuperation, studying, and career scrambling hadn't left him with much time for dating, via matchmaking or personal choice.

He was probably a nice, polite boy. He was dressed in a perfectly pressed business suit of modest price and sensible style, accented by perfectly sensible eyeglasses in smart, modern frames. He looked as bland and boring as the kind of boy that Bendi had been dying to find for her for years.

"Is this all of your family?" said Narain. "They all work in the restaurant?"

To own a business was considered successful in America—but in India, the caste system made this matter tricky to judge. How strict would this family be when it came to judging hers? Neither of her brothers had been interested in college—not a prayer of it for Rasha, either, who had practically skipped high school in her eagerness to move on. And her father's plans for the second branch of their restaurant were still on hold due to her mother's fears of spending profits irresponsibly.

"Oh no," said Ranjit hastily. "I have an older daughter married. To a very successful engineer."

"Our other son Nikil has his own business," spoke up Pashma. "Jaidev will take Ranjit's place someday in this restaurant."

Nikil's business was running a butcher's shop in one of Bellegrove's nearby ethnic districts—probably not the kind of trade likely to impress the couple sitting across from them, Ama thought. She wanted to smile at their possible reaction, but it wasn't all that funny, really. Surely this boy was going to see right away that she wasn't his ideal match and end this thing.

"What do you bake, Ama?" Tamir addressed a polite question her way, the first since their initial introduction. There was a little trace of an Indian accent in his voice, hardly noticeable in its presence. When did his family move to America? Twenty years ago or so—Ama hadn't been paying enough attention.

"Cupcakes," she said. "Mostly. And wedding cakes."

"She put a beautiful sari design on the one for her sister Nalia's wedding," supplied Bendi. "She's had so much practice in the kitchen, she is ready to bake her own!" She laughed—so did everyone else, although it was only polite laughter from Tamir's side.

Would it help them abandon this if they knew her mother was from a relatively poor Rajasthani family? Or that the Bhagut family's previous restaurant was a tourist trap in Himachal Pradesh? Ama racked her brain for every possible stereotype that could be cast against her as a marriage prospect by them, as if their impression of her weren't enough to make up their minds already.

"Don't worry about the American desserts—the important thing is she makes good *gulab jamun*," her father assured Tamir.

"I've eaten it before. It's a little sweet for me," confessed Tamir. "I guess I'm used to my grandmother's cooking. She was very... traditional."

"Did we mention that Tamir has been in India for the past year?" asked Deevana. "He helped my father in our family's business, design-ing its website. He also helped his cousin come to America, with a good scholarship at one of the schools. Tamir has a very respected influence in his university's technology department."

Was he hunting for a wife all that time in the prospective candidates of Tamil Nadu—and no interest from possible brides there? Ama's brain was picking up on the wavelengths from her auntie Bendi, maybe, who would be thinking this exact thought by now. That Tamir was discounted goods that could be had for a relative bargain, thanks to the disinterest among his cousin's eligible friends.

She made herself venture a nice smile toward him. "Do you have any hobbies?" Ama asked.

"He has no time for hobbies," said Narain with a laugh. "The boy works ten hours per day. And weekends. He's very dedicated to his career."

Tamir cleared his throat. "I like to read," he said. "I used to play sports, before I got sick, of course. That was around the time I started college."

"Sounds nice," said Ama politely.

"And before the accident. It made it hard to kick a football."

"Did we mention the car accident?" said Narain. "Three years ago a driver on his phone crashed into the car of Tamir's friend, when he was sitting in the passenger seat. He had surgery for the fractured bones—months of recovery for it."

"It set him back still further," said Deevana, as her husband shook his head sadly.

"Sounds painful," said Ama dutifully. She thought Tamir looked as if he was tired of hearing his various setbacks commiserated, although she couldn't be sure.

Their guests collected their shoes from the hall after tea was over. "It was nice to meet you, Ama," said Deevana, who didn't look particularly happy. That smile belonged to a woman who was desperately hoping to utter the magic word 'wedding' in connection with her son in the near future, Ama thought.

"We must all have dinner together soon," said Ranjit. "Come to our restaurant—I will feed you with the best Indian cuisine in the city. Banana leaves for everyone!"

Stop it, Ama willed him. Tamir shook her hand.

"It's been nice," he said. "I wondered if I could have your phone number? I thought maybe it would be nice to meet later on, just the two of us, to get to know each other better."

"What a nice idea," said Pashma eagerly.

"Sure," said Ama. This was standard operating procedure between prospective matches: to have coffee and scope each other out before the parents added their stamp of approval. Sometimes it never made it that far—Narain and Deevana didn't look ready to bless a courtship with her after today, so Tamir was only being civil to her now. The polite way out would involve deleting the digits he was now entering into his own phone as soon as he was safely outside.

"Thank you," he said. "It was nice meeting you." They shook hands again. He gave her another polite smile.

"Not a bad match for a first try," said Ranjit, after he closed the door behind their visitors. "Polite boy, good job—how could it be better?" He clapped his hands together. "Time to get to work again. Jaidev, turn the sign back so customers can come in. We have chicken seasoned that's ready for the fire, and tonight's special is tandoori." He gave Ama a smug look as he donned his apron. "Was it so bad to meet a boy after all?" he asked triumphantly. "Your father is a pretty good matchmaker, eh? A nice boy like Tamir instead of a stranger that Bendi met in the spice aisle of the grocery?"

Ama shook her head. "He's not going to call me, Papa."

"He will. You heard him. Why wouldn't he call?" insisted Ranjit. "You're a pretty girl, smart—we own the biggest Indian restaurant in this part of the city. What else does he want?"

"A girl with a degree and social background more like his own?" Ama guessed.

"This is America. You look for someone who has success here, good ties here," said Ranjit stubbornly, as if this particular fact of immigration in modern times somehow overrode those traditional cultural and caste ties. "You have all those things. You work hard and know about business and cooking and other things that are important in a wife."

This from a man whose thirty-odd years in America had yet to resign him to knowledge of the plot of *Star Wars*, the practicality of wearing denim, or the difference between Coca-Cola and Pepsi, thought Ama.

"She thinks every man isn't interested," said Pashma dismissively.

"I think he's perfect, Ama," said Rasha, who still sounded thrilled at the idea of Ama's suitor. "He's so cute. And he's successful. You guys will have a great time when you get together for coffee or something."

"I don't think you should get your hopes up," said Ama, shedding her hairpins and letting her hair fall freely in its usual style as she retreated to her room to be rid of the borrowed outfit's binding wrap as quickly as possible. "He's just being polite to get rid of a girl who was *obviously* not what they hoped for." Hadn't the rest of them seen that it was a disaster? Although, for once, she was actually grateful about her family's ability to make a terrible first impression.

"You're imagining things!" scolded her auntie.

"Trust me on this." She knew she was right. Even if a tiny chance might exist that maybe... *maybe*... she could somehow be wrong if this boy was really desperate. If he really did call, what would she do? Tell him that the matchmaking thing was her father's idea only—tell him that she wasn't interested at all in pursuing a match through the website?

"How can you say no to a nice boy?" said her father. "When he calls, make me happy and go, Ama. Please." To ask and not simply state this option as fact—that meant her father really wanted her to

change her mind. He had found her weak spot, and Ama felt guilty at
the thought of saying no yet again.

She sighed. "Fine," she said. "But there's no point, because he's
not calling."

He'll never call, she thought. Even a desperate and dull boy would
still have enough self-respect to avoid someone so clearly incompatible—and disinterested—as herself. At least she certainly hoped so,
since Ama was determined never to settle for less than sheer passion
and romantic sparks when it came to finding the love of her life.

Chapter Six

Tessa took a picture of the billboard as soon as it was pasted above the roadway. A softened photograph of a happy bride and groom hand in hand beneath a shower of confetti from smiling guests, with the Wedding Belles' logo to one side. *Let us make your special day all that it can be!*

At their headquarters on Thursday, Ama and Natalie were trying to disentangle some Christmas twinkle lights, finding a working set of cool white for the window display. "I think half of these are burnt out," complained Natalie.

"Try the other string. The plug looks less worn on it," suggested Ama. "We just need a couple of working strands in Christmas colors."

"Any calls?" asked Tessa, closing the door behind her as she tossed the business's mail on the entry table—all junk advertisements for high-speed internet and new cars. "Do we have a client?"

"It's only been four days, Tess," said Natalie. "Are you expecting a miracle?"

"I'm expecting someone to notice our snazzy graphics," answered Tessa. "The magazine ad came out yesterday—we're right next to a honeymoon airline package."

She unwound the scarf around her neck; at the same moment, the office phone rang. Tessa gave both her partners a triumphant glance before she hurried to the main desk and snapped it up. "Wedding Belles, this is Tessa speaking," she said. "Certainly. Of course. Tuesday at ten? Yes, that would be fine. No, thank *you*."

Ama and Natalie exchanged glances. "Dentist changed your appointment, I take it?" said Natalie as Tessa hung up.

"It was a client, thank you very much." A smile crossed Tessa's lips—she was bursting with pride, as if receiving this phone call was a personal accomplishment against the negative forces in the universe. "I told you it would pay off. The bride's name is Nadia Emerson, and she'll be here with the groom for the appointment." She made a note on the calendar. "Finally, our slump is over. I told you our bad luck wouldn't last. All we needed was a tiny push, and we're back on track."

"We'll have to tidy up the parlor," said Ama, almost tripping over the strand of lights and their box as she kicked the holiday decoration mess into a nearby cupboard. "I should make some biscotti or cookies or something." In the window, the only sign of the coming display was Natalie's beautiful gown on a mannequin.

"We'll have to cancel the buzz saw in the next room, too," said Natalie, as she stuffed the rest of the glittery fabric 'snow' into the cupboard as well. Blake's power tools were now buzzing through a wooden board, sending one end of it to the sawdust pile on the floor. Tessa glimpsed him through the doorway. She caught herself watching as if something fascinated her about this mundane carpentry act—maybe that's why she finished slowly closing the door between them.

✻

Nadia Emerson the bride was cute, smiling, and cheerful, although a tiny bit shy at times. She was a curator for a local art gallery who had met the groom when he was purchasing a canvas for his business's decor. Next to the dark-haired girl sat the groom, a sturdily built man named Lyle Kardopolis, around thirty, with close-cropped light brown hair. He owned a Greek restaurant across town that specialized in traditional dishes and modern fusion. Despite being engaged merely weeks, they had settled on a wedding date in December.

"This December?" Tessa asked, surprised at the tight deadline.

"We know it must sound crazy," Nadia admitted, "but we both agreed we don't want to wait for the New Year to get married." With a slight laugh, she added, "Every other planner in town has turned us down, so you're kind of our last chance, actually. Lyle saw your billboard and said we should give you a call before resigning ourselves to a spring wedding."

At the mention of their new billboard, Tessa sneaked a knowing smile in Natalie's direction. "Well," she told them, "I'm sure we can help you plan your special day, no matter the timetable involved. Tell us more about your ideas for it."

"So, we're thinking a medium-size wedding or so," said Nadia. "I don't have a big family really, just average size, but there's a lot of people I know professionally—Lyle, he knows everybody in the restaurant business, so he wants to invite them. Plus, he has a big family."

"Forty cousins," said the groom's mother. "Can you believe it?"

Her name was Paula, and she was squeezed into the short, antiquated chair beside her son on the love seat. Bright lipstick, brightly dyed hair... Tessa could sense a future loud and overly enthusiastic champagne toast from that quarter.

"That's a lot of cousins," said Natalie. "But I can sympathize. I'm Italian."

"Nadia has a far more... sedate... number," said Cynthia, the bride's mother. "I'm sure you'll notice that her side of the list is mostly professional? Our family doesn't like to make a scene on someone's big day. We like to keep it quiet and sensible, the way it should be."

Nadia's mother was seated to the left of the bride in an old wingback chair shoved as close as possible to her daughter. She was the complete opposite of the groom's mother if you judged by appearances, for Cynthia wore only neutral colors in her makeup and clothing, and her hair was drawn into such a tight bun it was a wonder it hadn't pulled itself out by the roots. She wore gloves and a hat that matched her overcoat and her sensible wool skirt and blouse, and spoke with the prim Southern drawl of a chaperone straight from the ballroom of *Gone with the Wind*. Give her a parasol and a wider skirt, Tessa reflected, and she would pass for a quintessential matron of the old South's 'ps' and 'qs.'

"What's wrong with a big family?" said Paula. "I hope these kids have a dozen in the future."

"I'm sure you would," said Cynthia with a sigh.

"Mother," whispered Nadia warningly. She recovered herself and smiled at the planners again. "We're planning to have the reception at Lyle's place. The restaurant has a huge banquet room."

"My place is doing the catering," said Lyle, who had been quiet until the subject of food. "Ever been there? It's called Olive Brook—converted warehouse, little grotto in the back with patio seating?"

"I've seen it before," said Ama. "Near the old railway station, right?"

Down in the old waterfront warehouse district, Tessa recalled a subtle, old-fashioned building with a limestone exterior, a row of high factory windows and a sign painted with graceful letters and a branch with a single olive and two leaves. It was right across from the riverfront Southern Steamboat Museum, which featured a mural-style billboard of a showboat chugging past the weeping willow-lined banks of a Mississippi River mansion, and a glimpse of an antique ship's steering wheel and naval compass through its glass entry doors—once, Tessa had taken her mother there for a Mother's Day outing. Now she wished they had had lunch at Lyle's restaurant instead of the little overpriced ribs place a friend had recommended. Gyros definitely would have been better.

"That's me," Lyle said. "Come by sometime, you can eat by the special rate as friends of mine—we've got a great chef whose antipasto platter and tzatziki mutton rolls are the best."

"You're not so bad in the kitchen yourself," said Nadia, nudging his side playfully with her elbow. Lyle's ears turned slightly pink.

"Yeah, well, who has time anymore, right? I got shipments, invoices, bookings—I got too much on for the kitchen these days," he said. "I won't even be around for half this stuff, so lucky thing that Ma's available to help out."

Lucky? Tessa wasn't sure that was the correct word, although Paula was glowing. "Isn't he the greatest son?" she said. "Handsome, charming, a big restaurateur—the number of girls chasing him was uncountable, believe me. I never thought he'd finally settle down."

"When I met Nadia, I knew she was the one," said Lyle, smiling at the girl beside him.

"It's not as if Nadia didn't have her choice of suitors," murmured Cynthia. Nadia gave her a warning look, as Lyle, unnoticing, opened one of the books on the coffee table, a picture volume entitled *Unforgettable Weddings*.

"Well, she picked the best, didn't she?" said Paula. "Lyle could have had *any* girl he wanted—all he had to do was snap his fingers."

Whatever prim little muttering came from Cynthia's lips this time—and it sounded like 'sausage rolls' to Tessa—was barely a whisper on the wind, but the wedding planner's glance nevertheless flew immediately to the former chef's thick digits, which might be a *little* fleshy from too many gyros... but surely she had misheard.

"Hey, look at that, Nadia. That's pretty sharp, isn't it?" Lyle was pointing to something in the book. "Maybe we can do something like it for our wedding."

"I like that," said Nadia, leaning closer for a look. A fluttering sigh of distaste from Cynthia's lips; a hardening of the eyes for Paula that reminded Tessa of a bull baited with a matador's red cloth. They looked like two rivals and not two future in-laws helping plan the couple's special day.

"This is going to be trouble," said Natalie, after the couple had set up their first appointment to discuss the wedding's theme, then taken their leave. "Did you see the look in Nadia's eyes every time her mom needled his mom? And he totally didn't notice his mom's words were an insult to Nadia, talking about all his ex-admirers."

"Maybe we're misreading things," said Tessa, as she slid her planning notebook onto her desk.

"Trust me. I know families," said Natalie. "This is just like my uncle Guido's relatives. They can't agree on the thickness of filling for cannoli, much less have a family wedding without a fight. They're constantly swapping little insults."

"We'll just ignore it," said Tessa. "We're supposed to be the buffer between all sides, the big negotiators and peacemakers for the wedding's plans, right? So we'll do our jobs extra well this time."

"If you say so," said Natalie. Doubtfully.

"Come on. It'll be fun. We haven't planned a wedding in weeks. This is the end of our bad luck streak, remember?" said Tessa. "We need to enjoy it."

"Or it's the latest jinx in our bad luck streak," said Natalie. "Don't be too sure we can just brush those two off, Tess."

"I don't believe in jinxes. Or in bad luck," said Tessa. "I believe we make our own luck, and, therefore, that there's nothing this wedding can throw at us that we can't confidently handle." She gathered up a stack of books from her shelf, all about winter-themed party ideas and Christmas and holiday entertaining, as well as one on innovative wedding celebrations. "Ten to one, Nadia will ask you to sew her dress. Isn't that fantastic luck, by your standards?"

"Fantastic luck would be if my mom stopped asking me to find Mr. Right," said Natalie, as she added a book on classic designer gowns to Tessa's stack. "You're talking situations with average odds."

"Maybe you'll meet him this afternoon," teased Tessa.

"Thanks," said Natalie sarcastically. "Remind Ama that Friday's takeout pizza and window dressing day, by the way. We can use any extra help that comes our way—say, if our contractor doesn't have big plans, he could pitch in, too." She added this part in a slightly louder voice than the rest.

Blake's strong arms hoisting an artificial Christmas tree into place, and helping Tessa untangle lights in a fingers-intermingling game of Twister: that was the last thing Tessa needed or intended to picture right now, and her brain quickly searched for a distraction, like the sudden need to locate her stapler. Why did these random thoughts about the handyman keep popping up after all these weeks?

"What do you need me to pitch into?" Blake had shut off his drill in the hall outside the office, where he was patching over an ugly light fixture removed from the wall.

Natalie and Tessa exchanged glances. "Nothing," they answered.

✳

Over a latte after her class on the fundamentals of garment embellish-
ment, Natalie studied a technical manual on using a sewing machine's
embroidery function, forgetting momentarily about her weekend
shift at the bakery, Mr. Right, or the fact that Tessa's face turned a
funny color whenever Blake the handyman's name came up in conversation. All that mattered at this moment was figuring out how to
size the pattern to fit the dress's bodice from her sketch, since her
machine was a finicky secondhand model vastly inferior to the one in
Kandace's loft.

"Number fourteen," called the barista. "One fresh apple muffin
to go?"

Natalie shoved her book in her bag and stepped up to the counter.
"That's me," she said, taking the bakery sack from the employee. She
turned aside, and found herself confronted not by the elderly man who
had been talking loudly to his caregiver about which pastry he wanted,
but a tanned, muscular blond figure holding a coffee cup. Fortunately,
his coffee cup's lid saved her hand-stitched sweater coat from ruin,
which Natalie was relieved about after spending hours pleating its
waist and sleeves like a poet's jacket.

"Whoa. Sorry," said Natalie. "Didn't see you there." How she could
miss seeing him was another matter, because he was pretty smokin' in
Natalie's book. Bronze complexion and blond hair that seemed just
a little on the long side for a white-collar career—which his business
trousers and pinstripe shirt obviously implied. Surfing enthusiast, she
guessed, based solely on his tan—but not that of the aging frat boy or
beer-swilling beach bum variety Natalie was generally fairly careful to
steer clear of in her dating life.

"No problem." He smiled. "Just trying to pick between strawberry and banana. My daily dilemma at this place." His head nodded in the direction of the pastry case.

"Get both. Then you don't have to decide," suggested Natalie.

"Too easy," he said. "I enjoy a challenge in everything but coffee."

"Let me guess. No sugar, one cream… and no decaf," said Natalie. "Am I right?"

"You are so close, it's scary," he answered, with another smile that parted his lips slightly, revealing the bottom edge of a perfectly straight row of white teeth. "Chad, by the way." He held out his hand.

"Natalie." She shook hands. "A pleasure to meet you."

"It's all mine," he said. "I think you might be the first grownup I've met in this place. Most of the employees look twelve—and is it just my imagination, or are college students now all tweens?"

"You noticed that, too?" said Natalie. "I feel like I'm surrounded by infants in the hall when I leave my grad school classes—all the freshman girls look like twigs and the guys are wearing skinny jeans in my size. I keep wishing my family had been Italian models in the fashion world and not Italian bakers." Not for the body of a twiggy twenty-something, Natalie knew, but didn't bother to explain.

"Who could tell the difference, looking at you," said Chad. "You mean you're not an Italian supermodel having coffee at this place?"

Blushes for flirtation were not Natalie's style, not even one of embarrassed politeness for such an obvious pickup line as this. But his tone of voice made his joke feel like part of normal conversation—not a corny punch line just hanging in the air for her response. She liked a guy who left the door open for her to decide.

As for the Italian model thing… corny, yes. But coming from a guy like him, definitely a little cute as well.

"Do you attempt that line with every stranger you meet?" she asked. He laughed, embarrassed.

"Not that often, I swear," he said. "But... since I wanted to ask for your phone number, I thought I should probably establish that I'm interested. The classic pickup line kind of points it out for me."

Smooth, Natalie decided, this transition from chitchat to asking her out. Much more gracefully delivered than the last pickup line offered to her.

"Like a sign holder on the corner?" she asked him. "Your pickup line's a big red arrow pointing straight to the truth?"

"More like a winking smiley emoji at the end of a text," he answered.

He glanced at the paper sack in her hand. "Are you in a hurry to be somewhere?" he asked. "I just got off work, and I think I've changed my mind and would rather have my strawberry muffin here than to go."

"Strawberry, huh?"

"The day they bake a blended recipe will be my lucky day," he answered.

They shared a table by the window, where they made casual talk for a half hour. Chad worked in marketing for a new startup brand that designed and sold athletic shoes, and had graduated from his college's business program seven years before. He preferred the office's laidback business casual attire Wednesdays through Fridays, khakis and polo shirts over ties, and he liked surfing, rock climbing, hiking, and zip lining in his spare time—thus explaining his tan. And he thought Natalie's fashion aspirations sounded fascinating, judging by the attentive look on his face when it was her turn to share.

"Not that you wouldn't make a great fashion model," he said. "Think about it. You would be the only one in the city who not only designed her own dresses, but showcased them personally on the runway."

"You don't have to use the model line anymore," said Natalie knowingly. "You have me interested, if that's what you're trying to do."

"Am I that obvious?" he asked, trying not to laugh.

"Yeah. You are. But it's kind of cute, so I'll ignore it."

They both laughed now. He reached for his cell phone. "Can I have your number?" he asked. "Maybe call you sometime to meet up after the holidays?" He shrugged, as if it was no big deal, this potential meeting. Not putting the importance and pressure on it of two people interviewing each other as prospective life partners, that zone of eager and nervous bouts of exchange. Music to Natalie's ears, that off-the-cuff tone for this proposal.

"Sure." She couldn't be so busy over the next couple of weeks that a fun evening or afternoon was completely impossible. She was already looking forward to seeing Chad again. The thought of rock climbing with his group on a Saturday afternoon was exactly the sort of fun she needed right now.

"See you soon," he told her.

"See you." She waved goodbye to him just before leaving the shop. There was something vaguely rugged in his overgrown hair and well-toned physique that resembled Blake Ellingham, minus the callused laborer's hands—although Tessa would probably vehemently deny that there was anything physical to notice about the carpenter, even in the strength and composition of his fingers. This from a woman who'd obsessively watched those close-ups of Matthew Macfadyen's in *Pride and Prejudice* a dozen times in the past. *Give me a break, Tessa Miller*, Natalie thought with a knowing smile.

Outside, the fresh, cool fall air tasted like cinnamon toast, thanks to the coffee shop's oven vents. Maybe Tessa was right, Natalie reflected—that their bad luck streak was over, not that Mr. Right had appeared in the form of handsome, hunky Chad, of course. But the latter possibility would be just fine with her too.

Chapter Seven

Over Thanksgiving, the window scene became a Christmas bride's paradise in red and gold twinkle lights, with a big bouquet of white poinsettias and silk and pearl bead mistletoe to match Natalie's second champagne satin wedding gown. More importantly, however, the firm's December bride returned to the parlor to choose her theme.

"I think I want sort of a… a snow bride feel," said Nadia. "Lots of white and silver and blue. I really love snow and frozen ponds and icicles—my favorite part of Christmas is the winter. The way everything glitters and sparkles."

This would be the perfect wedding for Stefan, Tessa reflected, thinking of the Wedding Belles' former wedding planner partner, who had ditched them for a tempting Paris job before they even began. The more sparkle the better had been his apparent motto.

"So it's like *Frozen*," suggested Paula. "Boy, I just love that ice queen movie. The big snow monsters, the big ice castle—say, maybe the cake can look like the castle! Wouldn't that be something? And you could wear a fancy gown like Elsa," she said to Nadia.

"Well… it might be kind of pretty," said Nadia. "I like the style—but I think—"

"My daughter is not wearing *blue* for her wedding," said Cynthia primly. "She's not patterning her ceremony after a children's movie.

I think we're talking about cool shades, pure white accented by some sort of blue flowers for the tables."

"I do like parts of the movie idea, Mom," began Nadia. "We don't have to rule it out just because the dress is blue. Obviously I'll want something a little more traditional, but—"

"We could put a big crown of snowflakes on you," said Paula. "Lyle always says you're his princess, so why not dress up as one? Can you do a snow princess wedding?" she asked Tessa.

"Only if that's what Nadia wants," Tessa answered.

"I don't think I want to wear a crown, Paula," said Nadia.

"Why not? It's your wedding, honey. You're a queen for that day. And, believe me, Lyle plans to treat you like one. Look how much he's forking out for this ceremony and reception."

Lyle wasn't here, or surely he would be embarrassed that his mother was almost bragging about how much the big day would cost, Tessa thought. Did he know that she was making such a big deal out of his role in the wedding?

"*I'm* paying for the flowers and the cake," Cynthia reminded her stiffly.

"Well, forgive me for forgetting *that* little detail," snapped Paula.

Nadia held up her hands. "Please, I think it's time we listen to the wedding planners," she said. "I'm sure they have some ideas about what a winter wedding should be like."

"I've actually been working on a few ideas that you might like," said Tessa. "I have some sketches here of some floral arrangements emphasizing white and silver, and some possible wedding favors."

Among the possibilities, Tessa had included a historic church outside the city which had windows big enough to showcase a snowy landscape, and a horse-drawn white sleigh for the couple's vehicle of departure. Nadia found this last suggestion enchanting, despite her mother pointing out how impractical it sounded.

"You'll need snow to have a sleigh, after all," Cynthia told her. "That's hardly the kind of thing you can guarantee for Bellegrove in December—even if we usually *do* have a white Christmas."

"I thought of that already, actually," said Tessa, before the bride could issue a comeback to this latest objection. "If it looks like snow is a problem, the best solution would be to rent a sleigh-style carriage. They look very similar to the real thing and it captures the spirit of a winter wedding without having to worry about any... technical difficulties."

"That sounds perfect," said Nadia—at the same moment as her mother let out a disapproving sniff. Turning toward her, Nadia demanded, "What is it now, Mother? You obviously disagree, so just get it out of your system." Clearly, the bride was feeling the strain of this meeting already.

"It's just all a little bit unorthodox, isn't it?" said Cynthia. "A carriage that looks like a sleigh, a snow bride without snow—"

"She has a point there, honey," Paula broke in, agreeing with the opposition for a change. "A limousine would be more fun anyway, don't you think? You and Lyle won't have to freeze that way and you could even get one that has a big flat-screen TV and champagne and stuff. Now that's what I call traveling in style!"

"But that's not what I want," Nadia said. "I like Tessa's suggestion. Put us down for the carriage," she told the wedding planner. Forcefully.

"Maybe we should move on to some other parts of the wedding now," Tessa suggested, putting a check next to the bride's preference on transportation. At this rate, they wouldn't be done planning the wedding until next Christmas, she thought.

"How about a big castle for the ceremony?" said Paula. "Lyle just has his heart set on a great big site for it. There's that big palace hotel with the fancy lobby. How's that for class?"

"Horrid," answered Cynthia in a crisp tone.

"What about bridesmaids in blue?" said Nadia. "I really like the thought of pale blue strapless satin, with maybe a little snowflake hair ornament for each girl. With the sort of silvery-white shawls..." She held up a photo on her cell phone.

"Those are nice," commented Natalie. "I can get you a break on the fabric for the bridal party gowns. And your own—if you want it tailored, too."

"You can sew my gown?" Nadia asked, amazed.

"She's the best," said Tessa proudly. "She worked for one of the designers in the city before she partnered with us." That designer had also been the worst in the city, but neither planner contributed this information, as it didn't do justice to how talented Natalie was.

"I can't wait to see," said Nadia. She leaned closer to the designer. "It's not that I want a *Frozen* wedding, exactly," she began. "But when it comes to the dress, I wondered if—"

"What about a nice quiet wedding chapel for the ceremony?" suggested the bride's mother. "I found a lovely one that says it's affordable and has seating for one hundred guests, and it's *very* sedate. Just what a medium-size wedding needs, really. Her dress would look far more stunning against a simple background."

Gloomy was the better word for it, Tessa thought. A dark modern interior of wood paneling and almost no windows, with hooded candle-style chandeliers above the pews and a plain lectern for the minister officiating the ceremony. The only artistic element being a large gold candle stand in one corner.

"Why not have the ceremony in a cave?" snorted Paula. "The castle's ten times better, and it's got real lights."

"We haven't decided *what kind* of venue we want for the ceremony yet," interrupted Nadia, inserting herself into the spat between her mother and her future in-law. "Lyle and I haven't discussed it yet. Besides, I think the wedding planners might have some ideas about it, if we give them a chance."

"Lyle likes the castle," said Paula stubbornly.

"He would." Cynthia sighed with this retort. Nadia nudged her.

"Let's talk flowers," said Tessa, opening her notebook.

She had made several sketches of possible flower arrangements using white, blue, mint green, and silvery shades in one, then another with pure white roses, poinsettias, and boughs of light evergreen needles. Cynthia was paying for this part of the wedding, and didn't seem pleased with any of the florists whom Tessa named as possibilities—surprisingly enough, Paula supported these objections.

"I had a bad experience with that one—it sent my mother's 'get well' bouquet all the way downtown to some nail salon," complained Paula. "And they didn't give me a refund, either."

"I do want nice flowers," said Nadia. "I want the venue to be simpler, but for the decoration to really stand out, and be wintry without being too Christmassy. You know?" She laid her finger on what was by far Tessa's nicest sketch, the one that would be priciest for any florist to create, Tessa knew. She had been hoping that the standard design might appeal, given their pickiness over the city's florist community. "I know it's crazy, but I really love flowers. I think the biggest expense in our budget will be the decor, but it will be worth it."

Nice flowers. Tessa made a note about its importance.

"I still think that castle's banquet hall would look just stunning in lots of white and blue poinsettias," hinted Paula.

Tessa tapped her pencil against her notebook. If flowers were among the top priorities for her client, then they needed to hire one of the top professional florists. One name had been at the bottom of the list precisely because of expense, inaccessibility, and niche design, although it was exactly the sort of place that Tessa had been dying to contact.

✻

Accented Creations was a modern innovation in floral design—'floral design' being how they described their work—in both the field of floristry and the city itself. Their business's appearance and mode of operation was like a hybrid between an art gallery and a floristry, complete with show rooms, exclusive appointments, and seasonal showcases which lucky clients bid upon for their events.

They were selective in their clientele, and an appointment to view one of their show rooms had become practically impossible to arrange after they were featured in *Modern Entertaining*. Artistry had its price after the unique business model had drawn the notice of the mayor, the governor, and even a famed actor whose wedding had taken place at the chic plantation hotel Willow Resort the previous year. After one of their 'floral artists' had supplied the gubernatorial ball with centerpieces, it would be difficult for a newbie wedding planner to get an appointment without producing a magic celebrity name. Or at least the name of someone who was friends with someone on the staff.

Wedding Belles was not the brainchild of a quitter, however. Thus far, Tessa's attempts to make contact with any of Accented Creations' florists, or even receive a list of quoted prices, had ended in disconnected calls and endless classical music loops, but she was determined to reach them this time.

"They hung up on me." Natalie slammed the phone receiver down in its cradle with more force than necessary. "Again. That makes twice in the same day."

"Would you rather be perpetually on hold?" asked Tessa. "I spent an hour yesterday listening to Brahms's 'Piano Concerto in B-Flat Major.'" No human being was ever coming to answer her call, she had decided, no matter what the receptionist claimed. "I think the key will be calling over and over, not waiting on the line forever."

"They can't be that exclusive—we're talking about flowers, not hand-cut diamonds," said Natalie. "How can they be this difficult to reach?"

"They did the flowers for the mayor's Christmas party last year, and I heard he was on a two-month waiting list," Tessa reminded her.

"Maybe this concept is overrated," grumbled Natalie. "We should go to a normal florist where you walk in and pick a nice centerpiece out of a book or a flower cooler."

"The flowers are important to Nadia," said Tessa. "That's what's going to create the atmosphere for her reception and her ceremony. You heard what she said at our meeting. Our client deserves the best, and I am determined to break through this wall of silence."

"How do you know they don't have another appointment with the governor?" asked Natalie snottily.

"Because this year Florinda's Petals is doing the flowers for the governor's mansion. Besides, there are no celebrity weddings taking place within a hundred-mile radius," said Tessa. "We should have as good a chance as any ordinary wedding planner of getting an appointment for a normal client… only I'm beginning to think it's impossible to get any human who works there to talk to you, even to explain that they have no interest in considering your client's request."

"So who do we know who would be friends with someone at Accented Creations?" mused Natalie, as she propped her feet on her desk. "It would have to be somebody who didn't run with a casual crowd, clearly."

"Someone sophisticated and snobby. Or who wants to be," said Tessa. She propped her chin on one hand—the latest dialing of the number had just landed her with Chopin's 'Nocturne in D-Flat Major.' "Someone willing to gladhand and fawn to make a connection with anybody who matters, so they have dozens of low- to medium-level contacts from every exclusive vendor."

"Probably someone with an over-inflated ego, who just *lives* for collecting those names," said Natalie with a snort of laughter—one which died short, suddenly. She met Tessa's eye.

"Do you think—?" Tessa said.

"You know it," said Natalie scornfully. "How could we not think of it before?"

Stefan Groeder, the firm's original fourth partner, had been exactly that sort of person. He had kept a color-coded Rolodex in his cubicle with numbers cross-referenced in his phone's contact book—all listed by their chic status or current ratings under Michelin, BBB, and the local *Hospitality Today* reviews. If anyone had wormed their way into a friendship at Accented Creations, it would be the planner behind the Cinderella wedding with a mouse-drawn white carriage designed exclusively for the rings. Of course, he was working in Paris now, but they couldn't let a little obstacle like that stand in their way, right?

"So if you wanted to infiltrate a business using Stefan's name, what would you do?" said Natalie. "Call and pretend to be his secretary?"

"It wouldn't work, unless it was his number on their call screen," pointed out Tessa. "They screen their calls, obviously."

"So you go there as his secretary. In person. Maybe you get lucky and whoever he knows at the business lets you talk to someone. His contact was probably somebody on the lower tiers of the company, anyway."

"Would that work?" said Tessa.

"Maybe," said Natalie. "I think subterfuge is worth a try at this point."

"Would you do it?" Tessa asked. "Pretend to be his assistant or whatever?"

Natalie laughed. "There's *no* way they would ever believe that Stefan would hire *me* as his secretary. I couldn't fool anybody for more than two minutes before something obnoxious blurted itself out. If you want this ruse to be convincing, it'll have to be you or Ama who walks into their headquarters on his behalf."

"Ama in tailored tweeds? His assistant would have to be impeccably stylish in the business sense," said Tessa. "They would have to look—"

"—amazing in a suit," concluded Natalie.

A thoughtful pause. "There's only one person I can think of who fits the bill," Natalie said with an impish smile.

Tessa was toying with the edges of a book on perfect bridal bouquets lying on the desk. "Do you think your friend Cal would do it?" she asked, lifting her gaze to her business partner's.

Another incredulous laugh came from Natalie's lips. "Cal?" she repeated. "Why would I drag him downtown to a snooty floral empire when we have a perfect resource in our fourth partner?"

"I just thought we might ask someone new," said Tessa. "I'm sure Blake doesn't want us bothering him *every* time we have a crisis."

"What's every time? There was one other time, Tess," said Natalie. "He won't mind. He walks in, he introduces himself, he makes an appointment for us. Ask him—I'll bet you twenty bucks he says yes."

"I don't think so," said Tessa. "You can ask, if you want. I hate to drag him away from his project."

"Why?" said Natalie bluntly. "You didn't mind before."

The lack of an answer from Tessa was a confession. "There's something going on between you two, isn't there?" said Natalie shrewdly.

"No," said Tessa quickly. The blush vanished from her cheeks almost before it became visible. "That's ridiculous."

"Then why won't you ask him to help us out for an hour?"

"I told you. I don't want to bother him again."

"Is that the only reason?" said Natalie. "If it is, then maybe we should find another contractor who doesn't need to be tiptoed around so carefully—"

"All right, fine. I'll ask." Tessa dropped the book on the desk again. "If that's how you're going to be about this." She flounced toward the exit with an air of seeming exasperation for this task.

"Tessa, what's gotten into you?" Natalie's amazed question went unanswered by her business partner, who had already left the room.

Outside the room under construction, Tessa took several deep breaths. Calm and collected. Nothing to worry about here, it was just a simple question, one that didn't call for clammy palms or a dry mouth. Why was she so nervous at the thought of asking Blake for a simple favor? He had agreed to this kind of thing, in a roundabout way. Hadn't he?

On the other side of the door, his Skilsaw whined through a sheet of lumber. Tessa gathered herself into a semblance of normality and pushed open the door.

"So what do you want me to do?" said Blake, after hearing her initial explanation.

He had powered off his saw, its cloud of wood chips and dust now settling over the front of his green flannel shirt as he faced Tessa. "Do you want me to pretend I'm him?"

It was a thought she knew he would find unappealing after his prior issue with assuming Stefan's identity, albeit only briefly. Not that Blake had complained about his false identity for that event, or even cast it up to her that she had created a fake reputation for him in their community as some sort of wedding genius—the successor to snooty Stefan with his Parisian promotion, even.

Blake had been nice about everything, in fact. So there was no reason to be nervous in front of him for these simple conversations, as if, let's say, their kiss after that wedding was a giant elephant in the room.

"Not exactly," said Tessa.

"Than what?" Blake asked. "Specifics."

"We need someone to be his personal assistant."

"His secretary," translated Blake flatly.

"That's one possible interpretation of it, yes," said Tessa. "But does anybody say 'secretary' anymore? Is that politically correct?"

Blake was quiet, albeit probably not in order to think of an answer to her question. For a sneaking second, she thought maybe he was sensing the same awkwardness as she was.

"Why, may I ask?" he said, taking off the safety glasses, and brushing the sawdust from their rims. "What do these people do that means you can't talk to them yourselves?"

"Does it matter?" she asked. "It's just for a quick little conversation with their receptionist." They might all be bounced out of the foyer ten seconds later if the business's front of house secretary had never heard of Stefan Groeder.

"I like to know all the facts," he said. "Humor me."

"We need an 'in' with this florist that we don't have," said Tessa. "They're very exclusive, and they're refusing to talk to anybody as low on the social scale as an insignificant event planning firm that's only been in business for a few months. But we know they'll talk to Stefan because of his reputation."

"But you're the wedding planner," said Blake. "You've had clients."

"Not ones who would impress this firm," said Tessa. "They're incredibly elite to the point of being inaccessible now for anybody but a customer who's lucky enough to get through the drawbridge. But if we could get them to work with us even once, they'll probably be willing to do it again. It would be a major boost for our reputation in the event planning community, bigger than any yet... it would mean an extra-beautiful floral arrangement for a client who wants her flowers to be extra special, too." The only client they had had in months who could afford something exclusive to garnish her tables. The last wedding's centerpieces were designed by Tessa, using wheat-colored broom straw and pink-painted daisies from a 'pick your own bouquet' business on a scenic highway route.

She sighed. "Stefan's reputation is worth more than mine right now, even with him in Paris," she said. "He wasn't one of the city's top planners, but he's helped organize events at Magnolia Manor, and he put together a tea for the Belles of the Ball society two Christmases ago. That's major stuff. His style makes a statement."

"I've seen his work. This Stefan guy just covered everything in glitter and dazzled his way to success, and if I can see that, I'll bet everyone else can. Don't you think you're overestimating his influence a little?"

"His talent, yes. His influence, no," said Tessa. "He *was* one of the city's fast-rising event planners. As impossible as it may seem to you." *And to me*, she added silently, although she would never have dared suggest it while Stefan was still around.

"Why not build your own contacts?" suggested Blake. "Make your own reputation. I know you," he said, looking at Tessa. "You can do this. I don't think you need anybody's help. Usually, you don't want any help, as I recall, since you can handle yourself in most situations. Prove to this florist that you're worth dealing with, or forget about them and use your judgment to pick somebody who's probably better."

Did Tessa blush? It was hard to tell. "Thanks for the compliment," she said, looking at the floor momentarily. "But this time isn't the same. Honestly, I'm not the planner Stefan is—I don't have his contacts or his clout in this city. Please, Blake. It would mean a lot to me—us, that is. And to our client, who's a really nice person." She glanced up. "This opportunity matters. Not just to my client personally, but to me as a professional. You would agree if you saw their work... or if you knew about Nadia's wedding."

"I'll have to take your word on it."

Tessa was now glancing at Blake, who rested both hands on the sawhorse behind him. This pause was awkward, she decided. It was the kiss that had done it. She never should have missed her mark and made contact with his lips instead. That kind of electricity couldn't disappear just because a couple of months had passed without saying anything.

He sighed. "Bring me the suit," he said. "I'll go with you to this place."

Tessa closed her eyes, hand clenching as if grasping this victory. "Thank you," she said. "Tomorrow morning would be perfect. We'll go early, before they schedule the showcase appointments and their potential customers are arriving."

"I will impersonate one of your coworkers only this one time, okay?" said Blake. "This is strictly a cameo appearance under our whole 'fourth partner' agreement." He tossed his safety glasses onto his worktable, beside the saw. "So where is this place?"

❄

'This place' was a snooty, dignified office space on the second floor of the Mercer-Howard Building, which had formerly been the city's bank. Its old-fashioned interior sported shiny marble walls, fawn carpet, and sleek chrome fixtures. This space was only the office for the floral artists' cooperative, with their greenhouse located on a four-acre garden outside of town, Tessa had read in *Floral Today*'s June issue.

In a Hugo Boss suit and tie begged, stolen, or borrowed from the storage warehouse by Natalie's friend Cal, Blake Ellingham approached the desk. He had offered to shave and even trim his hair before this morning's appointment, but Tessa had vehemently nixed this idea, much to his evident surprise. From somewhere, he had produced a pair of trim, stylish black-frame eyeglasses that looked almost exactly like Stefan's own. A perfect touch, Tessa thought.

The receptionist behind Accented Creations' desk was a college intern, Tessa pegged, who was probably hoping for a career at a city financial firm someday, instead of recording floral appointments for weddings and formal receptions. "May I help you?" he asked, looking up as he hastily stowed his cell phone's screen out of sight beneath a floral supply catalog.

"I'm here to set up a showing on behalf of Stefan Groeder's clients," said Blake in a crisp voice. "I assume one of your artists is available to discuss the pertinent details that my employer has in mind?" He held up a binder—Tessa's planning notebook—with these words.

The demeanor of the handyman had changed completely. His walk had developed a slight swagger, his posture becoming one of cool, slightly obnoxious command. It was the kind of bossy, intimidating look that fitted Stefan perfectly—and would fit his assistant perfectly, too, if such a person existed.

"I thought he moved to Paris," said the young man.

For a second, Tessa panicked—this person was a little *too* aware of Stefan's status, so it wasn't going to work after all. But Blake calmly replied, "Well, obviously I'm his assistant from the U.S. branch of Le Petit Fleur dans la Rue in Paris, working on behalf of Mr. Groeder's many clients here."

"I'm sorry," said the young man suspiciously… and snobbily. "I wasn't aware that Mr. Groeder had an assistant."

"I wasn't aware that a planner as eminent as Mr. Groeder needed to announce that fact," replied Blake, equally snobbily. Tessa and Natalie exchanged glances of amazement.

"And who are these people with you?"

"My own assistant, Ms. Miller," Blake said, after a pause to think of a suitable excuse for his entourage. "And our… style consultant, Ms. Grenaldi," he added, after a moment's pause. "They're both part of Stefan's creative team for his client."

"You have your own assistant?" asked the intern.

"Trust me. Anyone working for the likes of Mr. Groeder *must* have their own assistant, otherwise they would never accomplish anything," said Blake. "Now, do I need to call him to reassure you of this fact? Or will my word that I'm planning an *extremely* important event on his behalf be enough? Time is money, and we're all hoping we can make some today, aren't we?"

The intern wavered a little. "I guess I could see if one of the artists is available to talk to you," he said, reluctantly lifting the office phone's receiver.

"Mr. Walsh? The PA of that event planner you know is out here, waiting to talk to you. No, not the one you like... the one who used to bring you those organic lattes." The assistant was trying to keep his voice low, his face and body averted from them as he spoke. "Skinny... glasses... yeah, that's the one. The Cinderella and elf guy. This is somebody from his office, apparently. Is it okay to send them in?"

He hung up. "The fourth office on the right," he said in a normal voice.

"Fabulous," said Blake.

This magic card was enough to get them into the office of one of the firm's artists, who was clearly annoyed but relieved that it wasn't Stefan himself asking for a favor. He laid aside his last-minute prep on a showcase sample to give Tessa's sketches a cursory glance, and despite his assertions that they were 'extremely busy with several new clients,' reluctantly agreed to squeeze them into the business's schedule and set up a show room for 'Stefan's' clients the following week.

"It *worked*!" Natalie slammed the car door after sliding into the back seat. "I can't believe it! You were amazing, Blake," she added. "I totally believed in your performance, every word of it."

"You *were* amazing, actually," said Tessa, whose face betrayed how much so for a second. "Where did you learn all those snobby little inflections?" she asked playfully, after making a quick recovery.

"You were positively *diva*," continued Natalie. "I loved it. Bravo to your one-man stage act."

"I'm glad you enjoyed the show." Blake loosened his tie, then pulled it off altogether. "One performance only, since from now on my assistant Ms. Miller will be handling all matters pertinent to the Groeder account. Oh, and bringing me my morning coffee and wholegrain muffin."

"Thanks for that demotion," said Tessa with a touch of sarcasm. "Seriously. Where did you get the idea for your whole 'assistant image'?"

"Which is exactly what Stefan's assistant would be like, if he has one," said Natalie.

Blake folded the eyeglasses—obviously false ones—and stowed them in the pocket of the coat. "Maybe I watch a few interior design shows now and then," he said. "Some of the runway debacles like on *What Not to Design*. Decorators, designers, wedding planners—I figured they would be a lot alike. Call it a hunch, and I played it."

"I told you our luck was changing," Tessa said over her shoulder to Natalie, before starting the car.

"We owe him lunch as a thanks," said Natalie. "We have a budget for taking professionals to lunch in your PR fund, right?" she asked Tessa.

"You don't have to do that," said Blake, undoing his top button. "I can buy my own lunch."

"What, are you one of those guys who never lets a woman pay for anything?" Natalie answered.

"It's not that," he said. "But I don't have to see your account books to know this hasn't been a stellar month for you financially—"

"Thanks for making us feel extra small," countered Natalie. "So it's not that our money's no good, it's that we're not rich enough to keep you from feeling guilty."

"Did I *say* that?" he protested.

"Enough," said Tessa, as she shifted the car into reverse. "We're solvent financially, so it isn't an issue whether we can buy someone lunch. We can thank Mr. Ellingham for his concern and assure him that we are fine."

"I didn't mean to be insulting to either of you," said Blake. "I would happily drink any cup of coffee you generously paid for," he added to Natalie.

"Nice of you to surrender," she replied. Her phone beeped. "Great," she said, groaning after glancing at the screen. "My latest hope in the fabric department just collapsed. I swear, it's like we're—"

"—having a definite problem locating a good fabric warehouse, obviously," Tessa interrupted firmly. "I'll drop you off at Jimmy's, if you want." Jimmy Olander was Natalie's best contact in the garment world, and could sometimes scrounge up the names of vendors who supplied bolts of limited or discontinued fabric weaves.

"Just leave me at this boutique on the next corner. Cal has a friend working there, who's part-time at one of Kandace's rivals. Maybe he'll have a couple of thoughts on places I could try. Their selection of fabric was always pretty amazing compared to Kandace's. Then again, they were never trying to design garments made entirely from Velcro, either."

"Velcro?" echoed Blake, as if he misheard the first time.

"Just don't wear one inside out." Natalie emerged from the back seat and closed the door.

Tessa drove on, then pulled up a few streets away, in an open spot outside of a tiny coffee house where an employee was scraping the fall leaf motif off the picture window.

"Despite this month's poor revenue, I really do have the money to buy you a cup of coffee," said Tessa. "I owe you one, besides." She glanced at him. "Do you have a few minutes to spare?"

He would probably say no—he didn't look as if he was going to say yes, whether to having coffee with her personally or letting her buy it. Tessa suspected it was the latter.

He paused. "A cup of coffee wouldn't hurt," he said at last.

He didn't see the brief pink shade of Tessa's cheeks, which made her grateful. She pulled the keys from the ignition and tucked them in her purse as they stepped out of the car.

There was no way things were going to be normal between them unless she put things back the way they were supposed to be. A good start was sharing coffee with him as a friend. It should be easier to be normal with a table between them and a hot beverage to sip reflectively and keep one's mind on non-romantic subjects.

"You were actually pretty brilliant at the florist's," she said, as she steeped a paper teabag in hot water, letting it rise and dive on the string's end. "I know that none of us could have handled it that well. I think it's more proof that you have a talent for this business." She sipped her tea, finding it was still too weak. "Pretty soon we'll have to make you sign an agreement never to work for our competitors."

"What do you have in mind for me in the future? Designing a gown? Standing in for the best man?" He poured powdered creamer into his cup. "I need hints if I'm going to prepare. This gig could flex my creative muscle more challengingly than the one on Springer Street will."

His smile was a dry, sarcastic one really, which kept Tessa from turning pink again. "I'm—we're—not planning to strong-arm you into anything else in the future, I promise," she said. "This was for an emergency only. We appreciate your talents, but we don't intend to keep borrowing them in a crisis."

"I didn't mind it that much." His own face turned slightly red, as if embarrassed to think his joke had gone too far. "I didn't mean to make you think I felt... taken advantage of."

"I knew you didn't mind." Tessa sipped her tea again after these words, studying him over the rim. His eyes flashed with perceptiveness.

"Calling my bluff," he said. "Playing your cards with precision to make me guilty enough to volunteer another time. I can respect that level of savvy in the business world."

"You're not going to make me feel guilty in return," said Tessa. "But I *am* being sincere when I say that we don't mean to keep pulling you into our work. That's not what the fourth partnership was meant to be."

"Not a real partnership," he clarified. "Maybe I should admit that I didn't think your offer was fair. 'Too generous' being the better phrase. But so long as you've got it, it's not like there's any harm in pretending it's real now and then. Today was a favor based on our verbal contract. But if you'd given me some warning, I would have provided my own wardrobe. My suits may not be designer labels, but they fit—and it must get boring for them being stored in those garment bags."

Tessa smiled. "Thanks for saying so," she said. "I appreciate it."

"A cup of coffee's worth, sure," he said, sipping from his cup. "But not enough to ask me to fix the transom grate—"

"You know, I think I might be willing to buy you *dinner* if it meant we wouldn't have to talk about that," said Tessa. "Any place with plates under ten dollars."

"I'm not letting you buy me dinner," said Blake.

"So you really are the old-fashioned type, like Nat suggested."

"It's not an old-fashioned opinion. It's a preference for the gentlemanly gesture," he said. "I accepted the coffee you just paid for, so I don't think you can accuse me of chauvinism."

"Sorry," said Tessa.

"But if you do take me to dinner, I prefer Italian."

Tessa almost didn't see his grin because of the raised coffee mug, but his eyes were a dead giveaway. "Are you still laughing at me?" she asked. "I'm just trying to be fair." Thank goodness she wasn't blushing at the idea of taking Blake to dinner—or the idea of him taking her, either.

Blake in a suit like this one, with candlelight between them—Tessa added more sugar to her tea, stirring it furiously.

"I don't think either of us is laughing at the other. We just disagree," said Blake. "That's how you and I work together, apparently."

This idea did not sit with her as well as it should. "That's not always true," she said, shrugging a little. She sipped her tea, and managed not to gag at its sweetness now. "Not during Molly and Paolo's wedding."

"We made a good team for that event, it's true," admitted Blake. "On your career turf, we're good, so maybe it's only on mine that we run into problems. I think maybe you don't completely trust my skill, or my ability to stay within your cost projection for repairs."

"Don't be ridiculous," she said. "I trust you."

"Really?" he said. "That's not the impression I'm under lately. Are you sure you're not still holding the building's original estimates against me?"

She blushed. That was *not* the problem when it came to Blake. Was there any chance he was thinking of the incident after Molly and Paolo's wedding? No—that wasn't what he was suggesting. She was imagining things because she had let the incident of a harmless kiss grow too big in her mind.

"It's not you," Tessa repeated emphatically. "I don't trust myself. Not to make a mistake and topple our whole precarious business model, anyway." She sipped her tea again, not noticing the sugary taste this time. "I keep coming back to the image of money disappearing and no new clients surfacing, and feeling intimidated by it." Afraid was the better word, but one Tessa generally avoided. As it was, she couldn't believe she had said any of this aloud.

She never talked like this around Natalie or Ama. Why Blake? Why was it always him to whom she confessed these things?

"Starting something new isn't easy," said Blake. "The beginning for me was with a loan I wasn't sure I could pay back. It almost cost me everything."

This was news to Tessa. "I didn't know that," she said. "I pictured you starting from scratch with just your skills and some small projects." She thought of the handyman side of his work alone, not the big picture— the contractor who was a crew leader on Springer Street, for instance. Picturing Blake's work had always been a picture of him—his tools, his concentration, a kind of intimacy and closeness with his project in this image that she hoped wasn't some crazy metaphor from her subconscious.

"I paid it back ages ago. It took me longer than I hoped. But I didn't even have ownership of my own place at the time, so there's an advantage for your business decision," he pointed out. "Your payments are giving you something brick and mortar in exchange." He smiled.

"Every last rusty nail and termite-ridden timber," said Tessa.

Blake rolled his eyes. "Your place is in better shape than that," he answered.

"Or it will be when you're done with it. Right?"

"I'll drink to that." Blake lifted his coffee cup. Tessa touched her cup of tea to its rim. Her fingers brushed the tips of his own, but she managed not to make eye contact again. Remembering once before, when her hand was in Blake's for a brief instant, and a deep-rooted thrill had passed through her with the speed of lightning.

"I guess whenever you're ready, I'll drive us back to work," she said. "Unless you plan to wear the suit the rest of the day, since you evidently miss those formal dress opportunities so much."

"Are you kidding? I can't wait to get out of this. I'm afraid I'm going to spill something on it and become its owner for life." With one last swallow of coffee, Blake set his cup aside and rose from their table.

✳

On Thursday, the box from the wholesale novelty items company providing the cut-glass snowflake frames Tessa had ordered for the wedding favors arrived. The deliveryman unloaded it in the foyer, where Natalie and Ama cut through tape and burrowed through layers of Styrofoam peanuts to unpack them.

Natalie paused after scooping out two armloads of packing material. "Uh, Tess," she said. "I think we have a problem."

"What is it?" Tessa glanced up from her laptop, open on the foyer's reception desk.

"Is this what Nadia wants on her guests' tables?" Natalie held up a pair of zebra-striped sunglasses.

"What?" Tessa sprang up from her chair. "No. *No*," she said, digging through the box, which was filled with plastic novelty sunglasses, mini decks of cards, neon-colored slinkies, and cheap toy kaleidoscopes in zebra, tiger, and leopard patterns. *Congratulations—your Walk on the Wild Side birthday supplies have arrived!* said the invoice slip inside.

"How did this happen?" said Tessa. "This address is in Maryland. The name on it is Tolliver—that's not even remotely like Wedding Belles!"

"Call them," said Natalie. "And better do it quick. We got a fantastic deal from that company and it won't last forever."

"Great. We'll have to haul this box back to the shipping company and have it sent back," said Tessa, grunting as she moved it to a convenient hiding spot behind the desk. "It's heavy for a box filled with plastic toys for a kid's birthday party, and I would know. Did they order some rocks, too?"

"Maybe they could come pick it up. Some companies do," suggested Ama. "Don't you have a friend who's a driver for one of the big delivery companies?" she said to Natalie.

"No, I don't," said Natalie quickly. "Tess, let me help you with that." She began shoving the box's far end out of sight behind the desk's corner.

Tessa straightened her back again. "It's just a little mix-up," she said, taking a deep breath. "It won't take any time to fix it. I'll just call the company and they'll send our order in plenty of time for the wedding." She scanned the receipt for the customer service number.

"Just our luck," said Natalie.

"Don't say that," said Tessa warningly. "Things are going perfectly fine for us now, remember?" Her call connected, and she switched to business mode. "Hi, I need to talk to somebody about a mix-up on my delivery," she said.

Ama swept the stray packing peanuts into a nearby wastebasket. "Lucky for us it's an easy problem to fix," she said. "Not like something happening to the dress or the cake. Wedding favors—who cares if there's a problem with a souvenir that most guests won't keep anyway? If something has to go wrong for every wedding, this is the best possible thing, right?"

As she emptied the dustpan, her cell phone rang—a popular sitar tune that signaled the call wasn't from anybody in her circle of family or friends. An unfamiliar number popped up on the screen.

"Hello?" she answered.

"Hi. Is this Ama?" She didn't recognize the voice, although she could tell it was a man's. "This is her number, I believe."

It was a very polite voice. That's what told Ama it belonged to the would-be suitor from her father's ad. "It is," she answered. Her heart sank lower as she admitted this. Entering the parlor, she closed the door behind her softly, so Tessa and Natalie wouldn't notice.

"It's Tamir. I was wondering if you might possibly be free to have dinner with me this week."

"Dinner?"

It wasn't possible that he wanted to meet her again. Did he *not* notice his parents' disapproval? Hadn't they made him contact a more suitable choice by now—say, a girl with a nice college degree and normal, quiet Indian parents who were teachers or accountants instead of owning a somewhat kitschy restaurant?

"Yes. I thought I might meet you tonight, if it's convenient."

"Tonight? Uh—no. No, I have a... baking emergency," supplied Ama.

"Oh. Well, how about tomorrow night?"

He hadn't seemed like the persistent type when she met him. Ama racked her brain for another excuse that wouldn't be too rude. An excuse that wouldn't shame the Bhagut family, for instance. Tell him no, she thought—tell him that you have a boyfriend already, and the ad was a mistake.

"Tomorrow night," she repeated. "The thing is..." She hesitated. "I'm... free then, I suppose."

You great big chicken. We weren't going on any dates with arranged suitors, remember? Not even to make Papa happy.

"I would pick you up at your home, maybe around seven. Would that suit?"

Would it suit? He sounded so formal that Ama wanted to cringe. "Sounds great," she said. "I guess. I'll see you then."

"I'm looking forward to it. Goodbye, Ama."

"Bye." She let out a long frustrated sigh, and leaned back against the parlor wall.

In the foyer, Tessa hung up her phone with an equally loud sigh. "Can you believe it?" she said to Natalie. "They're out of snowflake frames. Completely out. They don't even have the white ceramic ones in stock."

"What about your order?" said Natalie. "The one that presumably went to Maryland?"

"According to them, it was just a packing mistake. There was no box for me to get mixed up in the shipping department with anything," said Tessa. "So now we have to lug the party supplies downtown to the shipping store, and we won't be getting anything in return." She glanced at Natalie. "What's the name of your friend who's one of the drivers?" she said, hinting. "The guy from your neighborhood you talk about sometimes?" An annoying childhood friend whom Natalie complained about in college and afterwards, in stories which clued Tessa into the existence of a complicated, unwanted crush in her friend's past.

"It's nobody," answered Natalie. "I'm not asking him for a favor. I'll take it myself, if you want." She cast an eye at the big box of plastic toys, where an inflatable giraffe's head was draped over one flap.

"I'll have to find a new wedding favor to suggest to Nadia," said Tessa, digging through the pile of catalogs that had came in that day's mail. "Those frames were so perfect. It makes me so mad that they're not available."

"Just our—" began Natalie.

"Don't say it," Tessa cut her off warningly. "I don't want to hear any more talk about bad luck or jinxes, okay?" She was dialing another number. "Hello, Novelties, Inc.? I was wondering if there's any chance that you have the name of the company who manufactured your snowflake picture frame ornaments, item number two-seven-seven-zero-zero-four..."

Chapter Eight

"Someone named 'Chad' called for you," said Roberto, as he poured milk over a bowl of puffed rice. Her brother was raiding their mom's pantry—again—and Natalie wondered if Maria ever managed to make a box of dry cereal last for more than twenty-four hours so long as Roberto was around. "He sounded like a loser and a jerk, but I took a message for you anyway."

"What was he doing phoning here?" Natalie snatched the piece of paper away from her grinning brother's hand. "I gave him my phone number."

"My guess is he dropped his cell phone while rappelling down the face of a mountain, like every other athletic man boy you've dated, and was forced to call from someone else's using… wait for it… the psychic powers of the city phone book in order to find your home number." Roberto rested his fingers against his forehead, as if channeling this answer.

"Please. Is that what this piece of paper says?" Natalie held it up.

"He says to call him at the number of some guy named Bebo. Number's written on the paper, so don't throw it away if you want to talk to this loser again." Her brother sprinkled two heaping tablespoons of sugar over his cereal.

"I've got to get a phone at my place, and get the listing changed in the city phone book," grumbled Natalie, as she dropped her embroidery manual on the table, beside a book on long-term small business strategy.

Someone knocked on the kitchen door. Roberto answered it. "Hey, Brayden, my man," he said, holding out his hand for a low five. "Just in time. Let me get my coat." He shoveled some more cereal in his mouth, speed-eating. Natalie was now intensely involved in looking for the paper her professor had returned in class today.

"No hurry," called Brayden. "I just got off my shift. Mom doesn't expect me at her place for dinner for a half hour." His gaze wandered toward Natalie, its natural homing beacon, she thought dryly. He ventured a smile of greeting.

"Hi, Natalie," he said.

"Hi." It was uttered with a sigh. "What are you doing here?"

"Mutrucksbrkn, gvn me a rud," said Roberto, as he wolfed down the last of his cereal. Translating this full-mouth speak, Natalie surmised that her brother's truck was in the mechanic's garage again, and that Brayden was the handiest person available to drive him to his job at the firehouse across town.

"Nice," commented Natalie. "You two have fun." These remarks from her professor seemed important to memorize. Very, very important. She frowned, trying to look deep in concentration.

"How's the new business?" Brayden asked. "Roberto says you guys are doing great."

"It's fine," she said.

"I drove by the other day. Your building looks super nice. Did you do the whole window thing, with the dress, and flowers, and stuff? That looked like you."

"Ama did some of it, too," said Natalie.

"The dress, though. That was you, right? You like to put those little tucks along the wide straps. I don't know what they call them. Like in the dress you made for Mom to wear for my cousin Shirley's wedding."

Shirring, Natalie thought. He noticed shirring in a dress?

"Funny story, Brayden," interrupted Rob. "Remember that weird billboard on the apartment building on Central? The one with the donkey painted on it? Well, they were making them take it down the other day, and they started by removing the middle of the sign—and there was this guy standing there in painter's coveralls, who was taking down that panel in the pic—and the angle he was standing at totally made it look like he was part man, part donkey for a minute there. Well, you really have to see it to get how hilarious it was," he concluded, shaking his head. "I sent a picture of it to Natalie. Nat, is that snapshot still on your phone?"

"Look and see." She held out her cell phone to her brother, who was pulling on his coat.

"I got my hands full, all right? Just text it to him," said her brother.

"I don't have his number."

"I can give it to you." Brayden eagerly dove his hand into the pocket of his delivery uniform's pants. "I've got yours in my phone—"

"Wait—here it is. In the old contact list from my last one," said Natalie, who did *not* want to add it to her new list as a result of Brayden texting her. She pushed the button to send the photo, accidentally hitting the 'call' button at the same time. A soft, tender melody buzzed to life from Brayden's phone.

A snort of laugher from Rob. "Is that Lionel Richie's 'Hello'?" said Roberto. He flashed a bemused grin at his friend. Natalie knew her expression was one of slight horror, but she couldn't prevent it.

Brayden's face was completely scarlet. "It's… um… let's see… that picture should be here any second," he said, hastily disconnecting the call from Natalie. "I saved it to 'My Photos' so…"

"Let's hear that again, shall we?" Roberto pulled out his cell phone and touched Brayden's name in his contact list. A Rolling Stones song played on Brayden's phone. Her brother shot a glance at her, as if confirming a secret suspicion. Natalie pretended not to see him.

"Come on, stop fooling around, Rob, all right?" Brayden's face was still slightly red. "Are you still going to show me that picture or what?"

"Find the file Natalie sent you," said Roberto, as he shoved his bowl in the dishwasher. "I deleted mine, so I can't send you one from my phone."

It *was* the Richie song playing a moment ago—and it was chosen just for her. Natalie had always felt it was a stalker-ish song, and now it felt even more so, knowing that wistful thinker Brayden had picked it to represent her number. Not that Brayden ever heard it play, since Natalie never called him, not even to ask him if his mom would like some of the leftover biscotti from the restaurant. And she liked Brayden's mom, one of the Grenaldis' oldest family friends, even if she was afraid that Mrs. Carmichael's sweet smile hid a secret reproach for her son's rejection by Natalie.

"I know it's here somewhere," said Brayden, searching for the photo, which hid the redness of his face better than his feigned normal tone did.

Natalie sighed. "Here," she said, confiscating his phone and opening the photo folder herself, in hopes that finding this picture would get him and her brother out of the house sooner. There were lots of photos saved there, mostly of friends, holidays, and places on Brayden's route. Natalie noticed with dismay that there were one or two featuring her, which had obviously been snapped at some of the Grenaldi friends-and-family gatherings.

"Here." She found the photo of the billboard Rob had tried to describe—not that hilarious, in her opinion—and handed the phone back to its owner.

Brayden chuckled at the picture of a man in coveralls bending over before a giant image of a donkey's back half—which did trick the eye into thinking he might be some kind of strange hybrid at first glance. Typical choice, Natalie thought, given Rob's juvenile sense of humor. "You should enter one of those photo contests with that one," he said to Roberto as he closed the file. "Um… speaking of billboards… isn't that new one on the bypass for your business, Natalie?" He sneaked a quick glance at her.

"Roberto, you're going to be late for work if you don't leave now," said Natalie.

"It is," said Rob, answering the question for her. "Though I think it looks pretty cheesy, having that giant ad for newlyweds walking in the woods, or whatever that's supposed to be. Hey, where's my sack lunch?" he said, checking the fridge. "Did somebody eat my salami and cheese on rye?"

"You need a sack lunch to go to work at five o'clock at night?" Natalie retorted.

"I get hungry, and I don't like to cook at the station," he answered. "I forgot my gear. Hold on a second, Brayden." He disappeared from the room again.

Roberto was so thoughtless, making a friend wait this long. But Brayden was used to it. He was the kid who always told the teacher that the playground bully had some victim pinned, and got pinned himself next time, the kind of guy who helped angry little old ladies at the bank teller's window. *But Brayden's just the type that doesn't put up a fight for himself… he just takes it like it is, even if it's unfair. A magnet for bad luck.*

Brayden cleared his throat. "So, I think somebody has a birthday coming up," he said. "Any big plans?"

"Me?" said Natalie. "You know me, Brayden. There's always something." Maybe chapter two of her textbook had some insight she should absorb during this moment. She opened its cover and tried to look engrossed in its words.

"Yeah, but this is special, Nat. We're talking special here. You're not doing nothing on that day… or that evening… are you?"

We're not going to dinner, Brayden. Get it through your head. Remember the dead dandelions? That was the symbol of our future, right there on the playground swing.

"I am sure I have plans, Brayden," she said, with emphasis. "I'm not available on that day. Or, for that matter, any day. You know me. That's how it is."

She met his eyes with a look that should shut down any further birthday hints that might be coming her way. Brayden was an adult, who knew how she felt about him, and that she was dating other people, so he had to assume she would make plans with one of them, and not be open to dinner at his mom's kitchen table, for instance. Right?

"I'll have to remind my mom about the day, since she won't forgive herself if she doesn't send you a card," he said, after a brief flicker of hurt or disappointment that made Natalie feel guilty. "I… uh… hope you find time to squeeze in some chocolate cake, though. Always your favorite at birthday parties." He smiled at her. "The richer the chocolate, the better."

Natalie managed a smile in return, though it felt awkward. "Like I need the extra calories," she said. "Um—you can wait in your truck for Rob, if you want," she hinted. "So you have a head start on delivering my worthless brother to his workplace. Fine with me."

"No." He shook his head. "What would Roberto think? I mean, a gentleman never leaves a lady sitting alone, right? It'd be pretty rude of me."

This lady would be fine with it, trust me, Natalie wanted to say, but instead replied, "You don't have to remind your mom about the birthday card. We're kind of past the age where celebrating them is a real thrill."

"Who's having a birthday?" Roberto had returned. Natalie rolled her eyes. "Not you, is it?"

Brayden shook his head. "You're hopeless, Rob," he said. "Ready to go, I guess?" He sneaked one more look at Natalie, who was busy paging through a helpful study guide on inventory logs. "See you around, Natalie."

"Bye." She didn't look up from her textbook until she was sure Brayden was gone, then she breathed a deep sigh of relief.

Lionel Richie. How *could* he make that her song? She shuddered and turned the page, trying not to imagine Brayden's fantasy about someday embracing her in his arms as part of his utterly hopeless romantic crush.

Chapter Nine

"I can't believe he called me," said Ama. "Why would he do that? Does anything about me seem like the kind of girl a straight-laced Tamil would like?"

"Will you relax?" said Jaidev. "It's a date. It's not like you agreed to marry him, Ama." He sniffed a sample of garlic powder from the vendor's stall. "That won't happen for at least two weeks."

Ama swatted him. "Some support would be nice," she said. "Please. You know how much I hate this idea."

"You were the one who said yes to him," said Jaidev with a protesting laugh. "What can I do about it? Look, you only have to go out with him a couple of times, then you'll probably both see that you're totally incompatible. He'll stop calling when his parents finally object, Dad will stop nagging you, and everything will be fine. You'll see." He tasted the garlic. "Try some of this, Ama. It's really rich, like browned butter."

"No, thanks." She drifted on in the Saturday market, leaving her brother deep in negotiations for his spices.

"Hey, Ama, it'll be okay." Deena linked arms with her now. "Romantic love is still out there waiting for you. This isn't going to crush your dream or anything."

"I know," Ama sighed.

"It's like the Bollywood movies where the second suitor she meets at random is always the perfect one for the girl. Your dream guy is going to sweep up and save you before you're in danger of getting married to some sensible guy who knows his way around software data or the family business."

"You watch Bollywood films?" Ama said, surprised.

"Sure. Jaidev and I have a BigFlix subscription." Deena hugged her closer. "Unlimited streaming. Ooh, look—is that girl over there wearing a pair of Louis Vuitton pumps?"

Deena understood certain aspects of Ama's personality better than her siblings, even though they had grown up with the same experiences as Ama herself. But her sister-in-law loved romance novels to the point of obsession, wore saris only when working as the restaurant's hostess, and lived for designer jeans. Her father had owned a hotdog snack truck down by the waterfront, where Deena had lacked a traditional Indian community to influence her upbringing—which meant there were other aspects of Ama's life that she didn't get at all.

"Make it one date, maybe," suggested Deena. "Tell him you have a… I don't know… a baking emergency or something, and you have to leave."

"I already did that," said Ama. Both she and Deena giggled. "Besides, how plausible is a baking emergency?"

"I'm trying to have your back," protested Deena. "Okay, maybe he'll pick someplace where you don't have to talk too much. Like a sports event. I think the Panthers are playing at the arena, only an hour away."

"An undignified sport like basketball? Isn't there a cricket match in the park?" asked Ama teasingly. "A rugby tournament at another stadium?" Then again, Tamir had mentioned playing football as a teen, so maybe it was unfair to assume he would consider this an inappropriate date site.

"How about a movie?"

"It'll be a Bollywood film," Ama guessed. "And with my luck, it will probably be a dull comedy about matchmaking somebody's daughter, with lots of *lungi* dancing and a *mridangam* soundtrack." Not even romantic, lovelorn scenes between couples at Indian train stations or exciting duels over honor or whatever else might give it some spice to hold her attention given the circumstances of this date.

"What's 'lungi'? And a 'mridangam'?" Despite whatever films she had been watching, Deena's awareness of Indian culture and music was still as low as her knowledge of denim labels was high, apparently

"You know. Dance style. Indian musical instruments, folk music types?" hinted Ama. "Isn't this in any of the movies you've watched?"

"I read subtitles," explained Deena. "I don't speak any language but this one, remember? It's all sitar music and belly dancing as far as I'm concerned."

"Never mind. I'm just making the scenario sound worse, probably, because I'm dreading it," said Ama. "What I really wish is that a knight would ride up on a horse, snatch me out of the marketplace, and take me to a beautiful Georgian manor, where we would talk about our future dreams while I baked him crumpets. Or scones, or something."

Deena giggled again. "Isn't a knight on horseback kind of a dated concept?" she said. "You need a modern figure for this fantasy."

A *beep beep* interrupted their conversation before Ama could reply, as a motorcycle eased its way through the marketplace crowd. A sleek retro black bike with chrome finish, and with a guy riding it who was possibly the most stunningly attractive man Ama had ever seen. Tall, dark, and handsome didn't even begin to cover it, as he parked near the stall selling imported pottery and climbed from the bike, removing his helmet to reveal a tousled mane of short, dark hair.

A Euro-Mediterranean hunk in an old leather jacket and denim, who would look equally amazing standing below a balcony in Verona as he did in the part of a rebel movie heartthrob walking away from his bike.

Ama had been watching way too many films on the classic movie channel lately.

"Sorry I'm late, George," he said to another man standing by. "Let's strap this thing on." He peeled off his coat and lifted a heavy-looking crate, then heaved it onto the back of the bike. Beneath the carelessly rolled sleeves of his white cotton shirt, well-defined muscles rippled.

"*Hello*," said Deena, in a dusky, soft voice. She nudged Ama.

"I know," said Ama, just as quietly.

"Here's the two hundred." As he tucked his wallet back into his pocket, he noticed them, and smiled. "Sorry, ladies," he said. "I'm taking up too much space, right? I'll move, so you can enjoy Jack's great selection of merchandise."

"No, no," said Deena quickly. "We can admire the view just fine with you there." Ama poked her in the ribs, hard.

"We're fine," said Ama, with a smile that was hopefully not *too* gushing. "We're just… wandering. Looking at these really nice pots." She gestured toward some glazed ceramics, which were painted with desert-style lizards.

"Those are great, aren't they? They're American-made, actually, from a friend of his in a tribe in Nevada." He lowered his voice and leaned closer. "Between us, I think he finger paints them in his basement, then charges a hundred dollars."

"I heard that," said Jack, who was making change for a customer.

"That bike is *awesome*," said Deena. "Is that a Harley?"

"Nope. Nineteen sixty-seven Triumph Bonneville T120," he said. "I fixed it up myself. I do restoration work at a shop downtown. If you're a Harley fan though, come check us out sometime. Or maybe if either of you have a boyfriend..." he said, glancing from Deena to Ama.

He would be impressed by Deena, Ama imagined. Guys always were—she had been engaged to an attractive but stereotypical 'all-American' boy before she met Jaidev at a local restaurateur's convention. That long dark hair, big coffee-colored doe eyes, and those long legs encased in tight denim tended to draw a second glance from guys of all backgrounds—whereas Ama was more the 'cute' type with her hair cut short at her shoulders, and her tie-dyed sneakers and denim overall capris.

"Married," announced Deena, flashing her ring. "Ama's not. And she has no boyfriend." She nudged Ama before she could say a word. "My husband's allergic to exhaust fumes, but Ama's *totally* into motorcycles."

"Are you?" he asked, hiding a smile. Ama blushed.

"That would be an extreme exaggeration," she answered. "But I kind of like the free and easy image. You know, wind in your hair, breeze against your face."

"Bugs against your helmet?" he said.

"Sucked the romance right out of it," said Ama, with a *tsk* of disappointment.

He laughed. He had a great laugh. "Come on," he said. "Come for a ride." He reached for the helmet strapped in a bag on the motorcycle's side. A spare, Ama realized.

"Oh, that's okay," she said, holding up her hands. Deena's elbow pierced through denim bib and tie-dyed t-shirt to Ama's ribcage. "You've got your box strapped in place. Some other time, maybe."

"No problem," he said. He lifted the box with a single heft, and placed it by the stall again. "Box gone, problem eliminated."

"Ama, go," said Deena. "You always wanted to ride one. Take a chance."

"Do you really want to?" he said. "'Cause I'm happy to give one."

Ama hesitated. "Maybe a quick one," she said. "Hold my bag." She handed Deena her sequined shoulder bag, receiving a discreet thumbs-up from her sister-in-law. She popped the helmet on her head and climbed on behind their new acquaintance.

"Wrap your arms around me tight," he instructed. "And hold on." He put on his helmet and started his bike. It purred through the marketplace's narrow pathway until it reached the street's opening, then zipped with speed into traffic. Ama felt a jolt as her body kicked backwards, then braced herself firmly against the stranger she was hugging as they sped along through the green light at the intersection.

His physique was strong and solid beneath her arms. Even without the speed of the motorcycle, her heart would still feel as if it were racing a mile a minute, she thought, at hugging someone like him. He was like a fantasy come true—the kind that was only in movies and the occasional romance novel cover on the rack at the corner grocery—and Ama might be in danger of the aforementioned swooning spell if her arms weren't wrapped so tight around him. Tight enough to feel the rock-hard abs beneath that cotton shirt.

She shouldn't be doing this, though. What would her mother say, Ama taking off with a perfect stranger without knowing where she was going or even his name? He could be a serial killer—an abductor who used his motorcycle as bait to lure unsuspecting women into his lair.

He pulled into the parking lot of a nearby fast food restaurant, and shut off the motor. He lifted off his helmet. "What did you think?" he asked as she removed hers.

"I liked it," she said. "It felt amazing." It had felt more incredible than anything she had ever done. So much better than the time her brother talked her into riding the whip at the carnival, which had ended with Ama's dinnertime dessert of *kheer* being showered on the pavement below. "No wonder you love this bike," she said.

"Yeah, it was more than a hobby," he said. "I don't do it for the money, not really." He glanced at her. "Are you from around here?"

Are you a serial killer? Then the answer is, I live at this restaurant, Ama thought, in a moment of silliness. "I am," she answered instead. "My family has a restaurant downtown. Ama," she added. "That's my name. That was my sister-in-law back at the market. The one who talked you into giving me a ride."

"Luke," he said. "And she didn't talk me into anything. I could see the gleam in your eye. I know an adventurer at heart when I see one."

"I'm not a very good adventurer," Ama confessed. "The only times I've gotten crazy are in the kitchen. But thanks for branching me out." She held up the helmet. "It was fun."

"It's not over yet," he said. "Here. Let out the chinstrap a little. It won't crush that knot in your scarf so tight under your ear this time." Gently, he adjusted it. His fingers were almost brushing her face, and Ama felt the lightest touch of his finger against her jaw as he moved his hand aside. She liked the way it felt; a shiver traveled deep inside her for the briefest second in response.

"All set," he said. "Let's go." He put his own helmet on. "Arms around me," he ordered.

Ama did not giggle, although a part of her was feeling silly enough to be tempted. "Yes, sir," she answered.

"It's okay to squeeze tight," he said. "I won't break." He clasped her hands in front of him, fingers intermingling briefly and igniting a bundle of fireworks inside her again. "I can feel that you work with your hands," he said. "Baker?"

"How did you know?" She was impressed.

"It's not hard," he said. "I used to live next door to a baker. She had flour under her nails, too. And the little mark on the inside of the index finger that comes from using whisks and spatulas. I know a baker's hands when I feel them." His hand was still covering hers, but only for a second. Ama felt that it was fine with her if it lasted for hours.

"Amazing," she said. "I've never had somebody read my profession from my hands."

"It happens to me a lot," he said. "Although they usually say 'grease monkey' if they're old, and 'ew' if they're young, hip, and have never changed a car's tire before." He started the bike and they rolled out of the parking lot. Ama shut her eyes for a moment, but opened them again as Luke wove seamlessly between two lanes of traffic, turning left toward the market again. He zipped past a truck unloading bolts of Indian textiles, sari silk glinting with gold in the sunlight, and a Mexican tortilla cart being wheeled toward the alley.

Deena was waiting for them. She hopped up and down as she spotted the bike making its way back. "Was it fun?" she asked, as Luke parked and Ama pulled off her helmet.

"It was," said Ama. "It was great. Luke's a really good driver."

"Luke, is it?" said Deena.

"Nice to meet you," he said, shaking her hand. Ama handed him back the helmet.

"Thanks again," she said. "It really was fun. You answered a lifelong curiosity for me."

"Answer one for me," he said. "Not a lifelong one, just a little one. Give me the name of your bakery, and I'll stop by and try some of your work."

The ground must be moving beneath her feet—that was the only explanation for why she was suddenly reeling inside. "I... that is... I don't have a bakery, exactly," she stammered. "I work for this wedding boutique—I bake their cakes and their pastries. But I..." She hesitated. "I could bring you something sometime. If you wanted to try it."

"Sure do," he said. "Are you busy next Saturday?"

She shook her head. "Not at all." Surely she wouldn't have a pressing bakery assignment that day, no matter what she'd told Tamir. "Next Saturday, I could bring something by."

"She's free all day," volunteered Deena. Ama pinched her.

"There's a park near the old train station switch on the east side," he said, as he loaded his box in place again. "Ever been there? I'll be dropping off a bike in that part of town, then I'm free for the day. We could grab some lunch, maybe hang out for a while. Say, around noon?"

"She'd love to," said Deena, at the same moment that Ama said, "Sure." She gave her sister-in-law a warning look. "I'd like that," continued Ama. "Noon sounds fine."

He started his bike. "Catch you then." He smiled at her, then drove off.

Deena hopped up and down again, squealing. "Isn't he great?" she said. "I like him, Ama. He's incredible. He's your knight—exactly what you need." She put an arm around her shoulders and hugged her. "I'm so excited for you!"

"Don't be too excited," said Ama. "And don't tell Jaidev. If the rest of the family found out, I would be in really hot water."

Bad enough to crush on a boy like this one, wild, impetuous, and a non-Indian to boot—worse yet, to agree to spend a day with him after she had already agreed to a date with her father's would-be match for her. She could imagine the looks on her parents' faces—part indignation, part betrayal for this impulsive act in the wake of such a suitable boy actually *wanting* to meet her—and it turned the curry inside her to a lump of ice.

"Lips sealed. I promise." Deena zipped her lips with two fingers, then unzipped them. "But what about the guy who asked you out tomorrow? Tamir?" she said. "How are you going to get rid of him?"

"I'll think of something," said Ama. Doubtfully.

❋

"Fondant designs… one hundred and one unique cake toppers… where's my book on marzipan sculpting?" Ama searched the bottom shelves of the Wedding Belles' reference library, a big bookcase that held the overflow from their various professional spaces' tiny shelves. "I know it's here somewhere."

"So what are you going to do about your problem?" Tessa asked, arms crossed.

Ama climbed to her feet. "I don't know," she confessed. "I don't want to hurt this Tamir guy's feelings. He seems nice… just dull. So do you think I should go on the date with him or just break it off before we have to spend the whole evening boring each other to death?"

"Are you sure he's going to bore you?" Tessa asked, as Ama stacked the books on the desk.

"Let me put it this way. If every Indian family had a nerdy cousin who only talks about tech, always brings his aunties a box of sweets and a polite kiss, and always spends Friday night reading the liner notes

to his latest CD from *World's Greatest Composers'* monthly release…
then that's the guy I'm agreeing to meet for dinner."

"You stole that from a Jhumpa Lahiri story, didn't you?" said Tessa.

"So what if I did?" Ama said. "It's still true. Tess, it's just going
to end up with my family being humiliated. They actually think this
nice, straight-laced boy with his proper, sophisticated parents is going
to give up the search for a sedate vegetarian from Tamil Nadu—so he
can date a girl whose family must seem undereducated and almost
crass by his standards. Do you know what the typical clichés are about
Punjabis, Tess? We're stereotyped as the noisy, overly opinionated,
overly flashy culture. If successful Punjabis were on a reality show, it
would be the equivalent of… of Snooki and the housewives of Jersey
Shore. Only less morally crude." She searched the middle shelves for
her missing book.

"You're exaggerating," said Tessa. "Every culture in the world has
unfair stereotypes. But you're also the culture of rajahs and gorgeous
temples, right? And besides… I'm guessing the other guy wouldn't care
either way. Probably *he* thinks your culture and your family is every
bit as unique and fascinating as they really are to the outside world."

Ama blushed. "There's… not another guy," she said. "He's just an
interesting acquaintance. My would-be knight on a motorcycle." She
toyed with the bent spine's edge on one of the tallest books.

"What's that?" A smile twitched Tessa's lips.

"Nothing." Ama quickly shoved the volume back into place.
"Where can that book be?" She scanned the shelves, her gaze resting
on the topmost one, out of reach. "There you are," she declared, rising
up on her toes to reach it, the volume eluding the tips of her fingers.

"I got that." Blake was behind her now, reaching easily to lift the
book perched on a stack of volumes devoted to flower arrangements

and designing your own invitations. "Pretty," he said, handing it to her. Its cover was of cupcakes decorated with forest trees.

"Thanks," said Ama. She brushed away the sawdust, which had sprinkled on it from the contractor's blue flannel shirt. "This is definitely the book I was looking for," she said, flipping it open. "It has tips for sculpting everything—flowers, animals, buildings…" A page of mini vehicles including motorcycles appeared, and Ama flipped hastily ahead, as her cheeks turned rose red.

"I liked the little London cabs on those cupcakes," said Blake, who had caught a glimpse of the page before it was gone, as he brushed away the sawdust from her latest page, one of Noah's Ark animals.

"You can make anything with marzipan," said Ama. "I should make you some cupcakes for your birthday, decorated with handyman tools." In her mind, she was undoubtedly sculpting little hammers and drills from colored marzipan.

"You have eight months before you need to plan for those," said Blake. "Any more books up there that you need?"

"No, thanks," said Ama, who added this latest volume to her stack on the table. "That'll do."

"Listen, about that old metal transom grate I took down in your office," Blake said to Tessa. "What are you going to do with it?"

"I don't know. It was a safety hazard, so I took it down," said Tessa.

"You're not throwing it away, are you?" he said. "Because if you are—"

"I never said I was," she protested. "I'm not that insensitive, Blake. I appreciate that it's pretty… it's just dangerous."

"But you wouldn't let me fix it," pointed out Blake. "It isn't impossible to find the decorative hardware that would put it back up above the door."

"Would it cost more than the new one?" Tessa crossed her arms and gave him a knowing look.

Evidence of defeat showed in Blake's attitude. Then, almost apologetically, he began, "I know I've said this a million times and you're probably sick of hearing it—" with a slight pause as Tessa rolled her eyes—"but as someone who restores old stuff for a living, I have to ask: will you ever make a decision simply for the sake of the building? Purely in the hypothetical sense, I mean."

"Do you know how much she paid for the billboard?" Ama asked him. "She paid for it herself, too."

"You leased a billboard?" he asked Tessa, amazed.

"Don't you ever drive down the new bypass to the business district? Then you'd know the answer," said Tessa, whose face colored a deep scarlet.

"Wasn't that a little pricey?"

"Isn't that none of your business?" she answered.

Tessa's phone rang, and she dug it from beneath the jumble of items in her purse. The number on its screen belonged to Accented Creations. "This is Tessa Miller," she said, answering it.

"Ms. Miller." The voice on the other end, that of the receptionist, sounded flat with disappointment. "Is Mr. Groeder's assistant available?"

"Umm... this is his assistant's assistant speaking," said Tessa. "Could I help you instead?"

"Only if Mr. Groeder wants me to cancel his show room appointment," sniped the receptionist. "I'm supposed to speak with the event planner himself on this matter. We're extremely busy, and we're going to have to cut someone from our appointment schedule, apparently."

Tessa covered the receiver. "It's the florist's," she hissed. "They want to talk to Stefan's assistant. It's an emergency."

"I thought you gave them your number," said Ama.

"I know… but the receptionist just asked me for him." She and Ama exchanged glances, then focused expectantly on Blake. "He says he'll cancel our appointment if he doesn't talk to someone with more authority." Tessa wondered if the handyman would now hold her previous arguments on the subject of their building's renovation against her.

They waited. Blake sighed. "Hand me the phone." He held out his hand. Clearing his throat, he lifted it to his ear, and when he spoke, it was with an affected, bossy accent. "Mr. Ellingham here. I *trust* I'm not speaking to anybody's assistant, am I?"

Tessa breathed a sigh of relief at the handyman's sudden snooty attitude. Blake listened to the conversation on the other end. "The show room time?" he said. "My client's availability, you mean?" He glanced at Tessa, who used frantic hand signals to communicate the best available date according to her appointment calendar.

"Let me consult my assistant's calendar. Please hold." Blake blocked the receiver against his shoulder. "He wants to know if Thursday at ten is good," he said. "What do you want?"

"Ten a.m. is fine," whispered Tessa. Blake lifted the phone.

"That arrangement will be satisfactory," he said. "Book that time for Mr. Groeder's clients. Of course. Ms. Miller will be representing our firm on that day. I am far too busy. *Try* not to give her a difficult time, if you please." With that, Blake hung up. "Satisfactory?" he repeated, this time to Tessa.

"Thank you." Tessa's tone was meeker than before as Blake handed her the phone.

"Brilliant," Ama said. "Was that really you, or were you temporarily possessed by Clinton Kelly from *What Not to Wear*?"

"It's an art form," said Blake. "I'm a man of many talents." A light, quick wink as his eye met Tessa's—but she was looking away now, and having trouble punching the keys to add the date to her phone's calendar.

"Sorry about the sawdust," said Blake, wiping it from her screen. His fingers brushed against hers—Tessa now accidentally punched the button that deleted her app for downloading coupons. "Next time, call my phone and spare yours from construction debris."

"I'll do that," said Tessa, whose voice sounded funny. "Good idea." She stuffed her phone in her bag again, trying not to pay any attention to her memory's instant recollection of Blake's phone's ring tone. That was just one of those little details that her brain had a *very* bad habit of storing away for no reason.

"The great news is, we're in," said Ama. "Thanks to Blake's help, we are now booked with *the* premier florist for our client. Sounds like good luck to me." She gave Tessa a smile.

"The best," said Tessa. Which, thank heavens, was exactly what they needed if they wanted to impress their latest clients and break their bad luck streak for good.

Chapter Ten

"You're wearing *that*?" Her mother sounded unhappy.

"It's nice. It's me," said Ama. "If I'm going on a date with this boy, I want to look like me." She spread her hands as if showcasing the outfit: a sequined, stretchy plum-colored skirt, a white blouse with tie sleeves, and a pair of black Mary Jane shoes with glittery kitten heels. "This is what me out on the town looks like."

Her family was decorating Christmas trees in the restaurant's lobby. As if the Tandoori Tiger couldn't possibly be more colorful in its decor, her father had decided that some holiday decorations would appeal to their customers. Now, there were two trees festooned with lots of purple, red, and pink lights, and decorated with tons of glittery, gold-swirled ornaments in neon colors that Ama *knew* Rasha must have chosen. The tree topper looked like a dome from the Taj Mahal.

"It's... so... understated," said Rasha at last, while studying Ama's outfit. "Don't you want to make a statement? You want him to notice you, not forget you ten seconds after the date is over."

"This isn't exactly camouflage," protested Ama. "At least it's not my zoo animal print skirt, right? No vintage print blouses or loud sneakers. Do you want him to remember me for the *wrong* reasons instead?"

"Show some cleavage," whispered Jaidev, before Deena swatted him. "Kidding," he assured her. "Guys like the mystery, I promise."

"At least put on some lipstick," said Rasha.

"Why not borrow your sister's blue *salwar kameez*?" suggested Ranjit, as he struggled to find a plug for the lights. "Do the lights blink?" he asked Jaidev, from beneath the tree's low foliage.

"Not blinking," reported Jaidev. "That must have been the wrong bulb we took out." Only half the tree was lit now, with the other half winking furiously every three seconds.

"I'm not wearing something borrowed from another person's wardrobe today," said Ama. "I want to be myself, like I said, so this is it. Now, do I look nice or what?" she asked, with a smile she hoped would ease the tension over this issue.

"Of course you do," said Rasha. "At least it's not your purple zebra-stripe dress."

"Or that terrible shirt with the buttons sewn all over it," contributed her auntie.

"Thanks," said Ama.

"You look great," said Jaidev, giving her a thumbs-up. "Knock 'em dead, kid."

"Jaidev!" Pashma scolded him.

"It's just an expression, Mom," he said.

Tamir's choice of restaurant was the new Indian Palace near the business district: Ama had seen it a time or two, a modern spot close to the waterfront, with an atmosphere at once austere on the outside and overly elaborate on the inside, in her opinion.

Folk dancers, sitar music—this place was more culturally accurate than restaurants like the Tandoori Tiger, where the staff wore loud saris, and there were glittery fabrics and cushions for the seating areas. Even so, its atmosphere didn't do much for Ama, as she discovered while seated across from Tamir, listening to a throaty folk singer covering a traditional Rajasthani tune.

The waiter brought them menus. "Welcome to the palace," he said, saluting them with a traditional Hindi greeting. "Tonight's specials are an infusion which melds the cuisine of Rajasthan and modern vegan cuisine in harmony."

Hence the *dhoka* music and the hostesses dressed in skirts and *chaniya cholis* in blue and yellow Bagru prints, Ama surmised, which put her aunt Bendi's mirrored and embroidered folk dress to shame. "They have some good Punjabi dishes here," suggested Tamir to her, as he perused the restaurant's signature dishes.

She wondered what he would say if instead of dinner she ordered a big dessert plate heaped with sweet and sticky balls of *gulab jamun* in their sugary sauce. Her lips almost twitched into a smile at this image.

"I'll just have the *dal bati*," said Ama. Her auntie's version of this dish of lentils and wheat rolls served with ghee was her favorite from her mother's family's traditional cuisine.

"And for you?" The waiter looked at Tamir, who was seated across from Ama.

"I'll have the *makki ki roti*," said Tamir.

"An excellent choice," the waiter said, bowing as he collected their menus.

"*Makki ki roti?*" she repeated, somewhat surprised at his choice. It was an exclusively Punjabi *roti* dish, and humorous clichés about Tamil Nadu proclaimed *roti* to be more of an indulgence among vegetarian dishes anyway.

"I haven't tried this restaurant's version," he said. "Maybe you can tell me if it's good, since it's probably a popular dish at your restaurant."

"Sure." Ama didn't really want to think about her restaurant's menu while surrounded by the palace's forced authentic atmosphere, though. What would Tamir say if he knew about the candied pumpkins topping

Indian desserts during November? Or saw the glitzy Christmas tree in the restaurant's foyer?

"How long has your family been in the restaurant business?" he asked.

Ama sipped her water. "As long as I can remember," she said. "I was born here, like all of my siblings. Before he came to America, my father owned a big restaurant in Himachal Pradesh," she added. "And before that, he helped run his father's restaurant in Punjab. But he and my mother had the chance to come to America, so they took it. The political situation in his home city was growing worse, and there were better opportunities abroad… you've heard the same story dozens of times."

Tamir nodded. Not the world's greatest conversationalist, Ama reflected.

"What about you?" she asked.

"My father worked for an American garment exporter based in Mumbai when I was growing up," said Tamir. "We lived in America for a while, then we moved back to Mumbai so he could manage the business's main outlet. He was transferred to the U.S. branch of the exporter's retail chain permanently when I was around fifteen. But I stayed behind for a couple of years, because my grandfather was the headmaster at the school where I was studying English and mathematics… and I was at the top of the class."

He hid a smile and, for the first time, Ama thought maybe he possessed a sense of humor. Maybe he was thinking, what Indian family wouldn't insist their son hold onto a first place ranking, even if it put an ocean between them? That was the kind of joke that their culture would chuckle over, and Ama almost did, to see if Tamir was really thinking the same thing. Just then, however, he spoke again.

"Have you ever been to India?" he asked.

"Me? No," said Ama. "I've been to Mexico once." It was a trip during her senior year, for which Ama had saved her meager tips from the restaurant—her father thought spending money on frivolous travel was wasteful, but Ama had loved the idea of lying poolside at a beachfront resort, with warm sand, broad-brimmed sombreros, and the colorful festivities of a Hispanic holiday that rivaled even the boldest Indian wedding celebration.

"Mexico?" Tamir repeated. A little frown wrinkled his forehead. That look of puzzlement irked Ama ever so slightly, as if he was wondering why anyone would want to go south of the border.

"It was the most fun I've ever had," she said. "I brought back a big hat, a sequined purse, and some beautiful fabric that I made into a skirt. I even put little mirror sequins along its hem—it kind of reminded me of my aunt Bendi's best blouse when I was done with it," she admitted.

"Is that your aunt's real name?" His brow furrowed a little more.

"A joke," said Ama. "It was my brother's nickname for her when he was a kid. She's a little... assertive... my aunt. She has a habit of bending circumstances to go her way, whether it involves a family issue or a new addition to our restaurant's menu." *Now would be a good time to change the subject*, Ama reflected. "You grew up in India, though," she said. "You must have some great stories. There are probably some really beautiful places in Mumbai."

"There are," said Tamir. "But I liked my grandfather's house in Tamil Nadu better. I've been to Rajasthan, though. That's your mother's family's home, isn't it?"

"You know that?" Ama wondered if that was why they were in a restaurant clearly hosting an evening dedicated to that state's culture—and if it had been the culture of Bengal instead, if they would be eating at the Punjabi Express across town.

"It said so on your profile," said Tamir, his brow creasing anew.

It did? It occurred to Ama to wonder what else her father had shared, inadvertently or on purpose. "What was it like?" she asked. "Did you see Jaipur or Jodhpur?" The former was the 'pink city' and the latter was the 'blue,' named for the colored stone and the paint that characterized their buildings, respectively.

"I saw Jodhpur," he said. "From the fort."

"So was it beautiful?" persisted Ama.

He shrugged. "It looked like the pictures," he said.

So was it beautiful or what? Ama was slightly annoyed. Tamir smoothed his dinner napkin, and now was busy cleaning his eyeglasses' lenses. Without them, his face looked different—less superior and oh-so 'I.T.,' as Jaidev would put it. When they were back in place, he offered Ama a glance and another bland smile.

Their waiter reappeared. "A sample of tonight's featured fusion dishes, with the chef's compliments." He placed two plates between them, one with *litti chokha*, the other with a spiced curry, he explained.

"Spiced with what?" asked Tamir.

"Our chef's secret spice," answered the waiter, before disappearing again.

Rats. Appetizers. Ama had been hoping the main courses might hurry themselves along. This evening would come to a merciful end if dinner was quick, especially since she and Tamir were running low on things to say to each other.

They tasted the first dish, then the second. "Can you tell what the secret is?" asked Tamir.

Ama let the flavor roll over her tongue. "It tastes a little like Hungarian paprika," she said. "Or maybe a mild Mexican chipotle." She took a second bite, but still wasn't sure. "It must be a cultural fusion outside of Indian spices."

"So much for authentic cuisine." Tamir returned to the first appetizer. "Last time I was here, the menu was a little more traditional, but maybe they changed chefs since then. My boss said it had the most authentic Punjabi menu in the city. That's why I chose it over Punjabi Express. I thought maybe it would be a good idea to try a less casual place."

You couldn't find a place less casual than the aforementioned restaurant, whose dancers and sitar soundtrack made the Tandoori Tiger seem positively sophisticated—and the Express's menu was twice as greasy and more like Indian fast food. Had he been planning to take her there because of that, Ama wondered? After having seen a glimpse of her own family's less than formal restaurant?

"Can I say something frank?" she said. Tamir looked up from his plate.

"Of course," he said, sounding surprised.

"I'm just surprised that you called me for a date," she said. "Actually, that you picked me from your list of matches in the first place. I mean, after you saw that my profile kind of exaggerated some of my background and qualities, especially." For instance, that a successful business couldn't cover for her family's lack of social status compared to his own, she wanted to add.

Her father's profile and not hers, that is. She didn't want a profile, or a match, or to be eating this dry curry dish in a restaurant that was way more expensive than her family's. Especially not with a guy who seemed so horribly wrong for her in so many ways—ones that had nothing whatsoever to do with class or cultural distinctions, either.

"I thought you sounded interesting," he said. "My roommate in college was Punjabi."

"Your roommate." She stated this flatly. This reason for finding her interesting seemed rather stupid to her. Maybe his friend had been one of those 'life of the party Punjabis' as Jaidev called them, and he had imagined she, too, was a talkative, fun-loving type who loved the night life. This theory was now replacing the possible mistake of him somehow assuming she was the daughter of a wealthy Punjabi businessman instead.

"He wasn't from Punjab. He was from New Jersey." Tamir moved aside his appetizer as the waiter arrived with their main dishes.

"Were you really good friends?" asked Ama. She wondered vaguely what Tamir did with his friends. If he didn't pursue outdoor sports anymore, what was his hobby? "Is he one of the people you hang out with?"

"I haven't seen him in two or three years, actually," said Tamir.

"I see." Ama picked at her lentils. "So what do you do for fun?" she asked.

"I see movies sometimes. There's an Indian theater near the cultural center. Do you like Rajinikanth?"

"I don't know. I've never had it," said Ama, confused.

"No, he's an actor," said Tamir. "His movies are some of my mother's favorites, although she generally prefers art house films over Bollywood. But I love Telugu films myself. Their stunts are hilarious." He dug his fingers into the rice on his plate—eating in the traditional right-hand fashion instead of using the fork beside his plate. Whereas Ama's fork was restlessly rearranging her food into perfect little piles. The lentils needed chicken stock, she decided.

"I don't watch many Indian films," she admitted. "Just a few on TV late at night. My mom and my auntie love the old classic ones, so sometimes I watch along with them. But I don't know very much about the differences between them, or the top Bollywood actors and actresses."

"Really?" he said.

"Unless you count *Bride and Prejudice*," said Ama. "I loved that one."

"What movies do you usually like?" She noticed Tamir wasn't that interested in his food, either. Maybe this restaurant's cuisine wasn't his thing.

"I like a lot of Hollywood romantic comedies," she said. "My favorites are the cheesiest. Old Disney romantic movies, black-and-white love stories... and the modern ones, those are the best. I've watched *Return to Me* more times than I can name. *Me Before You*, *Dying Young*—I pretty much keep a box of Kleenex beside the sofa when I watch."

"I've never seen any of those," said Tamir. "Don't they die at the end of those last two? The heroes?" he clarified. "I think my roommate used to watch the last one with his girlfriend."

"How about *The Way We Were*?" asked Ama. "Or *You've Got Mail*?" How could anybody not have seen a modern romance movie? Did no art house movies ever feature love stories?

"Doesn't ring a bell," he said. "You're sure you've never seen a Rajinikanth movie, though? They show them on some of the late-night movie channels, I think."

"I wouldn't know," Ama shrugged. "My auntie might." She tried to picture Tamir's mom enjoying the same kind of comedies her family did—ones about marrying off a dozen daughters to their true loves and suitable matches. Probably she watched them after spending an afternoon in a theater viewing some intellectual drama, like the French film industry's equivalent of *My Dinner with Andre*. Without subtitles.

He gave up on his plate of food. "Tell me about your baking," he said. "Your family said you run a baked goods by mail business part-time?"

"Not so much anymore. I'm a partner in a business, where I bake for weddings," said Ama.

"You make cookies for weddings?"

"Cookies?"

"That's what your father said you baked. Cookies," said Tamir. "I thought maybe it was a new wedding trend or something. He said it was sort of a hobby for you."

Trust her father to only think of the novelty birthday goodies she provided via her online shop Sweetheart Treats. "I guess I do bake wedding cookies sometimes," she amended. "But wedding cakes as well. And I wouldn't call it a hobby. It's my job. My real job, even though I still work at the restaurant, obviously."

"Baking sounds nice," said Tamir.

"Thanks. It is." Ama abandoned her lentils. They were definitely too dry. The restaurant was clearly having an off night.

"So what are Indian wedding cookies like?" asked Tamir. "Is it like a Punjabi dessert?"

"They're not really Indian wedding cookies. They're for any kind of wedding. They're just desserts. And I baked a five-tier wedding cake for the last client. It was just an average wedding cake like anybody might choose, only it was my own design."

"Oh," said Tamir. "That's nice." He smiled as he repeated this polite observation.

The folk music was suddenly louder—the *dhoka* player was on the move, along with the dancers, who were now gyrating beside Ama and Tamir's table, beginning the moves of a traditional Ghoomar dance.

It was kind of like being trapped in a Bollywood musical scene, Ama imagined, as she shrank a little from the loud musical notes coming from behind her left shoulder.

Tamir leaned closer. "Maybe we could try a different restaurant next time," he said.

Next time?

Chapter Eleven

Accented Creations' show room was an austere, modern room with staged lighting, resembling a Guggenheim art gallery more than the typical florist's showcase. The suspicious receptionist wasn't present, replaced by the florist's own assistant guiding them through possibilities for Nadia and Lyle's wedding. Fortunately, he held no animosity toward Tessa as Blake's supposed assistant, so the contractor's absence wasn't a problem today.

"This one is Margo's particular favorite. She calls it 'Winter Wonderland Walk,'" explained the assistant, referring to the florist in question. On display was an arrangement of slender, twisty woodland twigs decorated with a fake, sparkling crystal gel resembling ice, accompanied by fir boughs embellished with fake snow, glittery pinecone picks, and a strand of slender pearl lights for illumination.

"That's really nice," said Nadia. "That would look perfect. Lyle, what do you think? Lyle—" she poked her fiancé in the side, who was busy studying a weird modern painting on the show room's wall, one which resembled a jumble of calla lilies. "What do you think? It would look good in the middle of our tables, wouldn't it?"

"Sure, honey," he said. "I guess so. I mean, I don't know anything about this kind of stuff, so better ask Mom."

"But I want your opinion," said Nadia. "You know how important the decor is to me."

"Don't you think it's a little plain?" said Paula. "It's just a bunch of sticks in a vase."

The mothers were back today—Cynthia in a little pillbox hat that belonged to Jackie O's closet circa 1962, whereas Paula was doing her best impression of Gypsy Rose Lee's mother in heavy rouge and a sequined dress and faux fur coat that might have looked perfect at a burlesque show. Tessa's heart had sunk the moment they climbed out of Lyle's car, as if it was an omen for this day's progress.

The assistant bristled. "We prefer to think of it as a tabletop sculpture," he said. "Margo hand selects every branch herself and has it decorated by our team of artisans."

Tessa pictured a gang of little woodland elves decorating these branches with magic glitter in their tree house. The urge to laugh was the only thing that saved her from the feeling of impending doom, now that Cynthia was taking notice of the second possible wedding centerpiece.

"That design is entitled 'All Dressed in White,'" said the assistant, gliding into place beside the next exhibit. "Light, delicate, and reflecting the beauty of a traditional bride." Paperwhites and thick-stemmed white amaryllises filled the plain glass vase. It was simple with clean lines, and definitely very traditional in Tessa's estimate.

Tessa made a note in her planning book. "I like it," she said to Nadia. "Except I think the first one fits your theme of winter white a little better. Snow and ice are natural elements, so leaning toward nature—"

"I think frozen sticks would look terrible in the middle of the table. It's so cheap—Lyle, honey, tell them you aren't cheap like that," insisted Paula, tugging at her son's sleeve.

"Of course I'm not, Ma," scoffed Lyle. "Nadia and her family know that. It'll be nice, whatever you ladies pick." He wandered on to the third choice, not noticing the flurry of concern in the assistant's eyes at someone leaping ahead of the presentation.

"Well, *I* think the second one is far more tasteful," said Cynthia. "It's very you, Nadia. Don't you agree?"

"I like the flowers, but it doesn't really fit with my theme," said Nadia. "Like Tess was saying, if we book the church and go with the winter white theme like we planned—"

"I thought you were getting some big fancy hotel for the wedding," interrupted Paula. "Lyle, didn't you say you were going to get a real swanky place?"

"We got the restaurant, Ma. It's swanky, right?" said Lyle. "But we can do something bigger than the church for the ceremony. It's fine with me." He shrugged his shoulders. "What are these flowers called?" he asked the floral assistant, pointing to the third centerpiece.

"Those are Canterbury bells," said the assistant, rushing to prevent the arrangement from being touched by the groom. "Paired with lilies to create more clean lines and a feel of modern architecture, generous sprays of white roses and tulips, and for a little touch of *bling*, Margo has added some crystal snowflakes and a few delicate glass bells on sterling silver stems. It's called 'Bridal Blizzard.'"

"Now *that's* more like it," said Paula, joining him. "Look at this one, Nadia. This has some 'wow' factor, am I right? It's what you need for the wedding."

"Tell me you're not thinking about that hideous hotel downtown," Cynthia was saying to Nadia, in what she evidently believed was a quiet voice. "That modern white palace is simply tasteless—I've heard there are *gilded* toilet seats in the bathrooms."

"What's wrong with a little gold?" said Paula. "We need to ritz things up a bit for this ceremony, don't we? Nadia, honey, look at this thing. Now, this is a beast of a centerpiece. It'll really amaze the guests. Lyle, tell her this is the one you want."

"It most certainly isn't," said Cynthia. "Nadia has more taste than that. She wants something elegant, but understated. Which... this thing... certainly isn't."

"That 'thing' happens to be one of Margo's most expensive designs," said the assistant frostily. "I would suggest you show some appreciation for its delicate details."

"It's better than those boring little frou-frou flowers in that middle bouquet," snorted Paula.

"Are you referring to 'All Dressed in White'?" The assistant's jaw dropped.

This was going some very bad places, and it was only a matter of minutes before Accented Creations kicked them all to the curb—something Tessa could *not* have. In part because the winter wonderland bouquet showed strong potential as the perfect choice for Nadia's wedding, but also—at least a little—because it would be a major blow to the Wedding Belles precisely at a time they didn't need one.

"If that's the bland one, I sure am."

"I like the first one," said Nadia helplessly. "The one Mom likes is nice too, but..."

"How about we find a compromise?" suggested Lyle. "You know, put all three together or something? Hold on." His phone rang and he answered it. "Yeah. We're out of mutton? You're serious?" He made a face. "Hey, put Benny on the phone..."

Tessa drew aside the assistant. "Forgive my clients," she said. "I assure you that they are *very* appreciative of the opportunity to view Margo's work, and would be thrilled to have her design their centerpieces."

"Then tell them to refrain from insulting the centerpieces, if you would," snapped the assistant. "We do have other clients who are a little more appreciative of our efforts."

"I know. I know. You are very exclusive, and we are very appreciative of this opportunity for a showcase," repeated Tessa, who was ready to resort to groveling. "Please, just let me have a quick word with my clients."

She plucked Nadia's sleeve and drew her aside from the discussion of the second centerpiece. "We need to avoid too many personal comments on the designs," she said quietly. "This particular floral business is a little sensitive when it comes to criticism, and, believe me, we should make the most of this chance."

"I know," said Nadia. "I've seen their work in some of the magazines I read. I really like their designs, I really do. It's just that my——"

Cynthia had followed, and so did Paula, when her head jerked in their direction. "Nadia, you didn't answer me about the hotel," said Cynthia. "And what are you two whispering about? You're not talking her into that giant centerpiece, I hope?" She glared at Tessa anxiously.

"I think it's classy," insisted Paula. "Are you saying Lyle doesn't have taste?"

"Only for tzatziki," muttered Cynthia.

Nadia gave her a look. "Mom," she hissed. "Be nice." She glanced from one mother to the next. "Both of you, we need to dial it back a little. I haven't decided anything. The only important thing is for it to be something perfect for the theme, right? Please, just work with me, okay? I want to pick the right thing for me and Lyle's big day... and it's his decision and mine." She glanced toward Lyle, who had picked a leaf off the Canterbury bells' stem before the assistant could stop him.

Cynthia looked pleased. Paula looked injured. Tessa forced a smile to her lips.

"Let's focus on the best elements from each design," she said. "These are just examples to help us envision something extremely unique for Nadia and Lyle, so that's the important part to take away from this showcase. Which, by the way, is also *extremely* exclusive, so it would behoove us to keep that in mind." She couldn't say this part enough, in her opinion. Would they pick up on the hint that it was essential to be nicer to the artist's work?

"Of course, all of these creations will be displayed in Margo's specially crafted ice vases, with tiny snowflakes etched into the sides," said the assistant. "These same containers can be provided for votives as well, for a minimalist look. We have a relationship with an excellent ice sculptor, who does wonders with a saw."

"Those are gorgeous," said Nadia, looking at the pictures he provided of hollow ice blocks aglow with votive candles burning within. "And you can put flowers in them, too? Wow, I see so many possibilities for these." She glanced eagerly at Tessa, who felt the tingle of excitement she always did for a client's happiness.

"I think we could line the entrance with these," said Tessa. "And maybe with some icicle lights to decorate the church, too." She studied the photos, imagining the possibilities involving an ice sculptor for the reception's decor. Could the winter white theme come to life in the private dining room of Lyle's restaurant?

"Now, onto bouquets," said the assistant, who opened a special display case. "Margo isn't sure yet what direction your bride will follow, but she did have a concept she wanted to explore."

The bouquet comprised white poinsettias with paperwhites and frosted rosemary sprigs, the stems wrapped in white satin ribbon, leaving half the paperwhites' stems exposed. A definite start, although it lacked the blue and silver that Nadia had expressed an interest in showcasing. Tessa made a quick note about some possible adjustments, such as silver and ice blue colors for the ribbons, maybe.

"Isn't it pretty?" said Nadia. "I don't know how it will look with my dress... maybe with white roses instead?"

"Lots of roses," pressed Paula. "And maybe a big silver bow tied around it. Wouldn't it look nice with that big centerpiece?"

Cynthia closed her eyes with despair. "It's supposed to be simple. Nadia, this wedding will have a little dignity, I hope?"

Nadia sighed. "Of course it will," she said. "But what I want is—"

"You want something real nice," intervened Paula. "Lyle likes things big and bold, so don't pick some little bitty vase no one will ever notice."

"Even the simplest of Margo's creations attracts notice, I assure you," said the floral assistant.

"Of course," Tessa assured him.

Lyle was picking up some bits of fallen rosemary sprig when Tessa drew him aside from the group for a private word. "If you could help Nadia choose, it would really help," she said. "I think she needs some support. There are too many opinions in the mix, and only yours and hers matter," she told him. "Why don't you give her a little feedback on some of those flowers?"

He shook his head. "I'm no good at this kind of stuff," he said. "Ma knows more about flowers and cakes than I do. Besides, it's Nadia's big day. She should be the one to pick—isn't it the bride's thing? You know, flowers and pretty chocolates and all that jazz?"

"But it's your opinion she really wants, not your mom's," pressed Tessa. "Just give her a little hint." She was trying hard not to sound too pleading, but she wished Lyle would step up. Wrestle aside Paula and her insistent comments, she willed him, quietly—put Cynthia in the background for once, so Nadia feels she isn't torn between the opinions of two very willful mothers.

He cleared his throat. "Um, Nadia," he said. "That big one's nice." He gestured toward the fluffy 'Bridal Blizzard.' "But you pick what you like, okay? Those little flowers are nice, too. I like them too."

Paula's beaming smile withered, replaced now by Cynthia's turn at a crisp little grin of triumph. "Tell the florist you like the middle one," Cynthia said, giving Nadia's arm a poke. "Go on."

"I don't know," Nadia hesitated. "I still think the first one…"

"You heard Lyle, though," said Paula. "And you like the big one, too, don't you? Well?" she said, searching Nadia's face anxiously. Nadia was looking for an escape, judging from her eyes, which were locked solidly on an unperturbed and unnoticing Lyle.

"Honey, which one?" said Nadia. "Tell me which one you really like best, so I feel like I'm making a choice both of us want."

"You ladies work it out," said Lyle. "I trust you, Nadia. And Ma's got the best taste of anybody in my family, I promise. Hey, is there a coffee shop close by? I'm starved." He posed these questions to the floral assistant, who looked ready for them to leave. Tessa was mentally crafting an email to smooth things over and keep Nadia and Lyle from being erased from the potential customers list.

"I think for now… the middle one is the best choice," said Nadia with a sigh. "Can you ask the florist if she can email our wedding planners about costs and maybe some alterations?"

"Of course," said the assistant, making a note on his phone. "I can arrange for you to see the cost breakdown of all three potential designs."

"Thanks," said Tessa, who had made a note that number two was the winner—for now. "I look forward to that. And I'm very grateful for this opportunity. So is... Mr. Groeder," she added, at the very last. After all, it might not hurt to throw in the name of the annoying event planner who'd earned her this 'in' in the first place... or maybe it would be better to forget his part, judging from the assistant's expression in reply.

"You'll be hearing from us shortly," he promised.

Maybe an approving word from Blake would smooth things over instead.

✳

In her office, Tessa laid out the pages from Accented Creations' port-folio, admiring the carved ice votive holders, the delicate sprays of paperwhites and the simple amaryllises: a small arrangement, but still outrageously priced compared to the last florist they hired for a wedding. The one Nadia—or Cynthia—had chosen would probably work well with the possible theme with a few minor adjustments. But it would be nice if the discussion was between the bride and groom and not the warring third parties.

"We'll be lucky not to lose the florist after today," she told Natalie, who was sitting in the office's cushy rose-printed armchair, sketching some potential dress designs. "It was that bad."

"Are you sure?" said Natalie.

"I saw the little gleam of fury in the assistant's eye. I'm sure by now that Margo the floral artist is burning with resentment that her chief creation was referred to as 'a bunch of sticks' by our client's mother." Who had made it sound like the florist had gathered some refuse out of a backyard leaf pile.

"Just what we need—an enemy at the biggest florist's in town," said Natalie. "How are we going to fix that?"

"By finding a way to keep Cynthia and Paula apart," said Tessa. "Maybe we can suggest a 'one mother per outing' limit. Lyle has got to be the one to state an opinion to Nadia, not these Godzilla parents who keep interfering in every decision."

"How do you intend to stop them?" said Natalie. "If you ask me, if feels like this whole wedding is—"

"Don't say it," said Tessa warningly.

Natalie paused. "I was going to say 'trouble,'" she answered.

"Nice try. I know what you were really thinking," said Tessa, narrowing her eyes. *Jinxed. Cursed.* Those were not terms to utter here and now, when positive thinking was crucial to their survival.

"I think," said Natalie, leaning across the desk as she slid off the armchair's cushions, "that's because *you're* secretly thinking it with every new problem that crops up."

"I'm not listening to you." Loftily, Tessa stacked the portfolio pages from the florist and began making a sketch of her own, which included adding white tulips and narcissus to the centerpiece of 'All Dressed in White'. Natalie flipped her own sketchbook closed.

"Let's just hope that really expensive billboard you purchased brings us better luck in the future," she said. "By the way, the bill for it is still unpaid, I noticed."

"I'm going to pay for it," said Tessa. "I just need a few more days."

"Are you sure?" A little concern was in Natalie's voice. "If there's a problem, we can talk about it, Tess. Talk to me."

"There's no problem." Tessa gave her a smile. "I promised I had it covered, and I do."

"With your super-secret job?" Nat raised one eyebrow. "What is it, anyway?"

"Can't tell. It's my own private commission, and I promised that it would stay that way," said Tessa.

"Who made you promise?" said Natalie. A thud came from down below, where Blake was back in place, fixing an issue with the parlor's floor. "Not Blake?" she asked, in a way that suggested this was exactly what she was thinking. "Is that what your secretive little looks his way are about?" A sly smile flitted across the designer's lips.

"I'm not saying any more," said Tessa cryptically. "Let's just leave it at that." She sealed her lips and put on her best poker face to prevent any clues to this mystery from being revealed under Natalie's shrewd gaze.

"Fine. Be that way," said Natalie, giving up as she followed Tessa toward the staircase. They had started to descend to the foyer below when a familiar figure came through the front door. "Here comes trouble," Natalie muttered before they had reached the threshold where Paula now waited for them impatiently. "Hi, Mrs. Kardopolis," she said, greeting the groom's mother as she passed her in the doorway.

"Hi—have you found the dress for Nadia yet?" Paula asked, momentarily waylaying Natalie.

"Not yet." Natalie smiled as nicely as she could. "That is, she wants her gown to be custom designed. She picked out some special fabric from an online vendor, but she hasn't settled on a pattern yet."

"Well, good. I don't want her to get talked into something too plain." Paula was now hovering behind Tessa, who was willing her to go away. "I just wanted to give you the card for Lyle's head caterer," she said. "He forgot to give it to you, and he figured you need to talk with him about the menu."

"Thanks," said Tessa, tucking it into her bag. Paula noticed a folder that was open on the hall table with some initial notes Tessa had made about the centerpiece. She reached for a pen, crossed through 'All Dressed in White' and wrote 'Blizzard' below it.

"That's what Lyle really wants," she said in a hushed, conspiratorial whisper. "Don't tell that to Cynthia, though. Poor boy's so modest, he never gets a word in edgewise whenever she's around."

"But I can't—" began Tessa, with dismay.

"You make sure those flowers are real big and beautiful—I don't want my son's wedding to be some big snore because of somebody's froofy opinions on what's elegant," said Paula. "Gotta go. I don't want Cynthia getting suspicious that I talked to you on my own. This'll be our little secret, all right?"

"We really shouldn't—"

"See you later." Paula disappeared. Five minutes later, as Tessa was still trying to find the words that ought to have been her reply, Mrs. Emerson appeared.

"I only have a moment, Ms. Miller," she said. "I just wanted to be clear—it is the sophisticated second bouquet reserved for Nadia's wedding, correct?"

"It is, but—"

"Perfect." She sighed with relief. "I was afraid that dreadful Paula would try to talk Nadia out of it the moment my back was turned. Such cheap taste." She shook her head. "Don't tell Nadia I said that, however. I've promised her that I will be polite, and it wouldn't do to have her know I've been interfering behind her back."

"You *are*—"

"Just keep everything tasteful and delicate like Nadia herself, and it will be perfectly fine," assured Cynthia. "Well, I must run. We're all having lunch at some awful place that Paula thinks is the last word in Mediterranean cuisine." A limp little smile of approval was bestowed on Tessa, who was then left alone in her office to ponder how impossible it was going to be to get anything accomplished with these two women in charge.

❋

"*No*," said Natalie, releasing a long groan of frustration. "Look at this! How did this happen?"

The open box before her, which was supposed to contain the fabric she'd ordered for Nadia's dress, was filled instead with a bolt of fuzzy pink flannel printed with tiny sheep in pajamas. Ama whistled.

"Gorgeous," she said. "I can't wait to see the finished gown."

"It's not funny, Ama," Natalie snapped. "This is the only decision Nadia's made on her dress to date, the fabric she wanted. We spent three days looking at swatches, she took the book home before she picked this one, and we tried *three* different places until we located one that claimed to have it in stock. It took me forever to locate this vendor. *This* stuff is not the monumental decision I slaved over. It's a… a sheep slumber party." She snorted with anger.

"So it's a mistake," said Ama reassuringly. "We'll send it back. Just like the party supplies. And they'll send you a new bolt of fabric."

"Fantastic—if this wasn't the warehouse's last six yards," said Natalie. "I told you that this particular satin weave was discontinued. Something about the company's hand-dyed satin being made by an eighty-five-year-old artist who's retiring." She tossed the receipt into the box, where it drifted over a sheep snuggling a teddy bear.

The tiny snowflake ornament frames had been irreplaceable, even after an exhaustive search by Tessa, so Nadia had chosen a substitute in the form of silver sacks filled with shiny winter blue and white candies. Tessa was still trying to find a way to hang them attractively from the branches of the flocked Christmas tree they had already purchased for the foyer, where the guest favors were originally intended for display.

"Maybe you can still find some secondhand rolls," suggested Ama. "Try some of the online auction sites. It couldn't hurt."

"Why couldn't I have persuaded Nadia to pick something else?" said Natalie. She was mentally kicking herself for being the latest victim of this wedding's curse.

Natalie spent the rest of the day phoning every fabric supplier and warehouse she had ever met through Kandace's Kreations. Most of them didn't have anything remotely comparable, even the most exclusive website whose fabrics Kandace could never afford for her bizarre designs.

"Thanks anyway, Wanda." Natalie hung up the phone after her latest try, and returned to scouring the web. Lots of beautiful fabrics were available, with more than one tempting Natalie from purely a designer's standpoint. Exactly the kind of soft, rich material she had longed to sew with when Kandace was still obsessed with scratchy Lycra made from metallic threads and eighties synthetics.

What would it be like to see quality fabrics like these transformed into her designs… and, hypothetically, walking the runway at a show like the December fashion revue? Cal was forever telling her that she was good enough to create her own line of garments, but he was her friend and one of those supportive people who would always say nice things. As for her family and oldest friends, they did their best to be supportive, and more than one loved what she had sewn for them, but she knew that fashion design wasn't a subject any of them followed with interest… except for maybe one person, whose opinion Natalie wasn't dying to hear.

She clicked on a website specializing in wedding fabrics, as her phone rang. It was her brother's number on the screen, and Natalie rolled her eyes in anticipation of whatever favor Rob was asking.

"What?" she said. "I'm working, Rob, so it had better be good."

"Bad, actually. I have to bail on Uncle Guido this weekend. I can't help with the Christmas pasta, because I've got a training seminar upstate."

"Let me get this straight: you're spending this weekend putting out fake forest fires, and you need me to cover for you with our family. The way I did last year when you had to study for your promotion, and the Thanksgiving before, when you couldn't help with pies because your friend Tony had a bachelor's party in Vegas—"

"Are you going to recount all my wrongs?" said Rob. "Please, Nat. It's just a couple hours on Sunday afternoon, a little spinach ravioli. You could do it in your sleep."

"Yeah, and so could you." She clicked on a bolt of fabric, experiencing disappointment as she studied its close-up on the webpage. Poor quality—she could see that much.

"Just help me out, sis. You're the best, and you know it. I'll owe you one, and you know how much you love that."

"You want to do something for me?" replied Natalie, cradling the phone with one shoulder as she typed. "Then get Brayden to change that ring tone on his phone." She clicked the mouse on a new selection.

"What? Are you serious?"

"I am. It's creepy and weird, Rob. I'm uncomfortable knowing that's what he thinks of when my number comes up on his phone." Not that it ever did, but that wasn't the point. Natalie's tone was firm on this issue regarding Brayden's lovelorn gesture.

"Lighten up, Nat," said Rob with a dismissive snort.

"Seriously? I'm not joking, Rob. It weirded me out."

"Have a heart, Natalie," he answered. "It's not that weird, you know. Trust me, every guy on the planet has a fantasy at some point about a girl he can't get, and thinks about her when he hears some mushy love song. So Brayden's fantasy has just lasted a little longer than the rest, that's all. You don't have to make him feel like it's a crime or something to have a crush on you."

"I still don't like it," said Natalie, who was uncomfortable discussing it, although she couldn't pinpoint the reasons why specifically. It wasn't as if any of this was news to her, the idea that Brayden had feelings for her, as Rob would undoubtedly point out any second from now. Or that he had probably fantasized about kissing her, either. Why be frustrated because an awkward moment revealed that Brayden thought of her whenever some sentimental eighties pop hit played on the radio?

"Go easy on him," said Rob. "At least he's a nice guy, Nat. Some creep or jerk could be pining for you instead—especially after some of the guys you've dated. Just think about what good taste he shows by picking you as his dream girl."

"Funny." Nat's voice was now sarcastic. "So, you'll be having fun with Uncle Guido on Sunday, right?"

"Nat, please. Come on. Look, I'll give you my frequent flyer miles for your next vacation—I'll babysit your apartment next time you're out of town. Anything, just give me a break this time."

She sighed. "Fine. Sunday it is." She hung up the phone, then remembered that Sunday was her birthday. Not that she had plans yet, but her potential plans had not included spending yet another weekend working at the bakery, either.

Terrific. Thanks to Rob, she was roped into holiday cooking duty once again, only this time rolling tiny little pasta bites for her family's Christmas Eve dinner instead of baking Thanksgiving pies. At least she still had the promise of the handsome guy from the cafe, Chad, of a new Ecuadorian restaurant and a movie this week, and maybe he would like to make plans to see her on the evening of her birthday too... and maybe there would be time for a little piece of chocolate cake, then, since Brayden was right about her love for it.

Not that she wanted to give him credit for remembering that fact about her birthdays, after twelve years since her last real party. And she still had to find a way to make him delete that song from her number. Anything else would be better, she thought. Well, maybe not anything, given the number of songs about love, pining, and romantic dreams. How about something generic, safe, and a little bit depressing—say, Beethoven's Fifth?

Chapter Twelve

"So you hit a bad patch," said Bill, Tessa's friend and former boss. "It happens to everybody, Tessa. Deal with it. It's part of being a business owner. I thought you would have figured that out a long time ago."

"I thought so, too," said Tessa gloomily. "But everything's going wrong, Bill. It isn't just the little things, it's the big things too. If I fail, this is big time. You know what I mean."

"Turn the music off," said Bill. "The businesses along here have complained the last couple of times that it's too loud."

With a sigh, Tessa switched off the soundtrack playing through the dachshund-in-a-bun truck's topmost speaker—the music box version of 'How Much is that Doggy in the Window?' now dwindled to silence as Party 2 Go's vehicle turned onto the party supply shop's lane.

All of this felt eerily familiar to Tessa, who had spent years mopping up soda spills and donning a terrible T-Rex costume for Bill's birthday planning service before she found the nerve—and resources—to launch her own business. She would never forget the catalyst for taking that crazy career leap into the unknown: a humiliating birthday party encounter with her former childhood neighbor and college classmate Penny Newcastle. Standing before successful, stuck-up Penny in a pair of sneakers that were freshly festooned in neon icing from a dessert table mishap, the last of Tessa's dignity had demanded a change. The rest was history, as they say… except now history was repeating itself, albeit temporarily, for Tessa to earn a little extra cash.

"You know, I can't believe you actually agreed to help me out," said Bill. "You seemed pretty eager to turn in your t-shirt, frankly." He released a little chuckle. "I miss having you around, by the way. June's a mess at picking out cakes. Tina's got four new weird piercings, so now the kids are terrified of her when she dresses in the princess costume. Plus, that new guy Jared got busted for selling homemade wine out of the trunk of his car, so that's a huge headache for us right now."

"I feel your pain," grunted Tessa. She winced a little as she tried to ease into the only available parking spot on this narrow little street—couldn't One Stop Warehouse rent a building somewhere less crowded in the city? Worriedly, she cast her glance in the rearview mirror again and found, as usual, that the dachshund's camper shell bun blocked half her view.

"You must really need this money badly," said Bill, jotting something on the balloon-decorated notepad he had removed from his pocket.

"We just have a few extra expenses this month," said Tessa. "I needed some fast cash flow."

Natalie believed she was doing something for Blake, of course. A tiny part of Tessa thought she might die if either of her coworkers saw her today, while she was subbing for June, sick with the flu, as if seeing her go back to Bill's party service would signal the death knell for the Wedding Belles. Ridiculous, irrational, and somehow managing to entirely grip her mind as she eased the dachshund truck's nose forward a halting two inches.

She shifted into park. "Remember the plastic cups," she said. "That kid who had too much pizza at the party threw up in the emergency supply bag."

"Plastic cups, vinyl tablecloths, paper hats. Got it." Bill climbed out of the truck. "If the meter maid rolls by, you'll have to move," he said. "If you circle the block, watch out for the construction on Fourth Street."

"Got it," answered Tessa. She slumped lower in the driver's seat, catching a glimpse of herself in the side mirror. The ball cap emblazoned with Party 2 Go's logo was pulled low, and her red ponytail looked frizzy, as if hopelessness had turned her curls into a frenzied mess. There was a big glob of jelly sticking to the front of her company t-shirt.

Back where she started only four months ago. It was almost as if she had never left for her dream of planning magical wedding receptions and special ceremonies. Like the one for Nadia, that was getting botched as quickly as marshmallows turn to sludge in cocoa. Was it a terrible sign? Just when she had finally escaped the endless grind of vomit patrol, messy neon frosting, and screaming, crying birthday guests, she was behind the wheel of the same vehicle with which she had once accidentally pushed over a streetside popcorn vendor.

"What's happening to me?" she said, speaking aloud to herself. "Do I really think we're jinxed? Or am I just crazy?" The girl in the mirror didn't answer her, but merely brushed aside a few crumbs from the peanut butter sandwich that the last party's bully had hurled at her for ordering him out of the bouncy castle.

"Crazy about what?" Bill climbed into the truck, holding a paper sack from which a plastic bag of balloons was peeking.

"Nothing," answered Tessa. "Just thinking that you really need to disinfect that T-Rex head. It smells like mold inside."

"Kevin must've forgotten to spray it out last night," said Bill.

Tessa sighed. "Why did you hire me, Bill?" she asked.

"What? Because you asked if I had a couple of gigs you could help out with. I was being nice."

"No. I meant the first time." She lifted her head from the steering wheel. "Why did you hire me in the first place?"

He looked thoughtful. "I dunno. You needed a job. You were way overqualified, but I thought maybe I could give you a break. There wasn't much for you to do that would use your degree, but it was better than nothing at all." He chuckled. "I guess it didn't work out too well, did it? I kept forgetting to give you things to do, like pick out cakes or party favors."

"Other things got in the way," said Tessa. She had mellowed a little in her long-held grudge against Bill for always letting June have those prime opportunities—it wasn't as if he had taken her on to give her career ambitions a boost, was it? "You couldn't help it. You probably saved me from a life in retail."

Bill noticed Tessa's glum expression, and reached over and patted her arm. "Hard times pass, Tess," he said. "You know, when I first started out in this business, I was on the verge of failure myself."

"You were?"

"Yup. First month, I had two parties total. I had to hock the cool party dog sign I bought for the truck just to cover the truck's payment. Second customer stiffed me on the payment because he forgot to tell me his kid was allergic to strawberries, and there were some in the fruit cups. It was only me back then, cutting all those little Jell-O shapes and trying to frost dinosaur cupcakes."

"I knew you started it alone," said Tessa. "I didn't know your first few parties had been so awful."

"So see? Tough it out. It gets better," said Bill. "You'll figure out what you need to do to make it work."

"Okay. Maybe you have a point." Tessa managed a tiny smile and a shrug of improved confidence as she turned the key in the ignition again. "I'm probably being too dramatic and too worried this early in the game."

"And if something goes wrong, you can always come back to work for me," said Bill.

"You really know how to suck the mood out of a person, Bill." Tessa eased the dachshund's rear slowly away from the bumper of an expensive Mercedes parked beside them. If she came back to Bill, would he remember to ask her to pick up the cakes? Or would he stick with June's taste in neon frosting and gummy fillings?"

"Just trying to give you a safety net." Bill checked his list. "Make a left on Maple. The Phelps kid's party is almost over and we have to pack up the inflatable dinosaurs and the indoor mini golf stuff. I hope nobody put a golf ball through anything, because I'm sick of having to explain that liability clause to customers."

Tessa shifted the gears into forward and attempted to navigate her way out of the parking space while avoiding the front fender of the tiny car on the other side of her, nearly invisible in the mirror thanks to the hotdog's nose. That car would crush like a pile of empty aluminum cans if she hit it.

She pushed the truck's gears into reverse after the dog's tail eased its way into the narrow street without traffic, and an empty parking space on the opposite side. The gas pedal gave an extra jet of fuel when she tapped it with more force than she intended, and the tail of the dog narrowly missed the tiny car's headlamp in the neighboring spot to scrape against a light pole on the sidewalk instead.

A scrunching, crunching metal squeal. Tessa slammed on the brakes and pulled forward again hastily. The slam of brakes that followed jerked both passengers forward roughly. In the mirror, Tessa could see the tip of the dog's tail now dangling from the rest of it, and a streak of reddish-brown paint on the streetlamp's pole.

A long sigh from her former boss. "Good job," said Bill dryly. "Here I was, afraid that denting the dog's nose would be enough for your career."

Tessa turned off the ignition and unfastened her seat belt. "You drive," she said.

✳

Several hours later, Tessa pulled up outside a residential house with a lawn surrounded by iron fencing—in a car borrowed from a friend and *not* the hotdog mobile, since she had vowed to herself that today would be the last time she would ever again drive it.

Peeling off her old ball cap, she stuffed it and her cleaner's apron in the trunk of the car. She zipped her old canvas coat over her shirt to hide the jelly stains that had seeped through it, and the ones on the thigh of her jeans, and made an attempt to smooth her frizzy hair. Drawing a deep breath, she checked the result with a glance in the side mirror, and tried not to feel too disappointed by it.

Blake's renovation project was even more magnificent in reality, despite the scaffolding along the outside where it was being repainted, the chimney work in progress, and the construction work trucks crowded together outside its gate. There was an elaborately carved bookcase face and a beautiful walnut buffet partly covered by a tarp loaded in the back of one of them, which Tessa recognized as Blake's from its dents. As she approached the front gate she saw his worn red-painted metal toolbox in the back, and the familiar Skilsaw with flecks of white paint dotting its blade's safety guard.

Three workers were busy removing a ladder from the house's interior as Tessa ducked past them and inside the house itself. This was clearly a different kind of job from the Wedding Belles' renovation project—the elaborate chandelier, the massive carved fireplace, and the intricate crown molding all looked authentic and very nearly pristine, with the exception of a little peeling paint.

Blake was measuring the rails of the staircase, making a mark on a pad he now tucked in the back pocket of his jeans. He glanced up, seeing Tessa's approach, and smiled. "Hey," he said. "What are you doing here? Don't you have big plans for your client?"

"Not today," said Tessa. "I was just… running some errands." She zipped her coat a little higher and pulled its hem lower, in case the grape stains were still showing. "So I thought I would stop by. I remembered the address of this place, since you showed it to me online." It was hard to make an afternoon of wrestling Bill's inflatable stegosauruses sound more like a day of running errands—especially if Blake was noticing the finger paint on her shoes.

"Errands, huh?" he said. "That's, uh, not your usual look." He motioned toward her overall appearance. "Did your car break down by the road or something?"

"No," she said. "I'm going casual today. I can't wear high heels and dresses every time I go out. There's lots of times I wear jeans and broken-in sneakers. You don't see me every day, right?"

"Fair enough," said Blake. "Looks good. You in casual clothes, I mean." He made a note about something else on his pad, which spared him from seeing the quick blush on Tessa's face. "Maybe you should wear it around the office sometimes," he suggested. "Have a casual Friday."

"We'll think about it," said Tessa. "I'll take it up with my committee." She smiled at him when he looked up again, and managed not to blush while his eyes were on her. That would give him a very definite wrong impression about his compliment.

"So you came to see the place in person," he said, glancing around. "Not bad, is it?"

"I could live here," she said, shrugging her shoulders. "If I wasn't planning on owning a castle someday, that is."

"Then this place runs a little small for your tastes," said Blake.

"I'd take it. I live in two rooms now, after all," she said. "My old apartment wasn't much bigger than that. I don't know the technical terms for half this stuff, but I know it's all amazing." Her eyes traveled their surroundings, noting that the very elegant wallpaper was a shade between mint and jade. "It looks great. Did you—?"

"No." He shook his head. "We're just doing some touch-up stuff. It'll be a show home on the historic tour by Christmas, which is why we're rushing this place. Hey, Connor, have the paint crew check on that color for the dining room mantel, will you?"

"Sure thing, Blake."

"Is the furniture in the back of your truck for this place?" she asked. "Or is it salvage stuff?" Not that this looked like the kind of place where the wrong light fixtures or corbels abounded. Not like the Wedding Belles' headquarters, where plenty of architectural anomalies were present after a century or so.

Blake laughed. "If that kind of stuff was salvage, I'd be a pretty lucky contractor," he said. "No, that's the original buffet from the house. I was putting a new coat of finish on it in my workshop. Too much dust around here while they're cleaning the lights, and the fumes don't mix well with fresh paint."

"Oh. I see." Tessa looked around. "You seem... really happy," she said. "This really is what you love, isn't it? More than just fixing things, it's fixing them back the way they were supposed to be, I guess. Which is something we're not exactly giving you at Wedding Belles, are we?"

A wry smile crossed her lips, receiving a matching one from Blake in return. "Us girls, who defend the interloper metal staircase, and paint walls 'Romantic Blue.'"

"All right, I admit it. I like things done right," he said. "There's a kind of charm in turning back the clock in a place like this. In your building, too—which is what I'm trying to do by getting you to keep things like that transom grate in your office."

"As per our agreement, we're only paying to fix the really essential things and the really big ones for now, remember?" said Tessa. "We're paying you a share of our partnership too."

"Which I didn't ask for—"

"—but was fair," Tessa countered firmly. "But we probably can't afford whatever budget this place has to fix tiny pieces of hardware and wall lamps."

"A quarter of a million," said Blake.

Tessa's jaw almost dropped. "A quarter of a million *dollars*?" she echoed.

"People take historic homes very seriously in this city." Blake whistled as he made another note about the width between the banisters.

"Hey, Blake, Mac's here to see you." A man carrying two paint cans passed through the foyer, informing the contractor of this fact as he climbed the stairs to the upper story.

"Thanks, Tim." Blake snapped his measuring tape onto his tool belt. "We're finishing up the main rooms this week, so the furniture is coming sometime next week."

"Authentic furniture?" asked Tessa.

"Of course," he said. "Mac's tracked down some pretty incredible period furnishings for the parlor and the library. It'll all be festooned with big garlands right before Christmas."

"Need any help decorating?" Tessa teased.

"I think Mac's got it pretty well covered," said Blake with a smile.

"Good news—the paint crew has promised to vacate the dining room early, so we can have the table and chairs delivered by Wednesday," said a female voice behind Tessa. "Plus, I just got off the phone with the sandblasting service, and the hearth's surround is finally in the works, so all that gold paint will be gone in no time." She passed Tessa, a stylish wool coat draped over her arm, a professional leather satchel in hand. A polite glance of greeting registered Tessa's presence as she joined Blake at the foot of the stairs.

Stunning beauty. Those were the appropriate two words to describe the woman in question, from the toes of her high-heeled leather boots to the cut of her tailored business skirt and jacket, and the waterfall of dark hair that framed a face which might as well be that of an iconic fashion model. Tessa suddenly felt short, frazzled, and dingy by comparison. She drew her coat more tightly around herself, as if to hide any stains she might have missed.

"That's good news," said Blake, sounding eager. "I can't wait to get that thing put back in place. The whole face of the fireplace is bare without it."

"Can't have that, can we?" she said, and they both laughed. When Blake recovered himself, he gestured toward the woman by way of introduction.

"Tessa, this is Mac, our project's interior designer. Mac, this is Tessa."

The woman extended her hand. "Samantha MacNeil," she said. "A pleasure to meet you."

Mac? This was Mac? Blake's favorite interior designer in the whole city? "Likewise," said Tessa. Something was wrong with her voice again, and her hand was holding closed the flaps of her coat tightly, now remembering an old cocoa stain on it from a winter hike two years ago.

"I'm fixing up a building Tessa owns downtown. One of the old brick and limestone ones," said Blake. Mac smiled.

"You own one of those buildings?" she said. "What a beautiful architectural period that is—honestly, I would love to do your office decor, if you're looking for an interior designer." She produced a card from her jacket pocket and gave it to Tessa.

"Mac is definitely the best," said Blake. "Although she would probably tell you to pull out that spiral staircase and have the old banisters put back."

"There's a metal staircase in one of them?" said Mac, clearly amazed. "No way. You know, those vintage salvage models fetch a terrific price these days. People redoing old libraries, fixing up loft spaces…"

"I saw one sell for two thousand last week at the salvage auction for that old mansion that burned in Belleview," said Blake.

"And that's—what? Half the cost of restoring the original banister and stair rails?" suggested Mac.

Four thousand dollars for carved banisters. That sounded about as essential as the corbels that Blake had suggested when he first viewed their old fireplace. "Thanks, but that's okay," said Tessa. "I'm afraid decorating isn't currently on our horizon. Plus, we're event planners. We decorate people's big events for a living… so we do our own interior decorating. Mostly." She smiled. After all, they *had* painted their offices themselves. And found some creative pillows and throws to dress up the old secondhand furniture Tessa had salvaged.

"If you change your mind, I'm free for a few weeks after I finish here," said Mac. "Of course, that's if I'm not doing the Canton property's Christmas open house. Did I tell you they want *four* trees in the main hall?" she asked Blake. "Twelve foot apiece."

"Twelve foot?" he echoed. "I mean, the room can definitely hold them, but—"

"—it's going to completely overwhelm visitors, what with the big tree decorated in the parlor, right?" said Mac. "I can't talk the committee out of it. They want everything in silver, pearl, and mint green."

"It'll be gorgeous, though," said Blake. "You can do it, Mac. You should see the pictures of last year's holiday open house," he added to Tessa. "Mac had this whole thing going with a copper and royal blue look. You have to see it to believe it."

"So... Mac," said Tessa. "Are you working here for long?" *As in, the whole time Blake's here? Not that it matters, or I'm curious or anything...* Because she wasn't curious about this, right?

"Until the place looks finished and festive," said Mac with a smile. "Which should be another two weeks or so. Maybe less. This guy works like a racehorse when there's a deadline pushing him. I don't think we've ever worked together when you haven't finished at least a week early," she added to Blake. "Except for maybe the Thompson job."

"Ah. The floor varnish debacle," said Blake, one hand against his forehead at this memory.

"I guess you two must work together a lot," said Tessa. "The whole 'historic preservation' thing. You probably cross paths all the time."

"Lots of people who fix up old properties call on me to put the finishing touches in place," admitted Mac. "And, of course, they call on Blake first, because he just has an amazing instinct for what to keep and what to replace when it comes to any building." She touched his arm briefly, and flashed an open smile in his direction with these words.

"That's a little exaggeration. I'm no better than any other contractor in the city." Blake smiled back, a quick blush of modesty crossing his cheeks at the same time.

"He's definitely very good at his job," said Tessa, who forced a bright smile to her face. "I've seen lots of proof in what he's done for our building. Not that it's really anything he would brag about. The building, not the work—I'm sure Blake knows his work is great, because it is." Tessa shut up abruptly after this.

"Blake always says that no job is too small if a place needs a carpenter's touch," said Mac.

The light shone on Mac's hair like a flattering spotlight. Tessa was now wondering if there were little bits of plastic in her own from the T-Rex head. Its lining was beginning to slough off, something which hadn't seemed like a big deal until now.

"Hey, did you see the new wallpaper in the parlor?" Blake asked Tessa. "The crew was leaving just as you came in. If you didn't, you should take a look at it. It's from the same company that made the paper in that little sitting room at your place. Here, let me show you."

The paper had green parrots with coral-pink roses and tiny yellow buttercups, or something like them—Tessa barely noticed it as she followed Blake on his tour to show off the newest touches made to the majestic home.

"...and we replaced the big mirror over the mantel, because the original one was clearly bigger than what the restoration team found when they assessed this place," he said, then paused. "Are you okay? You look a little glazed over in the eyes. I've been talking too much about boring stuff like moldings and wood floors, haven't I?"

"What? No. Not at all," said Tessa. "I heard every word you said about fixing this place up. I mean, the work you've done is really, really gorgeous. It's just I have a lot on my mind right now, what with Nadia and Lyle's wedding and the advertising campaign for the business."

"How's that going?" he asked.

"Great," she said, as convincingly as possible. "It's all great." She put on her brightest smile once again as she brushed back her hair. Fantastic—she felt gummy bits of latex snagged in it from the disintegrating T-Rex's liner. Whereas Mac's looked like a Pert Plus Wash 'n' Go shampoo ad from Tessa's childhood. Not that it was in any way important since if she, Tessa, were in her usual clothes and her usual workplace setting, she would clearly feel less intimidated by someone who looked that perfect. They were practically equals, even if Tessa was still having to work odd jobs to pay her business bills.

"Are you looking at the lawn? 'Cause I promise it will be fixed back the way it was in the photo you saw after we're done here. That was its first public showcase, the Fourth of July opening. The old mantel still had its original paint on it then."

"The lawn? Looks great to me. I can't tell anything's happened to it." Tessa snapped back to her current surroundings. She realized now, however, that he was talking about the churned mud and tire tracks marring its grass. "I was just thinking about my errands from earlier."

"Blake, I need a quick opinion on the windows in the dining room, if you've got a minute," said Mac.

"Sure." He touched Tessa's arm in a farewell gesture. "Feel free to look around some more," he said to her. "There's a great view from upstairs—just watch out for the painting crew."

"Sure. Can do," said Tessa. But when Blake and Mac had disappeared to discuss renovations, Tessa didn't move from the front windows. The disheartened feeling from before had returned, when she'd slid behind the wheel of the hotdog truck once again. It grew stronger as she gazed at the parrot wallpaper, biting her lip as she listened to the sound of Mac and Blake's voices carrying from the next room.

So Mac wasn't a guy, as she had previously assumed. Big deal. It's not like Blake's life outside of the Wedding Belles was any of her business. She had far more important things to focus on than the details of Blake's other life and other coworkers. And by 'other,' she meant 'real,' because obviously Blake didn't think of his role as their firm's fourth partner as anything important.

With a final morose glare at the parrot wallpaper, Tessa made her way toward the open front door of the historic house. At least her building had real character in its eclectic nature, not some dime-a-dozen walnut banister that any historic home could boast. Someone like Mac couldn't appreciate that, probably.

Chapter Thirteen

For his date with Natalie, Chad had chosen a little restaurant with a casual atmosphere and special hand-sculpted clay serving bowls for its steaming pepper beef and rice. He liked to talk about nature and the outdoors, as well as his travels in Ecuador. He had been there several times in the past and seemed enamored with the culture and its native cuisine.

"Of course, my coworkers freaked out when they heard it was basically glacial volcanoes I would be climbing over there, but come on—it's the Andes. How could I pass that up? It's every climber's dream."

"Right," said Natalie. Although her experience with rock climbing to date had been limited to once at an indoor climbing wall with friends, far from matching the level of passion that Chad clearly harbored for it.

"You would love it in Ecuador," Chad continued, switching back to his second favorite topic so far. "The culture is way laid back compared to the kind of atmosphere you and I know."

He smiled and took a sip of wine before asking, "So what about you? Do you travel? I love South American culture. I guess it's like my home away from home, when I'm not doing the nine to five thing. When I'm not climbing the walls. Literally," he added, with a tiny outward movement of his lips.

Ecuador mustn't have any openings in shoe retail that would allow him to relocate, Natalie was tempted to joke. Instead, she answered his question. "Not much. See, until recently, I worked a pretty deadbeat job as a designer's assistant. Long hours, little pay, no vacation... it was about the prestige of working for a designer. Or paying your dues. Something like that."

"What happened?" he asked. "You quit and took life by the horns?"

"Exactly," she said. "A friend of mine wanted to start her own business, so she asked if I wanted to join her. Soon after—Natalie Grenaldi, wedding fashion consultant and independent designer, was born. Except when she's Natalie Grenaldi, part-time caterer and baker for her family's food emporiums."

Her fork cut neatly through the fish filet on her plate, ignoring the tradition of eating by hand that some of the restaurant's other patrons were attempting. Even chopsticks were not for Natalie, who had squished way too many calamari rings between them while onlookers giggled.

"Freelance, huh?" he said. "Is that what you want?"

"It's what everybody wants, isn't it?" said Natalie. "Nobody telling them what to do, somebody finding their work and appreciating it just because they want to. That's the secret dream that most of us never get to live."

"I get it. That's why I climb, whenever I get the chance," said Chad. "Having something to conquer personally is the only way to live life. My mom used to say, 'You're alone all the time because you're so obsessed with your goals, at least get a dog or something,' but I would always say, 'And who's going to feed him when I take off for two weeks just because I need to see the sun rise in Cotacachi? You know?'"

"I do," said Natalie. "Pursuing something not everyone can do is half the reward of a big dream. For me, it's the challenge of being part of a career field that changes constantly with the times—that's something my family doesn't get. Why not pick something steady, that you learn once and you're done?" This was the advice from Uncle Guido two Thanksgivings ago.

"I so know how that feels," said Chad sympathetically. "Everybody in my world can define their life goals by calendars, milestones, and schedules, right? That's why they don't get why I spend so much time climbing and get such a kick out of what's basically a sport to them."

"Not that reliable types aren't great," Natalie amended. "Take my mom. Ma, she lives to bake and fill a house with people. Nothing makes her happier than doing stuff that makes somebody else happy. And my friend Tessa is one of those total control freaks who micromanages her life and people's happiness on calendars and sticky notes. I think she would rescue a wedding from a burning building if she had to," she joked.

"She kind of reminds me of a friend of mine. Same way—only about portrait photography," said Chad, laughing.

"They're the kind of people who are always there though," said Natalie. "The people you fall back on, because they know the answers. They know the safe spaces you need that make you feel better."

She took a sip from her glass, suddenly feeling the humor sucked out of her. She had an urge for her mother's Italian Christmas bread, which was always baked especially for Natalie at the holidays, its scent filling her nose. Comforting things were missing from her life these days more than she realized, maybe. Having someone around to whom the little things mattered most.

"It's such a waste," said Chad. "Their lives are so wasted. I don't know how many times I've told family or friends who just live every day in their tiny world that they need to expand. Bungee jump—travel to

South America—do something new with your life, because it's totally devoid of meaning when you're trapped in the same old role in society. Why waste all your time and energy on other people, and what they need or think, when you don't have to?"

"And where would the rest of us be if everybody was like that?" Natalie asked with a smirk. "I'll bet you asked your mom to check your apartment and your studio while you were in South America. That dependable person you knew would be there."

"True," admitted Chad, saluting her with his glass. "Here's to the dependable people, then."

"Dependable people," echoed Natalie.

He was fun, charming, and easy on the eye, even if he was over-confident in his opinions on life at times—but Natalie could deal with a little shortage of modesty without too much hardship on her part, she decided. He even seemed interested in her life as a designer, and listened to her stories about it… and not in the polite way that a lot of Natalie's family made themselves request an overview, but in the way Natalie wanted, with an exchange of actual details like the style of dress she designed for an event, or the name of the horrible fashion line she first sewed for Kandace.

They talked for nearly a half hour after they were finished eating, and the waiter had taken away the handmade clay serving bowls, which was when Natalie suggested they have dessert at the bakery.

"You should try my mom's chocolate éclairs," she said, as she searched for Icing Italia's key on her ring. "I know we're not French, but she's really talented with pastry. She used to make these cool banana ones, but we kind of discontinued them after the blueberry ones became so popular."

"I can't wait to taste them," said Chad. "Good thing I gave up being macrobiotic last year."

"You were macrobiotic?"

"It was my doctor's suggestion. I had a major skin reaction to something in Ecuador. Probably just some plant growing near my apartment."

✳

Natalie slipped the key into the lock and pushed open the door to the bakery's front room, where the lights were dimmed, and the display cases—which usually held spiced and flavored beignets and crullers, fritters and sticky buns, alongside Italian cookies, sweet breads, and the occasional filled bear claws and Danishes that Natalie loved—were mostly empty. The only things not removed were two Italian cream cakes waiting for pickup in the morning, and this week's window display dedicated to the traditional Christmas breads baked in their buttered paper sacks and studded generously with dried fruit.

"The leftover pastries are in the back," Natalie was saying, "where we keep the day-old stuff, since my uncle uses the kitchen for the family…" She trailed off, because she heard voices now, and saw a light in the next room.

"Looks like somebody else is here," said Chad, pushing open the kitchen door. Light flooded from the room, where the scrubby old kitchen table was occupied by what seemed like Natalie's entire family, although it was really just her uncle, two aunts, her mother, her brother, his girlfriend Kimmie, and, of all people, Brayden. In the middle of the table was a big plate of half-finished spaghetti, and a tray of day-old bread drizzled with olive oil and rosemary. Her uncle was filling his glass from a bottle of red wine.

"Natalie! We didn't expect to see you," said her mother, who was busy cutting a lemon cream cake into slices on the counter by the stove.

"Ma? What's everybody doing here?" Natalie said. She wanted to back out with haste, maybe make an excuse about looking for one of her econ textbooks, but it was too late—Chad was right behind her, obviously her date for the evening since he was holding two paper sacks from the restaurant.

"Who's your friend?" This from Rob, who grinned widely. He knew full well that Natalie generally avoided introducing her dates to anybody. 'Getting their hopes up,' as she referred to it whenever one of her latest *amores* crossed paths with relatives, stirring up more wishful thinking about Natalie settling down.

"Natalie's latest young man, right?" Uncle Guido poured two more glasses of wine for his fellow diners. "Lucky him. He gets to meet everybody at once."

"Chad, this is my family," said Natalie, with evident reluctance for claiming them. "Everybody, this is Chad. We were having dinner together tonight."

She was trying to avoid Brayden's gaze as she made this introduction. Why was he eating dinner with her family? Didn't his mother have a nice casserole waiting for him when he finished work?

"Chad the rock climber, right?" said Rob. "We spoke on the phone before."

"Come in, have some dessert," said her aunt Louisa, who was passing out plates. "There's plenty of room, Natalie. There's an open chair by Brayden—"

"I'm good with standing, thanks," said Natalie.

"I'm Natalie's mother, Maria. That's my sister Lou, my brother-in-law Guido... that's Natalie's brother Rob... this is a friend of the family, Brayden..."

"Hi," said Brayden. He waved at Chad, then accepted a slice of cake from Natalie's mom."

"Chad and I really have to be going," said Natalie. "I just stopped to show him the place."

"Then show him it," said Guido. "Have some cake. My wife made it. She may not be much to look at, but she's a princess in the kitchen." His wife Dolores smacked him on the arm for this remark.

"You know, we never get a chance to meet Natalie's boyfriends," said Louisa to Chad. "You're the first who's been here in a while."

"Except for that guy Brock," said Rob. "The big one with all the muscles."

"Did I meet him?" Maria's brow furrowed.

"I didn't like him," muttered Brayden. "He was a real jerk." He cut into his cake with a tiny bit more force than was necessary.

Brock *was* a real jerk—he broke up with her after one of her worst fashion shows ever with Kandace, and a part of Natalie still recalled it with pain, but it wasn't something she wanted discussed here and now. Not as Chad awkwardly shifted the restaurant's take-home bags from one hand to the next, and Brayden kept stealing little glances at her and her date, as if trying to evaluate their level of seriousness. As was everybody else in this room, she suspected.

"Well, we say no other boyfriend. Brayden's here," said Rob, whose grin broadened, as if he were reading her mind. Brayden's face flushed fire red in response, almost as quickly as Natalie's own. Natalie wanted to kill her brother.

"Your ex?" said Chad—with evident surprise as he asked.

"There used to be an old joke in the family, saying they were destined to be together," said Rob, more wickedly than before.

"No. No, no," said Natalie hastily to Chad. "Rob is kidding. It's all a joke. Brayden is a friend, just a friend from a long time ago when I was a kid."

"Go on. He's practically family," said Maria, in her loving-scolding tone as she squeezed Brayden's shoulders. "His mom was my best friend when we moved to this neighborhood," she explained to Chad. "He and Natalie and Robbie grew up together, played every day on the sidewalk outside our house."

"Like family. Exactly," said Natalie, as if this erased any possible misconceptions about her and Brayden having any potential romantic involvement. "We have a habit of adopting a lot of people into our fold. You've been warned, so maybe it's time for us to grab some day-old doughnuts and say goodnight."

"Stay," urged Maria. "We treat people like family. Chad, have some cake. Dolores's recipe is *the* best, and I say that as a jealous baker." There was a chorus of 'oohs' at this sisterly challenge from the rest of the dinner guests.

"Chad could be the big brother you never had, Nat," suggested Rob. He had only survived thus far in life because mental telepathy possessed no truly murderous powers, Natalie had determined.

"And on that note, I think we should definitely go," said Natalie.

"Of course, when I say Brayden's like family, I don't mean I raised him," continued Maria, who was serving Chad cake whether he wanted it or not. "He had a perfectly good mother who did a fantastic job with her son. Do you have a big family, Chad?"

"Not really," he answered.

"Brayden was a better brother to you than I was," contributed Rob, sliding his arm comfortably around the back of his girlfriend Kimmie's chair. Could he *not* let this subject go? "Remember the incident with Bilbo?"

"A forest stump would have been a better brother to me," muttered Natalie.

"Bilbo?" Chad repeated with a half smile.

"He was a dog," said Brayden, who was actually blushing again. "It's nothing. An old story."

"The biggest, meanest dog on our block," said Rob. "His fence was posted for no trespassing, attack dog, and so on. No kids were allowed to go near him, 'cause he was a little vicious on his own turf. But he was always stealing stuff from the neighborhood yards and outside the apartments whenever his owner would take him for a walk. The guy never returned any of it, of course."

"Too bad," said Chad sympathetically. Natalie, who knew where this story was going, was really wishing they had stayed an hour at the restaurant and tried the Ecuadorian lime ice listed among tonight's specials.

"One time, the dog stole Natalie's favorite doll, which she had left on the steps, this old one of Mom's that she dressed up in a sparkly dress. Natalie called it her princess doll. So she's crying and crying and begging somebody to get it back, which nobody will, because Dad's working all day at the bakery and Mom's got a thing with my grandparents across town, and *I'm* not going in there. So Brayden here—"

"I don't think Nat wants to hear this story again," said Brayden, who was blushing down to his neck now, even his ears beet red with embarrassment. For her sake, Natalie thought, because she was squirming like a trapped animal as Chad tested a bite of her aunt's cake and listened to Robbie's narrative about her childhood. This situation was one of Natalie's all-time worst nightmares regarding dates meeting her family.

"—goes over the fence, and he's this scrawny kid who can barely climb on a garbage can without getting a nosebleed. But over he goes, tearing his t-shirt at the same time, and starts looking for the doll among Bilbo's treasure piles. So the dog comes out of its house about that time, and from two doors down we hear Natalie screaming, saying there's blood everywhere."

"There wasn't," said Brayden, shaking his head. "It was just a little nip on the arm. Nothing serious."

"You still have a scar, right?" laughed Rob. "Man, did Bilbo's owners and our folks chew you out for that dumb stunt. That's why I didn't volunteer to go over and get it, because I knew anybody caught doing it would be dead meat afterwards."

"You never volunteered to defend me from anything that I can recall," said Natalie.

"Do you still have the scar, Brayden?" said Rob.

"It's just a little one," he said.

"Let's see it," ordered Guido with a laugh, as the rest of the family echoed his demand. With a sheepish and reluctant grin, Brayden pushed up the sleeve of his shirt, revealing a little raised line on his bicep, the souvenir of Bilbo's legendary bite.

Twelve stitches. And it hadn't been that much blood, really. Although between the dirt and the blood, Natalie had been so sure that Brayden was half dead when Bilbo's owner hauled him over the fence again that she had almost forgotten about the doll.

"Did you get the doll back?" Chad asked her.

"Of course," said Rob, who volunteered to answer instead. "He didn't drop it until he was safe on the other side of the fence again. Of course, the princess needed a trip to the laundry, with all the blood and dirt."

"Wow. Can't say I would have done that. Dogs terrified me when I was a kid," said Chad. He left his half-finished cake on the nearby counter.

"But it was—" began Rob.

"—Natalie's *favorite* doll in the whole world," chimed in two or three more relatives who were part of this story, notably Maria and Louisa. Even Kimmie joined in on this one. Natalie wanted to sink into a big crack in the earth, but there was no possibility that an earthquake was going to rescue her.

"Why did they name the dog Bilbo?" asked Kimmie. "I thought dogs were named things like 'Rex' or 'Fido.'"

"I called my dog 'Raisins,'" said Rob. "What was the name of *your* dog when you were a kid?" Rob said to Brayden. "Was it Eddie?"

"Eddie was my dog," said Guido. "The big yellow-brown one that watched the back door at night. Brayden's was the one his mom gave him for his birthday one year—shaggy, only had half a tail."

"Samson," said Brayden, who was accidentally flicking crumbs onto the tablecloth from his cake. "He was mine. When I was twelve. I used to let him sleep on my bed, and sneak him your mom's cookies. I got in trouble for crumbs in the sheets." He brushed his mess into one hand, trying to clean it up.

"Not that much trouble. You were always a good boy—unlike my son," said Maria to Brayden, with a pointed look at Rob at these last words. "You used to fix Natalie's roller skates for her and take her down to that park where all the kids skated," she reminded Brayden. "She was an itty-bitty thing back then and fell over just about every time she stood up on those things," Maria confided to Chad now.

"Ma!" said Natalie in protest.

"Even I wouldn't take her down there," said Rob. "She was a mess on skates, and always cried when she fell down."

"Thanks," said Natalie dryly. "I appreciate you passing along that perspective."

"What? Everyone knows you cried all the time when you were a girl," said Louisa, as she passed Guido a dessert plate.

"Not Natalie. She was tough most of the time," said Brayden assertively. And admiringly. It was mean to feel exasperated by that, Natalie knew, although she wished he wouldn't be so… so *comfortable* with her family, at least not in front of Chad.

She wished her whole family seemed less comfortable, less involved, and less eager to talk about her in front of a guy she had only met twice, too. Chad looked as if he was feeling a little out of place as they stood here. *Out of the loop*, she thought, since he was the only one who hadn't heard these stories a million times.

"This one was a sucker," said Rob, putting Brayden in an affectionate half-hug—or headlock—as he rose to put his plate by the sink. "Always letting her tag along to make the rest of us miserable."

"Cut it out. You're just making stuff up now," said Brayden, whose ears were still way too red. "Rob's a good guy, don't let him fool you," Brayden continued. "Even Nat would say the same."

"Nat?" echoed Chad. "Is that what everybody calls you?"

"I prefer Natalie. Really, I do," she reassured him.

"I remember the time Brayden rescued those kittens from the drain pipe," began Maria, as she cut Brayden a second slice of cake.

"Another slice of cake, Ma?" said Rob incredulously. "You didn't cut me a second one. I'm your flesh and blood, too."

"Like you need it," snorted Kimmie. "You need to give up desserts if you want to pass your next physical," she pointed out.

"Me? I am a lean, mean specimen of physical prowess at the fire department," he answered, stealing a broken corner of cake from the plate, and popping it in his mouth. "Give me some more cake, Ma."

"And that old homeless cat that got hit by a car," continued Maria, who was ignoring Rob. "There was another time that Natalie was crying so hard—"

"Time to go," said Natalie. "Great seeing you all. Chad and I have plans for tonight, so we're going to split."

"Bye, Chad!" This was the chorus from half Natalie's family, the other half still coaxing them to stay. Natalie retreated after snagging a bag of day-old crullers from the sideboard, catching one last glimpse of Brayden's homely and wistful farewell smile before her brother turned and stuck his tongue out at her, and the kitchen door swung closed.

"Your family. Wow," said Chad. "I have to admit, I wasn't prepared to meet them in one big group." He shifted the restaurant sacks to the opposite hand, leaving his left one free, his fingers brushing against Natalie's.

"I know. I'm sorry," she said. "Honestly, they almost never eat at the bakery kitchen. I don't know if Uncle Guido just got carried away after making his spaghetti today or what... but I definitely would have suggested gelatos at the ice cream parlor down the street."

"I figured," laughed Chad. "Don't worry. I won't ask you to meet my mom on our next date."

"Good," she said. When Chad's hand brushed against hers again, she slid her fingers between his own. She could feel his light, warm grip, one that didn't hold too tightly or press too longingly. Perfect for what she needed right at this moment.

As they stepped into the street outside, Chad slowed his pace a little. "So..." he said, hesitating before speaking again. "Was he really your boyfriend? That guy having dinner with your family tonight?"

"What? No! No—I was telling the truth back there," said Natalie. "He's definitely not my ex. He's just a friend of the family." At no point could Brayden have been considered anything resembling a boyfriend, not in her world. Maybe to the perspective of an outsider, given the amount of time and the number of tributes he'd wasted on her since their grade school years, but that was different. "He had... sort of a crush on me. That's why they were joking about him like that, but, honestly, they were only kidding you."

"'Had' not 'has'?" joked Chad.

Natalie was grateful that lamplight was excellent at disguising blushes. "You think he'd seriously wait around for me?" she asked, pretending this was not the case. "We were kids. Nothing lasts that long."

"You seem worth it to me," said Chad. That casual-but-confident estimate of herself almost cost Natalie another blush. Chad was so smooth, so coolly matter-of-fact with compliments that you couldn't help accepting them. *See, this is what Brayden doesn't understand—his compliments are like cupcakes that have too much icing on them, so nobody in a million years would believe he actually feels that way about me.*

"Yeah, well, that's your opinion," she shot back, equally breezy. "Anyway, it was all a joke." Odds were, even if Chad was around long enough to discover the truth, it wouldn't matter that she presented this little white lie.

"Good," said Chad. "I kind of thought you were a little, you know... out of his league."

For one tick of the clock, these words were a pebble crashing through Natalie's life window, hitting the mark with perfect accuracy. A cruel assessment on Chad's part, but exactly how she viewed Brayden, even if she tended to word it somewhat differently. Brayden, awkward and bumbling—Natalie, confident and attractive. Two different people, but one lesser than the other, as Chad pegged after one meeting with Brayden.

Life was cruel, but that's the way it is, Natalie thought, albeit with a little grimness. And that's why people like Brayden never get what they want out of it when they try to defy fate's rules.

"You're not wrong," she said, though not with her usual sarcasm for this topic. "But he's a nice guy, and he's a friend of the family, which is why I still know him after twenty-something years. The Grenaldis are a pretty loyal group. We may fight amongst ourselves, we may criticize each other to the hilt and be too honest… but if somebody else tried to seriously hurt one of our fold, there would be definite consequences."

And that's why you should stop talking about Brayden right now, she added silently to Chad, in case he thought her agreement was an opening to elaborate on Brayden's hopeless candidacy to date Natalie. Because a little mean-spirited humor over Brayden's homely and-humble self might turn quickly into something deeper and crueler, and unleash a side of her that her paramours almost never saw—the lightning-fast, sharp-tongued temper of a Grenaldi whose friend was being abused.

Once, and only once, in a memory Natalie didn't like to relive, she had unleashed it to defend Brayden in a moment of weakness in her high school years, when a group of mean but popular senior girls chose him to be the target of a vicious prank. Their plan never made it to stage one after Natalie overheard it, and Brayden never knew how close he had come to public humiliation, saved by the same girl who treated his prom invite like a sample of Black Plague bacteria.

It was one thing for Natalie to despise him, but another thing for someone else to crush him under their heel like dirt.

"Let's not spend the rest of this evening on my crazy family or my fake ex-boyfriend," she said to Chad. "I plan for you not to experience *too* much time with them compared to spending it with me."

Chapter Fourteen

Ama had a thought board in her office: a corkboard on the harvest-gold wall, its crisscrossed pink ribbons holding the various cake designs that she had created this month, mostly inspired by Nadia's wedding theme. Inspirations for the event were also attached, including clippings from Disney's *Frozen*, and a Scandinavian ice hotel from her Pinterest album of exotic Christmas destinations.

A cake decorated with transparent candy-glass ice spikes. Could she make it look like an ice castle, with a little effort?

The Scandinavian ice hotel would be perfect for Nadia and Lyle's wedding, if it were only located a little closer to home than Europe. She sometimes thought it would have been a perfect compromise between boldness and simplicity for the two arguing mothers, too.

Nadia's vision for her cake was something that would match the winter white theme, Ama knew, in order to keep her vision alive despite the multiple criticisms it received from either side. The bride was still hoping for the country church and possibly a dusting of snow on the ground—but Paula was clinging fast to her argument in favor of the swanky hotel.

"I just think we should do things up," she said. "You may only get married once, you know."

"I'm planning on it, Ma," said Lyle, who was holding Nadia's hand in his own, and trying not to look befuddled by the many elegant wedding options Tessa surrounded them with. "Nadia and I are for keeps, and I want her to be happy. Go on," he said to Nadia. "Pick the nicest one. I don't care. Whatever you want is fine with me."

Ama watched as Paula nudged a photograph of the new hotel, inch by inch, in Nadia's direction, a hopeful look in her eyes. A second later, Cynthia set her handbag on top of it.

"I think the icicle lights you suggested for the restaurant's entrance are extremely attractive," she said to Tessa. "But do you think the frosted garlands are a bit much for the interior? I know that it probably needs some dressing up, but a little can go a long way."

"The restaurant will look nice, Mom," said Nadia reassuringly. "I want some atmosphere for the guests. It won't feel right if they leave a church with a frosty wonderland look just to come to a big dining room that only has twinkle lights around its windows and that's it."

"Now, if you take the big hotel ballroom instead, you won't have to worry about decorations," coaxed Paula. "They got it all! And if we put up some big gold Christmas balls in the restaurant's banquet room, it'll practically feel like they never left the ceremony site."

"Oh, please," said Cynthia, rolling her eyes. "I've seen its photos. The only way it could possibly look tackier would be to put up gold cherubs and a Cupid fountain carved out of ice."

"Say, that sounds pretty neat," said Paula. "Can you hire an ice sculptor who could make a big Cupid?" she asked the three wedding planners. They exchanged hasty glances.

"It's really up to Nadia and Lyle," said Tessa. "However, I was thinking it might be nice for the wedding party's dessert table if we—"

"No Cupid," said Cynthia crisply. Her refined Southern accent lost some of its smooth delicacy to give this statement a blunt edge.

"Mother." Nadia nudged her again. "Remember what we talked about?"

"Do you really want some hideous ice cherub on your banquet table? My dear girl, *I* don't think that's quite you, but I could be wrong, I suppose."

"No," said Nadia. "I don't. But Paula's right that an ice sculpture would look really nice."

"See?" said Paula. "I got good taste."

"The best, Ma." Lyle gave her shoulders a gentle squeeze with one arm. "Let's get an ice thing. How do we do that?" he asked Tessa.

Her brave smile was back. "It just so happens that I have some thoughts on it," said Tessa, producing a photo of a carved ice swan. "This would be perfect with flavored sorbet balls in Mediterranean flavors to accent your Greek menu, for example. Or even with scoops of seasonal ice cream or gelato, to let guests indulge in some with their cake." She smiled at Natalie, who had suggested this part earlier. "Or some beautiful fresh fruit prepared by the kitchen."

"That sounds just perfect," said Nadia. "I really like it."

"A giant swan?" repeated Cynthia.

"Very tasteful," Tessa assured her. And it was, compared to the Venus de Milo statue Stefan once had carved for a posh engagement dinner he planned.

"What about a big ice castle?" asked Paula.

"Like the one in Norway?" piped up Ama. "Actually, I agree that could be beautiful, too. We could put votive lights in it to provide illumination."

"I think an ice castle is a bit ridiculous, frankly," said Cynthia. "In my day, we believed an old-fashioned brick and mortar with decent architecture was good enough for anybody's wedding. Now, times change, but it still seems like the choice of good taste to me." The white gloves in her hand were being gripped with a bit more pressure than Cynthia's polite expression belied.

"My wedding, Mom," Nadia reminded her. "But I think I really like the swan. Lyle, what do you think of it?"

"I think… that I don't have a clue," he said, gazing at both pictures with a hybrid dumbfounded and I-couldn't-care-less expression. "Ma? What's your opinion on this?"

"I like the castle," said Paula. "Go big or go home is what I say. And how about with little colored lights instead of those bitty candles?"

The three planners exchanged glances again—this time, ones of dismay. "It would really clash with the wedding's decor," said Tessa. "We could use soft blue, maybe…"

"I think mixed colors are pretty, and they say Christmas faster than just some ice and snow," said Paula. "This wedding's got a Christmas tree already. The big hotel tree is full of purple and green and reds of all kinds…"

"Just like an Orleans Mardi Gras parade," Cynthia remarked—but quietly, so Paula didn't hear her.

"… but not in the ballroom—that one's all gold, of course," continued Paula. "What's wrong with those colors?"

"Weddings tend to stick to a specific color palette," explained Tessa. "Nadia and Lyle have chosen white, silver, pale blue, and pale green as their preferred colors, so we need everything to stay within those boundaries. Lyle's restaurant will be decorated the same way, of course."

"But it's all done up already with red and green," said Paula. "It looks nice like that. Why take all that stuff down if it looks nice?"

"Lyle." Nadia nudged him as he stared at his phone's screen. "Lyle?"

"What?"

"The restaurant's dining room will match the ceremony site, right?" said Nadia.

He looked as if he hadn't given this any real thought. "Umm… I guess so," he said. "Talk to Bernard. He's in charge of decorating stuff. I'm just worried about the menu, the inventory, and what kind of overhead we're going to have after the Leoni wine order ships."

"But Lyle, you promised you were going to take care of it," said Nadia. "You told me you talked to him weeks ago."

"Honey, you know I'm not good with this kind of thing," he protested. "I forgot, okay? The shrimp was being delivered, we had an issue with flour deliveries. I got caught up at work and I didn't think to tell him to change the dining room's decorations, okay?"

Nadia sighed. "It was one thing, Lyle."

"I have a hundred to do, though. That's why Ma's here, and why your mom's here, and why we've got these ladies here to help you out," said Lyle. "They know decorations and cake, while I know about what kind of food we're gonna serve at the reception. It's all working out, right?"

"Right," said Paula. "We can put a little red and green in this wedding's decor. What's it gonna hurt?" She beamed at the planners, who were feeling more uneasy by the second.

Cynthia started to protest, but Nadia seized her mother's arm in a firm grip. "Let's move on," she said—in a voice that commanded no arguments. "Do you have those sketches of the cake?"

"Do I?" Ama had been waiting for her cue. "I have been giving your cake some definite thought, and I've come up with a couple of ideas that I think are really good choices for your theme. First up, my white poinsettia cake." She propped the sketch on a little easel. "The silver berry centers are edible, and I can etch delicate little veins on the petals using a special edible metallic sheen glaze that will bind with the crystal sprinkles."

Fondant white poinsettias filled the spaces between each cake layer, ranging in size and all with a soft touch of glitter added to the page by some glue and craft glitter from Ama's craft supplies.

"Nice," said Nadia. "It's really pretty."

"My second thought has a little bit of blue mixed with silver, using more edible decorations," said Ama, now showcasing her second possibility, which featured an ice-blue frosting lace design trimming its edges and adorning its sides in swirls, with crushed candy glass sprinkling the surface and decorating the top with large decorative shards. "It's very minimalist and modern, but we can make it a little warmer by toning down the candy glass's icy look and replacing it with something cozier. Like a series of handcrafted chocolate Christmas ornaments, for instance, that have a metallic candy coating to give them a nice sheen?"

"I don't quite believe I like the second one," said Cynthia dubiously. "It just doesn't suit Nadia at all."

"I think that first one is a little too plain," said Paula. Ama looked slightly crestfallen. "Shouldn't poinsettias be big *red* flowers?"

"The wedding's theme is white," Nadia reminded her. "The cake's decor should definitely be simple and wintry, because that's what we want for our wedding."

"What about that ice cake?" said Paula. "Say, look—I got a picture of one from the internet. Do you think you can find one?" She held out the photo on her phone to Ama, who noticed right away that the generic bakery cake bore a striking resemblance to a birthday one for *Frozen*.

"Please," said Cynthia, pushing it down. A look of restrained patience appeared on her face. "Let Nadia choose her own cake. I'm the one who's paying for this little part of the affair and I'm not paying for some glitter monstrosity that looks as if it were built out of sugar cubes. Why not just have them make an igloo and be done with it?"

"I'd really like a marriage between these two designs," said Nadia, lowering her voice as she leaned toward Ama. "Can we have something that says winter wonderland and has some contrast, but keeps it mostly white? Kind of like the poinsettia cake, only with… I don't know… not snowmen or toboggans, I guess."

Nadia looked tired as she searched for words, a sign of how taxing this meeting had grown for the bride-to-be. "I can come up with something, absolutely," said Ama. "No Christmas, just winter beauty. How about I draw a couple of new sketches and email them to you?" That way, nobody but the bride and the groom would see them.

"Thank you *so* much," said Nadia, who looked relieved. Beside her, both mothers were still bickering over whether an ice palace cake was elegant or hideous.

She would definitely come up with a better design. Ama felt determined as she updated her notes, scratching out the candy glass and the concept for pale blue poinsettias. Snowflakes would be perfect—but not cookies, and not just fondant cutouts on the sides of the cake. It needed to look special.

❄

Her phone rang as she crossed the street from the Wedding Belles' headquarters. "What is it, Rasha?" she asked, answering the phone.

"Ama, what do you think of holiday lights in the restaurant's windows? I just saw the cutest ones in this department store. Do you think it would be too much, since Papa bought that big gold garland?" Her sister texted a photo to her, taken from inside a retail shop.

"Why not?" answered Ama. "Deck the halls, right?" Ever since her father decided that American seasonal holidays were a good restaurant marketing tool, the Tandoori Tiger had begun to feel like the neighborhood's glitziest holiday department store. No one had been able to talk him out of buying lots of big metallic pumpkins in October for decorating the hostess stand.

She entered the cozy eatery known as Sugar Pie, where the country classic 'Christmas in Dixie' was playing softly overhead while customers perused the menu of coffee, hot chocolate, and regional holiday favorites. She could already smell honey-glazed ham and sweet potatoes in brown sugar, and knew it would be served up with a steaming side of creamy green bean casserole garnished with French fried onions.

Checked and gingham tablecloths gave the diner a Southern sunshine feel even in winter, although there were countertop-height Christmas trees on display, decorated with pinecones and old-fashioned spice cookie ornaments, and one of the walls sported framed black-and-white photo art of dogwood groves, rustic chapels, and Appalachian trails. A toy cowboy dressed as a dancing Santa waved at customers who passed by the register on their way to the door.

Ama was perusing the chalkboard menu and still trying to decide between cinnamon bread pudding and a specialty red velvet Christmas funnel cake with cream cheese glaze, when she noticed a familiar face among the diner's customers. Nadia the bride was sitting at a table, leafing through Tessa's latest suggestions. With a smile, Ama approached. "Fancy bumping into you here," she said.

The bride looked up. "Oh, hi, Ama," she said.

"I'm already having some great thoughts about your new cake," Ama began, but her smile faded when she noticed the worry on Nadia's face. "Something wrong?" she asked.

"Everything." Nadia smiled halfheartedly. "I'm just so frustrated right now. There's so many decisions, and I feel like there's no agreement on any of them. I know what I want... but I'm not sure what Lyle really wants. I know way too much of what my mother wants, of course. *And* Paula."

"Sounds like you need someone in your corner," said Ama sympathetically. "You don't have to choose anything you don't want. Honestly, Tessa is the best when it comes to dancing around difficult relatives. She'll make your moms believe it was *their* idea to pick exactly what you want, if it comes to that."

"But it shouldn't come to that," sighed Nadia. "I want Lyle to step up and tell me that he agrees with me. Or say he disagrees with me. I want him to tell his mom not to be so aggressive, and help me ignore mine when she's giving me way too much grief. Is there anything really wrong with wanting a snowflake princess wedding?"

"So long as you're not an ice queen, no," said Ama with a joking little smile. Nadia laughed.

"Thanks," she said. "If I could only hear those words from Lyle, then I could tell myself that everything really will be okay for our big day." She pushed aside the pictures of the ice swan fruit bowl and the icicle garlands, as if her problem could be pushed aside with them. But it was evident from the look on Nadia's face that the solution wasn't so simple. Ama felt a tiny bit worried, as if it was somehow possible that the silly jinx or curse plaguing them was now going to strike the wedding couple themselves. But it was just silly superstition to think anything like that. Right?

❄

Ama sat on the bench at the metro train station, feeling the cool breeze against her cheek, and smelling the spices from her new apple and pear turnovers and the *gulab jamun* with its sugar syrup dusted with fresh-grated cinnamon. A sample of Western and Eastern treats for Luke, so he could taste both sides of her cultural skills. She had wanted to bring him some of her spice cookies and her double chocolate biscotti, but her brother Nikil had gobbled up most of them when he dropped off this week's meat delivery.

Nearby, a trio of musicians was playing an upbeat, jazzy 'God Rest Ye Merry Gentleman' for change as passengers disembarked from the west-end train carrying shopping bags and backpacks. With a smile, Ama flipped a few quarters into their guitarist's open case as she rose and stepped closer to the platform, scanning the faces of the disembarking passengers. Ama's phone trilled to life, her sister-in-law's number on its screen when she pulled it from her coat pocket.

"Hello?" she said.

"Are you still waiting?" asked Deena.

"I am." Ama glanced around. "He said he'd meet me here at one, as soon as he closed his shop. Ten minutes to go, I guess."

"Relax. Everybody thinks you're at the movies. I dropped a hint that you're seeing that film you and I saw at the mall last weekend. Perfect cover, don't you think?"

"I don't want to lie, Deena."

"You're not lying. I'm lying *for* you. It's a totally different thing." There was a rustling noise on the other end, the sound of Deena's sari brushing against the rack holding the restaurant's laminated menus. "You just said you were going out for the day. And you know what your family would say if they knew you were meeting a total stranger for a dessert date."

"It's not a date," said Ama. "He said he wanted to try some baked goods, and I'm supplying them."

"Yeah, and you are in no way interested in him," replied her sister-in-law sarcastically. "So, do you want me to tell your parents where you really are?"

"What? No. Of course not." Pinched, Ama retreated to the truth. Imagine if Ranjit or Pashma found out—with her father still basking in triumph over her less-than-perfect date. "I have to go. Bye, Deena." She hung up, seeing the latest passenger approach the train, one who looked familiar even in a crowd. Wool coat flapping carelessly in the breeze, an old scarf and hat that had seen better days covering part of his dark, rumpled hair.

Handsome. Definitely rugged, without question. Even sexy wouldn't be a stretch, despite the absence of the leather jacket and the sleek motorcycle he'd straddled in the market that first time she had seen him. Yet it wasn't his looks alone, but something about him as a person that tugged her in his direction without her feet even moving, as if the mere sight of his countenance, the slightest facial expression betraying emotion or observation on his part, had some kind of magic power.

Her heart was beating fast just watching him walk through the crowd. It was impossible for her to believe, but it actually skipped a beat at the mere suggestion he was glancing her way now. *Just like in all the romance novels and movies*, she thought.

When Luke saw her, a smile broke across his face. He paused to let a woman push a stroller by, then joined Ama.

"What's in the bag?" he asked. "Cupcakes? A slice of leftover wedding cake?" He took it from her and peeked inside. "Smells good."

"It's a little sampler of my best baking from this week," she answered. "I thought maybe you'd like to try some of my pastry work and a little something from my culture, too."

"Thanks," he said. "It looks delicious. What do I owe you, by the way?"

"Nothing," she said, shaking her head. "It's just my way of saying thanks for the ride last week."

He glanced toward the train. "Up for lunch?" he said. "My way of thanking you for the pastries." He held up the sack. "I know a great little stand that makes tacos and hotdogs on the far side of town, about twenty minutes from here. Any chance you'd like to try either or both?"

"Love to," she said. "I'm up for anything."

Ama liked trains, the way they rumbled and swayed whenever the rails met a rough patch, or slowed to reach the platform. Even when they were crowded—and the passengers a little weird or a little smelly—she still liked the atmosphere. People going someplace, people going no place, all lost in their own thoughts or stories. Even today, the middle of the afternoon, when the crowd riding to the end of town was sparse and even the window seats were vacant, she felt the same.

Today, however, she wasn't lost in her own head. Seated beside Luke, she had something to occupy her for a change, besides her own thoughts. He confessed that he liked the atmosphere of travel, too, so they made up stories about the only other passengers in their car, an elderly Asian man listening to music through an old Walkman's headphones, and a young man holding a skinny mixed-breed dog on his lap, which looked happy to be breaking the transit rules.

"It's a seeing eye dog," said Luke.

"It's too small," Ama protested.

"It's a travel-size one," he said. They both laughed. The young man with the dog was too busy looking out the window as he talked on his phone, but the old man turned his head despite whatever music he was listening to. Luke was trying her fruit turnover now.

"Mmm. That is heaven," he said. "You know your way around a pastry."

"You're just being nice," said Ama.

"Trust me. I know pastry. I used to live next door to a baker, remember? I grew up beside a French patisserie. This is way better than the *petit choux* I used to eat for free."

"Thanks," said Ama. "I try. I'm basically learning from a book I borrowed from the library, one all about classic pastry techniques. These were my first turnovers... well, not counting the batch that was a little soggy."

"What's the name of this dessert?" He opened the *gulab jamun* and tasted one of the dough balls. "It looked like *petit choux* until I tasted it. It's heavier... sweeter..." He licked his fingers. "That's really sweet. It's really good, actually."

"It's an Indian dessert—only with a little American twist on it that I added," said Ama. "Cinnamon, nutmeg, and crushed roasted walnuts. It's my family's favorite—a lot of Punjabi desserts tend to be sweeter than other Indian recipes. They're among the most famous in Indian cuisine, though Rajasthani cooking can be pretty rich in some regions."

"You're Punjabi?"

"My father is. But we live in a neighborhood with Indian families from several different Indian states. Among a few other ethnicities whom we pretty much outnumber, on our side of the street, anyway."

"I owe you a little apology," said Luke. "I don't know much about India. I once had a friend who was Indonesian, but I'm definitely sure that's not the same. You'll have to educate me, since I don't know the difference between your culture and the next one."

"It's okay," said Ama. "I have to admit that I don't know that much about it, either." She felt a twinge of regret as she said this out loud, though. Her family's heritage was a part of her life in so many different ways it seemed strange to her that she didn't know more about it by now. Perhaps if she did, it would give her a deeper appreciation for that side of herself and for the people she was closest to in her life.

"You must be second generation, right?" said Luke.

"How'd you know?" she answered.

"It was a guess. Something in your voice when you talk about your family. Maybe it's intuition," he said. "But you said you don't know much about your country? Even from your parents?"

"I know a lot about *their* cultures, sure. Their recipes, their families, some of the traditions that are important to them," she said. "But other things? Geography, plants, day-to-day life and catch phrases—I'm totally clueless. I can barely speak Punjabi anymore." What had been easy when she was little had gradually slipped away: in high school, Ama had rebelled against her parents' wishes by speaking only English. Fairly mild as far as defiant teenage behavior goes, but not something Ama was proud of, especially knowing how much it had disappointed them.

"I can speak a little French," said Luke. "Not much, but some."

"Cool," said Ama.

"*Ma petite amore*," he said.

"What does that mean?" she asked.

"'My little love,'" he said. "Not exactly impressive, is it?" He smiled. "Let's just say it doesn't come in handy very often. Not with motorcycle customers." He popped another of the sticky dough balls into his mouth.

Ama settled back against her seat. The scenery flew by, the ghost reflection of the girl in the window smiling back at her, in Ama's knitted multicolor cap.

"What are you looking at?" Luke asked.

"Nothing," she said. "I just like to watch the world go by sometimes. It's amazing how fast things travel. The blur... it's like something from a museum painting."

"The world looks like that from the back of a motorcycle," said Luke. "I took a ride when I was ten with my best friend's father. I used to dream about it afterwards. I kept this little die-cast motorcycle on my night table, and would look at it every night, imagining taking another ride. With me driving." He gave a faint smile after this remark. "It was a while before it came true, but I couldn't wait." He looked at Ama. "Did you ever have a dream like that?"

It was Ama's smile that became wistful now. "About baking," she said.

"Owning one?" he guessed. "A bakery, I mean."

"Baking," she said. "Period. The moment I opened up a book on desserts, I found what I loved most in life. I guess I started dreaming about bundt pans and cupcake foil and French rolling pins after that. Kind of like the way you dreamed about motorcycles."

"Did anybody have the heart to buy you an Easy-Bake Oven?" he asked.

Ama laughed. "Nobody," she said. "I was grown up enough for a real one when I figured out I loved it, though. So no big loss."

Luke tasted the last of the sticky syrup on his fingers. "You should open your own bakery," he said. "I could really taste the love for your work in those pastries. It's like the… I don't know… the nectar of human happiness is part of its ingredients."

"The nectar of human happiness?" said Ama. "No one's ever described my baked goods that way before."

"I always wanted to be a poet," he said, somewhat sheepishly. "It would make up for having no real musical talent."

"Do you write poetry?" she asked.

"Sometimes. I jot things down on old napkins and stuff. Probably nothing great, but who knows? Maybe there's a gift for words buried somewhere inside me. I've always wanted to find a way to express things that sound stupid when said out loud."

"I can't imagine you sounding stupid," said Ama, shaking her head.

"Plenty of dumb things come out of my mouth," answered Luke. "There are plenty of things I want to come out that don't make it. The story of the human experience, right?" He wadded up his napkin and tucked it in his coat pocket.

Ama was having a hard time imagining anything like that from Luke, although it was true of everybody on the planet. He was having no trouble with words around her that she could sense. *But could he say anything to me that wasn't utterly rude or inappropriate and I wouldn't find it amazing?*

"I can't write a poem to save my life," said Ama. "I would have flunked all my composition assignments if my sister hadn't helped me with outlines and suggestions. Words aren't really one of my gifts."

"You speak to people through food," pointed out Luke. "You don't need words. Communication through flour, sugar, yeast… it's one of the most ancient forms of dialogue besides hand signals." He made a series of mime gestures, being careful not to drop the paper sack of dessert at the same time.

"I think you're better at words than primitive communication," Ama said with a smile.

"That's why I wish I were a poet. I would've been happy being a violinist or something too, I reckon, but it turns out my fingers are only good at installing spark plugs and spot-welding metal. My mom paid for lessons once, but I was a failure."

"I was learning to play the *sarangi* once," said Ama, remembering.

"What's that?"

"An Indian instrument. It's sort of like a cello, but it has this really unique range of sounds," she said. "My aunt plays one, and she tried to teach me a few songs. I'm really bad at it."

"What were you born to do besides cook?" he asked. "Not that there's anything wrong with living solely for baked goods. But I think everybody craves pieces of other experiences."

"I didn't even crave to be a baker at first," said Ama. "I didn't have a lot of practical dreams as a kid. I think I was always dreaming of things that were impractical—or larger than life, sometimes. Needless to say, I didn't get that many of them, except maybe a trip or two to the seashore. A trip to Mexico once." Sand and shells there, too, but also excellent pastries that melted in Ama's mouth, so that the smell of cinnamon brought her back to that celebration in the town plaza where she had bought an insanely colored shoulder bag and lost twenty dollars to a pickpocket.

"Dreaming of the beach isn't silly," said Luke.

"I dream of other things, too," Ama said. "I like the idea of traveling. I want to eat pastries at a real Parisian patisserie someday. I want to make incredible wedding cakes that take people's breath away. I make cakes now, but... do you ever have that perfect design that you want to make real? You really want someone to share in how special it is, as more than just a picture you sketched." She tucked a lock of her hair behind her ear as she tried to explain it. It eluded words, like the thoughts and feelings Luke wanted to put into poems.

"Every so often, yeah," he said. "A very cool sketch I want to see painted on a bike somewhere out on the road, making its way down Route 66 or taking the open road to no place in particular."

"You make life sound pretty adventurous," said Ama. "Like it's waiting to happen around any corner."

"Lives are probably more like scrapbooks, collecting up all the things we do," said Luke. "There are more small things than big ones. That's how we fill up drawers and boxes, with candy wrappers from fairs, or coasters from restaurants."

"I have a coaster from a restaurant in Mexico in my wall collage at home," said Ama. *Coincidence that he made this comparison? I think not.*

"You prove my point, see?" said Luke.

"Fate did," she said. "Or the universe. Not me personally." But she bumped lightly against him at the same time. There were the sleeves of wool coats between them, but the feel of his arm was reassuringly real and solid. This was an adventure, this day out with Luke, she thought, if the feelings inside her were any indication. But an adventure that was more like a secret spy mission, with her cell phone switched off and Deena covering for her with the story about the movie, she remembered guiltily.

Luke settled more comfortably beside her, stretching one arm across the back of the seats. It wasn't touching her, but Ama imagined it settling around her, its fingers resting on her skin. The casual stretch and embrace—she had imagined it plenty of times when watching late-night movies with her mother and auntie, the old coming-of-age romance stories in which onscreen lovers shared their first moment of attraction.

Of course, she and Luke didn't have a pair of aunties watching them right now, or have to answer questions on suitable prospects, or worry about the first impression they were making on a whole family. And Ama was basking in the freedom of knowing that this moment, this afternoon, belonged to nobody but her and Luke. It was all hers, and it could be whatever and however she wanted it to be.

"So what do you know about modern Indian art?" asked Luke.

Ama smiled. "Nothing at all," she answered.

They arrived at the taco stand, where the food proved delicious. The little vendor's cart was near the waterfront, its sides decorated with paintings of tomatoes, sombreros, and dancing peppers. Ama tried one topped with pico de gallo and sliced jalapeños, then a chicken one with chipotle sauce.

"I love this one," she said, licking her fingers. "It makes me think of this bread I want to try. It involves chipotle, cheddar, onions, and this tomato paste sauce… anyway, it sounded delicious." She polished off the rest of her taco in two bites.

"Bread sounds like your favorite food, when you talk about it like that," he said.

"What do I love best?" she said. "I like… cupcakes. They're so cute and tiny, and can be decorated so many ways. And cookies—you can't beat them, because almost everybody loves them. But what I love best… the best is cake. It's a work of art, making a perfect cake. When it's finished, you just feel so proud. It's unique," she added. "No two are really alike. Are motorcycles the same way? Do you feel each bike you work on or rebuild is different?"

"Of course," he said. "Then again, they are. I don't get that many duplicates in the shop, since I rebuild a lot of vintage ones. Just the modern ones, but they can have a lot of character, too. You see all the different dents and scratches, and all the little character details. The decals, the symbols. A lot of the detail work people ask for is unique. Like… tattoos on metal bodies," he said, trying to explain it.

"Tattoos on metal?" said Ama, one eyebrow up.

"Expresses it better than just saying a paint job on a bike. Any canvas is art to me," he said. He pushed up the sleeve of his coat. "This one, for example, is my souvenir from the west coast. I saw it on the designer's board, and I couldn't help myself."

It was a phoenix-like bird, rising from a wisp of flame and smoke. Ama had never been wild about tattoos before, but something about this one spoke to her. It matched Luke's personality. The way she thought about him was summarized in those ink lines, channeling that aura of freedom and personal fire. Just like the motorcycle did… or maybe it was her imagination only?

"What do the words mean?" she asked.

"It's Spanish. It means 'live every day,'" he answered. "I'm part Spanish on my mom's side."

"Really?" said Ama. "Is that why you chose this tattoo?"

"Sort of. I got it to remind me to be more in the moment. I forget sometimes that the future can't be counted on, and it definitely can't be predicted. So all we have is right now, this moment, the one we're living in. You and me walking along this street—that's as much of the future as I can really know. So I remind myself to take it in. Enjoy it. Like this," he said, holding up the last of the dough balls from her pastry box. "It deserves to be savored and appreciated." He popped it in his mouth.

"They're called *gulab jamun*," she reminded him.

"That's a mouthful in itself," he said after swallowing. "Are they your favorite Indian dessert? Or just your family's?"

"Both," she said. She paused to consider what she would choose as her favorite dessert of all time. Lemon cream cake? Maybe for the summertime. Chocolate fudge cookies? Lately, she had been craving a nice batch of soft, sweet ones.

"You have a little something right there," said Luke, pointing toward the right side of his mouth.

"Right where?" Ama brushed her upper lip, feeling for a stray cilantro leaf or bit of onion from her last taco.

"Right there." Luke's thumb brushed the corner of her mouth. Rough, callused fingertips from physical labor, but ever so light against her skin, with a gentle pressure that made it totally unlike her imagination's version. Shivers traveled through her, sparked by this brief touch. She was breathless to think she had only read about it in fiction before now—yet it was so real in this moment, the physical and emotional chemistry between her and another person.

✳

The lunch crowd was gone from the Tandoori Tiger, and the evening crowd hadn't arrived yet. Ama could see the empty dining room as she slipped through the front door and stole up the stairs. The door to Ranjit's office was open, her father looking at inventory lists, his fingers pecking on a calculator slowly.

The step creaked beneath Ama's foot at the very top of the stairs. Ranjit looked up from his calculations, lowering his reading glasses. "Did you have fun at your movie?" he asked her.

She balked at the thought of Deena's excuse. "I didn't go," said Ama. "I went for a walk instead, since all the businesses are decorating for December."

"Did Tamir go, too?" asked Ranjit.

"Tamir?" Ama said with confusion.

"You went with him today, didn't you?" Ranjit looked pleased. "He called. He said he would call your phone to talk."

She had turned off her phone after talking to Deena, of course, to keep anybody from the family away for the afternoon. "I didn't talk to him today, Papa," she said. "Maybe he called here by mistake?"

"He's a nice boy," said Pashma, who passed Ama on the stairs, a basket of laundry in her arms. "See if he put a message on your phone."

"Maybe he wants to see you again," suggested Ranjit.

"No, Papa, I don't think he does," said Ama with emphasis.

"What are you talking about? He took you to a nice restaurant, didn't he?"

Only because the Punjabi version of McDonald's was probably too crowded that night, she wanted to counter, unfairly. "Look, Papa, we didn't have a very good time. We didn't have anything in common, so we had nothing to talk about all evening."

She had avoided describing the dinner in too much detail—especially the dull small talk that made Ama wish for the excitement of a fire alarm going off to interrupt the tedium. When she came back from the restaurant, she had made an excuse about being tired and hurried upstairs to bed to avoid questions from both a triumphant Ranjit and her aunt Bendi. Hoping that the subject of Tamir would simply go away, for instance, after he failed to ask her on a second date. But now he had called the restaurant for some reason—probably to break off any further matchmaking pursuit—and gotten her father's hopes up once again.

"The first part of a courtship is always hard," insisted her father. "It will be better next time. You'll see."

"Your father and I had nothing to say when we first met each other," said her mother, who was folding clean towels on the hall ironing board. "We did not say two words to each other. But we were still a good match, only we needed time."

"Time is not going to help me and Tamir," insisted Ama.

"Give him a chance," said Ranjit. "When he calls, talk to him. He may be calling you because he sees what I do—that you are a good choice for a nice boy who wants to be married."

"Nice boys do not come along every day," said Bendi, who was climbing the stairs with a second load of laundry. "*Shaadi* does not come to those who let good matches slip through fingers. I know."

"Marriage isn't everything, though, is it?" Ama replied. "Papa, honestly—"

"Ah-uhh." He held up his hand. "Your auntie is right. Make the most of this, Ama. Here is a chance for you to have the happiness that I have, that your brother and sisters have. What could be better? When he calls, tell him you had a nice time. What could it hurt? The next time you will have plenty to say. Listen to me, because I know about these things." He pushed his glasses into place again and tapped the keys on his calculator as if this discussion had come to an end.

"You can't just ignore the facts, Papa," she told him quietly. "Even if you want to, you can't change the fact that Tamir is a terrible match for me, and there's no way he's going to want to marry me. You have to let go, because it's not going to happen."

"You know the future, do you?" said Bendi with a laugh. Ranjit waved his hand dismissively, as if the subject had come to a close already. With a sigh, Ama went off to her room, since it was pointless to argue about this any further.

"He doesn't understand," she said to Rasha, as she curled up on the end of her bed. "It was literally the dullest evening of my life. Even the nights I spent studying for chemistry tests were better than that date."

"First dates are always bad," said Rasha. "When Sanjay and I had our first date alone, we were both nervous and awkward. He even had the old 'excuse' routine ready, with a friend to bail him out by emergency phone call. But he took one look at me across the table, and decided that I was a girl worth spending the rest of his life with. At least, that's what he told me after we were engaged," she said.

"You and Sanjay had talked online, though," said Ama. "You really knew him even before you officially met as prospective matches. Even during the whole awkward family meeting, at least you knew you liked *something* about him already."

"What's not to like about Tamir? He's nice looking, he has a great salary, and his family seems *way* refined compared to ours," pointed out Rasha. "Be flattered, Ama. He's a super great catch. The worst you have to put up with is Aunt Bendi reminding you that his complexion is '*sooo* unfortunate' for such a nice young man. And since none of us care about stupid cultural stereotypes, it won't matter. It's not like Aunt Bendi will be living with you two afterwards."

Ama giggled. "Stop," she said. "Don't talk about me and Tamir like we're a future couple. I don't want a three-year-long engagement while we get to know each other, and Papa talks about what good prospects the boy has. I don't even want a traditional Indian wedding."

"Do *not* let Mama hear you say that," said Rasha. "Don't even let me hear you say that. Ama, I wanted to help you choose your sari, and put on your wedding jewelry, with some new bracelets and whatever hair ornaments your husband gifts you, and all those great traditions. Maybe talk Aunt Bendi into playing a wedding song for you on the *sarangi*…"

"Stop it!" Ama smacked her sister with a pillow, then flopped over on her back as Rasha laughed. "I didn't say I wouldn't have *any* of those things for my wedding—just not the way Mama and Papa imagine it being, with everything based on their ideas alone."

Nobody understood her. After all, Rasha's mostly arranged marriage had worked out, and so had those of her siblings. It was great for them that they'd found somebody through semi-traditional channels, but it wasn't great for her. Couldn't they see that she wanted something different? She dreamed of spontaneity and sudden chances. Of looking into someone's eyes, even a perfect stranger's, and somehow knowing in that moment that a spark was kindled that could last a lifetime, if fanned by a kiss.

Spontaneous kisses, love at first sight, unpredictable sparks—the dreams of the hopeless romantic at heart. These things just didn't have a place in the world where Ama was expected to find her 'suitable match' who would fit certain standards of being a good spouse. Not perfect for her at heart, perhaps, but suitable in most respects. Not the love of her life, necessarily, but a future love of contentment and complacency after years of acceptance and compromise.

It was the more realistic picture of love and marriage in any culture, true; but not the once-in-a-lifetime romantic picture that everybody secretly dreams about, Ama believed. Taking a chance by waiting for it, to see if that impossible dream could really come true—that was something that would horrify all her relatives if she chose it.

Especially if 'suitable matches' like Tamir kept showing up to invite her on boring dinner dates.

"What would you do, if you were me?" she asked Natalie over the phone. She gazed through her open window at the stars, what little of them could actually be seen with the neon lights from the shop next door blinking madly in a pink-and-white haze. If you squinted, you could still see the little white diamond pinpoints in the sky, Ama believed, like a pattern on midnight blue fabric.

"Well, for starters, if I believed in true love and soulmates, I wouldn't be me," pointed out Natalie. "But I'm in the same boat, you know. My family still manages to pressure me sometimes on the subject of love. Believe me, I wish I had the answers, then I wouldn't have everyone asking me when I'm finally going to settle down."

"So we're stuck like this, you're saying," clarified Ama.

"Exactly," said Natalie.

Chapter Fifteen

"Happy birthday to me," sighed Natalie, as she gazed at the lone chocolate-covered cream puff in the fridge. She closed the fridge door and pondered whether to watch reruns of *Fixer Upper* or finish studying for her upcoming test on different fabric techniques.

Sunday afternoon had been completely consumed by both running the bakery's front counter while Maria was gone, and helping Uncle Guido crimp the edges on the tiny spinach ravioli which were now drying on racks in the bakery kitchen, alongside the spaghetti Guido had made the day before. Why he couldn't use his own son's restaurant to do this kind of thing, Natalie would never understand. Hundreds of tiny little pasta squares—no wonder Rob had signed up to fight pretend forest fires when he heard their uncle would be needing assistance in the kitchen.

Natalie had loved cutting the little ravioli when she was a kid, after pressing the soft shell closed around the spinach and dried cheese mound in the center. Today, maybe she would have loved it, too, except she was feeling disappointed about other things. Her plans for this evening with Chad had fallen through, thanks to a last-minute opportunity he had to instruct new rock climbers at some park halfway across the state. And with Maria gone, there was nobody to close the bakery that night but Natalie, who spent her birthday evening boxing up leftover biscotti and cannoli, and sweeping up crumbs.

"So where's Aunt Maria?" her cousin Chrissy asked when she phoned the bakery to leave Lou a note about an upcoming anniversary in the family. "Isn't she usually home for your birthday? I mean, your mom bakes for every occasion known to mankind."

"Emergency," answered Natalie. "The care facility is changing Gram to another room, so Ma's moving all her things to the new wing. She won't be back until tomorrow, so I'm holding the fort here." She locked the back door to the kitchen, glancing over the racks of drying pasta, the orderly chaos of baking pans and industrial mixers.

"Right. I forgot about that," said Chrissy. "So... are you seeing whatshisname tonight?" she asked teasingly. "Kimmie called and said he's *extremely* hot."

"I'll bet Rob called and told you he looked like a toad," said Natalie, shoving the flour canister back into place.

"By the way, you didn't answer my question. Is Mr. Hottie taking you out to dinner?"

"Not tonight," answered Natalie. "Tuesday. He wants to take me to this new Mongolian place that opened downtown. He has a friend working in the kitchen who swears it'll be the hottest place in town."

"Exciting. Tell me all about it afterwards," said Chrissy.

Natalie left the boxes of extra pastry on her mom's table, where she found a note scribbled to her on her mom's grocery pad. *Sorry about your birthday, baby. I didn't have time to bake, so I left a little something here for your sweet tooth. I'll make it up to you next week. Love, Ma.*

There was a sad little frowny face drawn next to the line about her birthday. Natalie opened the fridge and discovered the cream puff on the plate, one with a fancy drizzle of white chocolate over its milk chocolate glaze.

It wasn't her mom's work—it was obviously purchased from a different bakery, probably one of Rob's firehouse snack leftovers that her mom had confiscated on Natalie's behalf. It looked like the ones from Sugar Connection, the corner convenience store bakery where Rob bought greasy gas station-style food like corn dogs, pizza by the slice, and buffalo-style popcorn chicken to feed his never-ending appetite.

The pastry looked a little dry beneath the plastic cling wrap. Since it wasn't up to Icing Italia's standards, Natalie left it be.

She opened a plastic container of her mother's leftover lasagna, then opened her textbook on the table and flipped to the latest chapter her professor had advised reading before his lecture. Advanced silk-weaving methods—dry stuff for anybody who wasn't a diehard seamstress like herself. Propped next to it was her phone, since Chad had promised to text her tonight, and her mom would probably call with an update on her grandmother's new room.

The origins of silk have roots in myth and in history. Beginning with the discovery of the silk worm's properties in Asia during the... Natalie turned the page, jotting notes in its margins, her mind on Nadia's dress and not on the silk worm's humble career beginnings. What should a snow princess wear? The fabric Nadia had chosen was pale white satin... she had a picture of some really nice beaded bodice work in one of her scrapbooks, although that seemed pretty conventional and not unique to Nadia herself. So what would be?

Ice princesses wear tiaras that look like Ama's modern cake topper. Natalie's lips quirked into a smile. She heard the sound of the front door bell before she could finish this thought. Rob had forgotten his keys again, apparently.

"You should really keep a spare under one of those fake rocks," she said loudly as she unlatched the door. On the other side of it stood Brayden.

Brayden, in what Natalie suspected was the tuxedo he wore to Chrissy's wedding a couple of years ago, holding a plastic dessert carrier. He gave Natalie a smile.

"Mom sent you a birthday card." He took an envelope from his pocket and held it up.

She rested one hand on her hip and sighed. "What are you doing here, Brayden?" she said. "I thought you understood that I had plans for tonight." No plans had actually materialized, but she was deep in study for her next exam, right?

His humble smile twitched itself into place in response to Natalie's typical rejection of him. "Even if you're going to say no to me, don't say no to the cake," he said. "Death by chocolate with dark chocolate frosting."

"A cake?" She raised one eyebrow. "You brought me a cake. Just because you thought I needed extra chocolate?"

"I knew your mom was busy today," he said. "You know you can't have a birthday without chocolate cake."

"How did you know she didn't bake me one yesterday?" said Natalie.

"I read it on Facebook," said Brayden. "Your mom posted about it on her wall."

He was friends with her mom on Facebook? That was enough to kill whatever tiny part of Natalie hadn't dismissed Brayden as boyfriend material, although she still couldn't bring herself to close the door in his face.

"What's with the penguin suit?" she said.

"It's a special occasion," he said. "I thought I should dress up."

"Really?"

"Well... I thought if you didn't have plans... maybe we could do something," he hinted. "It's your birthday. You shouldn't be hanging around your mom's house. Some guy should, I don't know, take you to dinner or something."

"Look at me—do I look like I'm dressed for going out?" Natalie gestured toward her zippered sweatshirt and leggings.

"You look good to me." Brayden blushed after saying this aloud, as if she didn't know he was probably thinking it in secret lots of times. Dismay, however, did not bring a blush to Natalie's face.

"I ate dinner already," said Natalie. "Thanks, but no thanks, Brayden." Now he could take her hint and go. *Please don't make me hurt your feelings, Brayden.*

"So no Chad to take you to dinner, I guess?" said Brayden.

She sighed and averted her gaze. "Brayden," she said, trying to be gentle. "You know how I feel already. You don't have to... keep trying. 'Cause it's not going to work."

Brayden shrugged his shoulders. "I know," he said. "Happy birthday." He held out the cake.

Natalie stood there a moment. She could take the cake and close the door in his face, but even with Brayden at his nerdiest, Natalie wasn't that heartless. She sighed. "Come in." Begrudgingly she held open the door wider.

Death by chocolate indeed, with a molten chocolate sauce in the center and chocolate shavings on top. Definitely homemade—Natalie suspected that Brayden's mom had baked this at his request.

She took a bite from her slice. "Did your mom make this?" she asked.

"Yup." His fork cut into the slice she gave him, but he wasn't really eating it. He was mostly watching her enjoy hers. "Is it good?"

"What do you think?" She took another generous bite. "Your mom's a good cook."

"Yeah, but she's no professional," he said. He noticed her textbooks. "Studying?" he asked.

"Big test," she said. "Be prepared, that's my professor's warning. It worked out perfectly, having some extra time to study tonight."

"I can't imagine you need to study a whole night to know this stuff," he said. "You know fashion like—like the back of your hand." He turned the page of her textbook. "You were the only girl I knew who spent Saturdays at the fabric stores."

She shrugged. "It was just my thing," she said. "Like the kids who hung out at music stores."

"I guess it was more than that," said Brayden. "I always figured you'd become a big designer."

"I didn't, though," countered Natalie. "That was presumptive of you."

"Yeah, but you're halfway there now," he answered. "Give it a couple more years and you'll be the next big name."

"Yeah, right." She rolled her eyes as she swallowed the last bite of cake on her plate. Telling herself it was wrong to have another piece, although it was tempting.

"Bigger than the designer you used to work for, for sure," said Brayden. "Rob showed me some pictures of the clothes she designed once. I saw some in the paper's fashion page. Some pretty freaky stuff."

"It wouldn't take much to out-design Kandace," said Natalie with a short laugh. "A talented rock could do it." Thinking: *He read the fashion pages?* If he did, was it purely for the purpose of finding out what her workplace was like? He'd have seen the photos of the ugly dresses she sewed on Kandace's behalf, probably including the 'Easter Bunny Surprise' faux fur coat, as Cal titled it.

Great. Even her unwanted admirer had seen her most humiliating work.

She placed the plate next to the sink, and snapped the top back on the cake carrier. "Tell your mom thanks," she said. "For the cake and the card. It was nice of her to remember." Not that Natalie wanted anybody to remember these days, given the number of marital hints from family members, which seemed to triple with every birthday—enough to make her wish that everybody in her life would just forget she had one.

"You didn't open my card yet," said Brayden, who held out a second envelope. "I got you something."

Natalie studied it, reluctant to accept. His arm was weakening as he held it out as far as he could toward her, so the card wobbled slightly in mid-air as he waited for her to take it.

"Brayden," she began.

"Open it," he repeated. He looked pleased, excited, and embarrassed, all at the same time, like a kid watching his parents open some horribly wrapped Christmas gift, the kind that contained an unrecognizable artistic creation. Natalie lifted the flap and slipped the card out.

The figure of a tiny glamorous paper doll was on the front, slender and dark haired, wearing an evening gown with a plunging neckline. "Cute," she said. *Be polite.* "It kind of reminds me of me." She turned the card around to face the same way as herself in demonstration.

"I know," said Brayden, bobbing his head in agreement.

Inside the card were two things. One was a snapshot of her and Brayden when they were teenagers, taken at an amusement park. Rob had been the photographer—it showed Natalie with a half-hearted smile, seated on the far side of the Ferris wheel seat from Brayden, who was grinning ear to ear. The point when Brayden's childhood crush had become too much for Natalie, having gone from being the boy who always volunteered to put the wheels back on her Barbie's car to one who tried desperately to play Spin the Bottle with her at Izzy Patelman's birthday party.

"I found that in a drawer," said Brayden. "Thought you might like it. That was the summer you spent your birthday at the park, remember? The one with the fortune teller, and the bumper cars—Rob got that big lump on his forehead when he fell over the safety rails?"

"Sweet thirteen." The memory of coming of age, surrounded by the smell of roller coaster grease, stale peanuts, and the presence of her brother's dorky friends—including Brayden—tormenting Natalie's cool-as-ice girlfriends who were invited for the day.

The second item was a pair of tickets. She looked up. "Brayden," she repeated, this time in a voice that said no, even without the actual word.

"I know what you're going to say," he answered. "But I thought—"

"I can't. You know that I can't." She stuffed them back into the envelope. She didn't have to see what musical act or coming attraction they were for. This was almost as bad as the realization creeping over her that Brayden might have made a restaurant reservation tonight, just in case she gave in and agreed to go out with him.

"It's your birthday," he protested. "It's a present. You can't say no to a present."

"And yet, I just did."

"If it's because it's me… you could go with somebody else. I didn't expect you to take me, necessarily," he answered.

He did—or, at least, held a tiny bit of hope for it, and was disappointed again. That was the worst part of this awkward situation.

"Don't buy me stuff that costs real money," she said. "I'm serious. So take these back and get a refund or whatever."

"It's tonight. I can't get the money back. So see? You could still go. It'd be a good way to celebrate."

"Not dressed for the occasion—remember?" She took his plate—the slice of cake only half eaten—and set it on the counter, too. For all she knew, it could be a roller derby rink just as easily as the classical symphony behind Brayden's choice of a tux. At least it wasn't the one he wore to the prom, she conceded. It was a little better than that.

"You know there's a closet full of dresses upstairs," he suggested. "Your mom says you must have a hundred dresses up there that you've sewed."

"Not in my size," said Natalie. Lying.

"We're only talking about one time," he said. "That guy Chuck or Chad or whoever stood you up tonight, he wouldn't mind if somebody wanted to give you a nice birthday."

"He didn't 'stand me up'—he had a work opportunity," she said. "He teaches rock climbing on the side."

"If he liked you, he'd have said no to working on your birthday," asserted Brayden.

She shook her head. "I'm not going on a date with you, Brayden. If I wanted to go to dinner with somebody tonight, I could have gone, but I didn't want to. I don't need concert tickets or a plate of chicken marsala tonight because I'm fine on my own. I'm an adult who doesn't need entertainment."

She tossed the fashion model birthday card onto the counter—gently—then handed the envelope of tickets back to Brayden, holding it out until he accepted it reluctantly. She turned and brushed the crumbs from the table, sweeping them into her hand, then onto one of the cake plates on the counter.

Having her back turned for a moment gave her courage. "I don't like you that way, Brayden," she said, although her tone was softer

than usual, trying not to jab him with the painful truth of her words.
Words that needed to be said, if Brayden was ever going to move on
with his life and stop hoping for something between them. Knowing
this was for the best gave her the will to turn back around as she told
him, "You know that. Right?"

She looked into his face, although it was uncomfortable to do it,
just as it was every time the issue of Brayden's crush loomed between
them. She waited for him to say something, but he didn't. He just stood
beside the table, hands in the pockets of his outdated tuxedo jacket.

Nothing had changed since they were kids, but he never saw it.
Did she have to date every athlete or aspiring artist or globetrekker in
town to prove he wasn't her type? Did she have to turn these tickets
into confetti and sprinkle them in his face, the way she had left those
dandelions to wilt on the swing?

Brayden shuffled in place. "You could still change your mind."

"About going out to dinner?" Natalie raised her eyebrow again.
"After eating leftover lasagna and your mom's cake?"

Brayden shrugged. "Maybe," he said. "Or about me instead, maybe.
Either one."

That hopeful smile still wasn't cowed. It cracked itself one more
time, and that's why another sigh escaped Natalie—one of exasperation
and annoyance, followed by a laugh.

"You don't give up, do you?" she said. "Brayden, you are... *impossible*." No other word came to her. She brushed her hair back with
one hand.

"I've got no reason to." He grinned a little. Natalie didn't crack a
smile in return. Hands on her hips, she let a moment pass before she
opened her challenge.

"Do you want to give me something I'd like for my birthday?" she asked.

"Sure," he said, falling into the trap.

Natalie held out her hand. "Give me your phone," she said. "I want to change that ring tone."

She didn't have to say which one: Brayden's beet red blush returned, swallowing both face and ears in flame. "About that," said Brayden awkwardly.

"Yeah, about that," said Natalie. "I would prefer you to hear something else when I… very, very rarely… call your number. Something a little more appropriate. Is there a song somewhere in your music library about a girl being as cold as ice?"

"You're not that cold," said Brayden. Even being insulted like this, he *still* defended her?

She didn't withdraw her hand. "Change it or I will," she said. "Please, Brayden."

The 'please' got to him first. Brayden reached into the pocket of his tux—which had a slightly greenish cast in this light from its poor fabric and bad storage, Natalie noticed—and pulled it out. He pushed a couple of buttons, scrolled through his menu, then handed it to her, so she could see that the ring tone beside her name was updated.

She clicked the button. 'She's So High' from the nineties artist Tal Bachman played. Before it even reached the title line's words 'above me,' Natalie's lips were forced to smile.

"That's actually the funniest joke you've ever made," she said.

Brayden blushed again. "Thanks." Maybe she was wrong, but she thought there was actually a little bit of pain buried deep in his tone. Brayden took his phone back, and turned off the song. "I guess."

This would break anybody's heart. Why was it only for Brayden that she managed this edge of steel, designed to cut apart his hopes? Even Brayden must ask himself that question sometimes, she thought. He just couldn't see it as a sign.

Natalie opened the front door for him as she showed him outside again. She leaned against the doorframe as he crossed the threshold of her mother's house and paused on the stoop.

"Why?" she asked him. "What made you think I would ever give in and say yes?" She was curious to know, really.

Brayden thought about her question. He shrugged. "I'm a good guy," he said. "A guy who really loves you… who respects you… maybe he has a chance. I figure I'll still be here when the others give up, 'cause they don't really care. That's pretty much it."

The fire had gone out of Natalie's reply. The honesty in Brayden's had stripped away its fuel. Even if she didn't like him, it was hard not to be a little touched by those words. They had taken more courage than she believed he possessed, even when scrambling over that rusty chain-link fence hung with 'Beware of Dog' signs.

She put her hand on the door to close it. "Goodnight, Brayden," she said. At the last second, she added, "Find someone else to use those tickets with, okay? No reason to waste them just because it wasn't the right gift for me."

"Sure," he said. "Someone else."

He didn't say who that might be, but Natalie hoped there really would be a friend available for him tonight. Maybe someone at the shipping service, for instance. She didn't want him to spend a miserable evening alone, just because she had no wish to accept his romantic gesture. He was already walking away, though, so she could only take his word for it. Slowly, she closed the door.

She cut a second slice of cake and ate it while reading the end of her chapter on the history of silk. Each forkful melted in her mouth, although not quite as perfectly as her mother's double chocolate cake; but she tasted the past instead, a memory of salted popcorn from that night at the park on her thirteenth birthday, a box of it split by her and her giggling friends before they rode the whip twice in a row. Brayden tried to win a stuffed Garfield for her at the milk bottles booth that night, failing with every desperate attempt, as Natalie tried to pretend to be too interested in talking to her friends to notice him.

At least he hadn't been like Rob's other friends, who had dumped the dregs of their popcorn boxes like confetti over Natalie and her friends from the topmost car of the Ferris wheel.

A rueful smile crossed her lips at the memory of the shrieks and screams that followed, Brayden offering to pick the little pieces of husk and kernel out of her hair—at least she didn't make an awful face at that memory, although she *had* pushed him away at the time when he tried to help.

It all seemed a little sad to her now. Brayden had wasted his life pining for someone who would never love him back. And Rob was right about him. Awkward, physically plain, and hopelessly hopeful Brayden might always be, but he was a nice guy. A decent guy. That was the right word for him. He deserved better in life.

Could she ever fall for him? Natalie paused at this question, although she'd never entertained it in the past. A decent guy who really loved her, as Brayden suggested, and was willing to wait until she saw her shallower relationships for what they really were. But it was impossible, really impossible. He wasn't her type in the slightest—not just because he wasn't handsome like most of her other suitors, either. It was hard to explain, but she couldn't see herself with him no matter how hard she tried. To be with Brayden it seemed as if she'd have to be a completely different person in some way, and that would take years to achieve. Brayden would be an idiot to wait around for her to metamorphose into some regretful, romantically reformed person who wanted something deeper in a relationship... besides which, Brayden would never give up on these cringe-worthy gestures of his that had made her hide from him since their teenage years.

She had never told him thank you for rescuing her doll from Bilbo the dog. She never said thank you for anything he tried to do. Anybody but Brayden would have noticed that, too.

Chapter Sixteen

Ama had created two different sketches for the cake, each with three layers. One was roughly frosted—not quite 'naked,' but Ama definitely let the chocolate show through. The top of each layer was accented with sprigs of frosted rosemary, dappled chocolate shavings, mini chocolate pinecones, and crystal sugar sprinkles mixed with shards of candy glass in pale blue. 'Frozen Forest Floor,' she titled the busy sketch.

Number two was simpler, and, to Ama's mind, perfect for Nadia's vision: smooth white fondant, encircled by a flurry of delicate candy snowflakes of varying shapes and sizes. Some were made of delicate translucent candy glass; others of white chocolate or candy bark, dusted with edible glitter or lightly frosted with edible silver paint. They were affixed to a silvery wire frame, inserted in the bottom layer and spiraling up and around the cake until it reached the very top, where there was room for a delicate white chocolate snowflake and several decorative truffles.

"Ooh, pretty," said Tessa, leaning over Ama's shoulder. "I like it. I think Nadia will really like it, too. Even if Paula suggests we outfit it in twinkle lights with a pyrotechnic edge."

"I'm more worried about Cynthia's sniff when she points out the traditional bride and groom cake topper is absent," said Ama, suppressing a giggle. "But the important thing is, it works with Nadia's theme. I can even use a little pale blue metallic sheen to decorate a few of these edible snowflakes, if she so wishes."

She popped open the lid of the cake box on her desk. "Mini poinsettia cupcakes?" she offered. A row of tiny little cupcakes in silver foil wrappers were lined up inside it, each one decorated with a single green fondant leaf and a red marzipan poinsettia, with gold nonpareils for the center.

Tessa's hand dove into the box to claim one, taking a generous bite after peeling aside the foil. "Mmm, delicious," she declared. "And I missed breakfast. These vanilla cream ones are great, too. The exact flavor of yogurt I *should* have eaten instead." She licked a little of the cream filling from her lip. "Wait a minute," she said, pausing mid-bite. "You only bake mini cupcakes like this when you're depressed." She looked at the remains of the cupcake in her hand suspiciously. "Why are these here?"

An uneasy expression dimmed Ama's smile. "Well… I might sort of have this dilemma," she said, her sneaker nudging at the table's decorative foot—Ama's desk was an old kitchen worktable, scuffed and scarred and far more appropriate than the usual bland office desk. "I might have sort of… kind of… agreed to go out with Tamir a second time."

"What? The guy from the match site?" Tessa said. "But I thought you didn't like him. I thought the first date was horrible."

"It was. Truly. But—but he called looking for me. Twice. And when he finally reached my cell phone, he was just so polite I couldn't say no," she answered helplessly. "How do you tell somebody that your date with them was more boring than watching paint dry? Especially when they seemed like they were having a terrible time, too?"

"What about the motorcycle guy, though?" said Tessa.

Ama groaned. "Luke is perfect," she said. "Tess, he's funny, he's interesting, he's spontaneous…"

"He's *sooo* handsome," teased Tessa.

"That, too," said Ama. "He's this incredibly laid-back but passionate person. Everything I've been dreaming about when it comes to love—I really think he's the kind of person who could make it come true. He'd run away with me to places nobody has ever heard of… he'd kiss me under the stars, not caring if we were alone or everybody on the street was watching."

"Wow," said Tessa. "That sounds… pretty amazing."

"He definitely is," Ama agreed. "Which makes it kind of hard to believe he would pick me to spend time with. I mean, a guy like that would have lots of dating choices, right? Glamorous, exciting girls would probably go out with him. So maybe I'm reading too much into just one afternoon of conversation and baked goods."

"Yeah right," Tessa replied, rolling her eyes. "He's probably just spending time with you for the free pastries. Seriously though, Ama, don't talk yourself out of giving this a chance at least. Not if you want to experience that kissing in the street moment for real," she added with a knowing smile.

"Who's making out on the street?" Natalie appeared in the doorway, her tablet computer hugged against her chest.

"Nobody," said Ama. "Cupcake?"

"No, thanks. I'm the bearer of news right now," said Natalie. "Do you want the bad news first, or the worse news?"

Her two partners exchanged glances. "Now what?" Tessa said.

"Stillmeadow chapel? Booked through the entire month of December," said Natalie.

"Not Stillmeadow! I thought that would be impossible," said Tessa in shock. "It's a tiny little church with no reception hall!"

"Apparently, that was before they were featured in an article entitled 'Fifty Places to See Outside City Limits' in last month's *City Today*," said Natalie. "But it gets better. The sleigh and carriage rental company? Their horses are all under a veterinarian's care for some sort of equestrian virus—no harness time until spring, doctor's orders."

Tessa groaned. "You're kidding," she said. Gone was the rustic woodland chapel, the sleigh-style carriage in the hopefully snowy landscape pulled by a matching team of horses.

"Sorry. Wish I were," said Natalie. "But good news is, my cousin knows a guy who offers carriage rides in the park, whom he *thinks* has a sled stashed in his barn that he used to bring out to the park in winter."

"Work on it," said Tessa. "I definitely want to offer Nadia good news when we see her today." She noticed the computer in Natalie's grip. "Are you working on the dress design?" she asked.

"What do you think?" Natalie turned the screen around to face Tessa. "First thought—fabulous? Elegant?"

"Elsa from *Frozen*?" said Tessa.

Natalie released an exasperated sigh and lowered the sketch.

"No, wait—let me see it again," said Tessa quickly. "Maybe it will look different to me this time—"

"Forget it," said Natalie. "I'm still not envisioning something unique enough for Nadia's wedding, clearly. Back to the drawing board." She passed Blake in the hallway. "Free cupcakes," she informed him.

"I'll never say no to that," he answered. He paused before the open box on Ama's desk. "Okay if I take two?" he asked.

"Take them all," answered Ama gloomily. "What do I care?" Chin propped on both fists, she sighed and gazed at her wall board of creative bakery designs. Blake studied her quizzically as he lifted two mini cupcakes with one hand.

"Everything okay?" He glanced from Ama to Tessa as he asked.

"Fine," said Tessa. "Just a few minor issues with the wedding. You know, nothing that can't be fixed." She crossed her fingers behind her back.

"Not with the flowers, right?"

"Relax. I'm not going to ask you to be Stefan's assistant again," said Tessa. "Like you'd take orders from somebody you demoted to assistant-to-the-assistant in their own office, anyway." She reminded him of this with chagrin and a smile.

"Maybe I got a little carried away by the spirit of things," he replied, as he polished off cupcake number one. "Oh, by the way—about that transom in your closet—"

"Let me guess. You found hinges for it that only cost a hundred dollars apiece," said Tessa.

"No, that's not what I was going to say," answered Blake. "I wanted to offer to buy it."

"Buy it?" she echoed.

"Yeah. See, there's this door in need of replacing upstairs in the house I'm working on—it's way too rotten to save, which we didn't realize until we tried to adjust its frame, and discovered there was some damage from an old leak, which means we'll have to pull out part of the frame as well. So I was thinking—"

"This is the house you're working on right now?" said Tessa. "The historic district home?" She picked at a frosting crumb, which was melting to a sugary dot on Ama's table. "I thought you were almost done with it."

"So did I. But the door's gotta be replaced. A real shame, because we thought the whole house would be ready for Christmas, and now we'll have to tear out part of that bedroom's wall. The whole hall will be cordoned off for two weeks minimum." He pulled out his cell phone. "You should see the pictures from downstairs, though. It looks pristine, and Mac did a great job decorating it."

She had. Tessa looked at photos of the flawless powder blue paint in the dining room, the perfect arrangement of an antique love seat to one side, and an old sea captain's portrait framed on the wall perpendicular to the room's wide windows. Blake showed off the parlor with pride, where he and Mac had apparently struggled to move an incredibly heavy ornate sofa with green velvet cushions to face the doorway instead of the fireplace, for better aesthetic appeal. He showed the 'before' pictures of the house intermixed with them—patchy, dull paint, faded-out drapes in unappealing fabrics, the big velvet sofa looking like the victim of a gang of vicious wolfhounds with its worn fabric and leaky stuffing.

"This Mac is a miracle worker," said Ama, looking at the photos. "Which decorating firm does he work for?"

Blake didn't have to answer, because Mac appeared in the flesh now. "Hello, hello," she said, tapping on the doorframe. "I was pretty sure that was your baritone I recognized from downstairs, Blake, so I knew this must be the right place."

"Hey, Mac," said Blake. "Tess, Ama, this is Mac—Tessa, you've met before, obviously. Mac, these are the clients I told you about, who own the building."

"Oh, right. The wedding planners," said Mac. "Blake's told me a lot about you. And a lot about this building, which I can see is definitely impressive, even if it's a little rough."

A little rough? Tessa bristled, even though it was perfectly true. "I like to think of it as characterful, actually." She tossed her head slightly. Ama was giving her a strange look, but she ignored it.

"A little character goes a long way, right?" said Mac, laughing. "Those stairs—those are totally incongruous with the rest of the building. When did they put those in, the thirties maybe?" She was talking to Blake now.

"I'm guessing sometime in the forties," he said. "I found an old notice about the place being converted into some kind of artist's studio after the original store it housed had closed, so I figure somebody got artsy with the redecorating, or else bought the stairs off an old mansion after the original ones started to get creaky."

"But that molding above the upstairs windows is still original, isn't it?"

"It is in these rooms, but not in the hall. I had to replace it above the big window."

"A perfect match, though," said Mac, sounding impressed. "Blake is *such* a genius when it comes to wood," she informed them. "Isn't it incredible what he comes up with when there's a little problem on the job? Did he tell you about the plan to fix the upstairs bedroom?"

"He did," said Tessa. "Sounds like the two of you will be busy for several more weeks." No doubt Mac would appreciate his strong muscles when it came to moving heavy furniture. She noted the decorator had asked the contractor for help instead of the big, burly crewmembers who had been toting around the scaffolding the day she was there.

"Lucky me, having to work with this guy two more weeks, right?" joked Mac. "But that brings me to the reason why I tracked you down, Blake. I wanted you to see the photos of the downstairs, now that we finished decorating it last night."

"You didn't have to come all the way downtown, though," said Blake. "You could have texted them and saved yourself the trouble."

"I know, but I wanted to see your reaction firsthand," said Mac, as she pulled up the images on her phone.

"Wow," said Blake. "Tessa, Ama, look at these."

Fir trees dripping with authentic Victorian ornaments—paper cones, lace, and ribbons, with fake LED candles lit on all the branches. Shiny Christmas balls, tiny wax and hand-painted celluloid figures hanging from branches; big garlands of seasonal greenery decking the halls from the banister to the dining room's big white mantel, with nuts heaped artistically in silver bowls, and a trinity of pomegranates, oranges, and apples piled on antique serving platters.

Yep, it definitely couldn't be any more perfect. But at this moment, Tessa felt that perfection might be a tiny bit overrated. There should be at least one or two flaws in every so-called 'perfect' project, right? A pomegranate or two that wouldn't stay in the fruit pyramid… maybe a sagging battery-operated candle or two on those tree branches, held in place by wonky clips? How *did* she get them all to stand so infuriatingly upright?

"I'm having the outdoor garlands delivered today, so I have to run," said Mac. "I have an interview with the new bed and breakfast on Fifth. Wish me luck." She tucked her cell phone in her bag.

"Break a leg," said Blake.

Mac paused before Tessa. "I really do think your building has potential," she said. "If you want some help while restoring it, please give me a call. I gave you my card, didn't I?"

"You did," said Tessa. "It's in a safe place." At the bottom of the drawer where Tessa tended to pile paid bills and junk mail, actually.

"Call me up sometime. I can give you an estimate. I have connections to some of the best restoration fabric warehouses and wall decor people in the business. That big room down the hall, the master bedroom with the dressing room? I could find a sample of its original wallpaper and completely cover that modern blue paint."

She was talking about Tessa's office, maligning the 'Romantic Blue' she had personally selected. "Thanks, but we're really not in the market for a decorator," said Tessa.

"Still… you never know when you might change your mind," said Mac with a smile. She was on her way out now, almost bumping into Natalie in the hallway. Who, Tessa realized, had been standing there for several minutes, watching them all.

"So that's the famous Mac," Natalie said to Blake. "How long have you two worked together again?"

"Six or seven jobs. I've lost count," said Blake. He stole another cupcake from the box. "Mmm, these are really good," he said to Ama. "Let's see… first job with Mac was the house on Dillard Street… then the old city meeting house…"

"She seems like fun," said Natalie.

"She is," said Blake. "She takes her work seriously, but not herself seriously, if you know what I mean." He tossed the foil wrapper in the trash can.

"You should think about Mac's offer," he said to Tessa. "She could do wonders for that little room downstairs I've been working on. You wouldn't believe it afterwards; it would blow your mind when you see it come together. I could get you a pretty sweet discount," he hinted. "The kind only friends get."

"Thanks, but… I think we'll just stick to the original plan for the room for now," said Tessa. "You know, bargain paint and a set of drapes. Not that I don't appreciate the offer. From her or from you," she added hastily. "It's just she might be a little too… what's the word…?"

"Pricey?" suggested Ama.

"I was thinking 'perfectionist,'" said Tessa. "For our tastes, anyway."

"Look, she's not a stickler for the historic thing when a building's not becoming a showcase," said Blake. "She'll show you modern paint colors, modern upholstery fabrics that have a limited print and weave availability—basically, anything you want in a style she can help harmonize with your space."

She sounded brilliant. Tessa pictured Mac transforming this building into a magazine showcase, hovering close by Blake's shoulder as they studied catalogs of hardware, molding, and the ornate decorative touches that Tessa had routinely nixed for pocketbook reasons… Blake's muscles steeling as he lifted that heavy bookshelf away from the wall for the decorator…

"I have my heart set on the paint color already," said Tessa. "We're good."

"Even with a steep discount?" said Blake.

"Even with a discount. Strangely enough, I am unmoved," said Tessa. Her smile was becoming artificial, because being sincere about her feelings on this subject would endanger her working relationship with Blake. Maybe it was because the decorator had insulted her personal taste, she decided. Had Mac, an interior designer, no appreciation for a color as pretty as 'Romantic Blue'—for personal touches that made a room unique, like a chintz chair with striped pillows? So what if it was free-spirited, totally out of character with the building's origins, and maybe a *little* kooky with regards to the modern wall mural in Natalie's office…?

"Come on, Tessa," he coaxed. "You know you want to see that room at its best, don't you?"

"Oops, there's my phone," she said as it rang. "Nadia. Can't miss this call, since today's the day for the big floral unveiling and the cake tasting." She answered it as she escaped from Ama's office.

Accented Creations had submitted the final floral design for Nadia and Lyle's wedding. White tulips, paperwhites, glittered rosemary sprigs, and miniature powder blue bells in frosty, embossed ice vases formed the table bouquets. In between the flowers, votive vases made of ice with tiny LED candles flickering inside, with a shallow silver basin beneath each.

The biggest arrangement was destined for the altar, then the center of the wedding party's table, with smaller ones for either end, and for the guest tables in the dining room. The icy branch floral arrangement would adorn the cake and dessert table, with frosted evergreen boughs for the windows and doorways of both the restaurant's dining room and the site of the ceremony.

As for Nadia's bouquet, it was perfect: white tulips, white bud roses, and paperwhites, wrapped in white satin and trimmed with a pale blue and silver ribbon at the head of the stems. Nadia's bridesmaids had miniature versions of the same, only without the tulips. The florist was 'over the moon with the results,' as Stefan Groeder's false assistant was informed via an email to *his* false assistant.

So was Nadia, when she saw the pictures that afternoon. "It's so beautiful," she breathed. "I cannot wait. Does Natalie have a sketch for my dress, by the way?" she asked. "I was really hoping it would be finished soon. I'm kind of eager to actually see the fabric become my gown."

The replacement fabric, of course. But that brought to mind other replacements that Tessa had not quite found a good moment to discuss. "She's very close," said Tessa reassuringly. "By the way, there's been a little issue with the church, but I think we have something very promising in mind to take its place."

At first, Nadia was disappointed by the loss of Stillmeadow, but when she saw the photos of the replacement Tessa had chosen, it left her more breathless than the bouquet. From a list of small scenic churches in a fifty-mile radius, Tessa had located a newly built chapel constructed from insulated, reinforced glass, which was nestled in a wooded glen on the outskirts of the city. The closest thing to an ice castle in this part of the world, Ama had laughed—and with a perfect view of snowy oaks and evergreens, if only the weather would favor them with a surprise pre-Christmas snow in time for the wedding.

"Look at it, Lyle," said the bride, nudging his shoulder as he busily texted someone on his phone. "Imagine us inside on our wedding day. There's the altar, and the pews are gorgeous blond wood. Don't you love it?"

"Sure. It's nice," said Lyle, glancing at it briefly. "I mean, it goes with the white Christmas thing, right?"

"It's not 'white Christmas,'" corrected Nadia. "It's 'winter white.' Lyle, please. We've been over this, like, a thousand times. Are you not listening to me on purpose, or is the latest shipment of yogurt *so* engrossing that you can't remember anything else?"

"I'm listening. I swear. It's just that Ma's better at it," said Lyle.

"Don't you think this is a little too modern?" said Cynthia.

"Mom," said Nadia. Warningly.

"I'll finalize the details and have the invitations printed," said Tessa, making a note in her planning folder. "This is the biggest step in our process, and the only detail besides the cake that we really had left to resolve before your big day." She omitted mention of Natalie's struggle to finish the perfect dress.

"Which invitations are the ones you're sending?" said Cynthia. "Not the gaudy ones with the gold dove at the top, I hope."

Only one of the mothers was present today for the cake tasting. Ama had supplied four slices of each flavor she wanted them to choose from, so Tessa took the extra one—to be sociable, she told herself. First up was the white chocolate with a delicate vanilla cream mousse.

"I think this one is really special," said Ama. "The toasted coconut for the filling is optional, obviously, since a lot of guests don't like it. But this is something a little different from the traditional vanilla choice for a bridal cake."

"It's delicious," said Nadia. "What do you think, Lyle?"

"Not a cake person, remember?" he said. "I'm a baklava guy."

"We could make a baklava-inspired filling for the cake," suggested Ama. "What do you think?"

"I think it would be great, if it's possible," said Nadia. "Can you?"

"It's just nuts, honey, and a few spices," said Ama. "I'll tweak the flavors to balance with the white chocolate's sweetness. Or, if you choose vanilla, I can add a hint of cinnamon to the cake."

"I think the whole idea of it is odd," said Cynthia. "Vanilla itself is so traditional and elegant. I worry what guests will think about something so unconventional as extra spices and honey thrown in, of all flavors."

"You worry about everything," said Nadia. "Please, try to get over it. Lyle and I aren't trying to recreate the classic weddings of the past. We're creating our own traditions." She hugged Lyle's arm. "If he wants baklava filling, that's what we'll have."

"Vanilla's okay, too," said Lyle. Cynthia gave her daughter a look that said *see?* without actually speaking. Nadia wilted, then bristled.

Hastily, Tessa cleared her throat. "I think this flavor for the groom's cake is a winner," she said, smiling as she accepted a plate of Ama's dark chocolate special. "It's rich and warm and really offsets the sweetness of the white chocolate, don't you think?"

"I love dark chocolate," said Nadia. "What's the filling?"

"It's a dark chocolate mousse blended with crushed pecans and caramel," said Ama. "But I could make something baklava-inspired for it too."

"Let's try the vanilla," coaxed Cynthia. "Now, tell me—can you put traditional roses on it, instead of this unusual pointy little snowflake thing that looks like a music staff bent out of shape?"

"*Mother*," said Nadia, with partly checked fury at this insult.

"I can," Ama answered hesitantly. "But I really think the snowflakes will impress you when you see the actual cake decoration finished. It's completely edible except for the wire frame."

"What happened to the bride and groom for the top?" said Cynthia. "Didn't you get that picture I emailed you, Nadia? Of the one I saw in the bridal shop by the dry cleaner's?"

"Yes, I did, and I wasn't interested," said Nadia. "I want something different."

"I thought we were getting those shards of ice thingies," commented Lyle, who took a single bite of the groom's cake, then sneaked a glance out the window. "What happened to them? Those were kind of different."

"You and your mom didn't like the ice cake. Remember?" said Nadia, whose tone was taking on a slight edge now.

Lyle looked clueless. "Really?" he said. He shrugged. "I guess it doesn't matter, does it? Put ice on top, a big snowflake. Put the bride and groom too." He laughed. "People would definitely remember that cake topper, I'll bet."

"But not in a good way, Lyle dear," said Cynthia.

"I think Ma also saw a picture of a cute cake topper somewhere," said Lyle thoughtfully.

Tessa had seen it via email also, and it was not an option. A bride in a short white dress and fur-trimmed go-go boots hoisted a helpless, hog-tied groom in a tuxedo into her arms. It sent the wrong message in so many ways, and would definitely seem insulting to Nadia—and as for the other one, of the cartoonish Eskimo couple with the igloo and the penguin in a bow tie, all three members of the wedding planning team had vetoed it as a possibility.

Nadia pushed back her chair. "I need to talk to you," she said to Lyle. "Alone. For a moment." She waited for him to shove his phone into his pocket and lay aside his cake fork.

"Now?" he said. "Sure. Okay." They rose and left Cynthia at the table, who was tasting the vanilla slice with enthusiasm.

"Cinnamon would completely ruin the flavor," she assured Ama, who was trying not to look hurt regarding the previous comments about her work. "What else is Nadia supposed to discuss with you today?" she continued to Tessa. "I certainly hope it's not a conversation pushing that see-through chapel on her."

"Actually, we need to discuss the catering menu," said Tessa. "I've received the menu and the plate options to be listed in the invitations from Lyle, but I had a few thoughts about the dessert table. Namely, about an all-white buffet surrounding the cake, and some appetizers for serving before dinner."

The ice swan would be filled with pastel-shaded frozen sorbet balls in coconut, peppermint, and vanilla, while miniature vanilla cupcakes adorned with white fondant poinsettias would be presented to one side, along with 'winter white' truffles coated in confectioner's sugar or white chocolate. A white vegetable platter with tzatziki dip would circulate before dinner—a perfect complement to the Greek skewers and the marinated chicken being offered as the dinner's main dish choices for guests.

Tessa had planned it out perfectly, and was ready to send estimates on cost and inventory to Lyle's staff, but only after the bride and groom approved it, of course. Comments from Cynthia on this menu wouldn't be helpful in the least, Tessa sensed.

Nadia and Lyle's discussion had now reached earshot levels from the hall outside the parlor. "—but I need you to support me, Lyle," Nadia was saying. "Don't just parrot back what you think I want to hear."

"She's your mom, Nadia. I'm not going to tell her she's wrong to her face," said Lyle.

"But that's what I need from you," Nadia insisted. "This problem is on both sides of the fence for me."

"Wait… Ma's just trying to help out," said Lyle. "I don't get why it's such a problem, getting all these free suggestions. You don't have to pick any of them."

"But *I* have to be the bad guy who tells them their idea isn't going to be part of our wedding," said Nadia.

"Ama, don't you have some sample truffles we can try?" said Tessa brightly.

"As it happens, I do," said the baker, quickly pulling a white confectioner's box from beneath the rolling kitchen cart. "I confess I didn't actually make these ones—they're from a friend of mine who works at a candy shop and does *amazing* things with white chocolate."

"*More* white chocolate?" said Cynthia.

The two business partners exchanged glances.

The bride and groom returned—but not together, Tessa noticed. Lyle poked disinterestedly at his slice of vanilla cake, looking confused and hurt. Nadia was trying hard not to scowl.

"Nadia, you really should give this vanilla a chance," said Cynthia. "I'm sure that little white roses would look very Christmassy or wintery, or however it is you want it. After all, they are in the bouquet you chose."

"But I wanted the sticks covered in ice. Remember?" said Nadia frostily. "And I don't want vanilla with roses. In fact, I want something completely new. I want a coconut cream cake because *that* is my favorite flavor of cake. Ever. And with a coconut filling."

Her mother's eyes widened. "But you can't really be serious, honey—" she began.

"Why can't I? It's my wedding, isn't it?" said Nadia, her voice rising. "And Lyle doesn't object, does he? If he does, he can tell me right now. Tell me that he wants baklava filling and cinnamon vanilla."

"Sweetheart," began Lyle, looking totally baffled now.

"Then coconut it is," said Nadia, crossing her arms.

"Well, this will be a disaster," said Cynthia unhappily. "Stop being childish, Nadia."

"I don't think it's childish to choose my favorite," said Nadia. "It's *my* wedding, as Lyle says."

"Ma's allergic to coconut, though," pointed out Lyle.

"See?" This time, Cynthia's triumph was verbal.

"Fine," Nadia snapped. "Vanilla and baklava filling it is." Before her mother could object, she silenced her with a single glance. There was something dangerous in the bride's eye, the two uneasy planners noticed, although it escaped Lyle's consciousness. He was picking the nuts from the groom's cake filling and popping them in his mouth.

"Speaking of allergies, we had better omit the nuts from at least one cake flavor," said Ama, reaching for her notepad. "Just in case any more of your guests have an issue with certain ingredients."

"Let's move on to the subject of the hors d'oeuvres and chocolate truffles," suggested Tessa.

Chapter Seventeen

"Are you comfortable?" asked Tamir. "Do you want some popcorn or something?"

"No," said Ama. "I'm fine." She settled into her seat as the lights dimmed, tossing her cardigan and shoulder bag over the empty one beside her.

Date two was a Bollywood movie night, at the theater Tamir had told her about on their first date. The posters outside were in Hindi, featuring—Ama guessed—a film about a father with too many daughters and not enough suitable men with whom to match them.

Thank heavens it wasn't a Punjabi film.

Why had he asked her out again? Ama asked herself this question more than she asked herself why she said yes instead of politely telling him the truth. Niceness had its limits, and she was sure that Tamir had reached his after the dull conversation they had shared over curry. She had never imagined that he was actually serious about seeing her again, especially not for an Indian film, given her lack of knowledge about them.

The film was a musical comedy about a stingy patriarch and his family, filled with Gujju stereotypes, and, as Ama feared, at least one wedding in the mix. Beside her, Tamir was doing a better job of following the story than she was—of course, having grown up in India for part of his childhood, this all made sense to him in a way it didn't to her, except through stories and offhand comments by her parents.

"My mom loves this movie," he said to her. "It's her favorite, even though it's so—" He hesitated at the end of this sentence, and Ama realized he might have been going to say 'tacky,' then stopped himself. Thinking, perhaps, that it bore a slight resemblance to Ama's own family, with the loud and overemotional characters.

Tamir blushed; Ama's face reddened, both at his embarrassment and her own. Tamir cleared his throat. "My mother really does like crazy comedies," he said.

I'll bet she does. Ama reached into her bag and pulled out a spicy snack mix from the Indian grocery in the neighborhood. "Have some?" she asked Tamir, after opening its crinkly cellophane top.

He glanced at it. "No, thanks," he said. "I'm not really fond of the mild ones."

"It's not just *masala*," she said. "There's hot peppers and ginger in the seasoning."

He shrugged. "I'm just not a fan," he answered.

Ama munched in silence after this—as silent as you can be while eating crunchy nuts and puffed rice in a movie theater. She studied the other patrons in the dark as her mind wandered away from a dance number devoted to the son's courtship. This place was nearly empty on a weeknight, except for a couple in traditional Indian dress near the front row, and three giggling teens seated to her far left. This would be a great place for a criminal rendezvous Monday through Thursday, Ama thought. Nobody would be around to overhear your secrets.

"Does your mom watch Punjabi films only?" asked Tamir.

"I don't know," said Ama. "I don't think so. She likes romance movies the best but she watches action ones too. A couple weeks ago she was watching one with my Aunt Bendi. The hero drove a car that leapt over an elephant pen or something like that."

Tamir chuckled. "Sounds like a Telugu movie," he said. "Those are so crazy, you have to laugh."

Ama wished she could remember finding the movie funny. Then again, she had probably been reading a cookbook while watching it.

Onscreen, the stingy Gujju patriarch was tossing a servant out of the house for some minor offense. A few patrons near the back of the theater, unseen by Ama until now, were chuckling at the servant's comic relief role. Someone in the film tumbled into a courtyard cistern.

"What's supposed to be going on?" she whispered to Tamir.

"They just received word that a cousin brought shame to the family by getting conned out of the family fortune," said Tamir. "This is how he always reacts to bad news." He smiled faintly as he shook his head.

"But what happened to the son and the wedding?" Her mind must have wandered during the engagement scene—the last she had seen, a lot of aunties were dancing following the couple's announcement.

"Oh, that's been called off. Why did you think his mother was crying so hard in that last scene?"

"She was crying?"

From the look Tamir gave her, she realized she had been paying way too little attention to the story, since this was a big moment in the film, it would seem. "Sorry," she said. "I have trouble following classic Bollywood storylines sometimes."

"I thought you said you just hadn't seen that many," said Tamir. "But you had seen some."

"I guess what I was actually trying to say is I'm not a really big fan of them," confessed Ama. "Just a few here and there, like the ones I mentioned at dinner."

"Oh." Tamir accepted this with evident disappointment. "Do you want to leave?"

Leave and do—what? Sit awkwardly in front of coffee cups in a nearby shop? Visit a vegetarian grocery store and look at their selection of super-spicy snacks? Discuss names for the children they would definitely never have? Ama racked her brain for possibilities, and every suggestion that presented itself seemed worse than staying at the theater.

"That's okay," she said. "I'll grasp the plot if I just see a little more of it, probably."

Tamir settled back in his seat, although he still looked doubtful regarding this outcome. Ama dug her fingers into her snack mix and popped some more rice into her mouth. Another cluster of viewers, including a smartly dressed couple in the third row, turned their heads her way, their body language expressing disapproval for the crinkle and crunch from behind them. Even Tamir looked slightly annoyed by the noise from Ama's snack bag.

"Sorry," she mumbled. She repressed a sigh as she tied it closed again—with another disapproving glance from the front row—and tucked it back in her bag.

❊

"Look at this. This moment was hilarious, Nat." Cal skipped backwards on the video he had taken of the December fashion revue, which was now playing on Natalie's television. "Truly, Sandusky *must* have Kandace moonlighting with him part-time to create anything that ugly."

The model paraded down the runway in a military grunge look gone wrong—as if the bottom half of the jacket and pants had been fed through a leaf shredder, while the cap appeared burned by a chemical fire. Natalie stifled a snort of humor as the designer's next model appeared in a ghetto-fierce mix of eighties stone wash and spray paint.

Laughing at the weird fashions onscreen had caused Natalie to miss a stitch in the gown she was sewing—since it was Nadia's wedding dress, she quickly amended the mistake. Concentrating on the satin piled on her lap and the sketch propped as a reminder on her side table caused her to miss the next designer's line on parade, which Cal assured her was far more chic.

"That dress will be fabulous," said Cal, who admired Natalie's sketch of the bridal gown. "You know, you should really launch your own line someday. Your clothes could be a runway sensation in a show like this one. If even Kandace can actually sell garments after one of these events, just think what your designs would do—the crowd would mob you for orders, probably."

"Please." Natalie rolled her eyes. "When would I have time to meet those demands? If the wedding boutique stays in business, I'll have my hands full with bridal gowns alone. Which should be enough to make me happy, right?"

"But if you had your own *studio*, you'd probably have assistants," hinted Cal. "I know a really talented tailor who's totally ready to leave his boss for someone new. He works for cheap and he's pretty talented. If I do say so myself."

"Keep reminding me," said Natalie archly, as she hid her smile. "I'd have to be pretty successful to actually pay you or anybody else for their work. What if the line's a complete bust? What if my label fails completely?"

"What if a meteor hits the earth and we all die?" retorted Cal. "Those are excuses, Natalie. I think you have the talent, and you're just stalling."

"Whatever." She mumbled this through a mouthful of pins as she tucked the pleated ruches along the dress's bodice. Across from her, Cal shook out his garment in progress for display, a bell-shaped billow of slick orange fabric festooned with many heavy zippers.

"What do you think?" he said. "Is it totally chic, or what?"

Natalie almost burst out laughing. "What is it supposed to be?" she asked.

"It's the urban poncho," said Cal. "At least, that's what Kandace is calling it. *I'm* calling it 'camping tent couture.' The sleeves zipper off to turn the whole thing into a hideous orange vinyl cape, by the way."

Natalie was laughing so hard that she lost her grip on her pincushion, which bounced away across the floor. "Is she *actually* planning to market this?" she asked when she recovered her breath. "Does it double as shelter if you get lost in the wilderness?"

"I think her next line should be devoted to survival gear," said Cal, as he pulled some pins from what Natalie had mistaken for a hood, but was actually an oversized collar with pointy corners. "We'll sew sleeping bag trousers, glitter some rain boots—"

"—knit mittens from fiberglass for some *real* edge in her couture," supplied Natalie.

She and Cal both laughed at these ideas. "I miss working with you, Natalie," he said with a sigh. "It's just not as fun… or as bearable… to work with Kandace now that you're gone."

"I miss you, too," she answered. "Really I do." As much as she loved Tessa—and Ama too after only a few months of knowing her—it wasn't quite the same. There was certainly creative diversity and plenty of inspiration, but no one with whom she could talk about the complexities of couture fashion with complete understanding.

Her own fashion line. So what if it might fail? So what if no one bought her clothes after a big fashion launch? Nobody bought her clothes now, after all. It was true that her home closet was just a giant storage container for formal dresses, trouser suits, chic blouses, and everything in between that her sketches had captured. If she took a risk, and it worked out—if she were Kandace, only with skills and wearable garments, not just a reputation as an edgy visionary...

✻

She had draped Nadia's half-finished dress over a dressmaker's mannequin in her living room that night; now she was studying it in the late morning light as she perched on the back of her sofa. Imagining a faceted sequin here, a glimmering crystal there, and something more, something to make this dress worthy of Nadia's secret dreams for her bridal gown.

"Are you ready to go?" Chad appeared from the kitchen. "I packed some power bars, some energy drinks, and a guide about some of the city's best climbing spots, in case we want to plan our next outing when we're taking a break."

He had arrived bright and early for today's rock climbing date—or was it more like rappelling? She wasn't savvy enough about the sport to know all the technical terms the way Chad did, especially since she had a habit of tuning out some of his more involved jargon about the sport. If it wasn't for his apparent attention when it came to a mention of her interests, he might've seemed just a *teeny* bit obsessed with the subject in Natalie's book.

"Sounds great," she told him, as she finished lacing up her shoes. "I think I left my hoodie in the kitchen. Grab it for me, will you? And the trail mix bag by the fridge."

"Trail mix. How very health conscious of you," he teased. "You remembered I'm filling up on fruit-based antibodies before my next big climb in Baños, huh?" He disappeared toward the kitchen, hoisting his old rucksack higher on his shoulder. It was one that had seen him through most of his last climbing tour in South America, as Natalie understood from another story he'd told over their first dinner together.

Her coffee table was still cluttered with fashion articles Cal had brought over yesterday, along with his recording of the fashion revue. Kandace was quoted in one, talking about the 'horrible pedestrian taste' exhibited by the city's topmost retail designer. Natalie was considering having it framed for her workspace wall when a knock on the door interrupted her thoughts.

"Ma, what are you doing here?" Her mother was outside, holding a Tupperware container in both hands.

"I'm dropping off some cannoli because I love you and I missed your birthday." Maria kissed her on the cheek, and deposited the plastic food container on top of a runway model's photo. "Heard you had some nice chocolate cake, however, so my being gone wasn't a total loss."

"Ma," began Natalie, trying to sound patient.

"You don't have a Christmas tree? How many times have I told you to take the little one from the basement?" said Maria. "You loved it as a kid. It's just gathering dust down there and the box of ornaments is right next to it. You could come by for it today. Rob would help you dig it out and bring it over."

"Now's not a good time. I'm just going out, I've got plans."

"So what? Don't let me stop you just because I brought by some food," said Maria. "It's cold for walking, so take a coat. You're not wearing just that thin jacket, are you? And are you going out alone?

You know how dangerous those trails in the park can be, so take something for defense."

"You know I'm not going alone," said Natalie, who smelled a setup with regards to this visit, and how long her mother was lingering here with food in hand. The pastries were a ruse, a pretense. How had Rob known that she and Chad were going rock climbing? He wasn't her friend on social media, and never listened to anything she actually told him on purpose.

"There's the guy who's taking up my daughter's time these days," said Maria, as Chad reappeared with the requested supplies. "Chas, am I right?"

"Chad," he answered. "Nice to see you again, Mrs. Grenaldi."

"Why be so formal? Call me Maria," she said. "You're dating my daughter, after all. At least, I think you're dating my daughter—who's to know these days, since everybody's so casual about relationships."

"I'm definitely dating your daughter." Chad draped his arm around Natalie with a smile. "She's a really great person."

"I always thought so," said Maria. "I was hoping somebody would notice." She and Chad laughed at this joke, but Natalie did not. Her mother's expectant attitude always bothered her when it was directed at a guy she was dating. As if Chad was supposed to state his intentions up front, and list his prospects as a possible son-in-law.

"You two have a nice outing planned?" inquired Maria.

"Yeah, I thought we'd take in the sights along the new trail that just opened upstate," supplied Chad, glancing at Natalie as he spoke. "There's a great spot for rappelling down to see the natural falls."

"A waterfall in winter?" said Maria. "That's one I haven't heard before."

Not that she would ever admit it in front of her mother, but this wouldn't have been Natalie's first choice of activity on a cold day like this.

"That's one of the best times to see it," said Chad. "Winter brings you so close to nature, the silence and the raw elements really grip you in a stark environment."

Natalie hoped her jacket was insulated against the cold breeze. Chad was wearing some thermal parka thing lined with down that he had bought for a trip in the Canadian Rockies.

"Then there's a great Brazilian cafe near my yoga class's studio," continued Chad. "It's on our route back from the park so I thought we'd check it out afterwards."

At least the coffee might warm her up, Natalie thought. Then maybe she and Chad could talk about making their next outing to a little more winter-friendly place—like visiting an art gallery or taking in a movie, for instance.

"Sounds very active," Maria replied politely. "But that's what people do these days, right? Stay fit?"

"Here, Ma, let me put the cannoli in my dessert keep and give you back your container," said Natalie, who made short work of dumping the cream-filled rolls onto the cake plate in her kitchen, beneath a glass dome. "I'll just be ready in a few minutes," she told Chad, as she returned with the empty Tupperware. "Why don't you find the guide to the park that you left here last time?"

"Sure thing." He deposited his backpack on the sofa and went in search of the guide.

"What are you doing?" Maria asked Natalie. "I'm your mother, not a criminal. You don't have to act like you're trying to get rid of me."

"Ma, I just don't want Chad to be uncomfortable," she answered quietly. "Family members asking questions—it's a little too much too soon."

"So until you and he are serious, what are you going to do? Make us all hide in the closet if he comes by while we're here? Will you and he eat in separate rooms from the rest of us at holiday dinners?"

"No," said Natalie scornfully, as she rolled her eyes. "But those are things we don't have to worry about, because this is not a serious thing. Stop worrying about it—and stop trying to meet my boyfriends, all right? When it's serious, you'll know."

"Will I?" asked Maria sarcastically. "It seems to me that you don't know a lot about seriousness and relationships. How would you know it when you saw it?"

"Listen, I really wish you wouldn't spy on me." Natalie lowered her voice, glancing once to make sure that Chad wasn't suddenly about to reappear from the kitchen.

"I'm not spying on you!" protested Maria—but keeping her voice low, Natalie noticed, in order to ensure that she wouldn't cause a scene that would shut conversation with Natalie down completely.

"Yes, you are," Natalie said. "I'm closing in on thirty in a few years, Ma. I'm mature enough to know that my mother does not bring me baked goods without an agenda behind them."

"There's no agenda—"

"Ma."

"—except maybe a little bit of concern for my baby," said Maria. "You keep dating a string of strangers whom I never get to meet and might be the next Jack the Ripper for all I know—"

"Chad is not a serial killer. He's a rock climber," said Natalie. "And a... shoe salesman," she added, for lack of the more specific nuances of marketing sports footwear.

"I'm not talking about just him," said Maria. "Everything's such a secret with you when it comes to love. Everything's so loose, like untied shoelaces. Do you know if you'd like this boy's family? If you like his friends, even?"

"I don't have to, because that's not what I'm looking for," stated Natalie flatly. "What do you want from me, Ma? I'm happy, healthy, and employed, and that's enough for most mothers. Plus, you actually got to meet one of my boyfriends for a change, which I figured would make you happy." It had only piqued her family's curiosity, evidently, which was the reason for this cannoli delivery to her place.

"All right, sue me. So I wish you were dating a nice, marriageable guy," said Maria—still keeping her voice soft so Chad wouldn't hear, Natalie noticed.

Why did Maria always have to assume that just because a guy wasn't interested in marriage he was a creep or a loser? "Why isn't Chad a nice guy?" Natalie asked defensively.

"I mean somebody a little more mature," said Maria. "A guy more sensible, like Brayden."

"*Brayden?*" The snort of contempt and disbelief from Natalie's throat had no effect on Maria.

"Why not? Someone who's a decent, honest boy who likes your family and puts up gracefully with *you* when you're acting like a spoiled princess," said Maria bluntly. "You need someone to love you as much as I do, so they look past your thorns to the rose behind them. That takes a man who's either honest enough to throw it back in your face or tactful enough to bury the hatchet and move on."

"My *thorns?*" echoed Natalie, one eyebrow arched. "I'm sorry, but are we talking about my personality here?" She'd be offended, but she had heard this before—less nicely—from friends and family.

"I mean that blunt honesty of yours, the way you find people's weak points and needle them right there." Maria clearly had a mental list of Natalie's faults on hand. "Those are things half the guys you date probably couldn't handle. Does this guy you're dating know what you're like after a long day at the beach?"

Natalie rolled her eyes. "I've only been out with him three times. What do you think?" Maria had referenced one of Natalie's worst bugbears: hot afternoons and sunburn. "But it's not serious enough to worry about whether he'll love me when I'm red all over and savage the whole car ride home."

"Not that you'd either apologize or look for a guy who would put up with it, knowing you," added Maria archly.

That might be true, but Natalie was still stuck between an image of herself actually dating Brayden—Brayden, who probably envisioned a special date night at a local sit-down chain restaurant where they turned off the sports channel at 8 p.m.—and the image of Chad with a fake smile plastered on his face at one of her family's dinners, with a look of despair frozen deep in his eyes when her uncle asserted that sugar-free desserts were killing the population compared to full-fat gelato.

Surely her mom didn't actually think she should date someone like Brayden, did she? Someone who might as well be trapped in the victimhood department of saintly patience without having someone like her in their life full time? And as for her being trapped with him—

"Could you make an effort to stay out of my business?" Natalie asked in hushed tones. "For Chad's sake, if not for mine? I'd prefer for the guys I date *not* to know my family's opinion of them." A little of her sarcasm had come back now. "Now, if you don't mind, I have plans?" she hinted.

"Did I say that this Chad wasn't a nice guy?" began Maria. "Did I *say* that, Natalie?"

"There are customers in need of biscotti, Ma, more than your daughter is in need of an opinion on her love life."

Natalie's mother looked as if she had a reply ready for this one, but by now, Chad had returned with his guidebook. "I guess that's the last piece of gear we need," he declared.

"I should go," said Maria. "Nice to see you again, Chad. Don't be a stranger." She waved to him as she accepted her container from Natalie, who gave her mother a warning look.

"Sure thing, Maria," he answered.

"Bye, Ma. Thanks for stopping over." Natalie decided it would not be safe to go downstairs for at least ten minutes.

"If he's not serious in the end, you know that your cousin Janelle knows a very nice podiatrist—" began Maria in a quiet voice, before the door to Natalie's apartment had completely closed between her and her daughter.

"Are you expecting anybody else?" Chad asked. "Your brother or your uncle?"

"No. Relax. That was a very rare drop-in visit by one of my family members," lied Natalie. "She missed my birthday, after all. Mother's guilt."

"Then we're ready to go," said Chad.

"Ready," said Natalie. Although... for a few hours descending a cliff wall in the winter's cold? All to see a waterfall which, in reality, was more like a tiny spring guzzling out of a rock wall, if the picture in the park's guide was any kind of accurate representation?

Then again, Chad was attractive, smooth, a skilled conversationalist, and seemed fine with a no-strings-attached dating experience. Those were the best and most important parts of her relationship with him, and the ones Natalie chose as her focus during this particular outing. Besides, she could always look forward to maybe learning new and surprising facets of his personality as they shared a fine Brazilian blend of coffee afterwards. When he wasn't caught up in a long story about some climbing experience, Chad sometimes related interesting encounters he'd had with local culture. And when he'd showed her some rock climbing moves yesterday on his apartment's home-made climbing wall, she discovered that the activity had certain body-toning capabilities.

"There were fashion photos on your apartment table," he commented at the intersection light. "Are you working on a new line of clothes?"

"No. A friend brought some photos by of the latest fashion show in the city," said Natalie. "Keeping me abreast of what's been happening since I quit Kandace's team."

She thought he might ask her next about the dress in her apartment—if it was part of something new, or what inspired the bodice and the neckline. Instead, he asked, "Have you ever thought about using South America as inspiration?"

"South America?" she said.

"There are some really great ethnic fabrics that would make your fashions really unique," said Chad. "I have a friend who makes Ecuadorian jewelry. Maybe you could partner together for a market booth or an artisan fair. You create the fashion, she supplies the accessories."

"My knowledge of South America is kind of slim, though," said Natalie. "I had a couple of friends in school who were Colombian, and what they told me is the limit of my knowledge."

"Or Asia," said Chad, who was noticing the tiger on the restaurant sign outside the car window. They were stopped at the traffic light outside Ama's place now, with the Tandoori Tiger's exterior being strung with Christmas lights by one of Ama's brothers on a ladder. "They have some interesting fashions. I watched a documentary on Chinese imperial history last week, and I remember how their clothes really made a cultural statement. Bold colors probably inspire you, don't they?"

"Anything can inspire me," said Natalie. "That's the beauty of what I do."

"Probably not in my daily surroundings," answered Chad. "If it's not true nature, then I minimize my atmosphere to simplicity." Which was true, Natalie reflected. Chad preferred earth tones, and not just in his soft leather boots, wooden beads, and leather men's jewelry, or the green polo shirts and khakis of his semi-casual office days. His apartment's decor sported greens and tans for its upholstery, with a coffee table made from recycled bamboo, reminding Natalie of wood pulp molded into a crude packing crate.

"But you should think about Asian fabrics and design. I think it would be a new fashion experience that you would probably enjoy." Chad turned right at the same moment the restaurant's lights blinked to life in red and gold. Ama's brother waved to their car as he climbed down from the ladder, recognizing Natalie, apparently, as the friend who sometimes stopped by to see Ama. She didn't think he saw her wave back as he unraveled his next string of lights.

❄

As Natalie had driven past the Tandoori Tiger, Ama was inside, untangling some very different lights with Rasha. Her sister's latest purchase was a tiny string of novelty Asian elephants painted with bright purple rugs adorning their backs.

"Aren't they adorable?" said Rasha. "The second I saw them, I knew they would be perfect for the window. What says Christmas—but still says Indian—better than these little guys?"

"Nothing?" suggested Ama.

"It gets better," said Rasha. "Plug them in." As Ama stuck the plug into the electrical socket, the tiny elephants lit up, and began blinking like the twinkle lights her father loved so much.

"Aren't they perfect?" said Rasha.

Ama laughed. "Okay, I agree," she said. "Do we drape them above the window, or put them on one of the trees?"

"I think maybe both. The Mexican place one block over has little chili pepper ones hanging in the window where everyone can see them," said Rasha. "They're *so* adorable. Have you seen them when you've gone past? He draped them over the Christmas tree, under the Christmas tree…"

Ama's mind was far from the Mexican restaurant's holiday display as she looped the cord for the elephants over one of the picture nails tapped just above the window. Mentally, she was searching for a suitable replacement Christmas recipe for the autumn's creamy carrot *halwa* porridge, dressed up with cinnamon and other pumpkin pie spices. Now her father wanted something resembling plum pudding, causing Ama to rack her brains about the possibility of plum-flavored *gulab jamun*.

Luke had liked hers. He had eaten every last bite on the train. Remembering that made Ama feel special, as if he was one of the few people who had truly appreciated both sides of her life. Clients met with Ama the cake baker, while Ama the daughter forewent cupcake baking to worry about the consistency of *halwa* porridge for the restaurant menu… but how many people encountered both sides of her at once and simply accepted that both were equal? Her business partners came close, but they mostly saw her American side—the side that her parents still had trouble believing could be equal to their original culture and its traditions.

She and Rasha tucked the lights between the branches of the tree by the cash register, the one decorated in white and rosy purple shades. Her father and Jaidev were back inside and having a friendly argument with her mother over her brother's plans to put a Santa hat on the restaurant sign's tiger.

"It's going up as soon as I head back out," said Jaidev in teasing seriousness. "The neighborhood will love it. You've seen the German restaurant at the far end of the block, right? Their sign's dancers are wearing little Christmas outfits cut out of red and green foil." He stuck Santa's hat on his own head in the meantime, the floppy red velvet hood trimmed with white felt and a glittery silver and white pompom.

"How can you put that silly hat on our beautiful sign?" demanded Pashma.

"It's Christmastime, and most of our American customers will expect it, right?" he said.

"This goes too far," said Bendi, adding her two cents to the discussion in Punjabi. "It's enough that we have these trees all over the place—trees covered in lights and jewelry—"

"I like the trees," piped up Rasha. "These elephants make them look Punjabi, don't they?" She and Ama were giggling over the latest complaints this produced from their aunt as they tucked the last string of elephants in place.

The door leading to the restaurant's foyer opened, meaning a customer was coming inside, even though it was a half hour until opening time. A man in a black leather jacket and red scarf entered, stomping a little sidewalk snow sludge from his boots on the snow mat before crossing the threshold.

Ama's heart plunged like an elevator in freefall. It was Luke coming into their establishment, a paper sack in hand. His glance of greeting took in the members of the Bhagut family closest to him, her parents and her brother.

In telling him that she worked downtown at a restaurant, she hadn't meant that to be an invitation to stop by. If he was coming, why hadn't he done it for a nice lunch plate and not in pre-service hours, when it appeared that her entire family was standing in the lobby like a welcoming—or unwelcoming—committee? It was a bad dream, it was a nightmare—but if she pinched herself, she knew she would feel it, because this was all too real. *What have I done to make the universe kick me so many times lately?* she thought.

"Welcome," said Jaidev with a grin of greeting. "We're not open yet, but if you would like to wait at a table, you're welcome to stay."

"Come and sit. I am Ranjit, owner of the Tandoori Tiger," said her father, who scrambled for a menu—never mind that it was still several minutes until they opened. "Would you like a table near the windows or the nice holiday trees?"

"Thanks, but I'm not here for lunch," said Luke. "Though I'd love to try your food sometime. Ama says you're the best Indian home cook in the city."

"Ama?" repeated Pashma.

"That's who I'm looking for. She works here most days, doesn't she? I'm a friend of hers," he said, glancing from her clueless parents to Rasha in her workplace sari for serving as a hostess, then to Ama herself. She waved at him, although it felt like a hesitant move with so many pairs of eyes watching her.

"Hey," Luke said. "I brought you a present in thanks for the one you gave me." He held up the paper sack. "Pastries for pastries. Is that a fair trade?"

"Thanks. But you didn't have to." She approached, aware that confidence had been sucked from her in the seconds that Luke had occupied the restaurant's lobby. "I didn't realize you were coming by."

"I was on my way to drop a bike at a customer's place, and I thought I'd bring you something from that friend I told you about," he said. "My friend the bread baker. Turns out her recipes are Polish, by the way. Her grandparents brought them to America. I figured you'd like to try some after hearing about a fellow baker's work."

"You're a friend of Ama's?" Ama could hear the surprise and skepticism in Pashma's voice.

He was so... *bohemian*. That's exactly what her mother would be thinking, from the casual manners that assumed familiarity, the city accent, the leather coat and torn jeans and peeling vinyl t-shirt, to the disregard for the 'closed' sign on their door. He seemed exactly like the guys who always turned out to be trouble in the movies—Pashma had seen enough of them on Saturday afternoon television to recognize a 'bad boy' image when she saw one.

"Yeah. We met at the markets downtown," he said. "Luke Johnson. You must be Ama's family." He stuck out his hand to Pashma, who shook it, to Ama's surprise. He did the same to Ranjit and Jaidev.

"Thanks for the bread," said Ama, taking the sack from him. "You didn't have to do this, though, truly. Those pastries were just a gift. Leftovers from the restaurant. Honest." This sounded more like a justification to the Bhagut clan and not to Luke. Of course, she had made them especially for him, but there was no way she was declaring that in front of her family.

"That's some kind of Polish Christmas bread, by the way," he said. "And there's this cinnamon twist pastry in there that smells pretty amazing. She'll give you the recipe if you like it, by the way. I put her bakery card in the bag, since I had a couple extra at my place."

Maybe they will think she's his girlfriend, thought Ama.

"You said you were at the street market downtown?" said Jaidev. "I don't think I've ever seen you there." His puzzled smile proved he was trying to make the connection, probably mentally reviewing the faces of all the sellers he knew.

"I don't have a stall. I just shop there sometimes. I have some friends who are sellers, plus some of my customers hang out there." Luke tucked his hands in the pockets of his coat. The shirt underneath it said 'Challenge Authority' with stick figures locked in combat.

He couldn't be wearing a 'Smile' t-shirt the one day he encountered her parents?

"What do you do for a living?" asked Rasha.

"I run a motorcycle garage," he said. "I fix up bikes, restore classics—Ama and her sister-in-law were downtown one day the same time as me, and we got chatting about the classic bike I had with me, so we talked for a while about bikes and restoration."

"Do you have one with you now?" Jaidev was immediately drawn to the window to look for a Harley strapped inside of someone's trunk, possibly.

"It's the truck by the streetlamp. Bike's chained down in the back. It's an eighty-three Harley, nothing really special. I think they fixed it up for sentimental reasons."

"Cool," said Jaidev, with the near-universal masculine appreciation for things with engines and noise. "That must be a fun way to make a living."

"It pays the bills," said Luke.

Ranjit had been silent, except for when he introduced himself to Luke, as if not quite sure what to say to this friendly stranger. Situations seldom left him this quiet, but there was an air of worry and unease in his glance as it surveyed Ama's friend. Now he spoke up. "Do you like Indian food?" he asked.

"Honestly, I haven't tried it that many times," said Luke. "I used to grab a curry now and then, and I went to the Punjabi Express a few times when I lived on that side of town. I liked their menu, but their desserts weren't as good as Ama's."

Paying a compliment to the Punjabi Express, with its fast food-style menu and atmosphere—*not* a good beginning to a conversation with Ranjit. Ama was lucky she didn't groan aloud.

"If you would like lunch with *real* Indian food, then eat here," said Ranjit. "We have a special today on peanut chicken, a new dish on our menu. Friends are always welcome." Probably some friends were more welcome than others, but it was nice of him to extend this invitation to Luke. Not that it meant he approved of their connection or anything.

Missing was her father's customary hearty tone for coaxing visitors to try something new. He didn't act like this when other friends from her outside life showed up, like Tessa or Natalie. The simple knowledge that this stranger was a boy and knew Ama in the outside world had changed the whole atmosphere—almost as if her father and the others sensed there was some kind of secret involved, although that was ridiculous. Ama knew it, but she was still thinking it.

"I've got to go drop off my delivery," answered Luke. "I should let you get back to decorating," he added, motioning toward the string of lights looped around Ranjit's shoulders from the outside Christmas decor project. "Nice meeting you all."

"Nice to meet you, too," said Bendi politely.

"I'll see you around, Ama," he said. "You want to check out the bike before I go?" He jerked his thumb toward the truck. "It's not as good as the one you and your sister-in-law spotted at the market, but I'll show you the finer points."

Something emboldened her—maybe the thought of escaping this awkward situation. "Sure," she said.

She stepped outside the restaurant with him, being careful not to imagine her family watching from the dining room windows. She wrapped her arms around herself in the chill breeze, then quickly uncrossed them. What if Luke tried to give her his coat while they were watching?

Luke lowered the tailgate and ran a hand over the new paint job on the motorcycle, which was a deep purple. "This one was originally green, but the owner changed the color on me halfway through the job," he said. "The shell was rough but the motor was perfect except for the spark plugs and a little work on the steering pins. I'd give you a ride, but I'd have to undo about six wire cables and locks," he added as a joke.

"Not this time, then," she said. She tucked a lock of hair behind her ear. "Listen, uh…" She hesitated. "It's probably better not to come by here to see me. It's better to come to the address on that business card I gave you, the one for the building on the other side of town."

"What for?" He looked puzzled. She didn't blame him, after talking about her family and their restaurant. She hadn't meant to give him enough details to find it, or want to stop by… at least that's what she thought at the time.

"Because my family's kind of… busy," she said, using the only inspiration that struck her in the previous second's silence. "The restaurant's usually really busy. Friends never come by, because it's crazy when we're open, and even during setup and cleanup. But it's not that way at the wedding planning place." Tessa and Natalie wouldn't be concerned by Luke's rebel-like appearance. They would probably congratulate her instead.

"Okay. I'll remember," he said. "Hope you enjoy the pastries and the bread."

"I will," she said. "They smell great. I know a good bake just by the scent." She clutched the sack in her left hand, and tucked a strand of her hair aside from the breeze with the other one.

"Baker's instinct, huh?"

She nodded. "Exactly right."

His smile melted. "You must be freezing out here," he said. "Ama, I'm sorry. I wasn't thinking when I asked you if you wanted to see the bike." He was going to take his coat off, so Ama hastened to move toward the restaurant's entrance.

"No need," she said, waving—dismissively, though she hoped it looked like a farewell wave from the other side of the restaurant's windows. "I have to go back to work. I'll see you around."

"I'll call you," he replied. He waved to her as he opened the door to his truck and climbed inside. As it closed behind him, Ama went back into the restaurant. Whatever private commentary her family had been engaged in on her and Luke's possible conversation ceased at this point.

"That's a cool bike," said Jaidev.

"Sure is," said Ama lightly. She placed the sack of pastries on the cashier's counter, and began straightening the cord for the elephant lights, as if nothing unusual had just happened.

"This friend. You met him in the market?" said Pashma to Ama, as if confirming the facts behind what apparently sounded like a sketchy story on Luke's part.

"Yup. He had a nice bike parked by the pottery vendor, and me and Deena said to him how much we liked it," she said. "It was while you were at the Mexican spice stall, Jaidev," she added, speaking over her shoulder. "That's why you didn't meet him."

"When did you give him the pastries?" asked Rasha. Ama wished she hadn't mentioned this, since she was hoping to successfully avoid the fact that she had seen Luke outside of the marketplace.

"They were just leftovers from the restaurant for the Wedding Belles, that I had with me," she answered. "Like the ones I give Tess and Natalie sometimes. Free advertising for business, right? Giving out free samples to people we know and meet."

It wasn't anything remotely like that, of course—not how it happened or why she did it. The suspicion and curiosity was thick enough to cut with a knife. Her words and body language had an undercurrent of defensiveness that her feigned casual tone just couldn't hide.

Did it matter what the rest of them made of it? A rebellious part of her wanted to say it didn't, because it was her life and her friendship, and it wasn't anybody else's business. But she knew it wasn't that simple. Her family's opinions and feelings about this mattered to her, even when it was difficult to talk to them about her personal dreams.

"Free advertising is good," said Ranjit. Again, his tone lacked conviction, as if he wasn't quite certain it applied in this case. *Not to possible bad boys in black leather, who might be a terrible influence on his daughter.*

"Men with the motorbike and leather jacket are always trouble," said Bendi, expressing aloud Ama's previous sarcastic thought. "You shouldn't invite him to lunch, Ranjit. They don't know how to eat rice properly. They like big plates of it covered with fried chicken and that orange sweet sauce from the Chinese place."

"I don't think that's always true," said Jaidev, trying not to smile at their auntie's usual forceful opinion. "I see plenty of customers sporting that look who also love good tandoori chicken and roti."

"I didn't know you liked the motorbikes," said her father. "You like the idea of going *zoom zoom beep beep* around the city like boys on the streets of Ludhiana?" He sounded mystified by this. In his day, girls and motorbikes did not mix, and he still couldn't quite fathom a world in which girls wore skinny jeans, hopped onto motorbikes for casual transport anywhere in public, and sported tattoos that were not inked with temporary ceremonial henna.

Was he suspicious of her interests—or her interest in Luke? It was impossible to say which at the moment, so Ama stuck to the former. "Maybe I do," said Ama. "There's probably a lot of things you don't know about me, Papa. Nobody here bothers to ask me about my hobbies, or new interests I've developed. So it's not like I talk about them all the time."

She plugged in the elephants, the bulbs inside their plastic shells twinkling, then slipped on her apron and walked toward the kitchen. She knew her mother was watching her throughout this speech and probably had been since the first awkward seconds of Luke's arrival. Years of instinct taught her to know when her mother's eye singled her out among her siblings, which was why Ama made sure she walked from the dining room to the kitchen with seemingly unconcerned calm.

Nobody ever asked. Not even her siblings, who usually took it for granted that baking was her primary interest, except for crazy ideas about love at first sight and romantic first kisses. Her father would probably buy this explanation, and they would all argue over whether it was a bad hobby for girls, and forget all about Luke and his bag of pastries and his offhand knowledge of Ama's life.

She lifted down the flour tin from its shelf and set it beside her mixing bowl. Before she began sifting the flour for today's dessert, she opened the paper bag and took out the partial loaf that Luke had brought her. Breaking it in half, she studied the soft texture pocked by miniature bubbles of air, the pieces of sweet fruit dotting it like gemstones. She put a bite of it in her mouth and savored the mild sweetness and the buttery nut flavor of its grains.

At least Luke had kept his jacket on and her mother hadn't seen the tattoo on his arm. With some quick thinking, she had made sure that if he came back here, it was only to sample some *masala dosa* for lunch… and hopefully he would have sense enough not to ask to see the restaurant's dessert chef after she explained to him that she was too busy to take breaks while at the restaurant.

The kitchen door swung open and Jaidev entered, still wearing the Santa hat, and humming a Christmas carol as he took a roll of tape from the drawer. Before the door swung closed, the voices of her family drifted into the kitchen.

"—but they're so *dangerous*, those bikes."

"Papa, girls ride them all the time now."

Ama smiled and twisted off a piece of the cinnamon pastry from the bakery sack.

Chapter Eighteen

"Are you sure it's that serious?" Tessa asked. "Any chance it's just a cold?" She rubbed her forehead with two fingers as she asked this question.

"He can't even talk," answered the voice on the phone. "The doctor said two weeks until he recovers, at least. There's no way he could sing more than a couple of songs by that date."

"I see," said Tessa dejectedly. "I guess that's that. Tell him I hope he gets well soon."

She hung up. That was the end of her hopes that the wedding reception band was exaggerating their lead singer's symptoms. A nasty case of laryngitis, 'the worst the doctor had ever diagnosed,' meant weeks of salt gargles and rest and virtually no chance of an early recovery.

Backup options. Did they have any? Cynthia had been pushing for a string quartet, while Paula had voted repeatedly for a DJ spinning modern hip hop and dance mixes to 'liven up the party.' If it hadn't been for Lyle's old school friend being part of a local light jazz group that specialized in crooner's tunes, they would probably still be arguing about it.

The two warring mothers had learned nothing at all about minding their own business during the past few weeks. Tonight was no different, despite being separated by multiple places at the rehearsal dinner—an event that was being held earlier than preferable, due to unforeseen scheduling conflicts for the family. More bad luck? Tessa tried not to think about it, despite her worries that some member of the wedding party might forget their cue by the time the ceremony finally took place.

The groom's mother was dressed in red sequins tonight, a thousand bangle bracelets on one arm, and sporting a pink ball cap for photo ops, emblazoned with the words 'I'm the groom's mama, and this ain't no shotgun wedding!' which Natalie had attempted to discreetly steal and hide in the cloakroom. Cynthia wore neutral blues and sensible pearls, missing only a summer fan and a rocking chair to belong in a scene with the declining gentry of a Tennessee Williams play.

"I'm telling you, modern weddings do it right," Paula was saying to the person sitting beside her—Lyle's best man. "I saw this bride in a big pink gown on one of those TV shows about dream weddings, saying it was her favorite color, why shouldn't she wear it for the ceremony? And I thought, good for her. It looks better when things are all glitzed up and mixed together…"

"…and I've always believed that simplicity itself is elegance," Cynthia was saying to a bridesmaid beside her. "You agree, don't you? If someone suggested a wedding dress based on a cartoon character, surely *you'd* say something, too." The bridesmaid was trying to look sympathetic and not merely trapped.

Paula craned her neck in the direction of her rival. "You're not talking about that *Frozen* dress, are you?" she said loudly, in a hurt tone of voice.

Cynthia did a poor job of disguising her dislike of being interrupted. "I was only saying that cartoons have a place, and *real* wedding dresses have their place," she answered, after a polite pause to showcase her martyr-like patience.

"Are you saying a dress isn't a wedding dress unless it's white?" said Paula. "Do you have to earn it to wear it, too? 'Cause half the population would be in black now for their weddings." She threw back her head for a sarcastic laugh. A look of outrage and indignation filled Cynthia's eyes.

Nadia laid a hand on her mother's arm, yet again. "Let's not discuss this here," she pleaded.

"You heard what she said to me," said Cynthia in a half whisper.

"I know, but let it go. For my sake," said the bride. "We're having a lovely time tonight. All of our friends are here, the dinner is excellent. Italian is your favorite. You should be enjoying this."

"I *was*," said Cynthia. "Before your future mother-in-law insulted both public decency and the sacred vows of marriage."

La Bella Italiana was the site of the rehearsal dinner. They were down to the wire on this wedding, and Tessa was still debating when and how to announce that the band for the reception had fallen through, as she pretended to enjoy her linguine in light pesto.

"What's wrong?" Natalie whispered to her while pretending to reach for the bread basket.

"I'll tell you when we're away from the table," Tessa whispered back. She watched as Paula dug heartily into a plate heaped with spaghetti and meatballs, all while criticizing the spices.

"I don't see why we couldn't have dinner at your restaurant," she said to Lyle.

"We're having the reception there," said Lyle. "We thought it'd be nice to eat somewhere else instead."

"This highfalutin Italian place must be costing you a fortune, and the food's not that good. You call this stuff spaghetti sauce? There's no chunks in it and no little bits of cheese, either."

"I'm afraid real Italian pasta sauces simply don't have bits of dried cheese floating in them." Cynthia's remark could be heard from three seats away.

"Well, they should. 'Cause this is no better than canned ravioli sauce," said Paula, shaking her head. "We got the best chef in the city sitting right here, and we're missing out on his lamb *kleftiko* because of it."

"Ma, I'm not the best," protested Lyle with a blush. "Besides, Nick had another event to cater, so the restaurant was busy. I'm lucky that I don't have to be at the office until later, catching up on those inventory lists."

"Is that where you'll be later?" asked Nadia, glancing at him. "I thought you said the restaurant was closing early and that you and I were going to spend some time together."

"It is closing early, babe. I'm just going to take care of a couple of things, then we'll all go somewhere more relaxing."

"*All?*" Nadia's voice dropped to a whisper. Lyle glanced guiltily toward Paula, who was chatting to one of the groomsmen about Vegas weddings.

"Ma wanted to know if we were busy later tonight. She wants to give us her wedding present early. And I figured if your mom found out about it and wasn't there... well, you know what happens." He squeezed Nadia's hand. "Relax. It'll be fun. Couple of hours at most, I promise. Then I'll drive you home and you can get some rest while I finish taking care of some stuff for the kitchen."

It would not be fun, Tessa knew, and so did the bride. Nadia bit her lip and stared at her plate, as if trying to decide what exactly to say about this plan. Cynthia was growing unhappier as Paula's voice rose at the table, carrying with it a story about her own crazy wedding in

Vegas years ago, exactly the kind of story that would plant suggestions about rock bands at receptions and disco balls as decorations.

"I think now's a really good time for the DJ to start playing some music," said Ama, whispering to Tessa. "What do you think?"

"Go for it," said Tessa. Ama laid aside her napkin, and rose from the table to speak to the local DJ hired to help the couple make use of the restaurant's dance floor. Tessa laid aside her own napkin and telegraphed with a subtle glance and head nod for Natalie to follow her example.

Across the room, Ama was speaking to the DJ, who nodded at her request. Cynthia was watching.

"I don't know why you were so fired up to have people dancing at this event," she said to the wedding couple. "I've always thought it dressed down an occasion to entertain people with music that isn't live. Doesn't it seem a bit... well... pointless? Like watching a play on television or something?"

"Don't be ridiculous, mother," said Nadia, who sounded extremely exasperated. "It's been decades since people thought it was weird to dance to recorded music. *You* did when you and Dad used to host dinner parties."

"And I realized then how silly it was," said Cynthia. "How do you think I know? And I would appreciate you *not* rolling your eyes at me, thank you," she added to Nadia.

"I hope they're playing something to rev up this party," said Paula to Natalie.

"They're playing our song," said Lyle, putting his arm around Nadia's shoulders and giving her a gentle squeeze. "Nadia picked the song we heard when we first got together."

"How romantic," said Natalie.

Tessa pushed back her chair from the table and lifted her glass, tapping her butter knife against its side. "If I could have everyone's attention," she said. "In a moment, the future bride and groom's song will begin playing, and they would like to invite all of you to join them on the dance floor tonight in honor of their love." A smattering of applause from the guests; Nadia blushed and smiled, while Lyle's face turned a sheepish red.

The end of her speech cued the waiting DJ. His sound system boomed to life—not with the strains of Sinatra, but a hip hop song that Tessa knew from the radio, a breakup song about jealousy with a five-letter word in its title. Which was exactly what the guests heard before the music cut off as Ama hurried back to the DJ's station.

A second later, the appropriate love song began playing. Too little too late, in Tessa's opinion. Instead of sitting down, she exited the dining room, knowing Natalie would follow a few seconds later into the hallway of arched glass windows facing the restaurant's terraced garden.

"That was perfect," muttered Natalie, when she joined Tessa at the hall's end, in an alcove near the restrooms. "The DJ had the song ready to play, but punched the button of his personal gym workout playlist by accident."

"Why am I not surprised at this point?" asked Tessa with a sigh.

"Paula seemed disappointed that he turned it off," said Natalie wryly. "A few more glasses of wine, and she may be table dancing for the amusement of the wedding guests."

"We'll simply add it to our list of problems," said Tessa. "Good news from the band tonight—they've cancelled their engagement with us."

"What?"

"Laryngitis. Who else would get laryngitis right now except the lead singer of a band *we* needed?" said Tessa. "The drummer called

Lyle today, and he forwarded me a message. Nadia doesn't know
yet, apparently."

"What are we going to do? There's no backup band. These were
friends of Lyle's that wanted the gig."

"Looks like we'll be hiring a DJ after all," said Tessa. "I know that
will disappoint the bride's mother, but what else can we do? Maybe
not this guy though. We can't risk another wrong song situation… But
I suppose better him than no one."

She was trying not to sound frustrated, but she was out of ideas at
this point. If they started over with a new list of bands, they would have
to go through yet another endless debate on the subject of music tastes
and modern dance vs. ballroom. Could Nadia take any more bickering?
Tessa wasn't sure she herself could, and she was being paid to listen to it.

"Let me call a friend and see if they have somebody who would fit
the bill," said Natalie.

"Another friend?" said Tessa.

"My family knows practically everybody in town," said Natalie,
with a shrug of 'who else?' at this fact. "Somebody in my circle can
find a band on short notice. Half the starving population of Little
Italy consists of musicians anyway." She sighed. "So what else is new?"

"We have to tell Nadia," said Tessa.

"You are seriously joking."

"I'm not," said Tessa, with a very unamused expression. "Can you
imagine Lyle wanting to do it?"

"He pays us for it," said Natalie grimly. "But I'm not sure it's worth
it anymore." She grimaced.

My thoughts exactly, Tessa agreed mentally.

Natalie took her cell phone from her bag. "I'll call my uncle and ask
him to sniff around for someone who has a good band playing their

restaurant," she said. "And if you want, I'll ask the DJ if he's booked for that day, too."

"Sure," said Tessa. "We're not making another move without a backup." But if every backup needed its own backup, this plan could stretch into infinity, she reminded herself. Surely something was going to save them the trouble of its cancellation?

She couldn't help thinking of the snowflake frame favors right now—the first in a long line of disasters that were becoming hard to laugh off as coincidence. That was all it was... but it felt more like a jinx or a curse.

What if it ended with her behind the wheel of the hotdog mobile again—on a permanent basis?

Footsteps in the hall. Tessa stepped out of the alcove, half expecting to see Natalie returning with bad news. Instead, it was Nadia marching from the dining room, stopping halfway to plant herself at the central window, arms crossed. She might have been admiring the view, but Tessa didn't think so, from the impatient, restless movements of the bride's fingers, and the tap of her high-heeled shoe on the tiles.

Lyle appeared from the dining room, too. "Honey, don't be this way," he said coaxingly. "Look, it will all blow over by the time we have ice cream. The two of them never stick to any of these arguments for long."

"Do you hear yourself?" Nadia looked at him. "It'll always blow over, won't it? Just ignore it and it'll go away. That's really easy when you always look to someone else to fix it, Lyle. Like me."

"I don't expect you to make the two of them get along," he said. "When did I ever tell you to do it?"

"You just keep shoving the problem off on me," she said. "You put me in the middle every time to play tiebreaker between them. You don't want to hurt your mom, you don't want to insult mine... I've heard those excuses a million times until I want to scream, Lyle." Nadia's last remark came through her teeth, Tessa thought. She withdrew a little into the shadows again, cut off between here and the dining room.

"I just think you're better at choosing stuff," said Lyle. "I figured you'd tell the planners what you want and they'll fix it up for you. Then it doesn't matter what anybody's mom thinks."

"How is that going to help us in the future, when there's no planner anymore?" demanded Nadia. "When it's nursery colors, or... or where to spend Fourth of July weekend? Who decides then, when your mom has a plan and so does mine?"

Lyle shrugged helplessly. "I dunno. We'll figure it out then," he said.

Nadia shook her head. "No," she said. "I can't, Lyle. You leave me hanging all the time... I always have to be the bad guy in our relationship when it comes to disappointing someone. I can't do it anymore."

Her eyes were full of tears as she glanced at him. Tessa sucked in her breath. Was Nadia... *breaking up* at her rehearsal dinner?

"Honey, what are you so upset about?" he asked, mystified.

"We're never going to be a united force in our marriage, and that scares me," said Nadia, who was shaking a little now. "As much as I love you, I can't live like that. I can't go on like we've been acting ever since we started planning this wedding. I'm done, Lyle. Done. If that's how things are going to be."

"That's crazy, Nadia," he protested. "What are you saying? Are you saying that you don't want to get married?"

She shook her head. "I want to marry you," she said. "Just not like this." She pulled her ring off her finger. "So I'm going to walk away before I make it worse by staying."

"Nadia!"

She brushed past Lyle and evaded his hand as he tried to grab her arm, shaking off his grip when he tried to stop her. She was upset enough that he stopped after two attempts. He tried to follow her, then faltered, his expression that of a crushed man as he gazed after her instead.

Nadia didn't look back as she left, passing Tessa in the hall without even noticing her there. The exterior door that connected the restaurant with the neighboring art gallery opened, then closed behind the bride-to-be. Nadia avoided the main exit in the dining room, one crowded with guests who were supposed to attend her wedding in a week.

Tessa looked in Lyle's direction again. The groom was leaning against the windows, looking devastated and confused. He wasn't going after her, Tessa realized. He was going to stay right here while his wedding fell apart around him. Nadia was right—Lyle had no clue what to do about conflict.

An eternity passed, in which Tessa told herself to calm down. Nadia would be back after she cooled off, and they would fix this. Maybe she could intervene more on the bride's behalf. Maybe they could arrange a spa day for the bridal party and finish the wedding's last-minute details—and disasters—away from the two mothers. A dozen solutions could be offered that would save this car crash of a wedding. *Just think this through and smile when you go back to the dining room*, she said to herself. *And tell Lyle—*

But Lyle was walking out now. He passed her in the hallway without seeing her, and pushed open the door to the sidewalk outside. He fumed silently in the cold air, then struck off aimlessly into the night, shoulders hunched in defeat. Tessa felt the tight grip of panic in her chest. Was she hosting an engagement dinner at which neither member of the happy couple was now present? What excuse was she going to give people?

"Where are Nadia and Lyle?" asked the maid of honor, shouting over the DJ's latest song, a loud version of 'This Kiss.'

"They slipped away earlier," said Tessa, who was trying to smile serenely. "Don't worry, though. The party still lasts until nine."

Most guests didn't ask why a couple seemingly in love might leave the party early. As for the respective mothers of the happy couple, Tessa avoided saying anything more than that she had seen the bride and groom leaving sometime after the dance floor opened. She omitted 'separately' from the answer.

"Where are our clients?" asked Ama. "Did they leave without saying anything?"

"They left early," said Tessa. "I'm sure we'll hear from them tomorrow."

✳

Nadia did call the next day, but it was to leave a message asking Tessa to cancel the chapel and the flowers. It was waiting on the answering machine at Wedding Belles when Tessa arrived first thing in the morning.

She knew the blinking red light meant doom, even before she pressed the button. She sank into the foyer's velvet armchair afterwards, feeling despair. Now what? What could they possibly do in the face of a broken engagement except erase what pieces of the wedding they had actually managed to make perfect?

She called Nadia's number; it went to voicemail. "Nadia, this is Tessa Miller, from Wedding Belles," she said. "I just wanted to say that I'm sorry to hear this news, and I hope that things between you and Lyle can be fixed somehow. I would like to wait a few days before I cancel anything, just in case you both change your minds, if you'll let me. Please, call or text me at any time to talk about it. Or to just… talk… if you need a friend." It's not as if Nadia could go to her mother with these problems, after all.

Nadia texted her back. *Okay. Wait 2 days.* So they had two more days of pretending to have a client, at least. Maybe a miracle would occur and Nadia and Lyle would patch everything together. It was just a tiny fight, really. Just a minor disagreement over whether their marriage would be one big, long family argument.

She bit her nail, gazing despondently out of her office window. Should she tell the others that the wedding was cancelled? She could imagine what Natalie would say—something snarky about the billboard's lone client being a dud. And Ama had worked so hard on the cake, and in the face of such criticism—

"What's with you?" Natalie was in the doorway, a bridesmaid dress bundled in her arms, its light blue satin complementing the winter color scheme.

Tessa glanced at her. "You might as well know," she said. "Ama, too. We have a… slightly bigger problem than before."

✳

"They *cancelled*?" Ama's jaw dropped.

"I know, it sounds bad," said Tessa. "But I convinced her to wait a couple of days to see if this fight blows over. There's a chance they may get back together and the wedding will go on."

"And there's a chance we'll have to call our snooty florist friend and cancel the order after the terrific stink we made to land it," said Natalie disgustedly. "They won't be doing us a favor again, will they?"

"After all those sketches… nothing," said Ama. "I thought I'd finally designed the perfect cake, too."

"I'm halfway through Nadia's dress already. Now what am I going to do with it?"

"No one's going to do anything—yet," said Tessa, assuming command. "We're just going to wait a few days, as I said before. Everything will be fine, probably. It's not as if one tiny cancellation will be a black spot on our career."

"Did I tell you the DJ from last night is booked through the holidays?" asked Natalie. "So we can't depend on having him as a backup in case no one else is available."

Tessa gave her a withering look. "So we've had a few setbacks this time," she said. "It would have happened to any planning firm they hired. They just happened to hire us."

"Lucky us," sighed Ama. "We have to wait two days to find out if all our work is wasted."

"My best wedding dress ever, destined for the storage closet," said Natalie with a groan, thinking back on the multiple fittings and frantic sewing required to finish the gown in time. "At least it'll have plenty of company there."

"Listen to yourselves! We have to think positive thoughts," said Tessa. "How else will we come through this and find our next client if we don't focus? We have to take a deep breath and approach this calmly, one day at a time."

"Did Nadia make it sound like there was any hope?" Ama sounded as if the last of hers was floating on these words.

Not a bit. Tessa made a strong effort to smile, although it was hard with the ghost of Nadia's phone message behind it. "There's always hope when two people are in love," she said. "Right?" Her smile faltered again. "Just… hang on a little longer. Everything will be fine after this tough patch."

It was intended for herself as much as it was for her partners. They exchanged glances, the worry in their eyes the same as in Tessa's own. None of them needed to say anything more.

Since Nadia didn't call to confirm that the wedding was definitely cancelled—or suddenly scheduled again—Tessa focused on the wedding confetti and working on the wedding timeline from pre-ceremony to the reception. A few offices away, she could hear Ama's music playing, and could hear Natalie's sewing machine's high-speed click as it stitched through fabric for last-minute alterations on the bridesmaids' dresses that were now in limbo.

Seventy little bags of environmentally friendly biodegradable snow-flake confetti were tied with silver and white ribbons on Tessa's desk. As her fingers secured the last ribbon around the delicate sheer white fabric bundles, she glanced hopefully at the screen of her phone—no missed texts or calls, as the absence of any beep proved.

Lifting the box, she stepped outside her office to add the finished product to the wedding supplies downstairs in the storeroom. In the hallway, she found Blake removing his tool belt and safety glasses, tossing them into his metal toolbox. He was going to talk to her when she passed him, she sensed. Suddenly, Tessa's eyes were very busy studying the knots on the confetti bags, making sure they were attractively tied.

"Hey, you never gave me an answer on that transom grate," he said. "Can you let me know if you want to sell it or not?"

"What?" she said, racking her foggy brain for their past conversation about this.

"I wanted to buy the old transom from your office. Since you don't want to fix it up—"

"We don't have time to fix it up, or money," Tessa said. And managed not to sigh, because she was beginning to accept this bitter reality. "Give me some time to think about it." What was the going rate on antique transoms? Probably not enough to cover a month's electricity for this building—or the apartment she used to rent. Not that she wanted to charge Blake and recoup some of his hard-earned cash from this job.

"I need to know soon," said Blake. "I really do have a place for it."

"Better than sitting in our closet, you mean," said Tessa sarcastically. He couldn't see that she was busy thinking about something else right now. Did he *ever* think of anything besides his precious restoration project, anyway?

"If you were an antique fixture, would *you* want to sit in a closet for the rest of your existence?" replied Blake. It would be part of the historic renovation on the other side of town, while they would settle for the cheap, modern replacement she had purchased. That was all they could afford anyway, and if Blake was too busy with his new project, they would hire a cut-rate handyman to do it instead.

"By the way, the room downstairs is prepped for paint. I put in the new wall trim and put some spackle over the worst spots this morning. If you want me to, I can get started on the paint for you." His glance fell on the box in her arms. "If you haven't picked it, I can still match that color I told you about, and probably pick some up today for you."

"No need. I bought paint already," said Tessa. "It's the paint tin in the room's corner, under the tarps."

"The devil red shade, I take it?" said Blake.

"It's not 'devil red,'" said Tessa, with a flicker of annoyance, on top of everything else she was feeling today. "It's called 'Valentine Red,' a perfect choice for a wedding business. Although I'm sure you and Mac would still prefer your beloved shade of drab green for decorating its walls. Or bright purple."

"I only thought it would give the building a little extra charm to have your color scheme reflect its past, which is why I suggested that you let Mac come up with a color palette for your walls."

"So you can paint over 'Romantic Blue,' I suppose," said Tessa sarcastically. "I'm surprised your friend Mac didn't puke while she was in my office, surrounded by my tasteless color scheme."

A strange look crossed Blake's face. "Are you jealous of Mac?" he asked, sounding surprised—and amused—as he suggested it.

Red flashed quickly across Tessa's face. "What? No!" she declared vehemently. "Where did you come up with a crazy idea like that?"

"The little sneer in your voice whenever you talk about her, for starters," said Blake. "You were acting weird at the Springer Street house, *and* when she was in your office that time, too."

"I am *not* jealous of your friend, or… whatever she is," insisted Tessa. "I just didn't like the way the two of you talk about this building like it's a slum in need of a firm decorator's hand to save it."

"I never said that," protested Blake. "Look, I was only trying to help when I suggested any of those things. I thought maybe you'd like to have some historical accuracy in your decor for this place."

"Suggested? That's your definition of hounding me to give in?'" echoed Tessa. "You know what? I don't *like* dark green walls. I don't like oppressive woodwork that looks like it was salvaged from Dracula's castle, no matter how historically accurate it might be. Even if we made six-figure incomes, I still wouldn't hire your elite interior design friend to do the whole place in peacock blue and poison green. I happen to *like* my office walls, and mismatched chairs, and I *love* the spiral staircase, and I don't care what anybody else thinks. And if I want to keep that transom in a closet or mount it like a moose's head over the fireplace downstairs, I think that's my business, so mind your own."

She hadn't realized how forceful or loud her voice was, until she noticed both of her business partners had emerged from their offices. They were staring at her, just like Blake was, who looked both hurt and indignant as he listened to her.

She deflated. Why had she been yelling at him about furniture and the stupid spiral staircase over a snarky remark regarding paint color? What did any of it matter, since everyone, including their contractor, knew they were scraping together their decor from bargain bins and markdown shelves?

She was going crazy, thanks to this jinx. She had taken it out on Blake, who was the last person she should probably be yelling at. She shouldn't yell at anybody, because it was nobody's fault that their bad luck patch had tripped them up. The money wasted on the billboard, and the decision to spend money fixing up this place—technically, she had nobody to blame but herself for those decisions.

She brushed her hair back from her face, feeling how hot her cheeks were, knowing they must be visibly on fire. No tears, Tessa determined fiercely not to have any. Now that her anger and confusion were all mixed up inside her, she didn't know what she felt. The world's supports were buckling, just like the supports in these termite-eaten walls, probably.

"Everything okay, guys?" asked Natalie carefully. Neither Blake nor Tessa answered her, so her question hung in silence.

"You can have the transom grate," she said to Blake. Quietly. "It's still in the closet downstairs, so take it. I don't want anything for it." She turned away and went downstairs with her box of wedding confetti parcels, leaving the other three feeling clueless and confused in the hall.

Chapter Nineteen

The first aid supplies in her medicine cabinet needed replenishing, Natalie discovered, as she plastered a little extra antiseptic ointment on the scrape on her elbow. Discreetly, while she knew Chad was busy checking on the one-dish Ecuadorian rice stew that he had brought over for dinner, so he wouldn't know she was a wimp when it came to doctoring surface scrapes and bruises. Peeling off skin while rappelling down a rock bluff, all to see a trickle of water coming out of the base... telling him that experience ranked as one of the most tedious dates of her love life was something she planned to save for another week or two, when things would either be at their romantic peak or tapering off, according to Natalie's typical relationship cycle.

She might also bring up the fact that the cuisine of South America wasn't something she typically savored on a tri-weekly basis—but that, too, could wait. After all, it wasn't a lifelong commitment, this evening of sharing a rice casserole with some sort of weird chili spices in it. She and Chad had both agreed they liked to keep things casual, so it probably wouldn't break his heart to learn she didn't see a long-term future for them.

"Dinner's up," announced Chad. He lifted the dish from the oven and placed it in the table's center.

"Plates are in the cupboard by the fridge," said Natalie, tugging her sleeve over her elbow's bandage. "Grab some ketchup from the cupboard, too, will you?"

"Ketchup?" said Chad, with one eyebrow raised. "Give it a chance first, will you?"

"It's my go-to spice," defended Natalie with a lie, as she removed a serving spoon from the drawer. Her phone buzzed—probably a text from her mother. Again. She pretended not to notice as she poured Chad a glass of tea.

"I was just thinking your mom seemed a little stressed the other day." Her thought waves must be broadcasting themselves live for him to make this remark. "Did she stop by for something besides your belated birthday cake?" Chad asked, as he dipped a piece of crusty bread in the stew. This was the traditional way to eat it, he had explained to Natalie.

"Nothing important," answered Natalie. "Just standard mom meddling. She does it a hundred times a year."

"So it wasn't because of me," clarified Chad, as he sprinkled dried chilies over his bowl.

Natalie hedged. "Maybe a little." She dipped her spoon idly in her bowl. "Ma's chief preoccupation in life is whether I'm happy in the right way. In her book, the right way involves meeting a guy, settling down from my crazy dating life, and spreading happiness by sporting a large engagement ring." She wiggled her eyebrows as she tasted her stew, discovering that, just as she feared, the flavors were a little more exotic than she preferred. "Especially for the holidays. That's when my family finds my normally blissfully single state the most offensive."

"Families can be like that," said Chad, with an offhand shrug of his shoulders. "So she was here scouting to find out if I was finally serious relationship material, right?"

"Bingo," Natalie answered. She dipped her bread, mostly to soften it. "Don't worry. I told her to back off."

Chad stirred a spoon through his stew, cooling it. "You know," he said, "if you could give her part of what she wanted, you could probably make her happy."

"Is that your way of saying you'd actually eat dinner with my family?" Natalie retorted.

"Sort of," he said. "I mean, what if I actually came to dinner a couple of times? You could let them think we're kind of serious. At least until the holidays are over."

"What do you mean?" Natalie almost laughed at this suggestion, but the noise came up short of one, more like a snort. "Are you saying I should let my family think you're a serious candidate for… well, whatever." The word 'marriage' seemed a little too serious to actually say in a conversation this lighthearted, at least for her taste.

"It's a classic 'what if' scenario," said Chad. "Like in all the movies— you know, when two people make a pact to be a couple for a period of time, to make everybody they know happy. Like… in the song 'St. Patrick's Day.' That way you have somebody over the holidays, when everybody's sentimental about relationships."

"I've never felt pathetically alone at the holidays," said Natalie. "I'm not still listening to those John Mayer lyrics as a fully fledged adult, wishing I was walking through a Christmas card scene hand in hand with someone else. That's just my mom's wishful thinking."

"That's what I mean about doing it for your mom," said Chad. "And for my mom, too. Ever since my dad passed away, she's found the holidays a little harder to enjoy. It might cheer her up if I brought someone to a few of our celebrations, though. She keeps hinting she would like to meet some of my girlfriends, at least."

"That would be fine by me," said Natalie. "Better than doing it to appease the other dozen or so people in both our lives who think singlehood is horrible."

"And openly pity people like us during the holidays?" Chad suggested.

"Confession time. I am sick of pity," said Natalie.

"It would get your mom off your back for a few weeks if she thought you were serious about somebody," pointed out Chad. "And if that somebody is me, what do you have to worry about? We're dating, we both know how we feel about taking things too fast… so there wouldn't be an issue between us, right?" He left this as a question, as if to be sure that Natalie was on the same page. "Would there be?"

Of course not. She was as free as a bird, just like Chad with his long Ecuadorian treks in the company of some local cliff guide. It was ridiculous to suggest that she would even consider settling down at this point in life, much less so quickly in a relationship—and to consider it at all, even with someone as outwardly attractive as Chad, would prove she was certifiable.

Crazy. That was the word for it, in Natalie's book… yet, deep inside her, there was something appealing about the idea of not having her mom nagging her over the holidays just this once. No scolding from the other Grenaldis for showing up alone to every family event, or anyone telling her how sad it was that she didn't have anybody to share her life yet. How could they say it if there was hope, albeit a small one planted in her family's minds, that she'd finally found a chance for supposed romantic happiness?

They'd probably die of shock. No time to say "I told you so" with triumph at the sight of Natalie and Chad side by side at the dinner table. They'd be too amazed by Natalie actually being willing to *bring* someone to dinner to question whether it was the last holiday they'd be seeing him with her. Air castles would be built—who needed to know that she and Chad would blow them aside like clouds a couple of months later?

"What do you think?" Chad asked, with that tiny little joking smile that tended to betray the fact his lips were on the thin side. "You take me to one of your family's Christmas parties, I introduce you to my mom and a couple of friends as my 'serious' girlfriend. Since we're dating already, who would say we're lying?"

"Nobody," admitted Natalie, shaking her head. "Well, except for my shocked family members. But they'll all be struck dead the second I actually escort a guy into my mother's dining room."

"How far do you think we'd have to go to make them happy?" Chad mused. "Fake proposal? Fake ring?"

"How about a plastic diamond?" said Natalie. "Kidding. I think showing up at Ma's Christmas dinner would be good enough to impress."

"We have a deal?" asked Chad, holding out his hand, business style. "Seriously fake-dating until after the holidays? Exclusively seeing each other until our families are past the celebratory period?"

"Until St. Patrick's Day." Natalie held out her hand, shaking Chad's to seal the deal. "This might be the first Christmas dinner I actually enjoy in years, if we actually do it."

"See? Dating me is worth it, even if you're not much for rock climbing," remarked Chad.

"Or South American stew," added Natalie, pushing aside her bowl while making a face. "Is there any leftover pasta in the fridge?"

"Give it a chance, will you?" said Chad. "You need to broaden your horizons."

Not that much, Natalie thought. So long as this relationship lasted, they were eating Italian. Maybe they should lay down a few ground rules for their so-called exclusivity contract.

He collected her bowl and put it by the sink, and ladled a second serving for himself from the dish on the table, as Natalie found herself humming a song under her breath, the one that Chad had given as an example of how they could dodge their respective families' judgment over the holidays... at the price of further scrutiny and questions, she imagined, albeit cheerful ones. How could their relatives not ask what level of seriousness their relationship had reached, for instance? Or about the wheres and whens of all a serious relationship's milestones? Nothing would satisfy her mom for long on the subject of happiness, probably, except maybe commitment itself.

Then again, what if everyone believed it without question?

Chad was gone by nine, with a suggestion that they have lunch together next Wednesday at a vegan sandwich shop the company's latest shoe designer had introduced him to after a meeting. He took the stew's leftovers with him, aware that Natalie would toss them into the trash if he didn't—Natalie opened a leftover tomato pesto ziti dish from her fridge and dug in with relish as soon as he left, propping her feet on the kitchen table.

Her phone buzzed. *Can u help bake Christmas bread nxt wk?* her mom asked.

Maybe, Natalie texted back. *Busy at work. And stuff.*

She knew her mom would interpret 'stuff' as her personal life, including her love life, and waited for the usual text in reply, prepared to roll her eyes in response. *As usual. Make time for family, ok? Not just empty flings.*

This was Natalie's cue for a cutting reply about how she was content with her life. Instead, her fingers paused over the buttons.

Christmas Eve dinner at our house, her mom texted in the pause. *Can u bring bean salad?*

Sure, texted Natalie. Her fingers touched the keypad again. *Set 2 places for me.*

The long pause was worth it. The reply popped onto the screen. *Chad?*

Yes.

He's coming with u? If shock had a digital tone—or her mother knew how to insert emojis in a text—these words would express it in full force.

Natalie smiled. *He wants to see my family*, she added for effect. *He said so.*

The reply her mother fired back was lightning fast. *Why?*

Maybe he's thinking of the future? This was a bold reply. With a smile fully crossing her lips, Natalie left that answer on its own. *Salad is fine. Nite.*

She tossed her phone onto a sofa cushion, and leaned back with a smile, imagining what kind of rumors would now spread through her family tonight. She had just tossed a bomb into their lives, metaphorically speaking—and her mother's contact list would probably be a live wire for the next hour in the family phone chain. She might even be engaged by the end of that speculative exchange.

With a shake of her head, she finished off the pasta. Nobody would be crazy enough to believe *that*. Her, Natalie, not dating anybody else for two whole months would be a record in itself.

It might be a sacrifice worth making, putting aside her carefree life temporarily. Worth putting her dating life on hold, just one time, if she didn't have to hear her life choices as the butt of disapproval and jokes over cranberry Christmas bread at the family's holiday brunch.

✳

Deep, calming breaths. Tessa was not being forced to drive Party 2 Go's hotdog truck for a living again, not yet anyway. She could still find a way to keep Wedding Belles financially afloat, even if their only event for this month was disappearing fast and her dream career was stumbling on its shaky legs.

No shakier than her real ones at this moment, she thought. She owed Blake an apology—she owed Natalie and Ama realistic words about their future if business didn't pick up for them. If the billboard failed, if this wedding stayed cancelled... she might not like to think about those things, but she had to.

The little room's walls around her were off-white, dotted with graying spackle where Blake had patched them. The only decor was the pile of paint tarps, a scarred mantelpiece, Blake's aluminum ladder, and a worn armchair and card table shoved in there for the purpose of stacking up supplies for Nadia and Lyle's defunct ceremony.

Gazing around, Tessa remembered looking forward to painting this place, something that now seemed mostly like an additional expense they didn't need. Maybe Blake had a point about 'Valentine Red' anyway. She had thought of it as part of their unique 'ghetto chic' style which someone like Mac couldn't understand—but having four red walls closing in on her right now might be a little more than she could stand.

She should have bought the bargain green paint, called 'Mint Chip' or something like it.

She heard a double knock on the doorframe, and discovered Blake was standing there. "Can I come in?" he asked.

Tessa drew her feet out of the armchair and sat up straighter. "Sure," she said.

He sat down on the edge of the card table. "I think we need to talk about what's going on between us," he said.

Flames of rose colored Tessa's cheeks, along with the memory of her lips brushing against Blake's, tenderly. *The talk that wasn't*, she thought, flashing back to those words before his departure for Virginia.

"There's nothing going on between us," she answered, quickly and emphatically, as if he was the one being crazy now. She didn't want to discuss this, not now.

"Then you blew up at me just now for no reason?" said Blake. "I don't think so. Look... I want to apologize for calling you jealous a moment ago. That was a petty way to put things, and I didn't mean to make it sound like that."

"I'm not jealous, so you don't have to worry," said Tessa loftily.

"Then there's nothing to talk about?" said Blake. "Call me crazy, because I've had the feeling there's something we haven't been saying for a while. Since... well, since a few weeks ago."

Longer than that. But, in a way, it was nice to know it was that vivid in his mind. This was the fleeting reaction of Tessa's brain before she mustered the courage to reply. "About that," she said.

"Yeah," he said. "About that. Maybe it's time we cleared the air."

The elephant in the room, the subject they had been avoiding for months. Finally, it was at hand, and there was no way to escape.

She took a deep breath. "I know what you're probably thinking," she said. "I thought it wouldn't be awkward after a while, but I guess it is. I think it's—it's because I don't know what to say to you. I was being too weird about the whole thing. So on an issue like paint or fixtures, I just exploded, sort of. Especially when it came to your decorating friend Mac." She managed to say the name without a biting tone.

"I know the problem with her suggestions wasn't about paint color or whether we change some feature in your building," said Blake. "I already figured out that the problem you have with Mac is really about me."

The fire consumed Tessa's whole face as the emotions of confusion, elation, panic, and astonishment swept through her. Suddenly, her fingertips couldn't feel her skirt's fabric beneath them anymore, and unfinished thoughts were crashing into each other in her mind. *What* had he just said to her?

"I want you to know that working with her doesn't change things with us in any way," he said. "I know you probably assumed a lot of things when I told you about the Springer Street house, and how I was getting to work with a real crew again, and with somebody who knows their way around the home restoration community. But I didn't mean to make you feel threatened by it, or that what's going on here wasn't important to me."

"Are you—you mean that I—are you saying that we—?" Flustered, the words were not coming out right, because she didn't know which ones to choose. If her heart wasn't skipping beats, it would help her think clearly at this moment.

"You're too professional for that kind of jealousy, I know," said Blake. "But if you think that I'm going to quit this place, that isn't true. Even if I land another project like the Springer house, I'm not going to let you down. I'll still be around to see that this place holds itself together."

Professional jealousy. As in, fear that Mac was going to steal Blake away from Wedding Belles itself, with its desperate need of repairs for crooked joists and dry rot. Not Tessa's own personal fear of losing him to a smart, attractive professional woman who worked in his field. Relief flooded her and washed away the previous bonfire of emotion in a mere second's time… replacing it with another feeling that was strangely crushing and somber. Almost like disappointment, really.

"I didn't mean to sound angry," she said, after taking a moment to collect her words. What she meant was strangely lost inside her, at this moment.

"You had a right to be, if you think I'm bossing you around when it comes to this place," he said. "You're right when you say that it's your office, your fixtures. Your 'Ghost of Romance' wall paint, or whatever it is."

Tessa's lips twitched. "'Romantic Blue,'" she corrected him. "And… you're right. I was jealous, in a way. You are spending more time at your other work sites, and I felt like we were losing you, not just as a contractor, but as a partner. As a friend too," she amended. "You've helped us out so many times. Working without you at this point would just feel… weird. Almost like working without Nat or Ama."

"I won't tell you what to do with your office ever again," he said. "I'll put your devil—your 'Valentine Red' on these walls, and never mention those green paint samples ever again."

"Green *is* kind of a pretty color," said Tessa. "Maybe sort of a soft gray-green."

"So are we changing things? Because I'd like to know before I prime the walls."

Tessa shook her head. "No," she said. "'Valentine Red' will be fine. It was certainly cheap enough compared to having something mixed especially for us. We need all the cheap we can get, especially if we don't want to lose our very talented contractor."

They both laughed. "I'm glad we cleared the air on this," said Blake. "I was starting to be afraid that things were going to be pretty awkward around here."

"I was just under a lot of stress with the wedding and the tight business budget," she said. "I took it out on you instead of facing up to it." She laughed. "I guess I sounded a little crazy upstairs."

"I've heard worse," said Blake. "And from people besides you."

"Thanks," said Tessa sarcastically.

"Then we're good," he said. A smile twitched Blake's lips again. "You know, before, when you were acting weird around Mac, I kind of thought that something else was going on. When you ripped into her work upstairs, for a moment I started thinking something crazy about all this... that it wasn't just a professional problem between us."

He had been studying the floor until he lifted his eyes to Tessa's with these last few words. Even though his voice was casual, it was almost like a question had emerged now that Tessa was no longer expecting it to come, and was floating in the air between them. He had been thinking that 'something' wasn't strictly professional. That, for instance, there was chemistry between them, and that her feelings were not those of a coworker and friend.

"Because of what happened before..." she began.

"At the first wedding, yeah," he said. "And some of the stuff that happened afterwards."

"I guess we didn't talk about it, did we?" she said. *Here we go*, she thought, her body tensing, as if bracing itself for a sudden plunge on a roller coaster.

"No. But if there was something to say, then we could," he said. "Obviously."

Their eyes met, and neither of them said anything. A long second passed, and Tessa felt locked in place beneath those blue eyes, and the questions and fears inside her. Her tongue was stuck, and she felt the same sense of fear as when she'd stood on stage in the third grade play waiting to say her one and only line as a head of cabbage. Her knees would be shaking, except they were locked in this folded position with nothing to support.

Blake laughed a little bit; so did Tessa, although hers was from sheer nervousness. Her hands were shaking, as was the rest of her, although she supposed that could be attributed to her laughter to an outsider.

Now was the chance to say something different to him, and change the meaning of everything that had happened between them. Tessa's lips moved, fear welling up inside like an underground water spring.

"That would definitely be crazy, wouldn't it?" she said. Her eyes broke contact with his now. "I mean, for either of us to think that would be pretty ridiculous, right?"

"I guess so," said Blake. A short laugh. "Like I said, it was just for a moment."

Crushing disappointment. It was burdening Tessa, making her feel worse than before. She was shrinking away from the feeling, and from the impulse now deflated within her; it gave her laugh a hollow quality and made her feel strangely like crying, even more so than during her fit of temper upstairs.

Her cell phone trilled to life. Tessa answered it, recognizing one of the numbers for Accented Creations on its screen. "Hello, this is Tessa Miller," she answered.

"Ms. Miller, we have a problem," said a clipped—and extremely upset—voice on the other end. "It's a complete disaster. All the plants from greenhouse four through seven are completely ruined, including the ones intended for Mr. Groeder's clients."

"Ruined?" She motioned for Blake to wait as he rose from the table. "What happened?"

"An utter failure of the electrical system that operates the smart thermostats. Last night's precipitation apparently shorted out the electrical box, and caused the thermostat for the first three greenhouses to fall below twenty degrees. What's more, the explosion in the box shook loose one of the irrigation pipes inside and *flooded* the whole place before the temperature dropped. Every plant has frozen, and the floor is covered in ice—it's like a skating rink in there—"

"It's the florist," she said, covering the mouthpiece. Blake sensed something in her voice and sat down again. Tessa switched the call to speakerphone.

"—then the thermostat malfunctioned and ratcheted up the temperature in the last greenhouse to one hundred and fifty degrees," the voice on the other end declared. "The bouquets are wilted beyond repair. It's hopeless."

"Are you saying there are *no* flowers available?" Tessa met Blake's eyes, this time in an exchange of professional concern and not personal searching.

"It might be possible to do something for you," began the assistant on the other line, doubtfully. "But Mr. Groeder might prefer to contact another florist. We'll return ten percent of his client's deposit as per our disaster policy, and offer a discount on any future orders they place with us."

Ten percent? That hardly seemed fair, Tessa thought—not that it mattered if the wedding was canceled. "Surely all the flowers in your greenhouses weren't earmarked for someone's special event," she said. "Can't you simply redesign the centerpieces a little, with some substitutes for anything you don't have in stock? Even if you have to find another source to provide a few missing ones... they don't have to be from an Accented Creations greenhouse per se—"

"Really, Ms. Miller, wouldn't it be easier for your clients to go elsewhere for their special day?"

They were giving them the shove. No wonder he was content to speak with Ms. Miller, the lowly assistant, instead of demanding to speak with Blake again.

"Hold for Mr. Ellingham," said Tessa.

"Ms. Miller—"

She gave Blake a moment to gather himself before he had to assume the role of Stefan's assistant, a little afraid that this was too much to ask on split-second notice.

She needn't have worried. Blake cleared his throat. "Am I to understand that *you* are cancelling your agreement with Mr. Groeder without so much as a 'by your leave'?" he demanded, in exactly the sort of voice that Stefan's assistant would employ for this indignation. "Because of a little overnight wilting? You do have other greenhouses than these four, obviously."

"Yes, but we have a shortage of available flowers and several unhappy clients to contend with. Surely you don't think a wedding is equal to the mayor's holiday dinner, do you?"

"It's my job to assume that *every* wedding my employer plans is equal to a mayoral dinner," said Blake crispy. "I thought a florist's as elite as yours would be capable of finding some way to stretch its remaining flowers to fit the bill for its clients. Mr. Groeder will be extremely disappointed if you choose to fail—and need I remind you how popular he's growing in certain circles? How long until he's the one planning the mayor's dinner party?" Tessa bit her lip to hide a smile at this remark. A perfect touch by Blake's snooty alter ego.

"But—"

"I think your floral artists can find a way to resolve this without cancellation. Find some lilies, freeze some ice, and text us when you have a presentable substitute." He glanced at Tessa, who gave him two thumbs-ups. "Ciao."

Tessa disconnected the call. "You really are brilliant at doing that," she said.

"I try to practice now and then," he answered. But not in a serious way. "You think they'll come up with a couple of quick substitutions?"

"I don't know if it matters," said Tessa. "The wedding plans have hit a rough patch. There's a chance the ceremony may not even happen."

"They're canceling on you?" said Blake with surprise.

She shrugged. "I won't know for a little longer. But… the bride is pretty upset, and the groom hasn't lifted a finger to fix the conflict, so I won't hold my breath."

"What about the flowers and all those wedding favors you've been working on?" said Blake.

"They'll pay us for our time and expense," said Tessa. "Maybe we can recycle a few things later. Not the flowers, though," she said. "But at this point, it would be impossible to get back that retainer fee anyway. Frankly, given how many things went wrong for this wedding, it's amazing the plans made it to this point." It had been falling apart the whole time, with the three of them pasting its seams along the way.

"So what are you going to do?"

"The same thing any good wedding planner does," said Tessa. "Be disappointed over what happened, be realistic that things go wrong sometimes, then find a new client and hope the next time will be a smooth sail to a perfect day." She sighed.

If there was a next time, and their business wasn't doomed to fail no matter what. Tessa did her best not to think about it this way. *Cancelled orders, mixed-up shipments, last-minute changes—those weren't signs, were they?*

Nadia texted her at four. *No change*, she said. Tessa read it with a sigh, then texted back, *So sorry.* The time to pull the plug was drawing ever nearer, and she imagined the tearful bride was probably tossing all her plans—including those squashed by the quarreling mothers—into a wastebasket at home.

Me too.

Are u ok?

Sort of. A pause after this text. *No one understands.* Nobody in Nadia's world did, except maybe her closest friends—all of whom had paid deposits on their own dresses, Tessa recalled.

No friends?

They're busy. Not speaking to my best friend now. That would be Lyle, probably. Tessa wondered if they had spoken since the big argument.

Call me if u need 2.

Another text. *Are u busy?*

No, Tessa texted in reply.

Can we hang out?

Poor Nadia. Seeing the members of the bridal party was probably too hard right now. She was probably feeling lonely and dejected, surrounded by souvenirs of her big day that had fallen apart. Cynthia probably had a million *I told you so*s cued to share the moment Nadia emerged from her apartment to face the world.

Yes, Tessa texted.

Chapter Twenty

Cardboard versions of Nadia's cake had been decorating Ama's desk for days, but now she was packing them into a box from the hall closet. The sight of fake fondant and sugar snowflakes was turning her stomach, now that the finished creation was on hold.

Swiveling her chair around, she propped her feet on the edge of her wastebasket, piled with rejected sketches. Her phone rang, and she reached for it beneath the cover of the *Winter Cakes* cookbook.

Oh no. Was Tamir a glutton for punishment, that he was still calling her at this point? Ama was tempted to reject the call—better yet, to answer and ask him if he was out of his mind.

The phone kept ringing. She ignored it, and studied a recipe for making candy pearls. Now her phone beeped with its 'text received' signal.

It was from Tamir. *Busy tonight?*

Yes. That was all she typed. It looked rude, and felt the same way, but he wasn't leaving her with much choice.

Tomorrow night?

Ama hung her head. *Call me. We'll talk.*

About what a rotten couple we would make, she wanted to add.

Now her phone was ringing. "Hello?" she said, answering it.

"It's me, Tamir."

"I know."

"I thought maybe you would have an evening free this week. Maybe we could go to dinner, or to a gallery."

"Tamir, are you sure about that?" Ama stressed the "sure" in this question.

"No, not really. But I thought since you didn't enjoy the film very much last time, maybe we should try something new."

Completely missing the point. Ama wanted to smack her forehead against the desk—almost as much as she wanted to smack Tamir's for being so dense. "I don't think you had a good time, either," she said. "Shouldn't we just stay home?"

"Would your parents want me to come to your house? Or did you mean mine?" asked Tamir.

"Neither," said Ama. But so faintly that she didn't think he heard it. "I'm really busy this week, Tamir." Did he simply not want to understand her hints? Was that the problem?

"Are you free next Thursday?" he said. "I have a business conference in the first part of the week. I'll be back by then. We could meet and decide what to do."

Break up with me, Tamir. Please, please break up with me, so I don't have to tell you the truth, Ama thought desperately. What she said aloud, however, was, "I guess so." Reluctantly, which anybody but Tamir would sense. "We can meet then."

"I'll see you later." When the call disconnected, Ama's forehead thumped down on the cover of *Winter Cakes*, nose pressed against its glossy cover.

"I thought you told this guy already that you didn't want to see him," said Natalie, curled up on her workroom sofa, the second piece of Nadia's dress splayed across her lap. "Wasn't that the plan?"

"Plans go wrong," said Ama with a groan. "He's really nice. He's a nice guy. Deadly dull, but other than that, any girl would probably love to go out with him."

"Not me," said Natalie, snipping the thread from her needle. "But I'm probably not his type."

"Not his parents' type, anyway," said Ama. "I'm not, either. He just doesn't get it. He made a mistake, picking me from the matchmaker's site, and he can't see it. Everybody else can... well, except for my parents. They can't believe how lucky we've been to have a boy this wonderful show up on our doorstep."

"Is it that you can't look him in the eye, or that you won't?" said Natalie.

"Does it make a difference?"

"It's two different things," said Natalie. "If you're afraid, then I don't know what to tell you. If you're only reluctant to hurt his feelings, I have two words for you. Motorcycle. Guy."

Ama blushed. "That's... different," she began. "I don't even know if he likes me, to begin with. He might just think we're friends." He had never said anything to prove they weren't, come to think of it. A motorcycle ride, lunch on a train, an impromptu pastry delivery—those weren't actual dates.

"But you like him, and you don't like Tamir. Until you *tell* Tamir, you're stuck dating him when you want to date motorcycle guy, if he asks you out. There's only one solution."

"I wish it were that easy," said Ama. "Even if I tell Tamir the truth, I still can't date Luke." Not without sending shock waves through her parents and auntie. A perfectly good engineer tossed aside for a leather-wearing boy who probably believed in love at first sight and the magic of a first kiss, the most impractical of Ama's dreams. Dreams her siblings and even most of her friends had foregone when choosing their own mates.

"Would your parents be that upset?" asked Natalie. "He's not a psycho killer."

"You don't understand," said Ama. "You don't know how hard it would be for them to accept me being in love with someone who doesn't fit the mold. Who doesn't know our culture, our traditions… who would sweep me away anywhere in the world without a second thought about family ties."

If only Luke had been from India… or Tamir had been more like the kind of guy she always dreamed of meeting. Ama couldn't help wishing for an easier solution to the quandary she was facing now. As much as she wanted to find love, she also wanted her family to be happy about it when she finally did.

"Do you want to be swept away?" asked Natalie.

"Sometimes," said Ama. She nodded. "I think about being in love with someone, and having them as my whole world. I want there to be sparks for a first kiss… one glance to be a whole language, even though we've only known each other for a little while. Those are things my parents can't understand about me, even if I try to explain them. They're just not part of the story that they've known in their own lives."

"Mine had those things," said Natalie. "And look where it got me. The same place you are, with a mother who won't be happy until I commit myself to a nice boy and say, 'I do.'"

Ama sat down on the sofa, moving aside the long train of lace fabric trailing across it. "I have to choose," she said. "But it's hard. It's harder than I thought it would be."

Natalie folded the garment on her lap and stuck the needle into her ladybug pincushion on the floor. "Do you have plans tonight, or do you want to grab dinner somewhere together? *Not* Indian or Italian food?"

"Chinese?" laughed Ama. "Soul food? The flavors of South America?"

"Chad did introduce me to an Ecuadorian place with excellent lime garlic salsa," said Natalie. "I'll grab my coat and scarf and we'll choose someplace."

The funky embroidered coat and hat that Ama had worn to work hung on the back of her office door. She grabbed them and reached for her cell phone at the same moment it beeped with a new text.

Luke's number. *Hi, stranger. How are u?*

Ama's heart was beating strangely.*Hi there.*

Busy?

No. Going out with a friend.

Too bad. Wanted to chat. Got time?

A little. Miss seeing u.

I won't keep u. Have a cross-country delivery this wknd. Will u be at market Saturday of Christmas Eve?

I will.

See you then.

She closed the text window. Christmas Eve at the market with Luke—only, she would have to face her date with Tamir sooner than that. She closed her eyes and sighed.

She had to make a choice.

Ama and Natalie chose a Japanese place called the Koi Fountain, a quiet dining spot with a glass mural of Japanese goldfish swimming in clear blue waters, and tiny tearooms cordoned off with paper screens, and with window views of a moss garden. It was the first time in weeks that Ama had entered a restaurant that didn't have the heavy scent of *masala* in the air, and there was no pasta on the menu, much to Natalie's relief.

"So you're going to choose the one you want, right?" said Natalie

"Probably?" Ama's chopsticks picked through the tender slices of beef on her plate. The look on Natalie's face in reply forced her to add more words. "It's not as easy as it seems, trust me. Family pressure can be really tough to ignore. When I think about their disappointment, I feel a big lump in my throat that blocks the words I have to say to Tamir. I feel guilty that saying those things will hurt everybody in my life."

"I'm not exactly a stranger to the feeling," Natalie said, in a grimmer voice than usual. Her chopsticks were still wrapped in paper by her plate, her fork twirling her noodles Italian-style. "It's just because Luke isn't Indian, I take it?"

"It's bigger than that," said Ama, shaking her head. "I know they always pictured me with an Indian guy, but it's because they want me to be with someone who can be part of my culture, and accept it for what it is. There's an old joke about Indians marrying the family, not the person, but it's kind of true. It's a family experience in my culture."

"Are you sure you're not Italian?" joked Natalie. "Okay, it's not quite like that for me. But it feels like it, sometimes."

"At least you have privacy to explore relationships that might be doomed," said Ama. "If I dated someone who didn't get how my family thinks... who didn't understand them, or couldn't find a way to fit in with them... that would be devastating to my parents. It would really hurt them. I know it, and when I think about someone like Luke maybe saying or doing the wrong thing, I turn into a coward. He doesn't live in a world where you have to be near your family, or be part of their lives all the time. He doesn't have a family unit, he travels and lives wherever he wants."

Natalie lost interest in trying her soup after a fish head with an eye floated to the top from beneath a cucumber slice. "My ma has no clue why I wouldn't want to inflict all my relatives on every boyfriend I date," she answered. "Like every guy who ever meets me can't wait to find out I have an annoying brother and a weird uncle."

"The thing is," said Ama, "what my parents want for me isn't that different from what I want. A decent, kind, good-hearted person who respects me. They want me to be happy, and to care about the person I'm with—only difference really is how we think it should happen. They don't want me to leave it to chance, to risk maybe ending up alone."

This was the real problem—wanting the same thing, but wanting it in different ways. She knew they loved her, and wanted the best for her. They just didn't want to take the chance that her choices could hurt her.

"Lots of people who hold out end up alone," said Natalie. She would be one of them, she reflected, if nobody irresistible came along to change her mind at some point—since Chad probably wasn't going to slip a *real* diamond ring on her finger at the end of the holidays. Too picky, her mom would forever claim afterwards. And maybe she was, but that was her business alone.

"They could be right, and I could wait too long," said Ama. "But... I like the romance of waiting. That's the part that they don't understand. I don't want a safety net, a suitable boy who will 'do' because he's nice and he fits in. I want to take a chance... even if that chance means I end up making a hard choice."

It's not that she wanted to make one, but she wanted them to see she had a right to do it. Right now, she couldn't see herself compromising by settling for the first prospective guy who came along, not when the world seemed big and there might be a person in it who caused undeniable electricity to pass through her every time he so much as brushed her hand. She wanted it to be magic, not a match made by a checklist's columns, no matter to whom the list belonged.

"Or no choice at all," said Natalie cryptically, but with a smile as she finished off her last sushi roll.

✳

The scent of yellow turmeric was heavy in the Tandoori Tiger from her mother seasoning the rice on the stove for the second wave of dinnertime customers. Ama tucked her leftover sushi rolls in the fridge, then tied on an apron, preparing to help dice meat for curry, and mince vegetables for her father's secret recipe for stuffed veal rolls in garlic sauce.

Nikil was here, having a friendly argument with Rasha over a recent food delivery, while Bendi was doing her best as usual to add confusion to the discussion. Ranjit was pounding his cutlets to the thinnest layer possible, humming some song under his breath from one of her brother's contemporary pop CDs as he lightly sprinkled the meat with seasoning.

She felt a hand on her shoulder. "Somebody left this for you earlier," Jaidev said quietly, coming out of the storeroom with a bag of rice under his arm. From his tone, Ama knew who that 'someone' must be as he slipped an envelope into her hand. "I found it taped to the door when I opened the restaurant this afternoon."

He had tucked it out of sight before anyone else could see it, Ama surmised. She was grateful for this thoughtfulness on her brother's part as she retreated a little behind the shelf of pots and pans and lifted the flap. The light was bad in this part of the kitchen thanks to a burnt-out bulb in the lamp above, but she could still read the contents in the shadows of the vast soup and rice pots behind her.

She unfolded the slip of paper inside, finding a letter written by hand. It was her first glimpse of Luke's handwriting: quick, looping letters traveling in uneven lines across the paper like a highway's meandering borders. The top of the paper was ripped, where it had clearly been pulled free of a desk scratch pad, the bottom of Luke's business name and logo still clinging in ink remnants to the jagged edges.

Dear Ama,

I told you I wanted to be a poet, and say things on paper that are hard to say in person. Probably it's not my talent either, like playing violin or guitar isn't. But I'm pretending for a moment that it is, because I wanted to say some things to you without using a phone or showing up at your place of work again, where words have to be short anyway.

If I look in my mind these days, a part of you occupies it. You're planted like a flag in a sandcastle for the way you talked about loving the beach, or a postcard in my pocket from the Paris bakery you want to visit someday. Pieces of your scrapbook are pasted into mine now, even though we've only met a few times. I find myself thinking about you when I'm sitting alone in the shop, or working with my hands, and my mind wonders instead if you're in a kitchen making curry or pouring batter into pans.

What I'm really trying to say is this: I like you, Ama. So much that words don't easily express it.

You mentioned fate that day on the train. I can tell you right now that whatever fate holds in store for us, I'm glad we shared that experience, with conversations that only made sense in the moment, and pastries we tasted for just a few minutes before only the crumbs were left. That memory will make me smile years from now.

Sunset, steam rising, the quiet in the room seems expectant as I leave this line between us. That's the only poetic line I can manage in all this, but I thought you should know what's in my thoughts. Have a piece to keep for your life's scrapbook, even if this letter gets lost.

Until Christmas Eve, or whenever we talk again.

Luke.

It was a love letter. Ama's first. She folded it up carefully, as if it were valuable, and held it between the fingers of both hands. Eyes closed, she let the world reel around her in a dizzying cycle. Luke had said that he liked her. He thought about talking to her and spending time with her.

He really likes me. I didn't imagine it, that it was more than just a chance for free pastries or to impress Deena by taking me for a ride. He really wants to see me again. This magical feeling in response to a few lines on a piece of paper—was this what love felt like? It was different from the way she felt during one of her fleeting crushes in the past, or any little romantic fantasy that she indulged now and then while watching a movie. This had symptoms like surprise, anticipation, anxiety, excitement: all powerful enough to roll the floorboards momentarily beneath her feet. A little dance of happiness wasn't out of the question right now.

The soup pot clanging just behind her brought her back to the rock-solid earth. "What are you doing, Ama?" her mother asked.

"Nothing," said Ama. She quickly stuffed the letter into the pocket of her zoo animal skirt with one hand, the other adjusting one of the saucepans on the shelf. "I was looking for the skillet Jaidev uses for curry."

"It's on the stove," answered Pashma. She gave Ama another funny look, then carried away the pot she lifted down from the shelf.

Ama breathed a sigh of relief. Her fingers tucked the letter more securely in her pocket, feeling as if its words possessed a burning power that would shine through the fabric and reveal the truth to everybody, instead of remaining innocuously hidden. But maybe that's because she could hear Luke's voice reading them in her head the whole time she was dicing carrots on her cutting board, trying to look as if nothing monumental had happened to her mere seconds ago.

What if he can't understand the past or the culture that created me? she thought. *What if everyone else sees him as wrong, and only I see him as the right one?* The looks on their faces at his leather jacket and rebellious t-shirt... the cool and casual attitude that was so alien to her quiet world of cupcakes and novelty-print skirts—where rebellion was forgetting her Punjabi vocabulary in a youthful bid for independence...

What if it's too late and I'm falling in love with him already? She didn't dare ask herself this question. Not even as her knife missed its mark while dicing and shaved her onion as thin as carbon paper.

❋

While Ama was stranded in an island of thoughts amidst her family's busy kitchen, and Natalie savored one last cup of tea before the view of the koi pond and moss garden, Tessa was sharing a frozen pizza and a glass of pinot across town at Nadia's place. The young gallery curator's apartment was understated in its decor and also a little untidy—but a number of scattered bridal magazines accounted for some of the mess, Tessa noticed. Here was a woman whose spare time had been consumed by an event now destined for the recycling bin.

"Sorry, I haven't had time to clean," said Nadia, gathering up a few torn-out pages and a couple of empty fast food cartons. "I've been so busy the past few weeks, trying to sort stuff out at work and for the wedding. And survive my mother's complaints about it," she added wryly. She stuffed her armload in a pantry cupboard, slamming the door closed before it could escape.

"You had a lot of opinions offered to you—more than you wanted, I'm sure," said Tessa. "I can always see the stress building in a client's eyes whenever too many people are involved."

"Crazy eyes?" said Nadia. "Mine must have been. I must have been insane. Here I was, thinking it was supposed to be the happiest day of my life I was planning." She pulled the pizza from the oven, fumbling with a mitt that had a hole in its finger section.

"Careful." Quickly, Tessa rescued the pan's opposite side, using a dish towel as a makeshift potholder. Nadia set the pan on the stove.

"Thanks," she said. "There's another thing I should put on my to-do list, now that I have free time. Buy new kitchen linens." She opened a drawer and pulled out a pizza cutter.

"You didn't have crazy eyes," said Tessa.

"What?"

"Your look. It was very normal," said Tessa. "What went wrong isn't your fault, Nadia. Sometimes... sometimes you need a moment to step back from a situation and figure out why part of it feels wrong.

In relationships, we call it a breather. In the wedding business, we call it chocolates, wine, and maybe a couple of tranquilizers if someone hasn't slept in forty-eight hours."

Nadia laughed. "Do you really?"

"Not really. I just thought a joke might help." Tessa opened the bottle of wine on the counter, making the assumption that it was sitting there for use. She poured a glass for Nadia. "Humor helps. Especially if you work in a business that takes itself too seriously on occasion."

Humor helped Nadia, at least after they'd had a few laughs over some of the wildest ideas suggested for her wedding, especially by Paula. Between that, the pizza, and the red wine, Nadia seemed less emotionally rattled than when Tessa arrived.

Nadia took a sip from her second glass. "She called me three times every day about some part of it, my mother," she said, holding up three fingers for emphasis. "When it wasn't her, it was Paula. 'Oh, look at this fun idea for the reception, where everybody does the limbo with rubber chickens.' She wouldn't stop, even when I told her that I had my heart set on the winter white theme. Neither of them did, except my mother was *more* thrilled, because it fitted her 'simple is elegant' mantra."

"You needed a vacation." Tessa's thumb and finger stole the last pizza crumbs from her plate. "Sometimes I tell brides and grooms to just take some time away during all this. It will drive you crazy if you focus on one thing with such intensity. Believe me, I know—I do it every day. Over and over."

"You do, don't you?" said Nadia. "It's just like fitting out an exhibition. You're so in the moment for the artist's vision... then, three weeks later, it's on to the next artist, working with a completely different style."

"I never thought about it, but you're right," said Tessa. "We're a lot alike. Soul sisters separated at birth, maybe." They both laughed at this joke.

Then Nadia's laughter faded. "You know who didn't call me during all this?" she said. "Lyle. I always wanted it to be him. I wanted him to be supportive of the fact that I was trying to make this day about us. You know my mother hated the reception being at his restaurant?" she said to Tessa.

"Can't say that surprises me," said Tessa. She could imagine Cynthia wasn't enthralled with Greek cuisine.

"I was so firm with her about that. We had a huge argument and I told her that was the final decision, because I didn't want her to keep criticizing it and hurting Lyle's feelings. He doesn't realize what I've been going through with the two of them. That, or he just doesn't care." She burrowed deeper between two pillows cushioning the sofa's arm, brooding over her wine glass.

"Maybe he was afraid," suggested Tessa. "You have to be a little brave to be that honest with somebody."

Nadia sighed. "I didn't even have the chance to try on my fully finished wedding dress," she said. "Can you sell it for me?" she looked at Tessa. "Can Natalie just… sell it? No, wait—wait, maybe I don't want—I don't know." She set her glass on the coffee table and buried her face in one of the cushions.

Tessa set aside her own glass and rubbed her client's shoulder sympathetically. "You can still try it on," she answered. "Natalie will do whatever you want. You still need time to think about all of this, so don't rush yourself into making decisions."

"Can you unmake the biggest decision of your life in ten minutes?" said Nadia tearfully. "I did. And, of course, the only person who's going to clean it up is me." She wiped away a few tears. "Lyle hasn't even cancelled the booking at the restaurant. Or the band."

"Don't worry about the band," said Tessa, who possessed inside knowledge on this subject. "I'll help you take care of all those details." Undoing everything she'd worked hard to achieve in the face of the jinx, she thought gloomily.

A handful of gravel struck the window. Nadia sat up. "What was that?"

"A bird, maybe?"

Another shower against the panes. Nadia drew herself to her feet and crept toward the window, with Tessa behind her. Two stories below, they could see Lyle standing there, in an overcoat and scarf.

"He couldn't call?" said Nadia sarcastically.

"You turned your phone off, actually," said Tessa. "While the pizza was heating up."

Nadia's sigh was one of frustration as she opened the window and leaned outside. "What do you want?" she called below.

"I want to talk to you," he called back. "Can I come up?"

"I'm busy, Lyle," she said. "This really isn't a good time. Not after everything that's happened."

"Please, Nadia," he said. "Give me a chance. Honest. Just—a few words, and I'll leave if you want me to. But don't leave us like this, please."

Tessa glanced at the bride-to-be, who looked torn between sticking to her resolve and giving in to the man she still loved. "You could hear him out," she suggested. "I can stay in case you need moral support, if you want."

Nadia nodded. She leaned over the sill. "All right," she called reluctantly. "You can come up. But only for a few minutes." She closed the window and crossed the room to press the buzzer for the front door. "This is a mistake, probably," she muttered. "I don't know what I'm doing, Tess."

"One step at a time," said Tessa, who tried not to look too obvious or expectant as she perched on the edge of the sofa arm. Lyle knocked on the door. Nadia hesitated before answering it.

"What is it?" she said, sounding tired. "It's been a really long day, Lyle, and I have a lot to do, so let's just get this over with."

He shook his head. "I don't want to get it over with. Nadia, I love you. You know that, don't you? I didn't want to break up with you, I wanted to marry you."

"Please… let's do this some other time," said Nadia, who looked tearful again. "Just go home, Lyle." She started to close the door, but he stopped her.

"Wait," he said. "I've been thinking. Maybe you were right about me not helping you keep the peace and all that. Maybe our moms were kind of running things, and I was pretending that it wasn't all that bad. But I can change that. I can be better, Nadia. Please, just give me the chance."

Nadia's gaze was trained on the floor. "Those are only words, Lyle," she said. "I know you want to mean them, but… I don't know if I can believe you. I don't know if I can trust you." She met his gaze now, her eyes filled with regret.

"Would it help if I said I booked a ride for after the wedding?" he asked.

"What?" said Nadia in shock.

"What?" echoed Tessa nearly simultaneously—although hers was with a scheduler's panic.

"One sleigh and two reindeer to pick us up at that glass wedding chapel, and take us to my car," he said.

"Reindeer?" said Tessa.

Lyle looked at her. "Yeah," he said. "I know a guy who knows a guy. He's got a friend who has a Scandinavian lodge in Vermont." He shrugged his shoulders. "I called him up and rented one of his sleighs with a driver for the afternoon. They have little wheels on the sleigh, so even if it doesn't snow, we can still go in it."

"A sleigh and reindeer from Vermont? Lyle—that must be costing you a fortune," said Nadia. "It's only ten minutes from the church to the parking."

"We'll take the long way," he said. "I don't care about cost anyway. I care about making you happy. You want a winter-themed wedding, that's what I want you to have. It doesn't matter what cake your mom wants or what music my mom wants... what matters is you and me, like you said. I'll help you fix the rest of this wedding, promise. I'll be there for you, Nadia, no matter what."

He reached into his pocket and pulled out a Christmas ornament—a bundle of pale green silk mistletoe leaves tied with a red ribbon. A glittery crystal snowflake dangled from the center of the bow. "What do you say?" he asked Nadia. "Will you still be my winter bride, Nadia Emerson?"

Nadia blinked back tears. "I will," she said. She put her arms around Lyle's neck, the groom now holding her tight.

"Forgive me?" he asked softly.

She nodded, her face buried against his shoulder. "That's all I wanted to hear," she said. "That's all."

Neither of them was paying any attention to Tessa, who had become invisible in the room as she silently celebrated the look of happiness on the couple's faces now that their wedding was happening again. She made plans to slip away as quietly and politely as possible—when their embrace wasn't blocking the doorway, for instance.

No more unhappiness, no more cancellations. And no more bad luck curse for the Wedding Belles, either.

Chapter Twenty-One

Thursday evening in the city square—the shopping traffic was thick, and the holiday atmosphere permeated the air along with the scent of hot chestnuts and pretzels and coffee, and the sound of a Salvation Army band playing for donations. A little crowd was gathered there, and around all the window displays of mechanized North Pole workshops, sugar plum fairies, and chic merchandise in a winter wonderland of fake snow and glitter that reminded Ama of Nadia and Lyle's wedding theme.

She passed the green-and-red Christmas trees at the plaza entrance, their branches trimmed with twinkle lights and silver garlands. She searched the faces in the crowd until she spotted Tamir waiting on a nearby bench, a city guide in hand.

As always, he was overdressed for their outing, even with a knitted sleeveless pullover dressing down his pinstripe shirt beneath the coat he adjusted, tucking his wool scarf inside its collar. Ama glanced down at the skirt that covered her winter tights—printed with kittens and candy canes—then drew a deep breath and crossed the plaza.

He saw her approaching and rose to his feet with a polite smile. "Hi," he said.

"Hi, Tamir." Should they shake hands? Hug? Definitely not the latter, because Ama felt as if it would wrinkle Tamir's neatly pressed exterior. They stood there awkwardly, hands in their pockets against the night's cold.

"I thought we might choose something from this," he said, glancing at the guide under his arm. "There are some nice art shows listed for this month in the west end. The new Sixth Street Gallery has an exhibition of modern murals inspired by tapestries from Mumbai."

"It sounds pretty, but…" began Ama. Her smile was weak, at best, at the idea of pretending to admire abstract art in the form of wall rugs.

"We could have coffee somewhere if you like, before or after. I think there's a place near the gallery…" Tamir flipped through the pages of his guide, pushing his eyeglasses in place again. "Maybe I should try searching on my phone." He closed the book and pulled out his cell phone instead, searching the directory as he turned to go.

"Wait," said Ama. She didn't follow him, but remained in place while Tamir took a few steps forward, before he realized she wasn't coming. "Tamir, I have to say something."

"What is it?" he asked, puzzled.

"Tamir, I… I don't want to go out with you anymore." The deep breath in Ama's lungs escaped her with these words. "I'm sorry. But this isn't working. I don't think either of us are happy, and I don't think either of us are going to be, so long as we keep spending time together."

Her words trembled a little bit, but they still emerged. She couldn't bring herself to look him in the eyes yet—what if this hurt him? What if it felt like rejection, even if she wasn't the real girl of his dreams?

Tamir was perfectly still. He glanced at the lights on the Christmas trees, drawing a slow, ragged breath.

"Don't take this the wrong way," said Ama softly. "You're a nice guy, and you've been really kind to me. But I'm not interested in dating you. This whole—arrangement—was really my father's idea, and I never wanted to do it."

Tamir glanced back. "He made you go out with me?" he asked slowly.

She shook her head. "No—just the website thing," she said. "I went out with you because... well, because my family wanted it... and because you were a nice guy, and I didn't want to hurt you. Obviously I kind of failed that part," she added lamely.

Shaking beneath her coat, she felt both brave and terrible for saying any of this. She stood up straight, making herself look at Tamir with what she hoped was an apology in her eyes... but not any regrets for telling him the truth.

He released a sigh. "There's nothing to say, I guess," he answered at last. "Except that I... I understand what you mean. That is, I know what it's like to do something for your family's sake more than your own. It was like that for me too in a way."

"Really?" Her heart lifted ever so slightly with these words. "Then you didn't want to sign up for the match site either?" she guessed. Maybe this wasn't the crushing blow to his feelings she had feared it would be. He might be a little bit relieved even, somewhere behind that stiff demeanor.

Tamir hesitated. "It was more my parents' idea than my own, yes. I was willing to go along with it because they were so eager for it—but I wasn't sure I was ready for something like that. Or to have a relationship right now," he added somewhat sheepishly.

"So why did you keep asking me out?" The question popped from Ama's mouth before she considered its consequences. If Tamir was truly indifferent to her as a date and only pursued the relationship to please his parents, then it wouldn't matter much. But if he had started to like her, even a little bit, this could open a can of worms they were better off avoiding.

He looked embarrassed for a moment. "I liked spending time with you. And I thought we might actually be compatible, given the chance. I suppose I was wrong about that." His smile was wry but fleeting.

Compatible. One of Ama's least favorite terms for describing romantic connections, but exactly the kind she would expect someone like Tamir to choose when describing his ideal relationship.

"Maybe my first instinct was right, and I wasn't ready to meet someone yet," Tamir continued. "Maybe I was trying too hard—or not hard enough. I kept thinking with more time it might work out between us."

She hoped he wasn't holding out for the possibility that she would change her mind. She needed to be clear that it wasn't going to happen, just in case he thought there might be a chance for them despite this parting. It wouldn't do to have anybody trapped in wishful thinking.

"I really am sorry, Tamir," she told him. "I wish it could have been different, but it isn't. I don't think it will change in the future. I can't keep wasting your time like this."

There was a long pause as he absorbed this. After a moment, he nodded. "Thank you," he said. He looked so grave and serious—then again, he looked that way all the time, so Ama couldn't be sure how much this was actually hurting him. But his tone was one of acceptance, she thought, after spending time with him these last few weeks.

"I should go, I suppose," he said. "I don't want to keep you here too long. I guess you probably didn't plan to see the gallery after all tonight." This time, his glance betrayed a flicker of regret beneath the polite surface.

So he *was* hurt. Ama felt worse, seeing the pain in his eyes, but it was too late to change it. Whether it was his pride, dignity, or a deeper feeling that she had wounded, she would probably never know. But it didn't matter since she had been honest with him, about the fact that one more date or a hundred like the first two wouldn't change things between them.

"Thanks for understanding," she said. "I hope you find the right person next time." The cheerful rendition of 'Good King Wenceslas' in the background didn't fit this situation at all, even though Tamir managed a weak smile.

"I hope so, too." The smile, faint as it was, dissolved entirely as he turned away from her. "Goodbye, Ama."

"Goodbye," she said. "Good luck." That felt like a stupid farewell line, but she had already said it aloud. Tamir didn't look back to acknowledge it, however, as he walked away toward the opposite side of the plaza, his guidebook still tucked under his arm.

Ama sighed and hugged herself in the cold. As hard as it was to tell Tamir the truth, the hardest part was yet to come. How could she tell her family it was finally over between her and the matchmaking site's suitor?

❄

"How was your evening?" Bendi shut off the vacuum cleaner as Ama entered the restaurant's outer foyer. "You are home early."

Of course her auntie would be lingering here, waiting for the latest word on Ama's courtship—she should have expected it from the moment she came downstairs in her coat and scarf after dinner.

"I didn't go out to have fun," she answered, pulling off her scarf. She met Jaidev coming downstairs now.

"Hey, I thought you had a date tonight," said Jaidev. "That's what Dad said."

"I did *not* have a date," she corrected him.

"Didn't you see the boy tonight?" Ranjit appeared from the restaurant doorway, in his slippers and the Indian cotton ensemble that he wore whenever he hosted in the dining room. Behind him, Ama could hear the noise of customers eating, and the crash of a serving dish sliding off the table inside the kitchen.

"How was the former playboy of Tamil Nadu?" asked Jaidev.

"Stop it, everybody. Please." Ama held up her hands. "For the record, I did not have a date tonight. What's more, I'm not seeing Tamir anymore."

You could drop a pin and hear it bounce on the carpet in the second of silence which followed her words—then came the rush of replies, the exclamation of shock from her auntie, the dismay from her father which sounded like a wounded cry.

"But why?" demanded Ranjit. "Such a perfect boy for you. Ama, why?"

"He wasn't, though, Papa," she insisted. "I told you from the start that it wouldn't work, and it didn't. Now it's over, so everyone can forget about Tamir and me. All right?"

She turned to finish going upstairs, feeling Jaidev tweak her sleeve. "Nice move, sis," he whispered. She saw a sympathetic gleam in her brother's eye as he went below. She could hear her auntie and father's protests, the words being exchanged about her announcement, but she pretended not to notice.

Upstairs, she pulled off her scarf and coat and flopped down on her bed. She was supposed to finish making a list of ingredients for the dessert finger foods for Nadia and Lyle's reception, but she felt too tired to reach for her pencil and pad. Maybe sleep was what she really needed, now that her enthusiasm had drained itself in two confrontations.

❄

Chop, chop, chop. Ama's knife diced almonds for the evening's dessert amidst the morning kitchen's usual chaos, her mind on the chocolate truffles for the wedding, and the sugared coconut for their coating. Mini snowballs, she pictured—and mini peppermint cheesecakes to the side—

"Did you want apples for a dessert?" asked Jaidev, setting a sack on the counter. "Somebody said we needed apples, so I ordered a crate from the grocery guy."

"I'm using them to make a seasonal version of *halwa*," she explained. "Kind of like applesauce." Her knife slid aside the almonds in tiny piles on her cutting board. She glanced toward the stove, where her father was stirring a pan of chickpeas, looking morose and grumpy.

He was going to say something about their conversation last night, sooner or later. All morning everyone in the kitchen had given each other little looks when they thought she was busy, refraining from asking only because they thought she wouldn't tell them what happened. How did she break up with such a great suitor—more precisely, how did she manage to *lose* such a perfect suitor?

Her father's spoon clacked against the side of the pan the way it did when he was upset about something. Pashma looked up from grinding spices. "Let me make the chutney dip," she said to Ranjit.

"No. I want to do it." A childish tone of declaration—he must *really* be upset, Ama thought. She tried not to notice as she went back to dicing nuts, the rhythm of her knife matching the soft *shoof shoof* of her mother's pestle against the cumin seeds.

"Maybe there will be another boy," said Ranjit. "The website ad will last to the end of the month. Maybe there will be another nice date in a week or two."

"I'm not meeting another boy from the website, Papa," said Ama. "I just... can't. It's not going to work, so please don't ask me to do it anymore."

"But why? How?" he repeated. "Ama, he was such a good boy—he had a degree, he had a nice job—"

"He was soo cute," said Rasha. "Are you sure you want to break up with him?"

"Who said she broke with him?" Bendi interrupted. "Did she break with him?" She glanced at all of them sharply, as if sniffing for the answer. "Did she?"

"It was mutual, auntie," said Ama. "We weren't meant to be. That's all. It's just a fact of life for some people that they're not meant to be a couple."

"So try again," pressed Ranjit. "There are lots of nice boys on the internet account. Go look—one of them could be the right one. Maybe he writes, maybe he asks to meet you—"

"Dad, maybe we should let it go," said Jaidev gently. "Give Ama some time."

"She doesn't need time, she needs a nice boy!" declared Bendi. "Look how long she's been unattached. Men notice when a girl has been eligible too long."

"Not these days, Bendi," said Rasha. "Nobody cares anymore how long you've been single. You should look on the website though, Ama," she added. "Papa's right. Some of those guys sound amazing. I remember seeing Sanjay's profile after we were dating, and thinking 'wowza.' I would have totally dated him based on that."

"No, thanks." Ama pushed her latest almond slivers into a new pile.

"It is the fault of that other boy," said Ranjit vehemently. "The one with the motorbike. He's giving you ideas about wild boys being better than sensible ones, and you want to meet someone like him instead of a good boy like Tamir."

"That's not why Tamir and I aren't dating anymore," said Ama, with a guilty jolt at how close her father had come to the truth. "We weren't right for each other, Papa, and that's that."

"Why not?" he asked again. "What did you need that he didn't have?"

"I needed to feel something for him," said Ama. "Can't you understand just a little? I don't want to be practical about love, I want it to happen on impulse. I want to *feel* it happen to me—not try to feel it with someone because they're a suitable person, or we have a few things in common."

He shook his head. "A good boy shows up, you say no. I don't know what I'm going to do. You will choose some terrible boy and what can I do about it? What can I do, Ama?"

"You think a boyfriend I choose would be so awful that you could never like him?" she answered. "Is that what you think of me?" She was shocked and hurt, although it made sense, really. He didn't trust her, and that's why he wanted her to choose from a pool of candidates where he decided who was and wasn't acceptable.

"He didn't mean it like that, Ama." Rasha laid a hand soothingly on her sister's arm, but Ama shook it off.

"I think stupid movies and books have filled up your head," answered Ranjit. "Filled it with ideas about love that are not real. You think that boys should be like the princes and spies and—and superheroes—and that suitors should make long speeches and kiss you under the stars. Things are not like that in real life, Ama. But you will pick a boy who makes you think they are, and he will do it to trick you. That's what I know as your papa, and that's why I should be the one to decide these things for my children."

He clanked his spoon angrily against the side of the pan, as if the end of his speech should be the end of the matter. Ama's eyes burned with tears, although she didn't let them fall.

"It's not like that anymore, though," said Rasha. "You know that, Papa. Even Punjabi women in India can pick which matches they're going to date. Mama picked you, didn't she? She had other suitors who liked her, right?"

"In America, everybody does it like this nowadays," said Jaidev. "This is how all of our friends do it—they meet somebody, go out with them, have a good time, and marry them if they're a good person they like."

"That's not a good way," muttered Ranjit. Ama pulled off her apron and marched out of the kitchen.

He was never going to understand. She didn't expect him to, but couldn't he at least let her be herself? Couldn't he forget about Tamir and the website for a while—and try to believe that she wasn't a stupid person who believed in unicorns and fairy godmothers?

She pushed aside the sketches on her bed and sat on its end, struggling not to feel angry or hurt. The door to her room opened again—she expected to see Rasha or Jaidev, come to offer a little private sympathy, but it was Pashma instead.

"I'll come down in a moment, Mama," she said. "I want a few minutes to be alone." She didn't want another lecture on why being a good daughter meant making decisions that were based on what your family wanted. Or some such speech, like the ones that came when she and her siblings argued for holidays away from the family, or over what to do with extra profits from the restaurant.

Drawing aside her sari's free end, Pashma sat down on the bed beside Ama. "Your papa isn't angry with you," she said.

"What is he, then? Disappointed?" Ama asked.

"You are his last daughter. He's protecting you," said Pashma. "Once you are gone, he has no one to look after but me and your auntie… and there is only the one of us he wants to look after, we both know."

Ama almost smiled at this remark, but her unhappiness was stronger than that urge.

"Give him time. He will forget to be upset about the boy in a few days," said Pashma.

"But not about me," said Ama. "This isn't just about Tamir, Mama. You know that." A sigh of frustration escaped her, as her mother's arm tucked itself around her shoulders.

"I remember when you were six," Pashma said. "You drew the picture in school of what your life would be someday. You wanted to put it on the fridge box like all your friends did, by the list for the market."

"Did I?" said Ama listlessly. Another story about the past, to make her appreciate family warmth or security, probably. She didn't remember this particular picture herself, lost in a mental box of a hundred or so grade school art assignments.

"It was a picture of you standing on a beach. You had a little bucket and a little shovel, and a big castle made of sand," said her mother. "You told us that it was your dream castle."

"I hadn't learned to love cakes and cookies yet," said Ama. "It was too early for that dream to be reality." Maybe the point was that her dreams changed; and so, her dream might change to be that of a girl happy to have her father screen all potential boyfriends through a matchmaking site for Indian singles.

"I remember that picture, because it was different from the ones that your brothers and sisters drew," said Pashma. "I saw it was, even then."

"Jaidev's pictures always had race cars," said Ama. "Rasha probably drew fashion models."

"It wasn't the dream that was different." Pashma shook her head. "All the others had everybody in the picture with them, standing beside them. But not you," she continued. "You drew yourself only. You saw your life as separate. As something that was your own. You thought about your dream for you when they told you to draw it, and that's what you did. That's how I knew that you were not the same as all the others."

"What do you mean?" Ama wiped away the traces of her tears. "You mean more American, right? More love for fast food pizza and Nickelback CDs." Her mother didn't know who Nickelback were, of course. Then again, neither did the seventeen-year-old clerk at the corner mart when she had picked up a copy of their Greatest Hits out of nostalgia recently.

"Rasha was the wildflower that wanted to bloom and be pretty. Nalia was the obedient one. Nikil wanted his own place outside the home, and Jaidev can never be serious about life. But you are, Ama," said Pashma. "I know that you are. And I know that you are not trying to hurt your family when you say you are different."

"What are you saying, Mama?" Ama was dangerously close to crying again, but for different reasons from before.

"You are a good daughter," said Pashma solemnly. "You are a smart girl who knows what you can and cannot do. I will trust you, and we will see what we will see."

She drew Ama closer, and kissed her forehead. "Come down and finish your almonds," she said, rising to her feet. "We have only a few hours until we open, and customers will want some *halwa* after a big plate of spicy food."

Ama nodded. "I'll be down in a minute." She retrieved a tissue from her bedside drawer and wiped her eyes, then checked to make sure they didn't look red in the reflection of her compact mirror before she tucked it back inside. From the back of the drawer as she pushed it closed, two old worn crayons in faded paper wraps rolled into view, a green and a purple one, which came to rest against a package of cupcake toppers and a lone birthday cake candle.

It was almost like a sign, Ama thought, her mother's story about her childhood drawing still fresh in her mind. A sign that maybe some things can be different when you least imagine it's possible.

Chapter Twenty-Two

"How does it feel?" Natalie asked, leaning back on her heels as Nadia twirled in front of the mirror.

"It feels fantastic," she said. She laughed as she faced her reflection again in the mirror in Natalie's workroom. "Oh my gosh. It's so perfect. The sketch you showed me after you bought the replacement fabric was gorgeous and it looked great during all the fittings—but I didn't know it would look this amazing when it was finished."

Natalie shrugged. "I do my best," she answered.

This was more than her best: it was a labor of love that had stitched perfect ruches and embroidered a single silvery-white vine from bodice to knee on the surface of the smooth, ivory satin that felt like liquid between her fingers. She had worked all night just to finish the final details, but it was worth it to see the bride's approval for her efforts. The dress ended in a long train, a glimpse of a silver lacy underskirt spreading out from beneath its hem, while a single band of that fabric trimmed the top of the bodice.

"I love it," said Nadia. "Maybe I can buy a white satin wrap that matches it, do you think? Just to wear when we leave the church."

"I think we can do better," said Natalie. "Wait here a second." She rose and opened the second garment box on her sofa. Here was the second piece of her design, the one she had kept secret when making the sketches, the final touch that had eluded her until it was almost too late to create it. She had kept it secret for that reason, but now its moment of unveiling had arrived.

"This is the finishing touch your dress needs," said Natalie. "Fit for a snow bride, I hope."

The outer garment was a pelisse-like coat with an empire waist in a Regency-era style, made of sheer embroidered white lace. Silvery threads were woven through its fabric, with little pearl and crystal beads adorning the pattern's flowers. In the center of each flower, tiny ice blue rhinestones glittered in the light. It was the brainchild of hours of watching *Frozen* in her apartment, and the closest Natalie could come to capturing Elsa's dress without departing from traditional wedding couture.

A little cry escaped Nadia. She pressed her hands to her mouth. "Is that for me?" she said afterwards. "Are you serious?"

"Of course," said Natalie. "Perfect for a snowy sleigh ride through the woods to your waiting transportation." She unfastened the clasp, an ornate silver buckle with a tiny crystal snowflake in its center, and helped Nadia try it on.

They were meeting with Tessa today to confirm the last-minute details for the reception and the ceremony. Much to the chagrin of the wedding's three planners, both the bride's and the groom's mothers joined them at the table to go over the final menu and the layout for both the ceremony and the reception, as well as the seating chart.

"I think there are too many people crowded at these long tables," said Cynthia, lower lip pinched inwards with disapproval. "Smaller tables look so much nicer at receptions."

"Mother." A warning note in Nadia's voice.

"I'm only *saying*."

"I like a big family dinner," said Paula. "I think we should mix things up and have everybody's family and friends sitting by strangers. Meeting new people—that makes things interesting at dinner, and more fun when the music starts. Don't you think so?" She nudged Lyle in the arm.

"I think we should leave things the way they are, Ma," he said. "Tessa put a lot of work into this chart already."

"I did, actually," said Tessa. "So I think it would be a little late to rethink the seating plan for this many guests." She tucked the charts out of sight in hope the topic would be dropped. Besides, she still had the unfortunate subject of the floral centerpieces to discuss.

Thus far, this meeting felt a lot like the others, and all three planners were feeling nervous that it might end like the others—with the bride near tears and the groom looking awkward and befuddled. Paula's bracelets clacked noisily as she drew the seating charts from Tessa's stack of materials before the wedding planner retrieved them again.

"Now, I'm afraid we had to make a few small changes to the flowers," said Tessa.

"Really?" Nadia said, sounding disappointed.

"There was a slight issue with the original design, but the artist has found some substitute flowers that he feels will capture the same spirit as the previous choices," said Tessa, opening a photo file on her tablet with pictures of the new arrangements, minus a few of the roses and white tulip varieties from the original ones. "He's substituted more white amaryllis for the largest white tulips, and introduced a double-petal white narcissus for some of the bud roses. I know it's not exactly the same, but it's very close."

It was as close as the florist could come on such short notice, with a last-minute delivery from a greenhouse in the neighboring state to tide them over until the electrical snafu was repaired. The receptionist had been apologetic and surprisingly helpful when they spoke again on the phone, so maybe this new business connection wasn't as hopeless as it had seemed. Tessa crossed her fingers under the table as Nadia, Lyle, and their two commentators studied the new photos.

"It's still beautiful," said Nadia, in the end. "I think I can live with this."

"Live with it?" echoed Cynthia. "For the prices they're charging—which is highway robbery, in my opinion—how can you let them give you the cheapest bulbs in the floral world instead of roses?" She looked at Tessa. "Insist on roses when you talk to them."

"I think we should scrap 'em," said Paula. "Time to pick someplace less artsy, anyway. How about that real good florist over on Fourth?" she said to Nadia. "They made a great big bouquet for Una's wedding. It had about two dozen red roses in it and these great big sprays of baby's breath. Now *that* was a bouquet."

"I don't think so," said Nadia, shaking her head.

"It would really wow the guests," pressed Paula. "Don't you want things big for the big day of your life?"

"It would be tasteless and overdone," countered Cynthia. "This isn't a bulk order for a Rose Bowl float. This is a hand-held bouquet for my daughter to carry down the aisle, not stagger to its end under the weight of three dozen cabbage heads."

"You're ashamed of a little flash and glamour, aren't you? My son can afford to buy—"

"Enough!" The sudden declaration from Lyle brought silence from the warring mothers—or maybe it was his stern expression that did it. Nadia lifted her head from her hands and looked at him, too.

"Nadia wants these white ones," said Lyle. "They look good, and I can afford it, as Ma pointed out."

"You're not the one paying for them, though," Cynthia replied. "I'm covering those expenses, so I think I should have a say in the final decision, frankly."

"Well, I think Nadia should have the final say," Lyle replied. "So I'll pay for the flowers if that's what it takes for her to have the ones she wants. And nothing's too good for Nadia, so her mom should be pretty happy with things, if she wants her daughter to be happy. Besides," he added, lifting the tablet to look at the centerpiece more closely. "I kind of like it. Those little green things in the mix look nice."

A moment of silence followed. "I'll make a note to tell the florist you said so," said Tessa. "They'll be really happy to hear it." She reached for the tablet and swiped to her email inbox.

"Well," said Cynthia—but without the fire in her usual flustered tone.

"It's your wedding," said Paula, who sounded slightly injured. "I guess you know what you want."

"I think so," said Lyle. He pulled out his cell phone and dialed a number. "Hey, Ramon? It's me. I know we're busy today, but go ahead and strip all those red and green ornaments out of the private dining room, okay? Yeah, I know, Christmas is only a week away, but those don't go with the wedding reception's colors. Just stick 'em back in storage, okay? Okay."

He hung up. "So, what else we got on the agenda?" he asked Tessa.

No meeting had ever gone quite like this before, and it left Tessa momentarily unsure what to say. Lyle had never before expressed interest about anything except for the catering menu that his staff would be handling. Now, however, she sensed that he was braced for whatever topic she could offer.

She, Ama, and Natalie exchanged glances. "How do you feel on the subject of bands versus a DJ for the reception's entertainment?" Tessa asked.

❊

Tessa pondered this shift in the wedding's dynamics as she gazed at the fresh paint applied to the little parlor's walls. Blake had brushed the first coat of red over its surface, leaving no drip marks or smears, the way Tessa's roller typically did.

She was beginning to think maybe he was right. A change from these modern bargain shades might be kind of nice.

"Like it?" Blake was in the doorway behind her. "I think it's growing on me. Just don't tell anybody I said that," he added with a half smile.

"Don't ruin your professional reputation, in other words," she retorted, but with a smile also.

"It's essential in my business," he said, and his grin fully emerged, even if it faded away as quickly as it came. "What's that in your arms?" He gestured toward the notebook she held. She glanced down.

"The wedding folder for Nadia and Lyle," she said. "Now that it's back on, I have a lot to do if we're going to have this celebration in a week's time."

"Congratulations," said Blake softly. "I know you were pretty upset when it looked like it was canceled."

"Relieved is what I feel right now—but I'll feel happier when I have time to let it sink in," she said. "This was a sudden turnaround, kind of like a miracle. Or maybe… more like a sudden U-turn for a traveler on the road to matrimony." She was thinking of Lyle's sudden switch from passive participant to willing planner in the ceremony that marked his love for Nadia, which was a change she never would have predicted in a million years.

Blake smiled. "I guess we all make a last-minute turn now and then," he said, gazing at the half-dry wall.

"If that's a comment on my taste in decorating this place, I'm going to pretend I didn't hear it," answered Tessa. Blake's brow furrowed briefly, then comprehension crossed his face.

"I wasn't talking about that," he said. "No, I was... thinking aloud about something else." He shrugged. "You know, life in general. Maybe choices that come up when we think we know the answer already. That kind of thing." He gathered up some tools he had left in the room earlier: a chisel for opening the paint can, a screwdriver, some random hardware that must have been overlooked. He tucked the nails into the pouch of his carpenter's belt.

He was talking about life in general, Tessa thought. Or something more specific about life... "I suppose that's true," she said. "I guess I never thought about it in words before, but when you put it that way, it makes sense." She glanced at him. "Are you... thinking about something in particular?" She held her breath that this wasn't about something construction related, about Blake's job. What if it was about something more personal? More intimate.

"I don't know," said Blake. "Sometimes we think we see what we want right in front of us. It was there all along, in plain sight... then, just when we reach for it, something comes up to make us think it's a mistake. You know how it is." A sound like a sigh, possibly one of frustration, emerged like a deep exhale from Blake's lungs. As incredulous as she was about this idea, Tessa could swear that's what she heard.

Her fingers toyed with the corner of the notebook in her arms. "Sometimes change is good," she ventured. "Then again, sometimes the real problem is knowing what we truly want in the first place. Seeing it beyond the distractions." Here, she thought about the prime example in her own life, the one that had led to this moment with Blake, along with everything else these past few weeks.

"I almost turned around and walked away from Wedding Belles this year," she continued, aware of the glimmer of surprise in Blake's eyes at this confession, despite his intent expression. "But if I had given up, I never could have lived with myself. The 'what if,' the 'maybe'—it would have killed me, wondering if I gave up just when I should have given it my best. All because I couldn't see the turning point, where the light would shine through again."

It was Bill's advice for good business sense, but Tessa wasn't thinking of business at this point. She was thinking that maybe... maybe... Blake regretted that moment in the parlor, when they could have told each other about their feelings, but didn't. If she regretted not telling him that kiss was something more, maybe he felt the same way. The exact same way, from the tingle of magic to the sweet taste of possibility that came from one perfect touch.

Don't give up, she thought desperately. *What if it really is right in front of you, just waiting for you to say the word?* What insanity was prompting this utter change was a secret known only in the depths of Tessa's heart—her rational self was shouting for her to see how desperate this was after all she'd been through and all the chances they had dodged thus far.

"That's what I think, anyway." She shrugged her shoulders. "But what do I know, right?" She looked at him. Wanting to ask what this was all about, and if there was some way she could help. Saying that the idea of the two of them together wasn't so crazy seemed like a good start to her.

"I think you know a lot," Blake answered, with a smile that was tender, and allowed Tessa to feel a blush travel from her cheeks to her toes like a flame. "Maybe I should take your advice and figure out if my first instinct was right."

"Maybe you should." Tessa hoped the blush was gone from her cheeks by the time she replied. She couldn't do anything about the crazy way her heart was skipping beats at the idea that Blake really meant those words.

Chapter Twenty-Three

"Where are my pins?" Natalie rummaged through her emergency sewing kit. "Don't worry," she added, looking up at Nadia, whose face already betrayed slight concern. "I have them here somewhere. I'll have it fixed in seconds, I promise."

What a perfect start to any wedding day, she thought privately—with a perfectly secure dress seam giving way along the zipper, one she would swear was tightly sewn by her machine's closest stitch function. Her fingers pulled pins from the upside-down ladybug cushion, pulling the seam into place again.

It was one fifteen at Nadia's apartment, where Natalie was conducting a last-minute fitting before they were due to leave for the chapel's guest house—one which had turned out to be either a mistake or a providential revelation, depending upon how you felt about discovering a broken garment thread mere hours before the big moment.

The wedding was set for four o'clock, with the chapel just outside the city limits, in a wood bordering the forest park. Morning had dawned with a gray haze on its horizon, which had suggested doom to Natalie's mind the moment she opened her apartment's curtains, surveying the dusting of snow on the pavement from two days ago, which looked like grey sludge now, thanks to street traffic and fumes from the building's basement furnace. Thick, heavy clouds blanketed the neighboring rooftop in a storm band, the kind that looked ready to cause icy roads and zero visibility in a curtain of freezing rain. Natalie had stuck her tongue out at them. Defiance had not banished them from sight.

"Just a few minutes more," she said, as the maid of honor handed her the scissors from her sewing kit. "Good thing I decided to check the zipper before we left for the church, right?" Her emergency sewing kit included a mini seam surger, but if this dress's seam turned out to be worse than she thought, she wanted to be within range of a real sewing machine that would guarantee a perfect fix.

"Are you sure this dress will hold together long enough for her to walk down the aisle?" Cynthia's worried voice reminded Natalie of someone filing rust off cast iron.

The mother of the bride was sporting a short formal dress for the big occasion, a spotted navy blue silk that might have been borrowed from the Sunday church scene's costume rack for a Hollywood version of *Picnic*. Always refined and elegant, down to the white gloves, tiny diamond studs, and patent shoes—unlike Paula, who had chosen a magenta two-piece with a pencil skirt that swept the floor and enough sequins to light a casino billboard in Vegas.

"Completely sure," Natalie replied with a smile—albeit through clenched teeth holding her sewing pins. "Watch and see. And, *hey presto*, we're back in business." She pulled out the final pin after backstitching the end of the seam. It seemed sturdy enough now. It was just one of those rare sewing accidents, and not the dreaded curse that made Tessa's eyes harden whenever it was mentioned.

"I just pulled the zipper too hard when I tried it on again this morning," said Nadia. "I'm nervous. I'm really nervous. See how much my hands are shaking?" She showed Natalie the tremor in them. "Three hours from now, I'll be married. I just wanted to make sure that I hadn't gained extra pounds. I felt so bloated after last night's cannoli—now I just feel sick—and I *really* need everything to go perfectly."

"Hold still," said the bridesmaid who was styling Nadia's hair. "It needs two more pins at least in the back, to hold it until we get to the chapel."

"I'm having a hard time holding still," said Nadia. "I'm going to be married in a few hours. Can you believe it? I feel like I'm dreaming. Look at me in the mirror, I look so—glamorous."

"I just hope you don't freeze to death in that glass chapel you chose," said Cynthia.

"It has insulated walls six inches thick, according to the brochure," said Natalie. Maybe not in the nicest tone she could have chosen, she reflected afterwards. Did false cheerfulness count?

At the Wedding Belles' headquarters, Tessa was loading up the last boxes of extra wedding favors, snowflake confetti, and her own emergency repair kit: a plastic toolbox filled with masking tape, super glue, sewing pins, tack nails and a hammer-screwdriver combination tool, a stout pair of scissors, and a three-blade knife which claimed it had a blade for cutting any substance known to mankind. Arms full, she nudged open the door with her toes, and heard the trill of her cell phone from her handbag at the same time.

With a grunt, she eased the toolbox onto the entry table and pulled out her phone. "Is everything okay at Nadia's place?" she asked.

"No. I had to re-stitch part of the zip while Cynthia breathed down my neck and predicted the dress would come apart mid-ceremony," said Natalie. "Can you believe it? I have *never* had a seam split, Tess. Never. Not in all the miserable years of sewing for Kandace. Even the hideous clown cape I sewed while I had the *stomach flu* stayed together. But not a couture gown I labored over for weeks?"

The curse was back. No. It couldn't be real. Tessa shook off that idea. "These things happen, Nat," said Tessa. "None of us are perfect. Maybe the thread was weak, or the zipper's fabric was defective…"

"Nope and nope. I fixed it, but I have to say, I've felt better going into events other than this one. I mean, I know it's fine, but I don't *know*—you know what I mean. Nadia will probably be waiting for her skirt to drop off as she walks down the aisle."

"She knows you're a great designer and seamstress," soothed Tessa. "Where are you right now?"

"I'm at Nadia's place. Once the bridal party arrives at the wedding site, they'll finish dressing for the photography session at the chapel. I'll stop off at our building first to help Ama load the cake before I drive to the chapel."

"Where is Ama?"

"She's at the restaurant, helping the catering crew. There's a problem with something—I don't know what, because she didn't have time to talk. Try calling her. Maybe they have it under control now."

They didn't—Tessa felt sure of it in her sinking heart without calling the baker's phone. "I'm on my way there as soon as I load the emergency supplies here," she said. "Probably it's just something tiny involving the dessert table."

She tossed the emergency supplies in the trunk of the car she had borrowed, then headed in the direction of Lyle's restaurant. *Please, please, do not let this be a big crisis. Do not let this day be ruined.*

She clenched the steering wheel a little more tightly, trying not to imagine the kitchen floor littered with mini cupcakes, hand-carved radish boxes, and creamy dill dip. Already the floral delivery was down to the wire, thanks to the greenhouse debacle and a delivery date oversight by the florist. They had promised the centerpieces would be delivered first thing in the morning, and that their delivery team would have the dining room 'sparkling with floral elegance' in no time at all.

Of course, it was afternoon and they hadn't arrived yet. But any minute now, Tessa told herself. Maybe luck would be with her when she walked through the restaurant's doors. She was just glad she'd had the foresight to pick up the bridal bouquets yesterday for Nadia and her bridal party.

✻

While Tessa was on her way to the restaurant, the back door to the Wedding Belles' headquarters opened under Ama's key as she and Natalie entered. "Let's get the cart," said Natalie. "It'll be easier to move the cake by rolling it than carrying it, and we need to get it to the restaurant in double time."

The individual layers, covered in perfect white fondant, were chilling in the kitchen's fridge, with one on every shelf. The candies for the elaborate snowflake swirl spiral were in a box on the counter beside the transparent wire frame.

"I think we should carry it," said Ama uneasily. "It takes more time, but I'm a little nervous about handling the big one." The bottom layer was thick and felt slightly heavy to Ama despite the light sponge layers sandwiching its rich filling.

Natalie checked her watch. "Let's hurry, then." They opened the fridge and pulled out the biggest box from the middle of the bottom shelf, each taking an end as it slid free of the rack.

It *was* heavy. It sagged in the middle between them—only a little at first, but growing more noticeable by the second as they inched toward the van's open doors, Ama walking backwards through the kitchen's entrance.

"Walk faster," hinted Natalie.

"I can't," said Ama. "I can't see where I'm going. I'm afraid to look over my shoulder because I might drop this corner of the cake. Why is this box so thin? They never felt this thin before when I carried them."

"I don't know, but it had better hold together until we reach the van," said Natalie. "Hear me? Hold together, box." Ama slid her hand underneath, trying not to imagine that the cake's filling had somehow soaked through it and eaten the parchment paper liner within. It had never happened before in all her years of baking.

They both grunted with relief as the box touched down on the van's floor, padded by some foam strips Natalie had brought along. "Next time, cart," said Natalie to Ama, who nodded in agreement.

"We'll put the middle layer on the shelf since it has safety strips around three sides, and set the top layer on the tabletop," said Ama. "It should be pretty safe from escape since it's small, after all." She loaded the remaining bakery boxes with care onto the cart, then closed the fridge.

Halfway across the kitchen, the right-hand wheel dropped off. "Hold it," said Natalie.

"What? Why?" said Ama, who moved as if to join her on the other side.

"No, *literally* hold it, okay? The wheel came off. This thing could tip over," said Natalie. She crouched down and gingerly lifted the right leg, trying to shove the wheel's swivel base into its socket again. "This service cart is ancient," she said. "The wheel support is bent. How does it stay together half the time?"

"It never came apart before," said Ama. "Just stick it back together. Maybe Blake can fix it for us later." As Natalie seized the right-hand end of the cart, Ama pushed it carefully forward again, crossing the kitchen floor gingerly to the open door.

"Watch out for the rug," she warned Natalie, whose high-heeled shoe kicked backwards in response, sending the little floor carpet sailing to the opposite side of the room.

"No problem," said Natalie. The cart bumped slowly over the threshold and to the pavement outside, where it rolled along more easily without the rough patches in the kitchen's old floor.

"I think the wheel is loose again," said Ama, who was still feeling nervous.

Natalie glanced down, then moved to the side in order to see better. "It's just twisting a little, but it's still in place," she said. "It's easier this way, right? Smooth transportation."

"It is faster," admitted Ama. "We're almost home safe." The cart sailed smoothly, even without Natalie guiding its other end. That is, until the wheel struck a broken piece of rock lying on the pavement. The wonky wheel skidded and locked, the whole cart lurching forward. The box holding the cake's middle section slid forwards to bump against the side support on impact, while the topmost layer sailed free of the cart's tiny upper lip and landed on the pavement. Box open, smashed cake and fondant decorating the ground behind the van.

Chapter Twenty-Four

For a moment, neither of them said anything. A small cry escaped Ama's lips, building louder as she crouched by the remains of her cake, completely unsalvageable.

"How?!" said Natalie. "How is there a rock on the pavement in the middle of the city!" She ran her fingers through her hair in frustration.

"We really are jinxed," said Ama, groaning.

"Don't panic," said Natalie. "Think—think. We have to be calm. What do we do, Ama?" she said. "What do we do to fix this?"

Ama was picking up broken pieces of cake, although she hadn't any idea why she was doing it. "I don't know," she said. "I don't know—"

"Is there a backup cake?"

"No. There's nothing. Nothing in the fridge—" She scrunched the battered box on top of the cart again and marched inside, opening the refrigerator to reveal four leftover peppermint mini cheesecakes, two pints of cream, a stick of butter, and a jar of zesty pickles, none of which would assemble an emergency wedding cake. In the pantry there was a box of vanilla wafers and two packages of Twinkies—again, nothing that would save them.

Think, think, Ama. Her mind was blank, except for thoughts of cake mixes and fast sponge recipes, all of which were useless right now. There had to be a way to replace this in a half hour or less.

"There's a bakery two streets over," she said quickly, closing the door again. "Go buy any white sheet cake that they have, Natalie. Doesn't matter what it looks like, just buy it."

"They won't have one without frosting and decorations unless I have them bake it," said Natalie.

"Frosting's fine—just get whatever they have that they can put in a box for you," said Ama, who was putting on an apron. She opened a cupboard and took out a bag of marshmallows and a box of confectioner's sugar.

By the time Natalie returned fifteen minutes later, Ama was rolling out her shortcut fondant to the precise thickness needed for the cake. "Here we are," said Natalie, dropping her purse on the floor and opening a bakery box. "It was the only white cake they had, and it was covered in white frosting already. This kind tastes awful, though, Ama. It's like eating vanilla-flavored liquid foam." She made a face as she showed her the only available option, a plain vanilla cake iced with a pearly sheen, and a series of candied purple flowers garnishing its corners.

"It's fine," said Ama, who reached for her cake knife and began scraping the frosting and decorations off with sure strokes of its blade, until the cake was bare. Reaching for her smallest cake tin, she cut two circles from the sponge, using her pan like a giant cookie cutter. Slow, deep breaths kept her calm, while the process kept her mind focused on what came next.

"It's not the same flavor as the original," said Natalie. "This isn't your special recipe, Ama."

"I know. But once I sandwich it together with the cinnamon cream filling I made, it'll come as close as we can get," said Ama. "There's nothing else we can do at this point, and at least this layer isn't going to be served at the reception." She tasted one of the crumbs from the cut sponge. "We're definitely going to have to give Nadia and Lyle a big discount," she said. "Grab that second knife and start covering the top of this layer with the filling, would you?" she said to Natalie, as she skimmed the first cut circle free of the cake's filling.

Under a layer of smooth fondant, it looked identical to the first one. By the time Ama had smoothed it and trimmed the bottom ruffle of excess fondant, they were a half hour behind their intended delivery time.

Natalie checked the clock. "How much longer?" she asked. "I told the restaurant we'd be there twenty minutes ago. Pretty soon, that giant ice swan will be delivered, and there's nobody to scoop sorbet balls to fill it, since they're short-staffed today."

"Ten minutes," promised Ama. "Go ahead and carry out the top and middle of the groom's cake. I'll help you carry the bottom layer as soon as I'm done." She reached for another small bakery box and began assembling its sides.

"We are so late," groaned Natalie, as she eased out a bakery box containing one of the chocolate layers. "I'm guarding this one with my life."

❄

Meanwhile, across town at the Olive Brook restaurant, Tessa had arrived to find disaster waiting in the kitchen. Scattered trays of nearly finished appetizers lined the work counters, along with bite-size desserts in the process of being decorated, but the crew was busy dealing with a problem involving the stove's temperature regulation, which at the moment was refusing to light a flame beneath any of the pots on its surface.

"Everything okay?" Tessa asked, hoping against all evidence that this was a minor issue.

The catering chef looked at her. "Where's your food coordinator?" he asked. "Ama," he clarified. "She was supposed to come back and help us finish these trays. We haven't even started the main dish prep, so we're behind—we can't finish these on our own, we don't have enough people here."

"I can help," said Tessa bravely. Thinking, *Why can't Ama or Nat be here—somebody who knows what they're doing in a real kitchen like this one?* She reached for a knife and one of the rosemary stalks that was being diced to garnish the creamy dill dip.

The kitchen door opened. "Is the wedding planner here?" asked a restaurant employee, over the noise of the staff argument by the stove, its flame sputtering pathetically to life beneath a saucepan.

"That's me." Tessa laid aside the crushed peppermint candy she had been sprinkling over the mini cheesecakes.

"There's a delivery service here looking for you." He disappeared from sight as the door closed. Pulling off her apron, Tessa hurried from the kitchen, and smoothed her skirt in preparation for meeting Accented Creations' delivery team.

A delivery service was indeed in the private dining room for the reception, and in the process of unpacking decorations on the tables— shiny purple and green streamers and pennants, funky green, red, and purple baubles strung together on gold wire, and a giant crepe-paper piñata shaped like a donkey.

"What are you doing?" said Tessa, horrified. "What are all these?"

A deliveryman with a clipboard motioned toward the objects. "The centerpieces you ordered, the garlands, the piñata—"

"I didn't order any of this!" said Tessa. "These are supposed to be amaryllis and paperwhites—and where's my swan?"

"Swan?" he repeated, mystified. "Nobody said anything about a swan."

"Are you from Accented Creations?" They couldn't possibly be, not with these decorations and nary a trace of a flower among them. Something was horribly wrong here.

"This isn't the regional soccer champions party?" He checked his work sheet. Tessa noticed the logo on his green shirt—Events, Inc., a big chain competitor for Bill's Party 2 Go in the city. "You're not Hernandez?"

"No—this is the Emerson–Kardopolis wedding," she said. "So unless you have a big frozen swan in your truck to give me, you're at the wrong address. Now, please, get these things out of here as quickly as you can, because I have a delivery due any second now."

"Geez, what's with you and the swan, lady?" The clipboard guy motioned for the rest of the crew's attention. "Hey, guys—wrong address. We're supposed to be at 220 *South* Side. Let's move it." With grumbles of protest and dismay, the workers reversed their progress on unpacking the decorations.

Tessa pulled out her phone and dialed the number for Accented Creations. "Hi, this is Tessa Miller—the assistant to Mr. Groeder's assistant," she added, using her much-loathed false title. "The delivery to our reception site is late, and I was hoping that nothing was wrong." She crossed her fingers.

"Hold one moment." A long silence followed, as Tessa studied the dining room's stucco walls, trying to imagine them garlanded with soft, twinkling lights and greenery in mere minutes…

"I'm terribly sorry, Ms. Miller. Our big delivery van has a flat tire, and they're still working on changing it," said the voice on the other end.

"How long will they be?" Tessa checked the time. The wedding was due to begin in an hour, and she had to be at the chapel before then to make sure everything was in place for the ceremony.

"They expect to deliver to your address in a half hour's time," said the voice.

"You're sure?" said Tessa. "The reception is two hours from now, and guests will be arriving early."

"You have our guarantee, Ms. Miller."

She hung up. Hopefully, their guarantee was clad in iron and unbreakable, because that was the only way she could feel consoled about this situation. She tucked her phone in her purse again and hurried back to the desserts. Time was growing short, and *where* were Natalie and Ama with the cake?

A soft *foom* roared to life from the problematic stove in the kitchen as she opened the door, and witnessed a sheet of flames rising from a pan on the stove as several cooks leapt back, and someone ran for a fire extinguisher. The chef clapped a lid over it, leaving only a cloud of acrid, black smoke in the kitchen. Tessa coughed and fanned the air, peering desperately for a sight of the appetizers as she prayed they were covered in cling wrap and stowed safely in the fridge—and not turning grey beneath this cloud.

The kitchen helpers moving to and fro were carrying trays to the cooler and dishes to the sink—including one in a business shirt, sleeves rolled, and a Hugo Boss tie, wearing a chef's apron over both. Striking cheekbones and jaw line, chestnut hair slightly longer than the norm for kitchen work—

"*Blake?*" Tessa's voice couldn't contain her astonishment. He glanced her way.

"Tess," he said. "How are things out there?" He nodded toward the dining room.

"Um… they've been better," she said. "What are you doing here? What are you doing—*here?*" she gestured at the space around them.

"Helping out. They said those crab puffs needed some chives on top," he said. "But stick me anywhere you need somebody extra. I've got the afternoon free, and I'm already dressed for the part, as you can see." He placed the mixing bowl on the counter. "I can put in a hand here, or help you put up garlands out there."

"You don't have to do this," she said. "If you thought we were twisting your arm with that fourth partner arrangement just to steal your time when we hit a rough patch—"

"Look, I wanted to help out," he said. "I guessed that maybe you could use a hand for this one, so I stopped by in my official fourth partner capacity. Just in case something went wrong with the flowers last minute, say," he continued. "Besides, I'm kind of curious to see the end results of my performances."

"The flowers aren't here, actually," she said, still amazed by the sight of him. Her voice must be coming from somebody else's lungs—somebody who was slightly dreamy-eyed and distracted, not a professional like herself who had their hands full at this moment. "They're late... I'm late, actually. The chapel—the stuff for the ceremony—it's been a really crazy day."

"Go," he said.

"Go?" she repeated.

"Yeah. Take off. I can handle the flowers when they come," he said. "Like I said, I'd hate to miss my final performance as *assistant* Blake Ellingham. At this point, the florist would be disappointed not to see me here, making sure everything meets the standards of my exacting boss."

The world of horribly, crazily wrong events was a hurricane surrounding this one moment of perfect reassurance that someone had her back when she needed it. It almost felt as if she had been swept into a pair of strong, protective arms, but there was six feet of space between her and the contractor in his flour-spotted apron. A rush of gratitude spurred Tessa to cross the room, however, and throw her arms around Blake, hugging him tightly.

"Thank you. You're amazing," she said. Impulsively, her hand cupped one side of Blake's face to kiss his cheek, without thinking of what it meant to be this close to him until she met his eyes. This was how she had kissed him before, in the accident that wasn't entirely an accident. This time, if she kissed him, he would know she meant it.

This time, a kiss would truly change everything between them. It would be inescapable, their lips touching a second time, if she did what she longed to do.

His arm was encircling her waist, gently and lightly, as if returning her embrace. Holding her there without actually holding onto her. It had frozen Tessa in place, her lips mere inches from his own, with her hand caressing his face.

"Blake…" she began, although the words were dying on her lips without having formed any true declaration about how she felt. She wasn't escaping him, not his eyes or the protective curve of his arm. Not even when he leaned slightly toward her, as if to take the kiss they were on the verge of sharing. Hesitating—but maybe that was because Tessa herself had drawn back from that final touch by a mere fraction of movement, the briefest hesitation that had kept them from being locked together in an exchange of passion.

Her fast-beating heart only exacerbated this truth; her free hand touched his shoulder, but not to push him away. If she could stop gazing at his face, it would help. It would help her to pull her thoughts together, and say the real reason that being this close to him always tied her tongue in knots, one that terrified her to her very core just as it thrilled her.

"Sorry," said Blake softly. His hold on her relaxed a little, creating a space between their bodies. The only reason Tessa didn't blush was because mortification was sweeping over her. *Again* with this? Again she missed her mark when it came to this kiss? Was it for the best, or was it just stupidity that caused her to keep tripping over this moment?

"This... was a little over the top for a thank you, I guess," she said, her words stumbling, too, as if aware they were the wrong ones. "I keep doing that, for some reason." Did she *have* to sound breathless at this moment, of all possible times?

"You do," he agreed, his voice equally soft. "It's a habit with impulsive people, I'm told."

"I meant to say—to tell you—I'm really grateful that you're helping out."

If it wasn't for the beginning of a smile on Blake's lips at her reply, which might be followed any second by a laugh or a smirk that had not yet appeared, she would have hated how formal this sounded, and maybe hated that she was dodging the truth. Instead, her cheeks burned with a blush.

"No problem," he answered gently. And seriously. As she drew free of his encircling arms, he let her slip from his embrace completely. Once she was no longer touching him, or feeling his body making contact with hers, it was easier to think and breathe, she discovered. Easier to think that it was for the best that she hadn't crazily locked lips with Blake while precious seconds were ticking away before the wedding, and without so much as a hint that the situation between them was far from equally platonic.

"I should go. Thank you. For waiting for the florist," she clarified. She stepped back hastily and hurried from the kitchen, really, really hoping that the fire-red blush engulfing her face at this moment had yet to make itself visible before she turned away.

I almost did it again. What is he thinking? What am I thinking, because there's no way this is an accident that keeps happening. She was trying not to think about it, but was struggling to think of anything else, even the important events of the day.

Deadlines, big important details, and a ticking clock should be the focus of this moment—but even with the turmoil inside and out, she knew she trusted Blake to oversee the delivery with the precision of his snooty alter ego. It didn't need a second thought, because Tessa trusted him the way she trusted herself to finish the job.

If she could only trust herself that perfectly when it came to her behavior around Blake, then she wouldn't be catching her breath outside the kitchen door for a second, away from the smoke, the chaos, and especially away from his muscular arms.

Just breathe. Her calm and dignity returned to her as she focused on the task ahead and the chapel. Determined, she marched forward, not to escape herself but to meet the next round of challenges head on and prevent any part of this wedding from unraveling at its seams.

Time to secure Nadia and Lyle's perfect 'I do.'

❅

It was like a picture postcard: the glass wedding chapel in the cold winter light of the clearing, flanked by Christmassy evergreens and pale slender gray-barked saplings. Tessa hurried up the footpath, bundled against the cold—no dirty slush covered it, but there was a delicate sheet of white dusting the ground and lightly embellishing the woodland branches. True to their promises, Accented Creations' garlands adorned the doorway and the altar, with delicate white petals and crisp blossoms shining beneath the church's lamps. The roof was swept free of snow, but a delicate pattern of ice crystals etched the windows in the late afternoon light.

Tessa stepped inside. The guests were seated, there was still plenty of confetti in the basket beside the guest book, and the ceremony's official was chatting with Paula near the front of the chapel as they waited for the ceremony to begin. Lyle was standing in place, looking nervous but grinning as he spoke with his best man beside him, who was holding a small ring box in one hand.

The ring. The last thing on Tessa's list that could go wrong, short of Natalie's nightmare about the dress. Flowers, check. Confetti, check. Ushers, check. All that remained was the transportation, any little final issues that needed to be smoothed, and the music cue for the bride.

Glancing around, she didn't see Natalie anywhere. Ama would still be with the catering crew, Tessa suspected, but the Wedding Belles' official designer and seamstress had intended to be here in case of a wardrobe malfunction. She called Natalie's number. "Hey, Nat, where are you?" she asked. "I'm at the chapel, but I don't see you. Are you with Nadia at the guest house?" The bride, her mother, and the rest of the bridal party were waiting at the chapel's little cottage, which had been provided for dressing, last-minute champagne toasts, and privacy before the ceremony.

"Change of plans. The cake needed a little last-minute tweaking," said Natalie. "We're almost done, but I won't make it to the ceremony."

"What happened?" Tessa detected something in her partner's voice. A little element beneath that nonchalance that didn't *quite* fit the rest of her tone, regardless of Natalie's mastery for hiding things.

"Nothing. Everything's fine," said Natalie. "I swear, it will look perfect when the bride and groom stroll through the doors. After the edible decorations are in place, Ama and I are going to help lay out the appetizers and the dessert table. I just hope the main course is ready by the time they arrive—that's going to be touch and go, according to the kitchen."

"Call me if something goes wrong," said Tessa. Clearly, Natalie wasn't willing to confess what had already happened, which her partners had clearly handled on their own. "I'll be there as soon as the couple leave the ceremony."

She called Nadia next. "Are you ready to walk down the aisle?" she asked in her brightest voice. "I'm here at the chapel and everything looks perfect for the big moment."

"I am," said Nadia. "We're at the guesthouse and we're almost ready to leave for the church. Did you see the sleigh? It's beautiful, Tessa. It looks like it's been shipped here from some Scandinavian mountain village—can you believe Lyle arranged it?"

"He's a great guy, so of course I can," said Tessa. "I haven't seen it yet, but it's my next stop, and I'm sure it's just like you described it. Is there anything you need checked or changed last minute?" She hoped the answer was no, since her imagination was still occupied by Natalie's secret disaster.

"Nothing. Everything's great," said Nadia. "Thanks again."

"You're welcome." Tessa hung up. Taking a deep breath, she prepared to step outside into the cold again, wrapping her coat a little tighter as she trekked across the woodland path to confer with the sleigh driver. Making sure he was ready to collect the bride and groom when called was one of the final steps before the ceremony began. Already, Nadia and her bridal party were emerging from the guest cottage with Cynthia, who carried the bride's matching coat and a small clutch which contained makeup and other essentials, as they walked along the path to the church.

The sleigh and white reindeer were waiting in a small clearing in the grove a few yards from the church—it looked like Santa was parked there on a quick stop-off, Tessa reflected. The driver was bundled up against the cold, pausing in his texting as he confirmed the details of his part to Tessa.

"So we're clear on all the steps?" she said to the driver, who nodded.

"Absolutely. Soon as I get the signal, I'll drive to the front of the church, then take the long way to the parking lot." His two reindeer were dressed in black harnesses and silver bells, one nosing in a hopeful way against Tessa's pocket, suggesting it had sampled a few snacks from visitors at its home lodge. The sleigh was a beautiful white one with accents painted in silver.

"Looks like a storm's coming," commented the driver, pulling his muffler and coat around him more closely. Tessa hurried toward the church again, counting down the minutes until the ceremony.

"Just a few clouds," she called back. *It had better not*, she thought, feeling desperate enough to threaten the clouds instead of plea bargaining.

Thank heavens the church was warm enough inside, the guests cozy in their seats, the aisles decorated with simple greenery touched with fake frost. Tessa slipped to the front of the church and whispered to the organist, cueing her to play the wedding march as the doors opened for Nadia and her bridal party to enter.

The music was solemn, and the collective intake of breath at the entrance of Nadia and her party was audible in the room. The bride certainly looked stunning, and even Cynthia had a genuine smile as they proceeded slowly down the aisle to the waiting groom and groomsmen. Lyle looked as if he couldn't wait for this moment, Tessa thought, as he stretched out his hand for Nadia's.

"Dearly beloved," began the minister. Tessa relaxed a little bit—this part was all Nadia and Lyle's. Solemn vows, ceremonial candles lit, a touching and funny speech on what marriage means from the minister officiating at the wedding… these were the moments Tessa savored: the expressions of happiness, love, and hope in the eyes of the couple being joined together, and the friends and family sharing this experience with them.

This was the best part of her work, as she had told Blake at the very beginning. To think that her chance to share this moment had been slipping away… that was something she could no more put into words than she could define the sparkle she could see in Nadia's eyes as the bride said 'I do.'

Sometimes the perfect words don't exist, not for a blend of feelings that seem contradictory or overwhelming, like tears that mix happiness and excitement with the full spectrum of realization that one is taking a tremendous leap in life. Like the way it felt to touch another's hand, for instance, and realize that the feelings inside you are the electricity of attraction and fear of the unknown, all at once—

"I now pronounce you husband and wife," said the minister. "You may kiss the bride." Tessa snapped back to herself at this critical point in the ceremony. Seconds from now, the newly married couple would be presented to their guests, and the hour for the reception would be closing in quickly. It was time to check in with Natalie and Ama one last time.

Snowflake ice votives were lining the path outside the chapel by the time the couple was ready to leave. The first stage of twilight had darkened quickly, thanks to the clouds above; the lights woven in the simple, frosted greenery twinkled above Lyle and Nadia as they emerged from the chapel's carved doors to the party of guests waiting to see them off. All the guests held bags of snowflake confetti for showering the couple, but a flurry of soft, white flakes descended first upon the hood of Nadia's lace coat and Lyle's tuxedo shoulders, courtesy of the sky above. Real snow was falling.

Both natural snowflake and glittery confetti sprinkled over the couple as they hurried to the reindeer-drawn sleigh, its bells jingling softly as it reached the end of the path. From its carriage, Nadia stood and tossed her bouquet to the waiting crowd of single women, then the couple waved goodbye as the sleigh began its short journey through the woods.

Just like a scene from a winter fairytale, Tessa thought. She had never seen the couple look happier than now, even though the wood would be cold despite the white woolen lap robes tucked around them.

"The road will be a mess if it keeps snowing," said one guest, who was standing closest to her. "It's rotten luck that the storm actually came through."

"The weather radar shows it breaking up," reported a guest who was checking his phone's weather app. "Looks like it's just a little dust of snow, and that's it. Probably it'll be over by the time we reach the parking lot."

She couldn't have planned it this perfectly. Tessa smiled.

✻

At the reception site, Blake's powers of overseeing Accented Creations' delivery greeted her first in the dining room, with every centerpiece perfectly placed on the table. Ice vases gently dripped into their crystal basins as candles flickered inside them, and snow-white blossoms and cool mint greens shone between the shimmering woodland branches. Even the substituted blossoms looked beautiful; the centerpieces had lost nothing of their charm.

Visions of a cake leaning to one side or melting beneath the restaurant's soft lighting were vanquished—Ama's creation was perfectly in place, between the glittering ice swan of sorbet at one end and the chocolate groom's cake at the other. The trays of mini cheesecakes and chocolate truffles were in place, the crab puffs and Brie and Camembert savories ready and waiting.

"What happened?" she whispered to Natalie, who was tweaking the rows of silverware beside the serving platters.

"What do you mean?" Natalie answered innocently.

"Come on. I heard it in your voice earlier." Tessa glanced at the cake, seeing a quick flash of guilt in Natalie's eyes. One had to be quick to see it, but Tessa knew it would be there.

"Tell you later," muttered Natalie. "Before we send the bill." With that, she joined the catering staff, who were bringing out more small serving plates as the guests arrived.

Champagne corks popped for the first toast as radish boxes and creamy dill dip vanished into the mouths of hungry guests. Servers marched out with the soups and salads for dinner, beginning at the wedding party's end of the table, then the main courses, which Tessa tasted a little of in the kitchen as she helped garnish plates and uncork wine bottles for serving.

"Where's Blake?" she asked Ama, who was definitely in 'restaurant mode' as she drizzled the chef's sauce over the main dishes on the counter with an expert hand. "He, uh, was here when I left," Tessa added, to explain why she was asking. She was still searching the room for him with every new arrival to the reception, trying to sift him from the crowd of strangers belonging to Nadia and Lyle.

"I don't know," said Ama. "Is he here? I haven't seen him."

"He helped with the flowers, sort of," said Tessa. "There was a little fiasco with the delivery time for the centerpieces—" Ama glanced up sharply as she listened, as if anticipating another problem for them "—and he stayed behind to see that everything was fine."

"He came to help?" said Ama. She laughed. "Wow. I didn't think he'd ever set foot on wedding turf again after what we dragged him into the first time."

"I know. I guess he thought we were in a bind or something," said Tessa. "Then he said something about helping out the staff afterwards. Surprising, huh?" She laughed, but she didn't mean it. Something about it didn't seem funny, although she was afraid that she might keep laughing hysterically once she started—the way nervous people giggle uncontrollably when they're about to blurt out a secret.

"Like I said, I haven't seen him today," said Ama. "Since he was invited, he's probably still here somewhere." She grabbed a knife from the block on the counter and began mincing some herbs for a garnish.

He was coming, surely, Tessa thought. And when he did, she wondered if his mind would be occupied by the same thoughts as her own when he glimpsed her in this crowd. About near brushes with a kiss, and how it felt natural to be so close.

She could do it. She could tell him that it wasn't anyone's imagination responsible for the sparks between them, or the sudden moments of shyness or desire that completely changed their chemistry from time to time. It was real, because she was deeply attracted to him—therefore, that kiss between them hadn't truly been an accident.

So... Blake... is it the same way for you? These feelings, the sense that we have something more than just friendship? She knew he must, but she wanted to hear it from his lips all the same.

Tessa didn't spot Blake until the post-dinner toasts were being made. By then, the guests were standing, most of them ready for the DJ's records to begin to spin. Blake was still there, lingering near the back of the crowd, where casual friends and coworkers of the happy couple were paying less attention to the long-winded speech Lyle's uncle was making.

He caught sight of her and smiled as he waved. Tessa waved and smiled back, her heart beating faster at the same time, in anticipation of him drawing near to her, near enough that what didn't happen at the restaurant earlier today could become reality. Then Blake turned as someone caught hold of his sleeve and said something close to his ear that made him laugh.

It was Mac, in a beautiful maroon-colored dress with sequins on its bodice trim, her dark waterfall of hair stylishly embellished with one or two tiny crystal hair jewels. She laughed at Blake's reply in turn, and tucked her arm through his as the closest guests began conversing with them.

Had she come as Blake's date? The bridal couple had chosen invitations that allowed plus-ones for their single guests… but that was jumping to conclusions. Maybe Mac was invited separately and this was a perfectly innocent coincidence.

"Shouldn't somebody cue the music?" Ama murmured close to Tessa. Guests were applauding the toast and saluting with their glasses of champagne now that the speech was over.

"Good point," said Tessa, finding her voice with some effort. "I'll do it." She slipped through the crowd of guests, giving the spot where Blake and Mac were standing a wide berth.

Round two of champagne circulated, along with mixed cocktails on the serving staff's trays. Guests danced to love songs, then applauded as Nadia and Lyle cut the bottom layer of the snowflake cake, and sampled one of its crystal candy snowflakes for the photographer's latest snap. Tessa took a photo with her phone's camera, though she failed to adjust the focus, her usual attention to detail slipping momentarily.

"Nice job," said Blake. He was at her elbow—Tessa's next photo was a completely blurry mess as her hand jumped in response to his voice. "The party, not the pic," he said, as the image appeared on her phone's screen.

"Thanks." Tessa's tone was empty. She deleted the shot, her eyes trained on the phone's screen. "You stayed for the whole reception," she said. "I didn't realize you—I assumed you were leaving after the flowers were done." She hadn't assumed any such thing, actually. She was just trying hard not to think about that moment in the restaurant kitchen. The way Blake had almost reached for her kiss after she embraced him so impulsively—then hesitated, as if remembering that he shouldn't. Or couldn't

"I had an invitation to this event burning a hole in the pocket of my jeans," he said. "I figured it's good for your business's fourth partner to put in a public appearance at a wedding now and then. I thought you knew I was coming. Didn't I tell you?"

"No," said Tessa, trying to sound nonchalant now. "But you were invited, so it's great that you came. And brought a guest," she added. Her finger pushed the 'delete' button a little too firmly and accidentally trashed a photo of Ama smiling as her creation was being tasted by the wedding couple. "Did you lose Mac in the crowd momentarily?"

"She's waiting to sample one of your mini cheesecakes," he said. "I may've given her the impression that Ama's baked goods are not to be missed," he admitted, pretending to look guilty about doing it.

Tessa almost smiled in return. "That's nice of you," she said. "She'll be happy to have your endorsement."

"It's the truth. It's not like I had to embellish anything," he said. "Mac paid you a compliment the moment she walked inside. She wants to know who came up with the idea for the floral theme, and I told her you did."

This compliment left Tessa feeling strangely deflated. "It was Accented Creations who came up with the real design," she said. "And we owe you the rest for making sure they delivered the goods."

"I saw the sketches in your office before you called the florist," said Blake. "I know where the idea came from, even if they tweaked it."

A strange warmth swept through Tessa. "Maybe a tiny bit of it was me," she said, lowering her gaze, suddenly afraid there was a blush on her cheeks which hadn't been present a second ago. She studied the restaurant's carpet, as if checking for errant crumbs. "Wedding planners are meant to be jacks of all trades. We know a little about colors, a little about flowers, a little about food. Enough to get by."

"Maybe Mac will be hiring you in the future instead," he teased.

The color quickly vanished from Tessa's face. "I'm a little too busy to design flowers for people's foyers," she said, forgetting to watch her tone. The heat in her face had found a new home.

Stupid kiss. Stupid, stupid me for letting myself even think about it after the first time.

"Easy," said Blake, looking slightly puzzled. "It was a joke, Tess. I didn't mean anything by it, except maybe that you have talents besides the planning part of things."

She repented of that mistake now. "Sorry," she said. "I didn't mean—I wasn't trying to—" She hesitated. "Anyway, I hope Mac has a good time at the reception. You too."

It wasn't as if he would do anything else, probably, at a catered party in the company of a beautiful woman who was dying to say yes to his offer to spend an evening out together... if Mac hadn't said yes to that offer in the past already. The way she talked to him, touched him. The chance definitely existed that the two of them were beyond the strictly business side of things.

"You too," he said. "You said before this is the part you live for, when it all goes right and the client is living out their happiest moment. I don't think it gets much better than the one taking place out there right now."

He was looking behind her, toward the dance floor in the main dining room, where the newlyweds were sharing their first slow dance as husband and wife to the love song that was supposed to play in that semi-disastrous moment at their rehearsal dinner. Tessa watched as Nadia lifted her head from Lyle's shoulders, their eyes meeting as they swayed to the music.

This time, a smile found its way to her lips. "No, it doesn't," she answered softly.

She felt Blake's fingers on her shoulder, brushing against her sleeve. More like a nudge than a touch in its briefness, only gentler than Tessa felt that a friend's hand would offer it. "That's because of your work today," he said, as Lyle and Nadia moved together on the dance floor. "So, again, nice job."

"Thanks," said Tessa. Her voice was quieter than the last time she said it, with no trace of sarcasm or humor. Blake moved on, replaced by a groomsman asking Tessa to take a photograph of the bridesmaids posing with him.

From her place at the restaurant's main bar, Tessa watched the dance floor grow more casual for the second half of the evening, with the music become trendier and louder and the dancing crowd growing younger. Although she didn't admit it to herself, her eye was really on Blake and Mac, especially the interior designer, who was leaning into him as they posed for a photograph, her hand on his shoulder. Then she leaned against him on the dance floor, swaying gently on the fringes of the rhythmic couples, despite the upbeat love song playing.

Tessa turned away before they could catch her watching, and let her chin rest on her crossed arms for a moment. Her view of the world was of candles glittering on an empty table, the locked glass liquor cabinets behind the bar, and the remains of the nuts from the bar's crystal dish. The tip of Tessa's pinky finger nudged into place the pistachio shells piled around the base of her champagne flute, lining them up like little soldiers.

Someone sat down next to her. Natalie, too, leaned on a pair of folded arms, peering toward Tessa's face. "Penny for your thoughts," she said. "I haven't seen much of you this evening. I thought you'd be torturing me with needles under my fingernails for the missing details of the cake story."

"I trust you," said Tessa. "You said it was solved." Her fingernail turned the last nutshell's pointed tip to face the same direction as the rest.

Natalie said nothing. Tessa could feel her friend's gaze fixed intently, as if boring through her. "Blake was right," she said. "You *are* jealous of her."

A perfect guess. Not that you had to be one of her closest friends in the world, however, to see what was happening right now. Tessa felt her face crumpling slightly, something she struggled to prevent, just like the inner collapse of her walls.

She drew herself upright as she nodded. "But not professionally," she answered. She felt Natalie's arms around her shoulders as she closed her eyes, the best safeguard against any tears that might threaten to show up at this confession.

She was horribly, helplessly jealous. Those were not the attributes of calm, professional Tessa Miller at any other time, but no matter how hard she denied it, the sight of him with another woman had brought the truth screaming to her consciousness. She liked Blake— was attracted to Blake—wanted to fall in love with Blake. It could happen in any order of this process, but these things were definitely all happening to her, and had been from the moment she first walked into Wedding Belles' headquarters and laid eyes on him.

It was too late now. She was going to kick herself for this mistake for a long, long time.

Chapter Twenty-Five

The cake was down to leftover slices on plates on the dessert table. Empty glasses occupied most available table surfaces in both the main and private dining rooms at Olive Brook, as the staff cleared away the debris left by the wedding party. And Tessa's feet were aching as the tight leather of her high heels closed around them after a long day as she, Ama, and Natalie packed up the wedding gifts, flowers, guest book, the cake's top layer, and other belongings of the bride and groom for delivery to Lyle's place the next day.

The Wedding Belles' headquarters was quiet except for the usual creaks and groans of a building settling late at night, and the gentle hum from the kitchen fridge. Natalie deposited the box containing the guest book and the bride and groom's champagne flutes on the desk in reception, while Tessa placed the bridal table's centerpiece flowers in a chipped yellow vase stashed beneath it.

"I am exhausted, sore, and starving," Natalie announced, kicking off her high heels as she spoke aloud Tessa's first thought upon unlocking the door. "Please tell me there's something in the fridge besides those pickles." She flopped down on the sofa in the parlor, pulling its shawl around her and leaving exposed the sun-faded upholstery on its upper cushions.

"There's not," Ama called back, as she slid the bakery box containing the cake's topmost layer into the fridge. "But there's a pizza place two streets over that delivers until midnight."

"I'm calling them. I don't care if they only have anchovies and charge twenty dollars a pie." Natalie pulled her phone from her handbag and opened the city app. "I could eat one by myself."

Tessa plugged in the Christmas lights for the mini tree on the reception desk. The big trees in the window were dark, their brightly colored balls looking somewhat tarnished in the shadows. Even the little white and red twinkle lights didn't cheer her up. The thought of Christmas was depressing at this moment.

"Here's to happy occasions—and broken bad luck streaks." With this toast, Natalie lifted her water bottle to Ama's cup of tea and Tessa's coffee mug. "May next time be magical at every stage, and not just the end."

"To future good luck," echoed Ama.

Soon after, the 'Greek special' pizza was delivered, and Ama reached for a slice, the feta and mozzarella, chicken, and peperoncino olives wafting steam into the air. "Mmm, this is good," she said. "Pickled peppers and olives on pizza. I love pepperoni, but I think I totally love this too." She took another bite.

"So what happened to the cake?" Tessa set her coffee mug on the table and crossed her arms around her legs, hugging them from her perch in the armchair. Her two partners exchanged glances.

"Let's just say the top layer is not my finest work," began Ama hesitantly.

"Not your work at all," clarified Natalie. "Its design, however, should win some awards. You dressed that baby up so well that its own bakery mother wouldn't know it."

"That's *not* our cake?" Tessa said, her mouth dropping open. "Where's our cake's real top?"

"In pieces in the garbage?" said Ama. Her meek reply dissolved into a giggle after a second; Natalie snorted back a laugh, covering her mouth with one hand as she looked away in an attempt at self-composure.

"It's not that funny," protested Tessa. "What's underneath the fondant? Tell me it's not the Twinkies from the pantry," she added.

Natalie shook her head. "Just a plain ol' bakery cake from the closest place I could find on short notice," she answered. "But you can't tell by looking at it. I swear, after today I will always say that Ama's a genius with fondant."

"Maybe not a genius," said Ama, wrinkling her nose. "Just good in a tight spot."

Natalie smothered another laugh, but Ama was giving Tessa a look of scrutiny. "Wait a moment," she said. "You told me earlier there was a problem with the centerpiece's delivery. What happened in *that* situation?"

"Wrong delivery service—they brought us the decorations for a soccer team's party," said Tessa. "Accented Creations had a flat tire and an hour's delay on top of being late. It was half unpacked by the time I realized the wrong people were decorating the restaurant," she confessed.

"What was in the dining room when you walked out there?" Natalie asked.

"Purple piñatas, green streamers, giant sombreros. The normal decorations for a wedding," answered Tessa. When Natalie and Ama dissolved into laughter again, the same infection swept over Tessa too.

"This may go down as our most interesting time planning a wedding," said Natalie, taking a second slice of pizza from the box. "Definitely our most turbulent time."

"At least it turned out beautifully in the end," said Ama. "You would never know that it was full of disasters, watching it from the outside. We're lucky nobody saw what was behind the curtain except for Nadia and Lyle."

She lifted another slice of pizza as she rose from the sofa. "I think there are some leftover cheesecakes in the fridge," she said. "Be right back." She disappeared in the direction of the kitchen as Tessa studied her painted toenails, falling silent now that only two partners were left in the room.

"Hey," said Natalie softly. "Don't think about it too hard. Nobody but me noticed tonight that you were less than your enthusiastic self for a few minutes. You know I can keep a secret. You trust me, right?"

"It's not that," said Tessa. "There's no point in keeping it a secret except to keep from being embarrassed in front of him. Any more embarrassed than I've been recently," she corrected, at the mortifying memory of lashing out at Blake days ago—and nearly kissing him this afternoon.

"Except for him, I'm not afraid of anybody figuring it out who hasn't already teased me about the idea in the past. Me, the reformed romantic liking our sexy handyman." Her tone was sad and bitter, as if this idea was part of the past now, no more than teasing words at their first pizza party.

"Then what?" asked Natalie.

Tessa hesitated. "I was so stupid," she said. "I blew it, Natalie. After my bad string of crushes in the past, I said I wasn't going to fall head over heels for anybody again, and look what happened. And now… now he likes somebody else. As usual." She blinked hard, feeling the threat of tears creeping up suspiciously. "I shoved him away all the times in the past, and it didn't do any good for me. I probably shoved him into the arms of Miss Perfect."

"Who says she's perfect for him?" Natalie asked. "Mac's overrated. So she's a decorating genius with a résumé as long as a runway carpet? You have pluck. And a really great body."

Tessa snorted with laughter, failing to smother her response completely as Ama walked in. "Why are we talking about Blake's friend?" she asked, as she set the plate of cheesecakes on top of the pizza box's lid. "And Tessa's body?"

"Don't ask," said Natalie. But Ama had made the connection now, her gaze swiveling from the designer to the wedding planner. "No," she said. "You *like* him. You said it, didn't you? Oh my gosh, I can't believe I missed it. I've been waiting weeks for you to say something."

"Has *everybody* in this place just assumed I have a crush on Blake?" asked Tessa, who still managed to be miffed in the face of her predictions actualized. "Didn't anybody think I was telling the truth when I said I was through with romance?"

"No, not really," said Ama. "I just can't believe you actually admit it now."

"I knew you'd fall off the wagon someday," Natalie replied archly. "I only can't believe it took you this long."

"Why not?" Tessa mumbled as she sipped her coffee. "Now that he has another girl, what do I have to lose? Except my dignity, of course."

"Stop whining," said Natalie. "He never said he's dating Mac, so maybe it's just a passing phase. Look on the bright side: at least your one-sided romantic problem involves a hot guy who might still be unattached. I'm still trying to convince my unwanted admirer to give up on me and latch onto somebody else."

"Not Chad?" said Tessa. "I thought you liked him."

"I like Chad. I'm talking about… well, about somebody who shows up sometimes," answered Natalie vaguely. "My issue isn't the romantic disaster of a lifetime, believe me." She made it sound like she was joking. "Chad's still a great guy, just in case anybody is wondering." She snagged a cheesecake from the plate.

"I guess we all have romantic problems in our own way," said Ama. "I broke up with Tamir finally."

Both of her partners sat upright. "You did?" repeated Natalie. "Finally! You go, girl."

"Ama, good for you," said Tessa. "No more being miserable at restaurants or movie theaters. You're taking control of your romantic destiny."

"Sort of," said Ama. "It's a beginning. Let's stick with that for now. It felt like a disaster, but it will get better, I think. At least I'm not pretending to date someone I don't like, or hiding the fact that I don't feel the way my family wants me to about certain things. Right?"

Natalie lifted her water bottle. "Here's to happy disasters in life," she said.

Happy disasters. That's what this wedding represented best, Tessa supposed. Messy things sometimes tumble into perfect order at the bottom of life's staircase. Would other things in their lives fall into place eventually, like the winter wonderland ceremony? Working with Blake, thinking about him and Mac as a couple from now on—how good would she be at facing that situation? Clinging to their 'strictly professional' boundaries, pretending that she didn't think about him at all, or feel anything out of the ordinary when they touched… that had been the biggest miscalculation she had made since beginning this venture.

I'll have to go on working with him. I'll have to pretend it doesn't bother me, because that's exactly what he thinks after everything I said. Besides, I want him to stay. I don't want him to leave because he found out how I really feel. Having Blake quit would be worse, and she knew it, even feeling this mixed up inside.

"So, who is your unwanted admirer?" Ama asked Natalie.

"Nobody," answered Natalie. She passed Tessa a cheesecake on the plate. "Try one of these, Tess. They really are amazing." She took a bite out of her own serving, the crushed peppermint giving it a light crunch.

"No thanks," said Tessa. She didn't have an appetite for one, not after Mac's compliments, delivered via Blake. His admiring tone for the interior designer had been a big red warning flag to her emotions from the beginning, which she had refused to recognize at the time.

She felt Ama's hand on her shoulder, giving it a gentle squeeze. "Maybe Blake doesn't really like her," Ama suggested. "You are a little out of practice reading the signals, right?"

"Right." Tessa tried to smile, but it didn't go as planned, once again. As it wobbled into tears, she felt Natalie's hand on her other shoulder with the same comforting squeeze as Ama's, which made falling apart easier than at the restaurant. Maybe a few tears in sympathetic company was exactly what she needed.

Chapter Twenty-Six

"That's the last of my holiday shopping." Natalie let the door to Wedding Belles swing closed behind her on its own as she stomped the snow from her boots. "Nadia and Lyle must be on honeymoon somewhere warm, because I think they left behind their wedding's snowstorm in the city."

"It's a white Christmas," said Ama, who was peering through a hole in the picture window's frost as she rearranged the display's presents under its 'wedding tree,' decorated with invitations, cake ornaments, bunting garlands, and a cake topper to crown it. "That's my favorite kind. I love to go for walks on Christmas Day when it snows. Me and Rasha walk past the big church with the manger scene, then go window shopping even though the stores are closed, *then* we go listen to the band and watch the lights in the park at dusk."

"I thought your family didn't celebrate Christmas," said Natalie, depositing several shopping bags on the reception desk. She unwound her scarf and draped it over the shoulder of a half-dressed mannequin waiting for the spring display—one that she had promised to help put into place over the holidays, in order to escape endless leftovers and her relatives' questions.

"We don't. But we still have the day off," said Ama. "Nobody comes to our place on Christmas Day—even the Indians in our neighborhood always go to the twenty-four-hour Chinese delivery place a couple of blocks away. Usually, me and my sister watch the parade on TV, and my brother Nikil hangs out with his friends. Jaidev and Deena come over for dinner because my father *has* to cook something if it's a holiday."

"Sounds like my mother." Natalie rummaged around in one of her shopping bags. "At least you'll eat casual style. I'll have to dress nicely, eat a thousand of my uncle's traditional Christmas ravioli, and be prepared to eat a ton of cream cake on top of that when we come back from Midnight Mass. Plus, there's usually a big Italian seafood platter... my brother will make us all play touch football..."

"Still better than my mom's idea of roasting a turkey with turmeric and nutmeg," said Ama. "If she wants to roast one again, I hope she'll let me and my siblings help. My mom and American cooking do not mix."

"Ah, holidays with the family." Natalie smirked. She scribbled a note to send thank you cards to Nadia's wedding venue—and to the snooty new florist they had conquered, thanks to Tessa's creative substitute. Her phone buzzed noisily from her handbag.

"Do you want to answer it?" Ama asked, as she pinned the latest business Christmas card to a string of them hanging across the foyer mirror, clipped in place with tiny clothespins.

"It's probably my textiles class being canceled," said Natalie. "I heard my instructor has the flu." Ama dug the phone from the handbag and checked the screen.

A strange look crossed her face. "What?" said Natalie. "What does it say?"

"It's from your cousin." Ama hesitated, then took a breath and read aloud the text. "'How serious is Chad?'"

Awkward—it was *not* the college administrator texting her class. Natalie had forgotten all about those texts exchanged with her mother, the half-serious pact she and Chad had made to silence her family's meddling judgment. The look on Ama's face was proof that her brain had calculated matters and leapt wildly ahead to the subtext of this text—that there was something between her and Chad that was worth taking note of, regardless of Natalie's previous statements.

"You and Chad?" Ama echoed, before Natalie could speak. "The two of you are still dating?" Her eyes were alight. "I can't believe it—is this text genuine? Is your family really asking this?"

Natalie balked. "Uh—er," she began.

"He's so handsome though, right?" said Ama. "All that rock climbing... Oh my gosh, Natalie, I can't believe it. I can't believe you're seriously dating someone."

"It's... more the sort of 'feeling it out' stage," ventured Natalie. Did Ama actually believe this was true? After all she had said aloud about commitment, serious romance, even falling in love? "I wouldn't call us *serious*, in the strictest sense of the word. More like... exploring our potential as a couple." That was a good definition for her and Chad in reality, after all.

"Why is your cousin asking, then?" persisted Ama.

"Because..." Natalie paused. "Because that's what I told my mom the other night." The moment for fessing up to the reasons why she had done something this surprising was at hand. "Of course, I—"

A playful smile appeared on Ama's lips in reply. "You like him, don't you?" she said coyly. "I knew you did. He was everything you always said you liked in a guy, I just didn't think you were that serious about him yet. I wondered if there could be something, though."

"I like him, yeah," admitted Natalie, since this much could be stated honestly. "He's a great guy. But... but it's really new, this thing between us. You know me." She shrugged her shoulders and tried to act mysterious in order to avoid saying too much that would make it seem true, or crushing her pact with Chad this early in the game.

After all, she needed some practice before she confronted her family with her fake serious boyfriend. If Ama could believe that Natalie the uncommitted and unromantic would plunge into the heat of love after a couple of short weeks, then surely her desperate family would buy into the idea, too. Right?

After all, it's just until after the New Year... and maybe Valentine's Day. At least Ma won't try to set me up with one of the bakery's regular customers for this one.

"Oooh, this is exciting!" said Ama, clapping her hands.

"And a secret," added Natalie hastily. "I mean, at least so long as we're just starting out. Can't tell everybody everything, can we?" Oh, the flippancy of her tone. Her true self could have a wickedly good time with the double meaning of these statements, smiling at her own private joke. Maybe Chad would have as much fun telling his rock-climbing buddies that he had a steady girlfriend for New Year's Eve.

"We'll be planning your wedding next spring," predicted Ama with a grin. "You'll be our June bride, I'll just bet."

"I think I'm more of a December bride," said Natalie, balking nonetheless at the actual word 'wedding' in association with herself. "December of 2047," she added. "Don't get any ideas about putting me in a white dress yet, all right?" No way was she going to look at cakes or pretend to try on dresses just because her friends were romantics.

"Well, I for one can't wait to meet the guy who can change Natalie Grenaldi's mind about being single forever," joked Ama. "He must be pretty special." She held up three fingers. "Scout's honor that I won't tell Tessa. I'll let you do it. Besides, she'll totally flip when she hears this piece of news. I think you should wait and pop by with him, just to see what her reaction is." The look in Ama's eyes proved she was imagining Tessa's jaw dropping at the occasion.

Natalie couldn't resist laughing slightly as she pictured it, too—Ama's chuckle joined in.

"Mark my words, you're definitely a summer bride," said Ama, shaking her head in response to Natalie's look of denial. "If you're serious about Chad, you should really bring him by to meet us, so we can put our stamp of approval on him. As your closest friends, I mean."

"If I'm serious about a guy, he'll meet you both before I take any romantic plunge," said Natalie, artfully sidestepping the whole 'meet Chad' scenario. "You have my word. Scout's honor." She held up her fingers in pledge, unable to resist the return of her joking smile, one infectious enough that Ama caught it, too, although hers was for an entirely different scenario.

"Toss my phone back in my purse and let's finish tidying up so we can get out of here for the holidays," said Natalie, who sorted yesterday's mail from one of the many odd hiding places Tessa jammed envelopes when she was in a hurry to tidy up for clients. "I don't know about you, but I'm not working overtime today."

"We still have to finish touching up the window display, though," Ama reminded her. "You said you'd help me put up another white-lit Christmas tree in the corner."

"Sure," said Natalie.

In the back of her mind, be it ever so briefly, Natalie pondered what it would be like if a moment ago she had truly been talking about someone special who changed her mind about commitment and serious romances. *Imagine if this were real*, she mused. If she really cared about someone enough to share every family dinner with them for a lifetime, and had her friends' stamp of approval on him...

It wouldn't be Chad, she thought. Probably not, anyway. And it wasn't likely to be anybody else whom she'd ever met, judging by the string of texts and emails from her exes, who amicably surrendered whenever the romance grew stagnant. *Of course things can change overnight*, a tiny part of her brain reflected. *You'll be pretending to be romantically serious for two whole months. That's a lot of practice for the impossible, isn't it?* Just as quickly as this crept into her thoughts, Natalie's mind dismissed it as utter nonsense. For one thing, she couldn't eat any more Ecuadorian stew. And for another, rock climbing had left bruises in hard-to-treat places.

Putting aside thoughts of her holiday romance for now, Natalie held out a package to Ama, wrapped in candy cane paper and tied with a red ribbon. "Merry Christmas, by the way."

"What's this?"

"A Christmas gift. Go on, open it. It's nothing much." Natalie waved it away dismissively. "Just something that made me think of you when I was looking for a gift for Uncle Guido."

"A cookie cutter shaped like a Christmas tree light bulb?" Ama lifted the shaped metal outline from the torn paper. "I love it. Thank you. But—I didn't get you anything, or Tess. I didn't have a chance to go shopping, and my head was full of romantic problems—I didn't even think of you guys." Apology crept into Ama's voice.

"I have a hundred presents from relatives that I need to exchange," said Natalie. "Trust me, I don't need more. Besides… I think Tess would only be excited by one particular present that neither of us can deliver." She glanced pointedly at the construction ladder sitting just outside the little room undergoing its paint job, where the handyman's spare tool belt was looped around the paint can stand.

The front door opened and Tessa entered—Natalie and Ama both dropped the subject guiltily. She set her own shopping bags down in the foyer, glancing at both of her business partners. "Everything okay?" she asked.

"Fine," they answered together—a little too brightly.

Tessa looked slightly suspicious, but didn't choose to comment on this. "Any calls?' she asked, as she tapped snow from the sides of her boots.

"Someone called to make an appointment for the New Year," said Ama. "That brings us to a grand total of two for next spring, and potentially one more for next summer already, so our luck is definitely looking up."

"Good," said Tessa with a smile. "We have something to look forward to when we open after the holidays." She unbuttoned her coat and laid it on the chair. "We can close early today if everybody has plans. I told my mom I'd be there by dinnertime, but that could be any time after five in my book."

"Christmas at a Florida condo," said Natalie. "I'm so envious I could pinch you. You'll be watching the surf roll in, eating gourmet blueberry muffins while I'm listening to my family argue over whether Rob or I will be the first to tie the knot."

"Does your mom still decorate, even at her time share?" asked Ama.

"Of course. For every box of ornaments she gave us, she kept one," said Tessa. "She'll have twinkle lights and greenery all over the place. Plus, she's forever buying new ones at end-of-the-holidays sales." She spun a gold ornament on the foyer tree, an old one that Tessa remembered from her childhood. The wear on its gilded paint was the work of her fingers over fifteen or twenty years, probably. "We won't lack for Christmas at my mom's place."

"Will you have fun at the beach?" Ama asked gently. "Christmas in the sand instead of the snow?" Tessa stopped twirling the ornament and, looking lost in thought—while gazing off in the distance at Blake's ladder—her features rearranged themselves into a cheerful holiday smile.

"Of course I will," she said. "It's Christmas. I'll be with my mom, I'll watch lots of Hallmark movies on television while I stuff my face with chocolate truffles and brownies… we'll eat Chinese food and watch the parade. What's not to love?"

"Nothing," said Natalie, shaking her head.

"Chinese food," said Ama to Natalie. "Told you. It's the Christmas favorite, hands down."

Tessa pulled two tiny shopping bags from within her bigger one. "Merry Christmas," she announced to her partners. "Don't open these until tomorrow, okay? It's a rule in my house—no gifts early."

"Promise," said Ama.

"Scout's honor," said Natalie, holding up three fingers in salute.

Tessa glanced around. "I guess if nothing's happening here, I'll just go home and pack," she said.

"Good idea," said Natalie. "Beat the holiday traffic."

"No sense in hanging around, is there?" said Tessa, who was still lingering in one spot. Ama and Natalie exchanged glances.

Tessa sighed. "All right," she said. "I know he's not here today. He won't be back until after the holidays, and I'll be fine. Even if he's… dating Mac… I'll be fine. He's my friend, and my business partner, and I know how to be mature about this. I *am* a reformed romantic, after all. I just kind of… had a misstep."

"Come here." Natalie opened her arms and motioned Tessa forward.

"I'm all right."

"I know, but come here anyway," said Natalie. "You too, Ama. Reel it in. This is the last time we'll see each other this year." She put her arms around Tessa's shoulders and Ama's, the sleeve of Tessa's shirt sliding around the back of Natalie's sweater in return. Ama squeezed them both closer in the group hug, until a giggle escaped Tessa.

"That's enough," said Tessa, breaking the circle a moment later. "I have to go, and you both have plans for today, too. So I'll see you in a week, right?"

"A week," said Ama.

"When we're all living out our New Year's resolution to give up chocolate and sugar," said Natalie, who rummaged through her shopping bag, handing Tessa a box of truffles trimmed with a Christmas bow. "It's insane how many calories are in a chocolate truffle. And when I think of my mom's cream cake slices topped with those white chocolate ones—"

"Do you know how many cups of cocoa I drink during Christmas week?" asked Ama, echoing Natalie's dismay. "It's, like, a whole day's calories when you add in the marshmallows."

Tessa lifted her coat and scarf, and her shopping bags from the foyer. From the pocket of her coat, she slipped another package wrapped in holiday paper. She placed it near the back of the tree, hiding its tag from sight so the girls wouldn't see the capital 'B' at the beginning of the recipient's name. It was just a Christmas present to a friend, and there was a strong chance Blake would never notice it when he stopped by to collect his tools… but it wouldn't do to have them thinking it was a desperate gesture on her part. It wasn't as if a silly handyman-themed silk tie would make him see her differently.

She tucked it in place, then glanced back at her friends. They hadn't noticed. With a lopsided smile, she lingered by the tree a moment longer, then turned to go. Tessa's fingers stretched to touch the front door handle, but it suddenly opened as if by magic. On the other side was Blake. He had a coil of electrical wire looped over one shoulder, his cheeks reddened by the cool wind outside. A cheerful smile was on his lips, and the last of a whistled Christmas carol died away as he entered the building. One glance at those blue eyes, and she felt her own breath sucked away with a rush of feeling as strong as the surprise of him materializing before her.

Tessa took a step backwards. "Hi," she managed, when she recovered herself. Was she blushing? She hoped not. There was no good reason in the world to blush, just because she was confused and conflicted about Blake and Mac, and missing her chance for telling him how much she cared.

"Hi," he said, looking surprised to see her, too. "I didn't think I'd catch you before you left—"

"—I'm on my way out, actually," she said, trying hard to seem casual. "Just stopped to wish the girls a merry Christmas before I hit the road. Merry Christmas," she added to Blake, in a breezy, casual voice that she didn't feel was really hers at all.

"Hey, I have something for you," he said, his hand diving into his coat pocket. "Again, I didn't think I'd see you in time—"

Tessa's heart was pounding strangely as he pulled the box from his pocket. It was wrapped in perfectly ordinary red-and-green Christmas paper, a bow tied around it—but it was from Blake, and that made it different. He'd bought her a present? This, after her outburst—after Mac had become the girl in his life, if an arm around Blake at the wedding reception was any proof of togetherness.

"For you," he said, holding it out.

"You didn't have to." Her voice was softer, more honest in its betrayal of her feelings, as she accepted it from his hand. "I mean… I'm not implying that you… that I… I only meant…"

"Open it." The corner of Blake's mouth twitched with a smile of amusement at her bungled apology. Tessa knew her face was on fire now. Cheeks scarlet, her fingers dove beneath the ribbon, untucking the corner of the paper with a noisy haste that covered for her embarrassment and bewilderment. The folds parted, revealing a box underneath. Its flap lifted, and there it was: a little Christmas ornament of an old-fashioned brownstone house. A tiny little Christmas wreath decorated its door, glittering silvery-white with artificial snow. There was a tiny fir tree decorated in its window.

"I saw it and thought of you," said Blake. "It's your building. Not exactly, because the windows are different, and there's a basement entrance—"

"I love it," she said. "It's perfect. It looks so much like it, I wouldn't have noticed the difference." She held it by its ribbon, watching the miniature version of the Wedding Belles' headquarters gently sway over the gift paper from the open box.

"I thought you'd like it." Blake's voice had softened.

"You didn't have to get me a present, though," she said. He didn't, and not merely because she had waved away that last opportunity to tell him the real reason she had been jealous of Mac.

"I got ones for the other girls, so it would've been rude to forget you," he said. From his other pocket, he produced two more small packages, shaped differently. Tessa wondered if it was wrong that she felt disappointed by this fact. It was every bit as irrational as feeling jealous of Mac. Why was being rational such a hard choice these days?

"I—" she started to speak, then remembered the box behind the tree. "I have something for you, too." Her hand reached for the box under its branches, and she held it out to him. "It's nothing, really."

"You got me a present?" Blake sounded genuinely surprised, although he had just given her one.

"It's just a little thank you for all you've done for us," she said, shrugging her shoulders. Thankfully her blush had faded by now. "And not just for the building, I mean." Blake's snooty performance as Stefan's imaginary assistant was particularly vivid in her mind. Maybe it was in his, too, because his smile was still a faintly humorous one as he undid the taped corner of the gift-wrapped tie box. His fingers rustled aside its gift tissue, then lifted out the tie.

"I like it," he said. "I think it would look great with the Hugo Boss suit. Or maybe the Armani. What do you think?"

"Either one." A smile played at the corner of Tessa's mouth. "I'll let you decide."

He knotted it deftly and tried it on, although it looked ludicrous with his green flannel shirt. They both managed not to laugh, although the urge was strong. Then Tessa made the mistake of meeting his eyes again, and felt herself slipping into a tender state of mind. Thoughts of snooty Blake in those rectangular-rimmed glasses were being vanquished by a surge of other memories: of Blake presenting the antique altar for their first clients, Molly and Paolo, of him across from her in the coffee shop, talking about love and life's hesitations. Especially of his hands catching her when she fell off the ladder, holding tight to her.

Blake's gaze had changed in this moment, too, and for a second, hope rose in Tessa's chest, a quick pattering of heartbeats at the memory of the look in his eyes that she had seen—or imagined seeing—in the garden after Molly and Paolo's ceremony in the summer. Was his smile the same now as it was that day? Or was she telling herself so at this moment just because she wished for it?

He reached to hug her, but Tessa's arm was in the way, the one holding the ornament, blocking his embrace by accident. His arms drew back at the moment she automatically moved into a hug position—a laugh escaped Blake, and Tessa bit her lip, holding in her own smile of laugher and embarrassment. Awkward to the last, she thought to herself. A perfect ending, given how clumsily their connection began. It wasn't the one she wanted, however, no matter what she had suggested to Blake as recently as a few days ago, when he left the door open for her to confess her real emotions.

When he took a step toward her in the midst of these thoughts, Tessa thought she was dreaming. He lifted his hand and touched her cheek lightly. It was all she could do not to touch him back. Her fingers held the ornament tightly, as if freezing her hand in one position beneath the shock this tender touch brought her.

If her fingers moved to his own, with a touch that suggested everything she'd grown to feel for him, for instance… but before they could, an awkward expression entered Blake's eyes. Tessa's gaze broke from his own guiltily, as if aware she'd betrayed too much. Whatever crossed Blake's face was hidden from her as he glanced downwards, recovering himself as well.

He glanced at her with a smile again afterwards, one that Tessa returned. He had no idea what was really in her mind, she told herself. He probably thought she was sensing the awkwardness of his change in status with Mac or something like that—entering the 'be careful how you act around other women' stage of a relationship, for instance—and not that she was upset at herself for her own lack of decisiveness and self-control when it came to him.

He cleared his throat. "I guess I'll see you after the holidays," he said.

"Sure. After the New Year starts and we're back to our normal routines around here," said Tessa, although nothing would be the same next year. After all, things had changed for Wedding Belles, now that it was finding its legs as a business. And, of course, there was the thing about Blake being in a relationship. Not that it was supposed to have any consequence for life around here.

"Merry Christmas," said Tessa softly.

"Merry Christmas, Tess."

They lingered not even a breath's length after these words, their eyes meeting one more time in that instant, which felt like an hour to Tessa. Her mind had stopped the clock there. Then Blake offered her one last smile and stepped through the foyer to the reception area. He glanced back, and Tessa did the same—then Natalie and Ama spotted him, and it was over. She put her hand on the doorknob and opened it.

I wish I knew which one hurt more. That I let myself fall in love, or that I let my chance with him go by. If I could turn back time... if I could do just one thing over...

She sighed and stepped outside to the brisk cold and snowdrifts of a winter day in the city. In the bright sunlight, Tessa turned right and walked in the direction of her borrowed car. The windows of their neighbor were decorated with tinsel trees in assorted bright holiday colors, little lights twinkling among the branches of blue, red, and green. A toy steam train looped through a winter wonderland made from white cotton wadding and glitter, bearing tiny little gifts wrapped in metallic paper.

She glanced at it as she passed, and almost bumped into a fellow pedestrian approaching from the opposite direction. Turning quickly, Tessa was confronted by a woman in a well-tailored grey suit, a vintage-print holiday scarf adorning the collar of her camel coat. It was Mac, looking beautiful and model-esque as always.

"Sorry," Tessa apologized. "I wasn't looking where I was going, I guess."

"Same here," said Mac. "Going home for the day?"

"Leaving town for the holidays," said Tessa, holding up her car keys. "Are you in the neighborhood to meet with a client?" As if she didn't know why Mac was here.

"I was just walking to your place, actually," said Mac. "I took the day off, too, in fact—a little celebration time for me."

"Landed a big client, huh?" said Tessa, who was thinking of the glitzy Christmas display Mac had designed for the historic home. "They were probably impressed by your display at the Canton house, weren't they?"

Mac laughed. "I'm celebrating something other than work," she answered. "I had an early Christmas present this week." As she spoke, she drew her hand from her pocket—her left one—and held it up so the ring finger was facing Tessa, showcasing a sparkling princess-cut diamond.

The breath in Tessa's lungs dissolved. Her heart sank low as she gazed at the sparkling ring.

"Congratulations," she managed to say. "A proposal at Christmas. Who wouldn't love that?"

"Thank you," said Mac, blushing. "It's kind of sudden, but I'm getting used to it. Besides, how could I say no to the most perfect guy in the world?"

"How?" echoed Tessa, removing herself from here as far as possible emotionally—which was to say, a million miles, in order to be safe and certain in her replies and show no unsuitable feelings.

"I'm thinking a June wedding, so there's months of decisions to make. I'll need an event planner, too," said Mac. "Do you have a card? I'd love to use your business—Blake brags to no end about what a great job you always do."

Automatically, Tessa's fingers moved slowly into the pocket in the side of her purse, withdrawing one of the many business cards she kept there. "Here you are," she said. She managed to release it when Mac took it, though a part of her wanted to take it back and tear it up hastily… to say she was booked through next autumn, no openings for clients at all.

"I'll give you a call when we set the date officially," said Mac. "See you after the holidays. Merry Christmas." She continued on in the direction of Tessa's headquarters, a smile of anticipation on her lips already.

"See you," answered Tessa. She forgot to add her wishes for a merry Christmas, though it was the polite thing to do. She kept on walking, knowing Mac was probably on her way to the front door of Wedding Belles now, and would be inside in a few seconds, asking which room Blake was working in today. Would Natalie and Ama see the ring? Would they see Blake and Mac steal a kiss beneath the mistletoe, or would the couple keep their post-proposal reunion a private one?

She didn't want to know. She was fighting the tears as she walked to her car, keeping her head high and her heart as far away from the truth as possible. *I shouldn't cry. I shouldn't cry because Blake and Mac have a magical connection, the one that he and I missed. Maybe it wasn't meant to be for us. He was destined not to call, I was destined not to admit that day how much I cared about him.*

Carry on thinking this way and she could keep the horrible disappointment at bay for hours. Nobody would know how devastating it felt to see that diamond sparkling on Mac's hand, and know that 'the most perfect guy in the world' had sealed the deal with her. This explained everything about Blake's confusion the day of their near kiss, and this reason was even worse than what Tessa had formerly assumed.

This was the furthest thing from a merry Christmas that Tessa could possibly imagine.

❋

In the Wedding Belles' headquarters, Tessa's business partners were ignoring their last-minute work in an exchange of holiday well wishes with Blake. Natalie twirled the gift between her fingers—a novelty pen with a tiny fashion diva in impossibly stacked heels and a mini dress—while Ama admired the spoon rest that the contractor had carved himself from a piece of oak.

"Nice tie," Natalie informed him, giving the fabric a tug. "I didn't know you had such great taste in fashion. Although I'm not sure it really complements that shirt," she added with a wicked smile.

"Very funny," he replied. "I should've expected you to be the Grinch this holiday season. Just for that, maybe I should take back these presents I brought you."

"Don't take mine back," Ama protested. "I mean, I'm not the one who insulted your wardrobe, after all." She dodged a playful smack from Natalie's hand.

After a few more 'merry Christmases,' Blake made a quick check of his workspace and his tools, then offered them a quick goodbye and was out the door again. Only to be waylaid on the sidewalk in front of their display window by a gorgeous woman in a camel coat, as Ama and Natalie untangled yet another string of pearl white lights.

"Isn't that Mac?" Ama said. "The decorator from Blake's last job?"

"Yeah, I think so," said Natalie. "Same glamorous taste in clothing at any rate. That coat is no knock-off design, believe me."

"Trust you to notice," teased Ama. "Look, it is her," she added, as the woman turned so that her profile was visible. "And—is that a diamond on her hand?"

The hand in question lay in Blake's now, showing off its dazzling stone in the winter light. Mac's eyes were glowing as she gazed up at him, and brought her other hand to rest on Blake's shoulder. He was smiling down at her, saying something that made her laugh.

Natalie and Ama stared. Ama's jaw dropped slightly. "Is this real?" she said. "Did Blake—?"

"No," said Natalie. "No, no, no. This is not happening. This is… this is totally ruining things…"

"Ruining what?" asked Ama, who was now confused in addition to being shocked. She looked at the scene outside again, where Mac was now tucking her hands in her pockets, hugging her coat around herself for warmth.

"Wow. That was one impressive engagement ring on her hand," said Ama. A look of realization now dawned on her face at the meaning in Natalie's mind—Tessa's romantic confession. "Oh no," she said. "Did Blake *really*—?"

"Of course not. Blake would have said something if he just got engaged, right?" Natalie's tone was firm. "He's not a guy who keeps secrets. Not from his friends."

"Of course not," said Ama, still in shock. "But… are we really Blake's friends?" She left this question hanging as they watched Blake and Mac walk away together, the contractor never glancing back to notice he was being watched.

"Sure we are," said Natalie. But so softly she almost didn't hear herself say it aloud. Ama glanced at her.

"Why did you say this ruins everything?" Ama asked.

A pause. "No reason," answered Natalie.

Untangling lights had ceased to be fun. Even the distant strains of an instrumental carol medley being played at the newly opened holiday shop a few doors down didn't lift the sudden gloom cast over the Wedding Belles' foyer, its Christmas cheer vanishing like the winter sun behind a cloud.

Natalie stuffed the rest of the lights back in their box. "Let's call it done. That's good enough for my taste," she said, plugging in the lone strand that encircled the corner tree. "I better go soon. I promised my mother I would help cook. My brother is too lazy when it's his turn to help for the holidays. Let's just say that my phone would be ringing with pleas for assistance if I didn't show up on my own."

"I'll hold the fort here for a little while," said Ama. She rose slowly from her kneeling position, brushing the snow glitter from her skirt. "I thought about starting next month's window display a little early by finishing dressing that mannequin in your office... maybe finding some Valentine's Day cake toppers, and make a red-and-white bunting..."

"I thought it was your market day," said Natalie, as she wrapped her scarf around her neck. "Don't you usually buy spices and chocolate and stuff on Saturdays?"

"I'm not exactly planning to shop today," said Ama. "I have a little time to kill. I don't need any help, though, so you can go." Her smile was the same as Natalie's now, filled with regret for what Tessa would be thinking when she found out about this.

Neither of them asked if the other was going to tell Tessa. Neither of them would have the heart to do it, not during Christmas.

"Thanks," said Natalie. "Merry Christmas." She shrugged on her coat and grabbed her shopping bags again.

"Merry Christmas and Happy New Year," said Ama, as she opened the box containing the white dress from Natalie's garment stash, and fluffed its skirts.

❄

While Tessa was driving her way southwards in a borrowed car, fighting back tears as Perry Como's 'Home for the Holidays' played on the radio, Natalie was testing apple turnovers in her mother's kitchen as two of her cousin's kids raced around with paper reindeer antlers on their heads.

Chad had decided to tag along to dinner at Maria's that evening since he didn't have any prior holiday plans. In addition to the bean salad her mother requested, Natalie brought along a bottle of wine that her uncle would approve of, and had given Chad a few pointers about her family this time before they went inside Icing Italia's kitchen.

"Just be careful what you say to Rob," she had told him, as she unbuckled her seat belt. "He's the one with sharp hearing and a memory that won't quit—unless it's something you want him to remember. Stick to sports with him, and if he asks if we're getting engaged, just ask him when he and Kimmie are going to tie the knot. That'll shut him up."

"I can handle your family, no problem," said Chad. "It's just dinner, not a lifetime commitment."

"My thoughts exactly." Natalie lifted the wine bottle from where it was nestled between the folds of an old blanket in Chad's back seat.

"Did I tell you my mom invited us to dinner next Friday?" said Chad. "She's spending Christmas at her cousin's house in Raleigh, but she's really looking forward to meeting you."

"Of course," said Natalie. "I'll come."

"Great. She'll be excited." He opened the car door. "I don't spend a lot of time at her place these days, so this will be a good excuse to stop by."

"Not a close family, eh?" said Natalie. They had talked about family, of course, but not much about their feelings about family. That hadn't come up when they were having dinner out or at her apartment—or while Natalie was hanging from the face of a rock.

"I don't know. I guess we're close enough. I never thought about it." He closed the driver's door, and adjusted the collar of his button-down over his sweater's V-neck, combing a few fingers through the mane of hair sweeping against his jaw. "I guess we should go on inside and get this over with," he said.

"We have to tell them about us sooner or later, don't we?" joked Natalie. They both laughed a little, as if dismissing the last tiny bit of nervousness about testing out their relationship charade on real people and not just in their imaginations.

Good thing it wasn't a real relationship, or she might actually stay nervous. Her family could eat a stranger alive—only someone who was practically family could avoid the fierce criteria that the Grenaldis used to judge each other's romantic partners. Rob was just lucky that Kimmie was so adorable it was impossible not to love her.

Chad had taken Natalie's hand in the same careless, relaxed manner as always, and they walked to the front door. The bug-eyed look that crossed Maria's face when she answered the door proved how surprised she was to see Chad at Natalie's side.

"Chad, it's good to see you again," she said, recovering and giving him a friendly embrace in greeting, which Chad returned with a polite pat on Maria's back. "Come on in, everybody's waiting." Maria's smile was of pure happiness and amazement—but only at seeing Natalie

with the same man twice in a row, Natalie thought. It wasn't anything
to do with Chad himself, who was a stranger who didn't like carbs in
double portions, and had offered a smile both limp and nervous in its
politeness the first time he met the family.

If Maria only knew what he'd said about visiting his mother,
she would immediately question his priorities in life, too—that was
another pointer Natalie would have to give Chad for the next couple
of weeks, to make his family sound more important to him than they
might be in reality.

It was all worth it, Natalie thought, as she saw the looks on the faces
of her relatives when they entered the dining room. Even Uncle Guido
seemed floored at Chad's appearance. Her barely contained nervous
laugh and the brief squeeze of Chad's hand for their good-natured
pact, went unnoticed in the moment of surprise for everybody. A
quick whisper was exchanged between her aunt and Rob's girlfriend,
which Natalie would bet a hundred dollars was speculation about
Chad as 'the one.'

"… do you think they're shopping for a ring already?" Kimmie was
saying in a hushed voice, as Chad and Natalie sat down a few places
away. Natalie caught these words faintly below the clink of silverware
and the laughter of her relatives; Chad caught Natalie's eye and gave
her a conspiratorial wink, proving he had heard the same thing.

There was an old cubic zirconia ring in the bottom of her jewelry
box that would do better than a plastic diamond, Natalie thought playfully—and recklessly. Maybe she'd try wearing it a couple of times to see
if anybody noticed, and demur when asked if it was really a gift from
Chad. If nobody looked too closely, it might look like the real thing.

Pretending not to be romantically carefree could actually be pretty
fun. And if it wasn't, there existed a built-in failsafe to release her by

St. Patrick's Day, so life would go back to the way it was before. It was the perfect plan—though she still drew the line at tasting wedding cakes and picking out florists, even in jest, because a game of pretend couldn't fully erase the shudders that the concept of marriage tended to send down her spine whenever Maria joked about wanting a dozen grandchildren, or hosting a post-honeymoon family dinner for her newlywed daughter and spouse. To be safe, Natalie would have to tell Tessa and Ama the truth in the next couple of weeks before they got any ideas about building a portfolio of wedding ideas on her behalf—playing it safe was key to making everybody happy in this situation.

That's why the smile on Natalie's face was genuine, even when Aunt Louisa passed her the bread pudding and hinted that her younger cousin would *love* to be a bridesmaid.

❄

While Natalie was enjoying a temporary reprieve from family interrogations about her love life, Tessa was finishing off a carton of Chunky Monkey Ben & Jerry's ice cream with her hot chocolate, and watching the last few minutes of *Holiday Affair*. She was trying not to cry, but not because it looked like Janet Leigh and Robert Mitchum were missing their chance for love, or because she was being blinded by the billions of colored twinkle lights that decorated her mother's tree. She blinked hard as the characters onscreen swam into a black-and-white blur, to which the reflection of holiday lights draped around a nearby nativity scene added a neon haze.

"Everything okay, Tessa Mae?" Her mother paused in the doorway, her bedtime reading of Anne Tyler tucked under her arm, along with one of the many shopping catalogs she studied for potential presents this time of year—stocking stuffers were her mother's particular weakness. "You seem a little down. Is it because you miss the old house? I know the condo's not the same after all these years… but I still have all the ornaments, you know, so we'll decorate this place to the nines, starting tomorrow."

"It's not the house, Mom," she answered. "Or the ornaments. It's nothing." She shook her head. "Just a long week at work, that's all."

"You're sure?" her mother asked. "I can have the boxes out of the storeroom closet in a jiffy. I think all your school craft macaroni ornaments are in one. You remember how much you love them."

Tessa stifled a giggle, albeit a small one, at the idea that macaroni ornaments could solve her current blues. "That's okay. They can wait until tomorrow, when we decorate the kitchen tree," she said. Her mother would have a tree decorated in every room before New Year's Day, since she could never bear to leave any decorations in their boxes during the month of December. "I think I'll just finish my cocoa and see what the next movie is."

"Save the good ones for me," said her mother. "You know how much I love *White Christmas*. We just don't get enough of those in the south. I can't miss Bing and Rosemary, not for love or money."

"Sure thing, Mom. I won't watch that one until Christmas Day with you, I promise."

The cocoa had become dregs at the bottom of the cup, as Janet Leigh raced through train cars on New Year's Eve in search of future happiness. Tessa wished her own was that simple—a matter of chasing down love only to have it turn and give you a passionate kiss. But in her experience, chasing love just left you in the dust, while the one you pursued sped away with someone else.

First, all the crushes in college, and the boyfriends she clung to, who only ever loved her halfheartedly. Now it was Blake, falling for the devastatingly gorgeous Mac, leaving her behind in the dust like a fool. A big fool who had been proud and desperate at the same time, and let him believe that she found the idea of them dating to be a silly farce. A wild idea that had been planted in their brains temporarily by one tiny kiss.

If only Blake had called her afterwards, like he promised. If only she hadn't been too proud and too scared to say something herself, afraid that he had changed his mind. And when he hinted in the parlor that day that she was interested in him...

She pressed her hands to her forehead, wishing the pain in her head was brain freeze from the ice cream and not a headache from all the regrets and 'what if's in her mind. Why were the 'what if's she imagined always disappointing ones, and never happily-ever-afters for herself? Why couldn't she be happily in love, instead of being afraid that a chance for happiness would always lead to heartache?

The Chunky Monkey was a melted puddle at the bottom of the carton, but *Holiday Inn* was just beginning at a quarter past midnight. With a deep sigh, Tessa turned the volume up and sank lower in the cushions of the sofa, feeling drowsy. Hoping that any dreams that entered her head tonight wouldn't be of Blake.

Blake and Mac. Would she really have to plan their wedding? How could she do it and not go crazy? Right now, she couldn't think of a rational, sensible excuse to refuse, however, if Mac really asked her.

I can't plan your wedding because I'm in love with Blake, she informed the bride-to-be in her imaginary conversation. *That's why I have to decline. You understand, don't you?*

It made perfect sense to her, this explanation. And it was perfectly true, too, as she nodded off to sleep before the scenes of Vermont's Christmas snow, with visions in her mind of the handsome contractor helping her paint the parlor's walls with 'Romantic Blue.' His hand and hers were holding the same paintbrush as the white plaster surface became a pale violet, a shade that seemed just perfect for a newly broken heart.

Given a second chance, she would do anything to change things. If a miracle gave her one, she would tell him exactly how she felt about him. Reformed romantic or not, she wouldn't be stupid twice.

Now, if only a miracle would come her way.

❉

Back in Bellegrove on Saturday afternoon, Ama was helping rub the tandoori chicken for cooking, something she never did on her free weekends.

Her knife minced garlic in a steady rhythm as her father ground spices beneath his pestle. Working at the same rhythm, her father concentrating on his recipe, Ama felt a sense of harmony in the kitchen, which had been lacking recently. Not that anybody had mentioned the controversies involving her love life or Tamir. Even Ranjit had held his tongue on this issue.

"Not too much garlic," he said, stopping her knife. "And small. Small pieces."

"Like this?" The sharpest edge of her blade turned a minced square into slivers.

"We make a smooth paste first," he said. "It brings out the flavor. Our special way of doing it, different from all the other restaurants."

"From the Punjabi Express, too?" said Ama teasingly. A snort from her father.

"That place. Dry chicken, overcooked rice, too much tomato in the *masala*—and no flavor to their *halwa*. It tastes like the little jars of food that Nalia feeds the baby. Squashed pumpkin from a can."

"It kind of does," Ama admitted with a laugh. "But I like that potato thing they make. The one with the turmeric sauce."

"It's not bad." Ranjit began crushing her garlic now. "I would use *masala* to give flavor to it… or make a spice sauce with those smoked peppers your brother buys. The ones from Mexico."

"And maybe honey to sweeten it," suggested Ama.

Her father smiled and nodded. "Good idea," he said. He added a sprinkle of pepper to his mortar dish. "Good thinking."

Reaching over, Ama laid her hand on her father's. "I love you, Papa," she said. "You know that, don't you?"

Ranjit's hand was still beneath hers. His right hand laid aside his pestle carefully, then covered Ama's own with a gentle, trembling grip. "You're a good daughter," he said. He patted her hand at these words, then released his hold on her.

Ama smiled as she began mincing the garlic even smaller. It was the closest she would come to receiving an apology from her father. This was a tentative truce on the subject of her life and how she planned to live it. Maybe it was only a beginning, but it was still something.

During the car ride to the market, she thought about her mother's words. Her mother trusted her to do the right thing, even while following her heart. Of course, she didn't say what that meant, but it was nice to hear those words, especially without the stipulation that her heart would lead her to someone else's idea of a perfectly acceptable suitor.

She took a deep breath and closed her eyes. So why did today feel like some kind of betrayal, after her mother's promise?

Deena pulled up to the curb on the ethnic market's street, checking her rearview mirror as she shifted into park momentarily. "I think that Hispanic vendor you like is just now setting up," she said to Jaidev.

"See? We're not late. Plenty of time for you to have your pick of the fresh cilantro."

"I still think you could've decided to visit that holiday festival another day," he grumbled, as he unfastened his seatbelt. He leaned over the back seat to look at Ama.

"Listen," he said. "I know what you're going to do…"

"Deena!" She looked at her sister-in-law with indignation, who shrugged helplessly.

"… and I only have one thing to say to you," said Jaidev. "Just… be careful out there, okay? Dad's not the only one who worries about you. Be sure this guy's a decent type before you get too serious with him."

Ama rolled her eyes, but she was smiling. "I won't do anything stupid," she answered. "Satisfied?"

"That's all I had to say." He opened the car door. "Pick me up by six at the coffee shop down the street, okay? I promised Dad I'd man the kitchen tonight during the rush."

"See you later," answered Deena. Jaidev closed the car door and jogged swiftly toward the Hispanic family unloading bushels of smoked peppers, bundles of green leaves, and sweet ground spices in paper bags.

Ama took a deep breath. Her hand was on the car door's handle, but she hadn't lifted it yet. And not just because Deena hadn't unlocked the door.

"Relax. Jaidev only knows because he guessed after the letter came," said Deena. "I filled him in on the details so he wouldn't jump to any stupid conclusions. Other than us, your secret is still safe."

"Secret," repeated Ama. "That's the problem. How long can I keep it this way? It feels too much like lying *not* to tell them. If something actually happens, I mean. And I have no idea if it will, so maybe I'm worrying over nothing."

"Stop," said Deena. "For the first time, you have the chance to choose what you want. Your father finally admitted that it's your life. This is the first step, Ama. You don't want to go back to dating guys that your father picks out, do you?"

"No," admitted Ama. "I guess I'm just afraid of what comes next." What if she fell in love? What if Luke truly fell for her and wanted to meet her family? Those were huge hurdles that she couldn't imagine facing right now.

"Take happiness one step at a time," said Deena. "See what happens next before you worry about the future." She lowered her driving sunglasses. "Speaking of which, destiny has arrived."

A motorcycle was pulling up to the lone parking spot left on the street. The figure riding it, bundled in a wool coat and worn jeans, could only be Luke. Ama knew it by the way her heart's rhythm shifted into a new gear, its speed outmatching the slowness of her fingers and body.

She lifted the handle of the car as Deena unlocked the door. Stepping outside, she approached the rider as he dismounted. He removed his helmet and turned around, a smile dawning on his face.

"You're early," he said. "I didn't think you'd make it for another fifteen minutes. I was going to check out my friend's pottery booth and see if he had anything new, but this is better."

"I had extra time today, so I caught a ride with Deena," said Ama. "I guess I was excited to see you." Deena's borrowed car was easing out onto the street, its driver waving goodbye as she set off for a day at a holiday festival in the next town.

"I wasn't sure you'd show up," Luke said, smiling. "I would've hung around at the restaurant a little longer the other day, but I got the sense you didn't want me to. Then I left that letter, and I started thinking I had overstepped my bounds. Maybe I misread something."

Ama shook her head. "No," she said. "No, the letter was... was so like you. It was real and honest and kind of incredible. It wasn't a mistake or anything like that. It's only that things are kind of complicated for me."

"Complicated can be good or bad," said Luke. She could tell from the way his smile had changed that he didn't know which one to expect.

"Can I tell you something?" Ama asked. She had waited until Deena's car was out of sight, until there were no witnesses who knew her, even at a distance. "I need to explain. My family—they've never seen me with a guy who wasn't part of our culture. Part of the ideal image they have in their heads for my perfect boyfriend. I was afraid to let them see anybody in my life who wasn't like that."

He didn't take a step backwards as if accepting this as rejection, but Ama took a step closer to him anyway, as if to keep it from happening. "But I'm really sorry I didn't let them see more of you that day. Because... because I think you're really amazing. In ways I really wish they could see and understand, and I'm really trying to show them why."

Shivering with nerves and fear, not with cold, she wrapped her arms close around herself. She wanted him to understand, and she hoped that he did. *Please understand, Luke. See how hard I'm trying to make this work.*

"Can I say something?" he asked.

She nodded. If he couldn't accept this situation, that would be the end. If so, she had turned her back on the concept of matchmaking for nothing. No, not for nothing—for the chance to find her own path to happiness, not someone else's, for a change. For that alone, it was worth it.

"You know what I'm like," he said. "I'm not a big planner, I'm not a guy who has a lot of ties or traditions. Hence the tattoo. It says it all, really. I keep things loose, but I'm still a serious guy. I hope you can see that."

"I'm okay with the tattoo," said Ama. "I like free spirits. I don't need perfect plans or perfect details for life decisions."

"You didn't seem like you did," he said. "And I get that you're from a pretty straight-laced background. But you don't assume things about me. I like that."

"You didn't assume that I only eat Indian food, or listen to sitar music, just because my family's still traditional," she said. "It was nice to have somebody not assume things about me, either."

"I tried to say things in the letter that I have a hard time saying in person," he continued. "Mostly, that I'm thinking about you a lot these days. I feel like I'm myself when I'm with you. There's no pretending or changing, even though we're different people. I want to get to know you better because of it."

He drew closer. He lifted his hand, and Ama felt it rest against her cheek, cradling it softly. It was the first time Luke had touched her like this, deliberately, romantically, and her skin was alive with a thousand pinpoints of electricity. Those callused fingers were sure and steady. Unlike the tremor in her own before she laid her hand over his, holding it in place as long as possible.

"I like you, Ama," he said. "Very much. Not just because you like my bike, or because I like your desserts, either. Is that okay with you?"

The cold was making tears form in her eyes. "Really, really okay," she answered. She felt him gently tuck a strand of her hair behind her ear, the one the cold wind had been whipping against her cheek all this time.

His lips kissed hers. A shiver traveled deeply through Ama in response—one of surprise, amazement, and disbelief. It was nothing like she had imagined it would be whenever she pictured her first kiss with him. The roughness of Luke's sleeve cuffs beneath her fingers, the taste of mints on his breath... cold wind in her face, no starlight above. But the energy—the incredible sensation of being this close to him—that couldn't be imagined in a hundred years of fantasies behind the Tandoori Tiger. How could anything so soft and so strong, firm, and tender at the same time, possibly be real?

He drew back and looked into her eyes. "Do you want to go for a ride?" he asked. "I brought two helmets. I was hoping you'd say yes."

Recovering, she nodded. "I do," she answered. "More than anything."

"Do you want to go to dinner tonight?" he asked.

He was officially asking her out. It was really happening. An official date, with the two of them as more than friends taking a train together on a Saturday afternoon. Though it was cold, Ama didn't feel it at all. "Absolutely," she answered. "I would love to."

"There's this little place on the other side of the city that makes incredible Italian food. If you don't mind, we can take off in that direction and see what happens. We can spend the day together, take the long way. Maybe go past the park, catch some of the street performers there. You like Italian food, right?" He grinned.

"Who doesn't?" she answered.

He tossed her the second helmet. "Come on," he said. He climbed on the bike and helped her on behind him. When she wrapped her arms around him, she felt his hand clasped over hers, checking the strength of her grip beneath his own. A brief caress from his thumb traversed the curves of her own.

"Hold on tight," he said. He glanced over his shoulder and smiled at her, then started the motorcycle. It purred to life, zipping into the street a moment later. The cold wind pushed against Ama as they raced along, her heart matching the speed of the wind.

The world was dizzying her with the first taste of love and independence, spiked with fear and uncertainty of the unknown. She might be on the verge of happiness or heartache, but she was going where she wanted to go, and with the person she wanted to be with. At this moment, she was traveling on the wings of the wind with her arms tight around Luke and adventure lying immediately ahead of them.

Anything could happen. Eyes closed and heart pressed close against Luke, Ama hoped that it would.

A Letter from Laura

Thank you so much for reading *One Winter's Day*, the second book to feature the adventures of Tessa, Ama, and Natalie—aka the Wedding Belles. I hope that you found it to be a cozy Christmas read, perfect for curling up with by the fireside with a cup of warm tea (or hot chocolate!). To stay up to date on the latest details for the series, be sure to sign up below for notifications about upcoming releases. Your email address will remain completely private, and you can unsubscribe at any time.

www.bookouture.com/laura-briggs

I'm so glad you chose to spend the holidays with my characters in Bellegrove, the fictional Southern setting they call home. It's a beautiful place year-round, and I hope you'll be ready to visit it again soon for more excitement surrounding the personal and professional lives of the series' three heroines for a new season and new adventures next spring.

I also hope that if you loved this book you'll leave a review sharing how you felt about it. To learn more about the series, please join me on social media using the links below—I can't wait to tell you more about the next story for Tessa, Ama, and Natalie!

Thanks for reading,
Laura Briggs

authorlaurabriggs

PaperDollWrites

paperdollwrites.blogspot.com

Lightning Source UK Ltd.
Milton Keynes UK
UKHW020618051019
351068UK00008B/190/P

9 781786 816757